11/08

Lucky Billy

Books by John Vernon

Lucky Billy

The Last Canyon

A Book of Reasons

All for Love

Peter Doyle

Lindbergh's Son

La Salle

Money and Fiction

Poetry and the Body

Ann

The Garden and the Map

Lucky Billy

JOHN VERNON

HOUGHTON MIFFLIN COMPANY

BOSTON • NEW YORK

2008

For ANN,

and in memory of

PATRICIA WILCOX

◆

www.houghtonmifflinbooks.com

Library of Congress Cataloging-in-Publication Data
Vernon, John, date.
Lucky Billy / John Vernon.
p. cm.
ISBN: 978-0-547-07423-8
1. Billy, the Kid—Fiction. 2. Outlaws—Fiction.
3. Southwest, New—Fiction. I. Title.
PS3572.E76L83 2008
813'.54—dc22   2008017924

Printed in the United States of America

Book design by Victoria Hartman
Map by Jacques Chazaud

DOC 10 9 8 7 6 5 4 3 2 1

The tintype of Billy the Kid is reproduced courtesy of Palace of the Governors (MNM/DCA), negative number 128785.

Excerpts from the letters of John Tunstall, Robert Widenmann, and Huston Chapman, cited from *The Life and Death of John Henry Tunstall* and *The Lincoln County War: A Documentary History*, are used by permission of the author, Frederick Nolan, and, acting for the family, Hilary Tunstall-Behrens.

The letter written by Lew Wallace to Billy the Kid in chapter 13 is reprinted by permission of the Indiana Historical Society, the Wallace Collection.

· CONTENTS ·

· TINTYPE ·

THAT'S HIM. They say that's his picture. The cocky little cowboy strikes a tintype pose, probably assisted by a hidden stand whose metal collar restrains him for the long exposure; you can just see its leg behind one foot. Still, he looks draggle-tailed. This may be more attitude than posture. I picture his mother propping him up with a death-grip on the back of his neck, though his hips nonetheless appear to sling forward, his arms to bow apart, his insolent mouth to slackly unhinge, as though most of him were an irrelevant sack hanging from her clenched hand. But Catherine had died in 1874, six years before this picture was taken, and a species of coat stand with one projecting pincer-arm had to substitute for her. She never saw him as we do, when we gaze at this picture, with his front teeth so prominent he could eat pumpkins through a fence, as a wag once said — or with arching black eyebrows, sticking-out ears, scraps of black hair hanging down his neck. He surely didn't own that weaponry when she was living — the holstered pistol, the cartridge belt, the Winchester rifle on which his hand rests — because when she died he was only thirteen and he hadn't yet become Billy the Kid. The side-creased hat looks as though he's been clubbed on the head by a washboard. The sweater, though, two sizes too large, could be a hand-me-down — he did have an older brother — and the shirt. The shirt! On its placket just visible through his buckskin vest is what appears to be an anchor with a rope loosely coiled around its shaft, and does that not make it one of those ubiquitous sailor shirts that doting mothers used to buy for their sons? It could be the same shirt he'd worn as a boy.

The Anthony four-tube camera had a six-second exposure and produced four images, for which the Kid paid twenty-five cents. Two survived. One disappeared years ago. The other was given to the Lincoln County Heritage Trust in 1986 by the descendants of Sam Dedrick, a horse trader at Fort Sumner, New Mexico, where the picture was taken. But the Trust displayed it under bright lights, a serious blunder, and the tintype darkened, and all we have now are reproductions of a vanished original. Even the scratched and spotted surface is a copy of a scratched and spotted surface, as are the marks of the tacks on the four corners and the photographer's corrosive thumbprints at the bottom. The only known image of Billy the Kid, then, the one you are looking at, is a shadow of a ghost, a photograph of a perished tintype of a young man who perhaps had it taken in the first place to prove that he wasn't a figment of his own imagination. But what was he thinking of, to tilt his head like that and pooch out his jaw, looking every bit like Gomer Pyle, thus defying our attempts to make him a figment of *ours?* He looks nothing like the Hollywood Billies, the Robert Taylors, Buster Crabbes, Paul Newmans, Kris Kristoffersons, or Emilio Estevezes.

Nothing like Billy Conlon, either, the boy who stole my three-speed Schwinn bike when I was ten years old, then had the chutzpah to offer to search for it with me and our playmates. As our posse scoured the backyards and alleys of north Cambridge, he looked up at my face — like his namesake, he was short — and framed his desire to "find" what he'd taken as a thrilling adventure; this was the Wild West and we'd string up the horse thieves. For a moment, his eyes were convincingly plaintive but, slipping to the side, they lapsed into cunning. Billy Conlon, too, had an exigent mother (and a missing father), a tall, indolent syrup of womanhood who wore shoulder pads, hairnets, and high heels, and who often poured herself across her shabby couch and asked her son to scratch her back in his friends' presence. When I'd all but despaired of reclaiming my bike and lay on my bed sulking one day he brought it to my door, having found it, he said, in the marshes beside the Dewey and Almy Chemical factory where Route 2 made its swing into Boston, the same industrial wasteland at the edge of our neighborhood where he'd once tortured bullfrogs and turtles. His mother had made him return it, I guessed. And, talk about brass, he expected a reward, despite having gouged his initials on the fender!

He was always Billy the Kid in our games, for unlike the tintype Billy he looked the part: gash of black hair across his freckled forehead, fetching grin, not too big a nose, no buck teeth, close dark Irish eyes. His face was a cherub's. Yet, he'd set his room on fire; he'd forced his sister Nancy to drink range oil and eat an entire package of Ex-Lax; he would fight anyone at the drop of a dime. And later, when I'd finished college and had begun writing novels, I heard that he'd stabbed a man on the street, viciously killing him, exactly as the first Billy was said by his nemesis and friend Pat Garrett to have done (because the man verbally abused his mother). And that's when I learned to look back on my childhood as though it had become an abandoned film set, a back lot obliging my fond inclination to sentimentalize bad behavior. Or a discarded comic book, or a Big Little storybook, for I read everything then, I even read torn newspapers on the street and labels of cans of peaches in the store, and pictured myself as an extra in the story that the Billies of the world acted out in books and movies.

Most longings fizzle. The point about Billy was he always died young. He did not have to make emotional adjustments, watch his language, rearrange his priorities, wonder what was stirring inside him, be punctual or dignified, harbor guarded intentions, or care what people thought of him. Those of us who color inside the lines and wash our hands before eating and finish our vegetables and floss and remain faithful to our spouses — we nice, regular people who shrink existence to the size of a nutshell and live out our biblical three score and ten with diminishing zeal — where would we be without him?

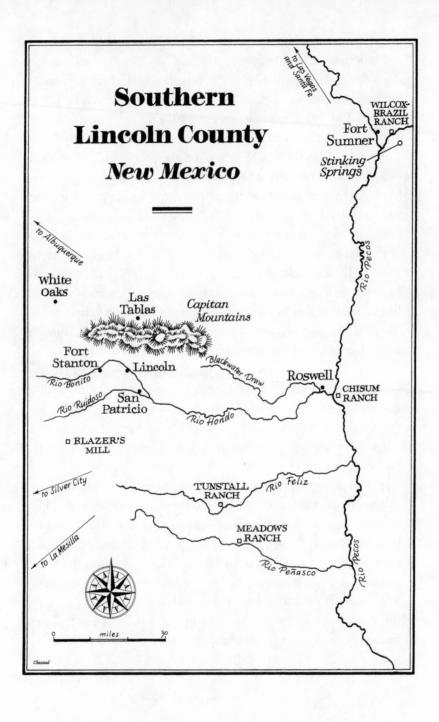

Southern
Lincoln County
New Mexico

to Las Vegas and Santa Fe

WILCOX-
BRAZIL
RANCH

Fort
Sumner

*Stinking
Springs*

to Albuquerque

white
Oaks

Las
Tablas

*Capitan
Mountains*

Rio Pecos

Fort
Stanton

Lincoln

Blackwater Draw

Roswell

Rio Bonito

CHISUM
RANCH

Rio Ruidoso

San
Patricio

Rio Hondo

□ BLAZER'S
MILL

to Silver City

TUNSTALL
RANCH
□

Rio Feliz

to La Mesilla

MEADOWS
□ RANCH

Rio Pecos

Rio Peñasco

0   miles   30

Chazaud

April 28, 1881

Escape

HELLO, BOB."

Bob Olinger looks up at Billy in the window and freezes on the spot. He's a large man of vinegar aspect, a burly, dumb, squint-eyed giant with red hair, curiously infantile features, meaty hands, reeking breath, and, the Kid knows, a heart of pure lead. Two years ago he murdered Billy's old friend John Jones by shaking Jones's right hand with his left and squeezing it tight, which prevented Jones from drawing, and shooting him cold. Now he's a deputy sheriff in Lincoln. There's just no keeping some men down. For the record, his first name is not Bob but Ameredith, inflicted on him by a patriotic mother who wanted a girl. It was only yesterday that Bob had told the Kid he had no more chance of escaping under *his* guard than of going to heaven. Thanks for the *aviso*, Bob. From his perch in the window, Billy spots the prisoners Bob had escorted to the Wortley Hotel across the street watching from the hotel grounds. They won't flee, he knows, even after Bob's killed, for unlike the Kid they are trustees, they've even been allowed to wear their weapons at the courthouse, since their acquittal is all but assured. No court in New Mexico will convict five men for killing four others who'd fired on them first in a dispute over precious water rights — not when the accused men's alfalfa fields needed irrigation. They're being held at the courthouse in the room still referred to as Mrs. Lloyd's room, named for Lawrence Murphy's former housekeeper. And Billy's being held, or was long enough for him to savor the irony, in the late Lawrence Murphy's bedroom, for the Lincoln County Courthouse not that long ago was the Murphy-Dolan store, headquarters of the Irish ring against which he'd fought for the last four years. They'd started this mess. They'd killed John Tunstall. Dolan and his crew had once disarmed the Kid right here in the store and made him eat crow, and now look at him! It *was* the only two-story building in Lincoln, that's why he can look down at poor Bob for a change instead of the latter toploftily sizing up his famous prisoner shackled to the floor before kicking his slats, as he'd done every morning for the past seven days when it was wake-up time.

Yesterday, when Sheriff Garrett left for White Oaks to order up the wood for the Kid's gallows, he'd double-checked Billy's shackles, called his deputies in, Olinger and Jim Bell, and warned them to be especially vigilant. If he's shown the slightest chance, if he's even allowed the use of one hand, if he's not watched at every moment, he'll effect some plan to murder the both of you and escape. Lip-labor, said Bob after Garrett left. The sheriff ought to save his spit. Bob's response to his boss's absence was to gloat over Billy, to taunt him all the more. Wake up, dearie, potty-time, dearie, can I get you something, dearie? The Kid in turn had greeted the two deputies at breakfast that morning, *Ameredith* and the more pleasant Jim Bell, with a cheerful "Morning, girls." They passed the time by playing poker in the sheriff's office. "I never did enjoy killing a person," Bob said as he dealt.

"I did."

"But I'd love to kill you. It would give me great pleasure."

"Is that so."

Bob poured himself his first midday whiskey. Usually when the bottle was half drunk he offered Jim some. And Jim in turn, if Olinger had to use the privy, would wait until Bob had left the room and, due to the short chain on the Kid's manacles, hold the bottle to his mouth. Is there kindness in hell? Jim asked Bob, "What do you mean you never did enjoy it?"

"I never had a weakness for it. It didn't take with me."

"Didn't take?" Billy said. "You make it sound like the cow pox."

"What is it then, sweetheart?"

"It's just pulling a trigger. You're the messenger, that's all. The bullet was assigned and fired long ago, before you ever come along."

Bell said, "That's a crazy idea."

"What about you?" Bob asked Billy. "Was your bullet assigned?"

"Everyone's was. You can't duck it, either."

"You've ducked plenty."

"They weren't mine."

"In other words, do I have this straight? The bullet you dodge isn't yours. But the one you don't is. That's — there's a name for that. It's un-American. No matter what you do, it just had to be. That's a piss-ant philosophy."

"I'll tell you why," said Billy. "My stepfather said it. Your bullet's coming after you all through your life. It follows you around, takes every turn you take. Spend too long in any one place, sleep too much, it's bound to catch up."

"I myself sleep a lot."

"It's best to keep moving. *Look out!*"

Olinger jumped up, knocking over his chair. He threw his cards on the table. "You little cunt-garbage," he hissed. "Back to your hole, maggot!"

"Shoot me, Bob, and get it over with."

"I'll get it over with! I'll get it over with!" With one arm, he grabbed Billy's chains and dragged him out the door to the head of the stairs. The other held his ten-gauge Whitneyville shotgun. "Go ahead. Run." He released his prisoner, opened the shotgun and looked inside the breech, then closed it with a *shlang*.

"How can I run with these shackles?"

"You'll run if I tell you." He kicked him in the ass and Billy slid down the stairs, protecting his face by skidding on his elbows, and managed to break the fall halfway down. Then he turned and mounted the steep flight of stairs with baby steps enforced by the heavy shackles. "I was hoping you'd do it," said Bob. "If you'd of just reached the landing I would have blasted you to hell. I'd love to see you make a run for it. They would have to collect the little pieces in a jar."

"I wouldn't give you the satisfaction."

"In that case, my satisfaction shall be watching you hang. I'll be right in front with a smile on my face."

"That's a lie and you know it. You never smiled in your life."

Mrs. Lesnett on her walks past the courthouse heard these daily altercations. She'd once hidden the Kid in a grain bin in her barn during the Lincoln County War. When she walked by that after-noon, Bob, to cool off, had wandered out onto the balcony and lit up a cheroot while Bell and the Kid, with Bob's half-empty bottle to pil-fer, resumed playing cards inside. Bob shouted down, "Annie! Mrs. Lesnett! You ought to come to the hanging. Watch his neck stretch. You used to cook for him, ain't it?"

"He's a nice boy."

"And your husband didn't know. You hid him in a mash barrel, I heard, lest the Dolans burn you out."

"You should mind your own business."

"Well, come to the hanging. It will be fun."

And from inside the courthouse Billy's voice shouted: "If I'm not there they can't hang me!"

Playing poker with the deputies while wearing fifteen pounds of shackles was a cross to bear for Billy, a caution to Bell. Sheriff Pat Garrett had had the shackles special-ordered from a blacksmith in Santa Fe after capturing the Kid. No bolts or brads. Fused single-piece manacles connected by a short chain; leg irons also linked by a chain; and both manacles and shackles chained below and above to a permanent chain around his waist. Nights, the entire harness was padlocked to an iron ring anchored to the floor in his room. Days, he couldn't walk; he shuffled, he dragged, he heaved with both legs as though in a sack race. Eating, he had to lean into his plate, affording Olinger the chance to push his face into his eggs. He couldn't deal monte with his hands manacled, it impeached their smart pace, so he and the deputies stuck to poker. To show, he seized his cards in his teeth and spit them onto the table face-up. Bell's complaints about seepage on his cards were taken with a grain of salt. Better slobber than boredom.

Bell and the Kid were still playing cards when it came time for Olinger to walk the trustees across the street for their supper at the Wortley. When they were through Bob would saunter back first, carbine hanging from one hand, with the Kid's and Bell's meals in a box in the other. Neither Bell nor Billy talked. Poker could not dispel the tedium, just give it method. Everything about waiting to hang was tedious. With a finger, Bell rubbed his ear-to-mouth scar, the result of a dispute over cards in a mining camp, which had gentled his temperament — at least that's what Billy thought. Unlike Bob, who wouldn't hesitate to ear down their prisoner if he looked at him wrong, Bell never lorded it over Billy. When the Kid announced he had to use the jakes, Bell pulled out his Colt's Army and waved him to his feet and followed behind as Billy awkwardly bunny-hopped toward the stairs. The leg irons allowed just enough tormenting slack to take baby steps down; one foot found the tread then the other caught up. Halfway to the bottom, the Kid grasped the banister and gave it his weight and went two legs at a time, and this new protocol spiced his day, Bell couldn't help grinning. At the door, the Kid paused and Bell stepped out first and looked left and then right then led the Kid outside to the privy, Billy hopping with a festinating shuffle.

"Can you free my hands? I'll have to wipe myself." Bell unlocked the short chain that linked the manacles to his waist.

Hollow-eyed Godfrey Gauss, gray of face and beard, was hoeing his vegetable patch near the fence. He'd once been a coosie for Billy's boss, the late John Tunstall; now the county employed him to keep the courthouse floors swept and the windows clean and to lock up at night. He gestured Bell over, reached in his coat, and pulled out a slip of paper. "That order came in," he said.

"Which order?"

"The spit cups." He held it up. "'Three dozen spit cups which we hold subject to your order. Bill herewith enclosed.'"

"Does that mean they're here?"

"In Mesilla," said Gauss.

"Then it didn't come in."

"What do you want me to do?"

Bell glanced beyond Gauss's shoulder at the privy. "Wait till Garrett gets back." The door was hanging open. He looked over at the courthouse where Billy's after image vanished inside, spilling forward bent in half, humping it to beat the band. Halfway to the building, Bell heard his prisoner's chains thump and rattle up the steps. He ran for the stairway, which was already empty and eerily silent, and took the steps flying three at a time, his last lunge whipping him into the hallway where the world came crashing down. He was on his hands and knees. The *whang* in his ears had a logic, he felt: it pulsed with each blow, flashed orange and yellow. Each time he pushed up, a manacle hammered the back of his skull but couldn't crack the hard nut. Always the thickwit, as Pap used to say. But he had to push up, if he were closer to the source of the blows the force would lessen. This coolheaded observation gave him hope. He raised up again, something slipped through his hip, it felt like a hand sliding out of a glove, then he knew it was over, his gun had been taken — it all happened too fast — so he didn't resist the kick down the stairs, despite not much oomph, the Kid's legs were still hobbled. The first shot completely missed, and Bell was still rolling. The second missed, too, but shattered off the wall where the stairs made their turn and nearly sawed him in half, for at last poor Bell had managed to stand — nearly made him two people, a top one and a bottom one, weaving out the door while carrying himself like a vase on a pillar. He was *coming apart at the seams*, Jim Bell, and felt like the village sot with his mortifying groans. *My little body. These vasty wilds.* He spilled through the yard into Gauss's arms and died.

"Hello, Bob."

After that, the upshot merely took minutes. Billy hobbled to the armory, put his shoulder to it, softest thing he ever struck. Doors opened before him! He looked around at the Springfields, the Remingtons, an old Henry, a fine selection of holsters. He picked out a holster for Bell's Colt's and here was a Winchester and there the .50-caliber Sharps with the octagonal barrel that suffered from wind drift. But the thing that caught his eye was Olinger's Whitneyville. Double-barreled, loaded, propped against the wall, ready to right all the wrongs of the universe. He grabbed it and bunny-hopped to his cell — Lawrence Murphy's old bedroom — and waited at the window.

"Hello, Bob." The voice smooth and playful. Below, the big ox freezes on the spot. Approaching the courthouse, he never thought to look up. What lovely revenge, what head-splitting joy! Billy has killed men before, he fully expects to kill them again, but it's never the same from one murder to the next. It's different each one. These two, ushered in by an internal free fall, by a rope snap signifying release from control, are the product of seven long days of vigilance. Bob standing there below just ten feet away with a load in his pants, or so the Kid surmises. The carbine hanging from his fist; too late to raise it. Billy thrusts out his tongue and almost bites it in half, watching Olinger squirm like a bug on a pin, though he doesn't move at all, he *internally* squirms. "The Kid has killed Bell!" somebody yells out back — maybe Gauss — and Bob's response comes just before or just after the blast from the Whitney strikes his chest, his right shoulder, his arm, his cheek and neck — rips off his ear, pulps an eye, cracks his jaw, unfingers his hand — turns his body flesh, his bones and mapped blood into a fountain of Olinger-slop, as though thrown from a pail. Both barrels, thirty-six buckshot, all that smoke, the Kid can hardly see. Then he hears it: "And he has killed me, too." As the smoke clears, he spots the shadow of blood and fat stretching more than twice Bob's length behind his sprawled body. The man was just hog fat.

Now what? He's not happy or content, if anything more livid. He smashes the shotgun on the windowsill, splintering the stock, and throws it down on Olinger's corpse. "You son of a bitch, take that with you to hell." If he could kill him again he'd gladly do so. He stops, thinks. "And save me a place." He clanks back to the sheriff's room, steps out on the balcony, looks down at the crowd beginning to assemble. "Hold it right there," he shouts at Bob Brookshire, waving Bell's pistol hip-high. He never has liked Brookshire. "Cross the street and I'll kill you." So Brookshire wisely stays across the street with J. A. LaRue, Sam Wortley, and others, any one of whom could draw a bead on Billy but evidently cannot summon up the spunk. Below the balcony, it appears, every Mexican in Lincoln has gathered to watch. Godfrey Gauss, too — he catches Billy's eye — and Mrs. Lesnett. The Kid finds himself speaking. He paces back and forth. Every movement he makes pounds and rattles his chains. "Olinger, I don't care. Nobody liked him. Was there a single one of you liked that gorilla?"

No reaction from the crowd. His voice feels funny. He has no control over how it sounds. Is it loud or soft, can they even hear him? They're all maddeningly quiet.

"I could never see where he was an asset to any community. But as far as Bell goes, I did not want to kill him. I told him to surrender —" Billy's little white lie. "— But he refused. It was him or me, and so it was him. And that's that. I done him up. I'm sorry he's dead but I couldn't help it. Anyway, he's famous now. His claim to fame is all wrapped up for being someone I shot."

No one says a word.

"Don't all speak at once. Whoa. Calm down."

They look perfectly calm watching him from below.

"Somebody here got an ax or something I can use? I can pry off these irons?" Gauss leaves the crowd and walks around the courthouse while Billy keeps on talking. "I'm worked up so watch out. If anyone tries to stop me I'll kill him. You know me. I shoot first and ask questions later. It feels like I weigh a ton, my mind's racing all over. I got to take a piss but I can't in front of people. I feel like . . . I feel . . . Do I look all right to you? A little pale around the gills? I'm not going back to that snake hole in there." He nods to the room on the corner of the courthouse. "Thank you, Dad." Gauss tosses him a pickax and Billy sits and puts down his pistol and works on a leg iron. "These fucking things are strong." He inserts the pick into the first link, fused to the iron, and works it back and forth. "All right. Hold on. This goddamn head's loose." He holds the head of the pick, not the handle, but because of the manacles has to lean forward and twist to one side. "Dad, get me a horse. Maybe one of Judge Leonard's." Gauss walks off. He scurries up the road.

For a good fifteen minutes Billy works on his shackles and succeeds in snapping the short chain linking them — no more baby steps. The manacles are harder; he'll need Gauss's help. Gauss, below, now holds Billy Burt's pony, saddled and bridled. The Kid jumps to his feet and tucks the chain in his belt and leaps in the air and kicks and whirls around as though at a *baile*, and the skittish pony tries to pull away from Gauss. "He's on his way to hell," Billy announces, waving at Olinger, "and me, I'm free." He grips the balcony and leans out and shouts. "Freedom beats all! That's what makes this country great! I'm as good an American as anybody here. It's not many countries you can be free in anymore. I'm free and white and my blood's red and no one can stop me. Give me some room, for Christ's sake. Give me room, give me room!" His wild eyes dart everywhere searching the crowd, which backs off as though he might actually leap. "And this fucking country can easily spare men like Bob Olinger. My only show was to kill the stupid bastard. You ought to thank me for it. The town's a safer place. Alls I ever wanted was a fair shot at getting those bastards that murdered Mr. Tunstall. Mr. Tunstall was good to me. He gave me a horse, a saddle, a gun. He brought some class to this place and what did they do, they shot him in the back. Then I hired to Macky Sween who never paid me a penny and they killed him too and I hired to John Chisum and he still hasn't paid me. These jackleg lawyers and mealy-mouthed cattle barons do everything on tick, understand? If you owe them, why, it's everything you got. And if they owe you they punch a hole in a barrel of kill-me-quick red eye and offer you a swallow, thank you very much. Then it takes two days to straighten up again for business. They don't want you to be free. Isn't that right, Annie?"

Mrs. Lesnett just stares.

"Then they say I killed Brady. Well, it wasn't me. It was somebody else named Billy the Kid about the same size as me. Why am I the only one that stood trial for Brady? I'm for myself now. The hell with them all. I'm on my own hook. Hold on. Don't move." Wrists still manacled, he waves his gun at the crowd, at the sky, across the street, then twists his body and holsters the gun and grabs the pick and exits the balcony. He races down the stairs and through the old store and out the front door, eyes searching the world when he's out on the street. "Help me with these bracelets, Dad." With the pick, Gauss and Billy break the chain on his manacles. Gauss holds the pony but when he tries to mount, his hanging chains spook the animal, who bolts up the road. "You. Alex." Billy points the gun across the road at Alex Nunnelly, one of the trustees. "Catch that horse and bring him back."

"Hell, no. That would make me an accomplice."

"Well, you can just tell them I forced you to do it." Alex reluctantly starts up the street. "Move!" Alex runs.

As Alex shacks the horse Billy scans the crowd and spots José Sanchez and walks up and shakes his hand. "José." He hugs Godfrey Gauss, pecks Annie Lesnett on the cheek, and now a queue has formed: all the Mexes in Lincoln line up to shake his hand and nobody smiles. "Hey. Buck up. Go ahead, dance for joy." Even Bob Brookshire joins the line and manfully, somberly grasps the Kid's still-manacled hand. "Don't beat the drums or nothing." Then, festooned with chains but liberated — free! — Billy mounts the skittish horse and canters out of town. "Tell Billy Burt I'll send his pony back!"

They mill in the street and watch him trot off. And is that singing they hear? Yes, the Kid is strangling "Silver Threads Among the Gold" and Annie Lesnett tenuously joins in with a muffled quaver. At last they come to life, they're beginning to talk. A few even laugh. They glance around, shake their heads. There ought to be a band. Look, he's waving his hat. "Adios, boys!"

Then he's gone.

Five miles west of Lincoln he turns up into the Capitans, hardly conscious of direction. It's the trail to Las Tablas. Spring snow along the horse path, a soft hum in the air. The hum, he discovers, comes from his own throat. Must be the jitters. The hums are indulgences, little throaty grunts that rise through his spine with each thud of the horse and pleasantly vibrate inside his glutchpipe, and they work to calm him down. This is how famous outlaws mosey out of danger. Hum, sing, leap. *Whoop 'em up, Liza Jane!*

He clams up and looks back. Keeps on looking back, eyes forever searching tree trunks, brush, boulders.

He feels his tongue sticking out. Sees his stepfather, Antrim, coming at him with a shovel, then his mother's lips trembling — out of nowhere, these memories. Ma has that look, the one preceding tears, the expansion of face as before a pot boils. I must obey my mother.

Won't Garrett be floored! And Lincoln without authority of law, having lost its two deputies, so there's no one to chase him. Just the same, to be safe, Billy moves off the trail and rides inside the maze of tall ponderosas, thick enough to stop the undeviating bullet. The comfort of these trees, the firs and ponderosas, cannot be overstated. Real trunks for a change, the sort that reach for the sky, instead of the empty grasslands and desert whose rare stunted piñons in folds and arroyos hardly reach a man's shoulders.

He usually sees these mountains from below. Sees them pull their green fabric tight to their bulk like disgruntled sleepers, shorting the foothills, completely baring the llano.

The chains spook his mount but what can he do? The climb into the Capitans now begins to taper off but the Kid's horse won't give up limping, bad actors can't stop. Then comes the ridgeline folding into the canyon down the other side and the pony opens up. And the Kid, the young hotblood brimming with funk, the hard case, the desperado, the tough little pine knot, the canny *pistolero* of the sure aim and sixth sense, finds his mind racing as he descends, as it looks like he really and truly has escaped, racing and skidding and hopping around like spit on a hot stove. *Que hombre*, what a man! *Muy señor* — very much the gentleman. God knows he didn't *want* to kill Bell, who treated him fairly, but he had no choice. Oh, my goodness. The Kid has killed Bell.

Yes, he killed me, too.

What the Faber-pushers won't say. What the rag sheets won't print! Well, I'm short, they can't figure me out. My lack of facial hair is a deficiency that nature is still laboring to correct. Don't laugh. Let's slay that little shit, he looks like a nancy, wait till I give the signal. But fate decreed otherwise as the saloon lights blazed brilliantly in the pitchy inky darkness and the stranger fogged out. Last night you boys had "Billy the Kid" creeping around here, did you know that?

He knew the shooting would disturb the poor children in the orphanage. He'd once rescued a prayer book that a little girl had dropped — there you go, sweetie.

That frank, open countenance. *Look at me, Ma!* Note the roguish snap about the blue eyes, the brown curly hair, the slight but wiry frame clad in common garments. Hell, I'm just a person. A boy. I'm sort of normal for my age. I like to go to *bailes* and other such affairs where there is lots of noisy fun. At times I feel like smashing things. Everything tastes the same. Quite a handsome-looking lad and with an eye for the ladies, relaxed, light-hearted, playful with children, gallant to the *viejos*, attentive to his ma. You'd of been proud to know him. The tender heart of the coolest young outlaw who ever trod the trackless west — this Claude Duval of the wilderness — this good-natured Knight of the Road, always cheerful and smiling —

William H. Bonney, Billy Bonney, Billy the Kid, Kid Antrim, the Kid, El Chivato, William Antrim, Henry Antrim, Henry McCarty, Henry McCarthy, Patrick Henry McCarthy, what a prodigy of cognomens! And with each new name a piece of past washed away, with each one his selfhood loosened its grip. My goodness, there were days I never even existed.

How do you like it, Bilicito?

Don't move. Just like that.

Oh, Chivato, it's so *beeg*.

You think this one's big, you ought to see the '73. Single action, sure, but good Christ — it's got a .45-caliber center-fire cartridge and the goddamn barrel's near eight inches long!

What will Garrett do when he finds out? He will sit down and smile and be perfectly collected and eat himself inside. I'd like to see his face. Or Governor Wallace, I could pull for Santa Fe and lay for him there before the news arrives. He's the big toad in a small puddle, or so he thinks, but he is about as estimable as a heap of shit. The man is swelled up over his position and needs to be taken down a buttonhole. All of them do. To see their tongues hanging out, their petrified jaws —

They'll be on me like a stink. Let them come. Let them come. Who was it betrayed me to Garrett in the first place? Who told him where to look?

Once approaching Las Tablas, Billy calms down and his palms

begin to dry. The trees thin out, trail grows sandier. A cottontail at the base of a ponderosa is perfectly still, thinks no one can see him. Now it's evening, almost dusk. As the trees give out he can spot with greater keenness the brown-green plains below and the volcanic cones and blisters and domes, the ridges stacking up against the gray distance and the gray raised rim of the faraway horizon streaked with long shadows from the setting sun. The smells have changed, too. No more pine needle compost, moist pits of ghost rain. Now, rising with the heat against his descent comes the coal-oil cinnamon throat-scrape odor of the dry plains below. He rides down past needle rocks and flatiron crags with tall fins and flukes, as though, two thousand miles from the nearest ocean, without consideration of nature's proper arrangements, gray whales here had swum into the mountain and found themselves stuck.

The brownish plains turn red. Like a grassfire: hot, quick, finished. On a crumbling shelf in the many folds of hills, the Kid spots the first cholla. Now it's junipers and piñons comfortably arranged with scalds of free dirt between isolated trees. Around a quick bend, the scratch-ankle town of Las Tablas emerges.

April 29, 1881

Garrett

Hudgen's was a long-bar brass-rail place. I've a sensitive nose and could detect each distinctive component of its smell: beer, sawdust, sweat, old leather, pipe tobacco, coal smoke, and gamey foodstuffs. On a table near the bar were stacks of sliced meat, piles of bread, pickled beets, boiled eggs, warm biscuits, a hog's head, and canned tomatoes sprinkled with vinegar and sugar. The beer came in washtubs in back of the bar, into which the underskinker dipped the frosted mugs, and towels hung from nails pounded into the tables to wipe the thick foam off your beard when you drank it. Sand and sawdust on the floor, cattle brands burned into the paneled walls, a painting of a thinly veiled odalisque, yellowed by smoke, on the wall behind the bar. I couldn't bring Apolinaria into this place. It wasn't just the painting; bean-eaters weren't welcome, especially women. Too many encounters with out-of-town miners. White Oaks was a mining community, they had the quality miners, the scabby gap-toothed ones. The ones that swung shovels at each other from underneath the earth and considered every Mexican to be fair game. Among the acts of aggression these gentlemen committed, one asked a man to pass the butter at this very saloon and, not being heard, he immediately drew his pistol and presented it to the man's head, saying, "Pass the butter, *please*." They thought I was to thank for this new civility. The marshal, Pinto Tom, when arresting malefactors took special care now not to hurt their feelings any more than was necessary.

If asked, the men at my table would probably have called me the apotheosis of the changes that were sweeping the territory. The railroad, which ran all the way to Las Cruces. The Apaches, which gave up their war against the world. The bad men, who I supposedly broke of miswending and taught how to sing patriotic songs. Thanks to Pat Garrett, the Lincoln County War was over. Somehow I'd been credited not only with catching Billy the Kid but with wiping out smallpox, whorehouse manners, decayed people, and unbridled fornication. Folks paid their taxes now; I was in White Oaks to collect them. Also, to obtain the wood for his gallows. They'd offered to contribute all the lumber I needed and a wagon to carry it. This was what they called community spirit. The pillars were there, Pinto Tom, Joe Tomlinson, Fred Kuch, even Israel Jones, the parson who once accused me of being an atheist. A nullifidian is more like it. Also at the table was a drummer from St. Louis who wrote for the dailies as well as sold stoves, and he hadn't heard the story of the Kid's capture yet, so all of them would get it one more time tonight. Being seated at table leveled our disparities. You'd never have known the drummer was five-foot-one or I was six-six or Jones had a wooden leg. My legs being half of me, my fingers and arms came from the same tree and they were lengthy, too; that's what they called me, "Lengthy." The Mexicans made this into Juan Largo. At Fort Sumner in the old days, I'd already told them, I was called Big Casino, the Kid Little Casino. We sometimes partnered up at the faro tables. At that time I'd just arrived, I was years from being sheriff. Likewise he wasn't yet Billy the Kid, he was Antrim, Kid Antrim. It was a newspaper man that gave him the sobriquet Billy the Kid. And that was only last year — not long before I collared him at Stinking Springs.

"Weren't you a bardog at Sumner?" asked Jones.

"Yes, Reverend Jones, in the old days." He inspected me with an eyelid that drooped at half mast, having been ripped off in the same altercation in which he lost his leg, then sewn on with fish line. His puttylike face had not one scrap of facial hair, thus stringing out the mouth. "Do they still call you Reverend?"

"Israel will do."

"Fort Sumner?" said the drummer. "They had a saloon there?"

"It hasn't been a fort in ten years," I said. "More like a starve-acre town. I used to live there. What happened to me was a thousand-pound porker ran me down on the parade grounds, damn near killed me, but instead of dying I married the woman who nursed me back to health, Apolinaria Gutiérrez. She and her family moved to the fort when Lucien Maxwell bought it. You've heard of him, I suppose? Lucien Maxwell of the Maxwell Land Grant? He's dead now but his son Pete still brags up his daddy's two million acres, enough land to contain a fat curve of the planet. Had to sell it all to pay off his debts and with the leftover he bought the old fort, which was decommissioned in '71. Converted the officers' quarters into a home, elegant by the usual standards. By the time he died and his son Pete took over, the family empire was sadly diminished. Pete still manages the place, the sheep herds and stables. He's a well-known friend of the Kid, or a foe, depending on the hopes of his sister, Paulita. She was the Kid's sweetheart. She now carries his child. Pete rents the old hospital and barracks and storehouse which his father chopped into lodgings for his Mexican clients and friends from Cimarron. He runs the weekly dances and leases the shops and stables and saloons, Bob Hargrove's saloon and Beaver Smith's saloon, where I first met Kid Antrim. Beaver Smith is the one you should ask about Billy. His ears are jingle-bobbed. You're a drummer, you must get around, have you ever heard of that? For twenty-five cents Beaver will show you the long rail on his hams from where Chisum's men branded him. Get him drunk first."

"From bardog to sheriff," the drummer observed, looking at me. I gave him my bullet-hole-eyes look of being startled, fooling him by seeming somewhat up a tree. That's what I always do for strangers. You never know who they are. The effect of the mustache covering my mouth, I knew, was to lessen my jaw, and with my reedy twangy voice, mine was the most Texas drawl he would hear in White Oaks. "The secret to being a bardog, I learned, is to keep your mouth shut."

"You must be catching up," said Jones.

"I do talk more now."

"Why is that?"

"Because I'm done with doing."

"With the Kid in irons, you mean?"

"With the Kid in irons, I mean."

The drummer piped up. "What's he like?"

I kept my voice lofty. It comported with a stiff-jointed sandy sheriff who wished the world to think he was slightly loco, or maybe nervous as a hen, when not coldly efficient. "A very pleasant, fun-loving gentleman, quick with the handshake or quip or laughter unless he thinks he ought to kill you. I believe his hands and feet, being delicate and small, are more like a woman's than a man's. He's fairly much a chameleon of a person. He's just a boy. He changes stripes often. He once gave me a horse when mine come uncorked and I did not ask its provenance. George Coe told me something once told to him by the Englishman Tunstall. It was John Tunstall's murder that began the war whose final chapter will be the Kid's hanging. Tunstall said to Coe, 'George, that's the finest lad I ever met.' We might have known what he meant if he'd lived. In my estimation, the Kid wants you to think he's a cocksure reprobate. That was his downfall. He swung a wide loop and that put him in chains. Be happy he's scheduled to die in two weeks. He overwent the norm when it came to taking risks, plus he always desired to put in a gay time. Then again, he strikes fear in the average person's heart, mouth-fighters especially, so I guess he has a reputation to live up to. You can thank those who wield their Faber's number two. Have another glass of meat." I reached for the drummer's tumbler with my whiskey. "I should mention as well he's a famous lady's man. It's not just Paulita Maxwell. That's what rouses Pete's ire. The Kid has planted babies all over the territory. Just like a squirrel — hide the seed in a hole. A year later you forget where-all you put it."

So as not to scale down his heroic proportions, I didn't add what I could have about his behavior in those Fort Sumner days. Back before the Lincoln County War, before he stopped drinking and would get quite a jag on most every night at Beaver Smith's saloon. He'd sing his favorite song, "Silver Threads Among the Gold," and would not stop singing it despite all our efforts, which included throttling his neck, he still sang through squeezed pipes. One night, Pete Maxwell, whose hands are large as shovels, exclaiming, "Shut your damn pie hole," clamped his hand across the Kid's mouth for a full five minutes, and when he let go, the Kid, instead of continuing to sing, flipped his lips with a finger, making a sort of sputtery baby sound in one endless aggravating babbling scroll. Some fool then dared him to continue and to our dismay he did, even when every blessed person in that place screamed at him to stop. Beaver Smith then emptied a trunk in his room and carried it out and we loaded him in it and still we could hear him through the shut lid. And the next morning, when I arrived for the day's business and asked Beaver, "Is he still at it?" and he answered, "Look and see," I lifted the lid and there was the Kid folded up like a coffined grasshopper, his hard blue eyes round as buttons looking right at me, still flicking his bloody lips with his finger and making that sound. "Ain't he a piece of work?" asked Beaver. He's some for his inches, I acknowledged. If he caught himself a pig he knew damn well to hold him. The stubbornest jackass west of the Pecos.

"You captured him last December, you say?" asked the drummer.

"We set out in mid-December five months ago, yes. I knew his habits well. His haunts, his temptations. And my posse were reliable.

We started from here, White Oaks, from this very saloon — Frank Stewart, Lon Chambers, Lee Hall, Poker Tom Emory, Louis Bousman, the latter called 'The Animal.' Who else was it, Fred?"

"Bob Williams."

"Bob Williams. Barney Mason, of course. Jim East joined us later. It takes an army to catch a little fly. We took off across the prairie, cold-camped in a gulch, and made Puerto de Luna the following morning. We spent the day putting up at Grzelachowski's store, warming our flesh at mesquite-root fires and eating dried apples and drawing corks. From that place we struck out for Fort Sumner in a terrible snowstorm. Arrived at Gayheart's ranch twenty miles above the fort and sent a Mexican fellow, Juan Roibal, to see whether Billy and his boys were at Sumner. He returned the news they were. Next morning, Barney Mason and me snuck into the fort but someone must have tipped them off. They'd racked out, we learned, to Wilcox's ranch, about twenty miles east. Tom Wilcox and his partner Manuel Brazil on the Texas Road. The same road I first traveled into this territory, being a brush-popper from the *brasada* by way of Louisiana."

"Louisiana?" A burst of laughter came from a nearby table. Someone rolled a barrel in, wagons passed outside. Hudgen's was full of clinked glasses, loud shouts, low growls, sharp heel-thumps.

"So I concluded on a subterfuge. You see, Billy had lots of Mexican friends who were carrying reports to him all the time. There was Ignacio Garcia, José Valdez — tools of the Kid. I traded Valdez out for his assistance, convincing him to show a note to the Kid, addressed to Manuel Brazil, stating that our plans had disarranged and that, as we'd thought better of the situation, we'd ridden on to Roswell. My intent was to suggest that we'd been scared up. Then we sequestered our horses in Pete Maxwell's stable. We forted up in the old Indian hospital on Sumner's east side, a few doors down from Charlie Bowdre's wife, whom we were forced to restrain. Poor Charlie! His heart was not set on riding with the Kid. He'd already written to Governor

Wallace promising to change his evil ways and forsake his disreputable associates and requesting the governor to extend the pardon he'd granted for others to him, Charlie, and give him the opportunity to redeem himself. Charlie'd met me in secret to plead his case but he evidently thought I was playing a game to get him in my power. Quit those curs or surrender, I frankly told him, if not you will certainly be caught or killed, as we are after the Kid and the gang that runs with him and will sleep on the trail until we take them all in, dead or alive. Whether he remembered this conversation or not that night is beyond my surmise. If he had, would they not have been somewhat leery? I posted Chambers outside, to the east, on guard. The remainder spread a blanket on the icy floor and Mason had his cards and we sat to play poker. This room held old saddles, harnesses, traces, spurs, and ropes, mostly hung on the walls, and sacks of feed in the corners. Now and again I went to the door and cracked it an inch to peer out into the night. It was wintery and dark but not so dark as to be black. Warm air had blown in from the south and the snow gave off fog which obscured determined vision. The snow was a foot deep and the moon shone through the fog, mixing light and dark in swirly gusts of wind. About eleven o'clock, Chambers rushes in and announces a party is coming from the east. That can only be them, boys, I say, and we slip out, me, Chambers, and some others, and conceal ourselves amid a row of harnesses hanging on the porch. Mason and the rest go around the building in case they come that way. Soon, they heave into sight, emerging through the fog. The lead horse thrusts his head directly onto our porch. 'Halt!' I shout and up pops my Winchester and Chambers and I fire in concert. In the subsequent fusillade on either side, amid the swirl of black smoke and blue fog and moonlight, I heard cries of mortal agony. Their steeds pranced and curved and vanished in the fog, but one of them come back — made a circle and returned. 'Don't shoot, Garrett,' a voice I recognized says. 'Don't shoot. I am killed.'

"It was Tom O'Folliard, Billy's joined-at-the-hip man. Stuck to him like glue. But if you want to find out what sort of person the Kid is, I later learned that as they were approaching Fort Sumner, the Kid and Tom cheek by jowl in the lead, Billy all to sudden has an infusion of caution. A strong suspicion arises in his mind that they are riding into unforeseen danger. I'll say this much, he's quick. He decides that what he wants is a chew of tobacco and knows that Billy Wilson has some that's good and Wilson's in the rear, so he swings his horse around at the very last moment after the tobacco."

"Who told you that story?" asked the drummer.

"The Kid himself, from his jail cell. Told it with a wink."

"The coward."

"One man's cowardice is another's wile." I widened my eyes and fixed them on a fly grating my nerves in a puddle of beer. When my hand walloped down, beer fountained the table, and Fred Kuch got it in the eye. I smeared the pastry of fly guts and beer to the fat of my thumb and flicked it on the floor. "O'Folliard's sagging in the saddle. Our rifles are upon him. 'Throw up your hands!' 'I can't, I'm too weak.' We approach him with caution. He begs to be assisted. The rest of his gang has disappeared in the night. Mason slips his carbine out of its spider, we help O'Folliard from his horse and, to his cries of mortal agony, carry him inside. Not an easy task. He is a large mulish man with a flatiron face and porthole eyes. Been shot below the heart and creased across the chest and begs me now to finish him off. 'If you are a friend of mine you'll put me out of my misery.' 'I am no friend to men of your kind,' I tell him sternly. 'You sought to kill me because I tried to do my duty.'

"We lay him on the floor, sparing our blanket, and resume our game of poker. The chicken pie's large — almost ten dollars. But our play is distracted by O'Folliard's groans and I for one grow peckish. 'Oh my God, is it possible I'll die?' We've had to move the blanket to avoid his track of blood. 'Goddamn you, Garrett!' he screams when I've just drawn to a flush. 'I hope to meet you in hell.' 'I wouldn't talk that way, Tom,' I very calmly tell him. 'You'll be dead pretty soon.'

'Aw, you long-legged son of a bitch,' he wails, 'suck my cock.' 'Take your medicine,' says Mason and shows three nines and reaches for the pot. The oil lamp broadcasts a broken wheel of light into which our arms dip. Tom's back there in the darkness. 'Your time is short, Tom,' I say without turning. At the same time, I lay my hand on Mason's wrist. Directly behind me, Tom by now is breathing shallow and changes his tune. 'The sooner the better. I will be out of pain.' He asks for a drink of water. Having already folded, Jim East sighs and stands up and gets him one. As the poor fellow drinks I show Mason my flush, much to his disgust, and rake in the pot. Tom gags on a bubble and when it pops he's gone. I gather up the cards and shuffle. My deal."

The drummer asked, "Was this before or after Wallace posted his reward?"

"Governor Wallace announced his five-hundred-dollar reward for the Kid's capture on December fifteenth. The day we struck out. Are you suggesting I was doing this for mercenary gain?" I stared the man down. His disconcerted smile showed one broken tooth beneath his mustachio. "Don't be such a squitter-ass. Is that what you're suggesting?"

The poor fellow shrugged. "I suppose."

"You suppose? You suppose?" I produced my snippy smile. "What the Christ else would my object be?" The rest at the table nervously tittered and the drummer looked around in baffled relief. He grabbed the Old Towse and poured a double shot and drank it down chewallop. "After Tom died and we put him in the ground we had another heavy snow. I was in no particular rush at this juncture. We lit a warm fire and played some more cards. I knew Billy and the others would go back to Wilcox's ranch. If they caught on they'd been betrayed they never told Brazil or Wilcox. In fact, the Kid sends Brazil to Fort Sumner to scout out the lay. This was his one lapse. It could be he was distraught over losing O'Folliard. The next day Brazil rides into Fort Sumner and comes straight to me without batting an eye. He describes the condition of the crestfallen band, now reduced to five: the Kid, Charlie Bowdre, Dave Rudabaugh, Tom Pickett, and Billy Wilson. Rudabaugh's horse had been wounded in the shootout and died underneath him on the way back but he got another from Brazil. So it's five men, five horses, Wilcox and Brazil pretending to be friendly, and I give Manuel some more good manure to spread when he gets back, that we're shaking in our boots and want no more violence, then send him on his way. I tell him if the gang's not there when he returns, to come back and inform me. If they're there, just stick around. I and the posse will start for the ranch at two in the morning and if we don't meet you on the road we'll know they're still there.

"He went home and turned around and come back to Sumner, arriving at midnight. Snow on the ground, cold enough to piss icicles, frost in his beard. They taken supper, he said, then mounted and left. We climbed on our mounts and pulled out for the ranch. I send Brazil ahead to see if they're back and go around by Lake Ranch and come down from the north just past Wilcox's, where Brazil meets us. He shows me their trail in the snow, heading east. After following it a short distance I know their destination: a deserted forage station made out of stone hard by Stinking Springs. When we're half a mile away, I caution my companions to preserve silence, as we have them trapped. We leave Juan Roibal in charge of the horses, divide the party, and circle the house. I'm inside the dry edge of a snow-filled arroyo scarcely fifty, maybe forty, feet from the door. Three horses are tied to the projecting vigas, which means two are inside with the five men. Shivering with cold, we await the dawn.

"I'd coached the posse regarding Billy's togs, in particular his hat: wide-brimmed, light-colored, a Mex sugarloaf with an artistic braided green band around the crown. Some señorita wove that band for him. If he makes his appearance, fire at once, I said, and the rest will surrender. Shoot the Kid down first, ask questions later. He'd sworn that he'd never yield himself a prisoner but would die fighting with a revolver at each ear, and I knew he'd keep his word. Being in position to command the doorway, I said, When I raise, you also raise and fire.

"Faint light. Cold dawn. We're shivering with cold from lying on the earth and a man appears at the open doorway wearing a hat which corresponds to my description. A nosebag in his hand to hang upon a pony. The doorway, understand, has no material door. It is just an opening. And there are no other openings save the window that faces us. I raise my rifle, the others do too, and seven bullets speed on their errand of death."

"Did you give them fair warning?" The drummer again.

"I take no risks. I'm fond of my hide. And the reason I'm sheriff and have not been killed is I never give the other fellow a chance — not if I can help it."

"Admirable," muttered Israel Jones.

I looked him up and down, amused. His face darkened; he lit a cheroot. I was a little hoarse by now so I nodded to the drummer, who passed the bottle, and I medicined my throat. "I see it's not the Kid when he reels back toward the door — it's poor Charlie Bowdre, who wanted out so bad, if you recall, that he'd written to the governor. My heart bled for Charlie. God bless him, poor man. His ready-made conscience just didn't fit. I suppose Mrs. Bowdre had insisted he wear it, maybe even 'took it in' so it wouldn't be baggy." I hung quotes on the words. "But it's hard for some men to unglue from dear companions if they come to your ranch and ask to be fed and taunt you for demurring when they ride to depredations. Let that be a lesson. As to why he was wearing Billy's hat, I presume he just grabbed it. Or is this another instance of that savvy or luck for which the Kid was justly famous? Did he throw the hat at Charlie just before he stepped out? Here, warm your head. If so, the bitter pill must be hard to swallow now. To save his own hide, he sent the two men who were closest to his heart to die in his place. When everyone around you lives outside the law, when no rules exist and mayhem is common and every sort of debauchery and cruelness is run-of-the-mill, then survival depends on forgotten skills like knowing who-all to sacrifice.

"Wilson shouted out that Bowdre was killed and wished to surrender. We laughed in our boots at this appositive. The young wounded brigand staggered at the door, not quite dead yet. I shouted for him to come out with his hands up but from behind him the Kid caught Charlie's belt, drew his revolver, placed it in his hand, and said to his friend, 'They've murdered you, Charlie, but you can take a few with you.' Bowdre come out with both arms in the air, the gun dangling from a finger, and him walking tangle-leg, left and then right, his head rolling like a melon. He wobbles in my direction, motions toward the house, and with a mouth full of blood, purls, 'I wish . . . I wish . . .' He'd been shot in the groin, the gut, the neck, shot up so bad it was a wonder he could move. Each of his prints in the snow was pooled with blood. He falls in my arms and I roll him to the side and after a while when I reach out to feel him I find him frozen already, solid as a block of ice.

"It's full daylight now. At the house, I see, one of the riatas is being pulled through the door. I drop on the fact that what they wish to do is lead the remaining horses inside then emerge at full gallop and make their escape. As the horse approached the door I shot him in the brain and he fallen like a stone, barricading the outlet. They couldn't now make a break, even two on a horse, as in leaping over this large obstruction the riders' heads would strike the lintel. I believed we had them trapped. To be on the safe side, I shot the two ropes which held the other two horses and they trotted away about a hundred feet and started pawing at the snow.

"I now opened a conversation with the besieged. 'How are you boys fixed in there?' 'Pretty good,' said the Kid. 'We need some wood to make a fire.' 'Come out and get it; be a little neighborly.' 'Go to hell, Lengthy. I'd freeze to death first.' Then they're talking to theirselves and after a piece, he asks for some tobacco. I say again, 'Come out and get it.' 'Just pitch it in here,' he says, and I think, at the risk of seeming soft, why not? I toss my pouch through the door. 'Where's the papers?' says he. 'Now you're asking too much. Come out and get them.' 'Fuck you, you lengthy bastard.' 'Then toss my tobacco back.' 'Go to hell, Garrett.' 'Toss it back, Kid!' 'Just wait a pissing while.' They seem to have a confab. Chattering like magpies. Soon, the bag flies out the door but something tells me not to catch it. Mason picks it up and looks inside and exclaims with a prune-face, clamping his nose, 'Don't that beat all.'

"Billy asks if we have cards. 'Sure,' I answer. 'I know,' he says. '*Come out and get them.*' 'You're catching on,' I say. All this time, *sabes*, my bead is on that door. 'Well, how about some sipping whiskey?' says the Kid. 'Come out here and take a sip.' 'Sip on this, you long-legged cocksucker.'

"We guarded them all day. Bad names were applied, each to the other, but it was all sort of sporty. Along to noon, they turned out the two horses which were inside. I concluded they'd grown tired of living in a stables. Around three come a wagon from Wilcox's ranch with provisions and firewood. We build a big fire and roast a lot of meat and the bubble and spit of the fat and the skin rides the smoke into their hole. It proves to be too much for the famished lads. Rudabaugh fixes a stick to a hanky that once had been white and waves it out the window and calls out they want to surrender. He emerges first. All will give theirselves up, he's been deputized to say, if I guarantee them protection from violence. This I did. In a few moments they slunk out of there, were disarmed, shook our hands, got a big meal, warmed themselves at the fire, then we took them to Wilcox's. I sent Brazil and Mason back to Stinking Springs to fetch Bowdre's body. Then we started for Fort Sumner in the dark.

"First thing at Sumner, Manuela Bowdre come rushing out her door whacking me with a skillet and kicking my legs until the boys pulled her off. 'You son of a bitch,' she screamed over and over, 'you killed my husband.' As we brought the body in she struck me on the shoulders with a branding iron, and I had to drop Charlie at his widow's feet chachunk. I told her I'd buy him a brand-new suit and dig the hole myself but she spit in my face and called me a name I shall not repeat to you, for it would be quite useless. I did pay for the suit. We sat to supper at Beaver Smith's saloon and the Kid gives his Winchester to Jim East but Beaver Smith raises such a roar about accounts he said Billy owed him that he switched the gift to Beaver. He gave Frank Stewart his fine bay mare, saying that he expected his affairs to be confining for the next few months, and he wouldn't have time for horseback exercise. Then Deluvina Maxwell come in the saloon and asked if we could go to Pete Maxwell's house so his sister, Paulita, could say her goodbyes in private to the Kid. I let it be understood that this was out of the question. Dirty Dave Rudabaugh was shackled to the Kid and they would not be parted till we got to Santa Fe and were safely in their cells. We did go to Pete's and I let the two sweethearts say their farewells but in front of everyone, not in private, and with Dave along for the ride, leaning as far away from the lovebirds as the chain would allow and bending over like he's sick. It did not seem to bother the sweethearts that their farewell kiss was such a public event. It got Pete's mad up, though. He pulled his sister away. But not before they'd indulged for time without end in one of those soul kisses of which the novelists tell us but which is rare if you're an outlaw wading in blood or a waddie always sleeping in fields of cow patties. Paulita wasn't showing yet and only her brother knew she was pregnant, but my guess is she took that opportunity to whisper the news into Billy's ear. He seemed somewhat abashed yet prideful after that. Then we hit for Las Vegas but on the way out of Sumner all the Mexes gathered to wave goodbye to Billy, though it was Christmas Eve. My sister-in-law, Celsa Gutiérrez, was off to one side, and I noticed she and Billy blew kisses at each other, him with lips blushing fresh from Paulita's mouth.

"The next day in Vegas, we had another little adventure. The

Mexes there hated Dave Rudabaugh because he'd murdered Lino Valdez earlier that year, in a futile attempt to spring John Webb from jail. We boarded the train to take the prisoners to Santa Fe but a mob blocked the tracks and surrounded our car and made murderous noises. They were brandishing weapons. We stood on the steps and threw down on the crowd and told them we were taking Rudabaugh to Santa Fe, where he would be jailed, come what may. I went inside the car and announced to the passengers, 'Gentlemen and ladies, there is going to be a fight and if you don't want to join it you better get out.' All left with the exception of two rusty hackums who said they hadn't killed a Mexican in two weeks and would fight to pass the time. They pulled from under their seats two enormous .50-caliber Sharps buffalo guns and knelt at a window. Our posse, too, knelt at windows as the mob seethed beneath, but I noticed their seething had diminished. Each of us picked out a greaser to aim at. I told the posse, 'Don't burn powder for nothing,' and to the prisoners I announced that I would unchain them and arm them as well, if it came to that. The Kid said, 'Fine, arm me now.' Then he looked out the window. 'Hell, they won't fight. Just look at their faces.'

"He was right. Waving his pistol, Deputy Marshal Morley mounted the engine and pulled the lever wide open and the crowd dispersed when the wheels begun to spin.

"On the train, Billy the Clown amuses the passengers by placing a slice of apple pie in his mouth then pulling it out in one piece. Well, he's got a big mouth. This was the extent of his rollicksome performance. In the Santa Fe jail, the whole kit and caboodle attempted to escape by digging a tunnel and hiding the soil inside their mattresses but a deputy discovered it. Billy was put in solitary confinement where he spent all his time writing to Governor Wallace and asking him to act on his promised amnesty. That promise was made two years ago and since then the Kid has murdered, stealed, passed counterfeit money, and generally deported himself in a lawless manner, so what did he expect? His trial was in March down to Mesilla and we taken him back to Lincoln after that to be jailed until his hanging. Where he is now."

"Is it true what he said in Las Cruces," asked Tomlinson, "on the way to Mesilla? The crowd's at the station watching as they take him from the train to the stagecoach and somebody asks, 'Which one's Billy the Kid?' And the Kid puts his hand on Judge Leonard's shoulder, saying, 'This is the man.'"

"True as taxes."

"And the quip about the papers," Tomlinson added, providing versicle for my response.

"I believe you mean the easterner who asked the Kid, 'What do you think when you read about yourself in the papers, Billy?'"

"That's right."

"The Kid looks at this man with a twinkle in his eye. 'I think what a hard case, what a bloodthirsty killer, he does not have a drop of mercy in his blood. I'd sure like to meet him.'"

All laughed. "So he's a wag."

"The most dangerous wag you could imagine. I for one will not laugh at his antics until he's safely hanged. He'd shoot off your balls just for a merry prank. He's a likable sort who helps himself to whatever he wants, a woman or a horse, but hanging won't atone for half of what he's done. As the good book says, we roar like bears and mourn like doves and look for judgment and there is none."

"Isaiah," said Jones. "Not bad for an atheist."

"Atheistic thinking has never led me by the nose. I grew up with the Bible."

"Too bad you don't believe it."

"Too bad you don't believe anything else."

"Now we're talking. Your feet run to evil, your hands are stained with blood, your lips have spoken lies. We look for judgment and there is none."

"You may look for judgment, Reverend Jones, but I suspect you love your whiskey better than your God."

"Least I have a God to love."

Outside on the street there was a sudden commotion. A young buck burst into Hudgen's Saloon and bellered, "Garrett! Garrett! Is Pat Garrett here?"

All gazed at me. I smiled.

"The Kid has escaped! He has killed Bell and Olinger! Oh my God, he's escaped!"

Leaning back in my chair, I checked the diamond rings on both of my hands and the gold watch chain at my waist. My smile didn't fade. I drank calmly from my glass. My long neck stiffened. My tongue was dried up now. I raised my brow and pulled out my watch, noted the time, continued smiling, tucked it back in, reached up the sleeve of my fine worsted coat and tugged down for all to see my silver cuff buttons. They gladden wanton eyes. My face felt warm. My pupils may have crossed. The Lord will take away their tinkling ornaments, their chains and their bracelets, their bonnets and headbands and tablets and earrings, their rings and their nose jewels, their changeable suits of apparel, and their hoods and veils and fine linen and crisping pins. For outside are dogs and sorcerers and murderers, and outside every mouth speaks consummate folly, and outside in the desert men squat on their haunches and drink blood and eat flesh and pick at scabs and lice, all manner of filth, and feed each other's mouths, and feel satisfied, and laugh, and then shall it be for a just man to burn.

· 3 ·

1877

Tunstall

Lincoln, New Mexico
23rd March, 1877

7 Belsize Terrace
Hampstead,
London, England

My Much Beloved Father,

McSween & I left Belen (where I wrote you my last) after many detentions last Sunday morning; we traveled all day & night reached a place called Abo, it is just above the words *El Salad* on the new map I sent, & lies about 50 miles southwest of Belen. "Abo" consists of about a dozen mud huts, the people are miserably poor & had smallpox in every house (I was vaccinated when at Belen but it did not take) & we slept in one that I supposed from what they said had as little as any of them. Our next drive was to have been to the Gallinas spring which is about 60 miles (there is a waterhole marked on the map which does not exist) & there is not water between the two points. We were under

· 32 ·

the impression that a man named Dow had a ranch at Gallinas spring & we took no grub save a loaf we had in our mess-box, we got to about 30 miles on our road when our offside mare wanted to lie down. We unharnessed her & she started going into convulsions, rolled & kicked at her stomach. McSween said "My poor Molly! Oh, Tunstall, I believe she is going to die right here." I went up & looked at the poor faithful beast, struggling in agony, & commenced calculating how we were ever going to get straightened out, for it necessitated that one of us should go back for help & the other remain (at the shortest) 18 hours alone on the prairie. We sat down & watched her, & the carrion crows came around & watched her, & soon many came, to wait for their promised orgie. The sun was high & hot & we stayed in this spot from 11 in the morning to late in the evening when a mighty rumbling reached our ears & an ox wagon came rolling down the hill. *"There you are, Mac!"* I said, *"I told you that* I was not going to be left in the lurch, I told you my people believed that Providence had a special commission out to protect me & you see, there it is, come just in the nick of time." (I really had told him that before & I reminded him of it.) The Mexicans (for such they were) had a little scrub pony behind the wagon, which we hitched by the side of our sound animal.

We reached the house of our friends Livingstone and Winters, but 40 long miles had to be travelled first. The next day we reached Lincoln at about 5 pm where I received a number of your letters. You will be able to judge from my previous anxiety how much these letters relieved my mind. My friend Widenmann has come down to this country. I was very pleased to see him as he is a man I can depend upon & whom I like *very* much. I introduced him to Mr. & Mrs. McSween & he left for his room about 9 pm.

Oh, did I mention Molly recovered and a Mex brought her to us.

We have traveled over 700 miles, looking for the best ranch land. I don't like this Rio Grande country atall, it is a complete waste land & in my opinion one long den of thieves & cut throats, at the present time they are getting somewhat scourged with smallpox & by that means a number of the young male fry are being prevented from developing into horse thieves & the female fry from developing into fit mates for the same. The situation in this interminable wilderness is the same everywhere: a few lone white men in control of trade, legitimate and otherwise (mostly the latter) — an immensity of desert & canyons & mountains — and fitful little pockets of brown-skinned natives, both Mexican and Indian, whose intentions are inscrutable.

Placita (or Lincoln) seemed *welcoming* this time even if it is in miner's parlance about the "toughest" little spot in America, which means about the lawless. You'd never know this from its peaceful demeanor, a small collection of adobe (or mud) homes scattered up a pretty creek called the Rio Bonito (which means Pretty River). The single dirt street is either dust or mud, depending on the weather, and a haze of wood and charcoal smoke hangs above the town. I must be growing fond at the advanced age of 23 because the clang of the blacksmith shop, the sound of children at play & the barking of dogs & grunting of pigs not to mention a fellow playing piano in a saloon (if that's what you can call it, it sounded more like banging the keys with his elbows) made me feel as though I'd arrived home again. I have to remind myself (as I remind you) that a man can commit murder here with impunity. All countries more or less thickly populated with a *needy, ignorant* population are unsafe in a measure. A look may, if it have sufficient malice in it, justify resort to firearms in the minds of people here.

Of course, you aren't to worry. As regards my getting shot, well this is a fine country & people sometimes use others as targets, but I am not going to get shot so don't be uneasy about that. If formerly I had not the knack of making friends, I seem to possess it now to a sufficiently useful extent; & then again I have a presentiment that I shall *not* get killed but that I *shall live* to accomplish my schemes & will give those three Pets my sisters (whom you must read this to) such a time as will make their heads swim (as we say on the frontier).

Of my friends, lawyer McSween is in particular a blessing. A lifelong teetotaler, a Presbyterian, he never carries weapons and has both the outward appearance and the inward temperament of an honest man & has succeeded in persuading me to go into stock. His wife Susan I find a very pleasant woman in every way, she told me as much about this place as any man could have done, she is the only white woman here & has a good many enemies in consequence of her husband's profession. Everyone in my circle is fond of her to distraction, she keeps us well entertained. Her husband with his long stringy moustache down to his knees (all American males have prodigious facial hair), who seems often to be frowning by the angle of his lip-whiskers, absolutely dotes on her with an aspect of rapture in his eyes and a foreboding air of longing as though they'd just made acquaintance (they have been married 4 years).

Robert Widenmann is common looking but a man I place great confidence in. I have executed a small deed, constituting him my legal representative in case of my death, until you write, come over, or instruct some other person, to attend to my affairs and your interest. Both as regards to his ability & integrity, I feel sure that in case you ever need his assistance, that he can save every cent that I "have out" for you. The history of his interest & mine would be somewhat lengthy, but I consider them parallel & not at all liable to clash. Two of Widenmann's leading traits are obstinacy & combativeness, he will hold a point longer & fight harder to keep it, than any man of his age I ever met (He is 25). And he has consequently a great deal of what I call "force" in his character; if he decides that a horse wants throwing down, he throws him; & if a mule gets its own way with someone & he concludes that she has to learn that she can't do it with others, he teaches her. I consider myself very lucky in meeting him, he so exactly suits me we stick to each other like brick & he takes care of me, we sleep in the same room. His parents are German & live in Georgia, he was educated in Germany, he weighs about 175 lbs & he stands six feet & is very broad. We are sufficiently good friends to be able to get as mad as we like with each other, without its affecting our friendship in the slightest. People say we are like man & wife.

Both Mrs. McSween and her husband have told me that the whole of this country (New Mexico) is under the control of a ring composed of two or three lawyers, & their practices & power throughout New Mexico are quite astonishing, they are more powerful than the priests & that is saying a great deal. The local store is owned by low Irish, part of this ring, & they buy local produce by extending credit on their store merchandise & thus get the Mexican farmers in their power. They advance both goods and credit against future crops and stock & when the poor fellows see they're in a trap they balk or move away, & if it's balk the House uses the law to attach their goods and property (most particularly, cattle and horses) for debts owed to them. They are known as "the House" but also called the Murphs or Dolanites or Murphyites, for the owners, Lawrence G. Murphy & his partner, James Dolan. They "carry" local settlers until they (the settlers) are so extended that their benign benefactors have no choice, their poor hands are tied, but to foreclose on their property. Their real money is made by contracts to supply the local army post, Fort Stanton, which both men served at, their ties to the command being part of this "ring," & by stealing supplies contracted to the Indian Agency & selling them in Las Cruces, Albuquerque, & other places. In placing people in their debt they force them into thievery to pay off the debt, no questions asked. So of the beef that Murphy and Dolan supply to Fort Stanton and the Agency much of it once belonged to John Chisum, the largest rancher in this area. John Chisum here is "the man behind the scenes." He knows that Dolan and Murphy, or their agents, steal his stock and he pays men to steal D & M's horses, *pari passu*. The "Dolanites" also "sell" ranches & land to incoming settlers without themselves having title, which has happened to a friend of mine here, Dick Brewer, a young rancher whom I highly esteem. He is called the handsomest man in Lincoln Country & he is as true as steel.

Before I came to this place two men highly regarded by the citizens, Robert Casey and Juan Patrón (one of the best educated Mexicans I have met, he is quite intelligent & appears to have good principles) were shot and Casey killed, after they had become outspoken in political meetings against "the House." Patrón was wounded and crippled for life, he was shot through the back about 1/2 an inch to the left of the spine, in about the hollow of the back the bullet was taken out from just under the skin of his stomach, & strange to say he survived it, though it seems to have touched the nerves that command his left leg, he has very little control over it, this is the only ill-effect he feels from it & at the time he was shot, he thought he was shot in the leg & not the back, is not that odd?

To the House's dismay they caught the man who shot them, William Wilson, & *By Jove!* you would like this story if I could just build a fire and dry the ground for you to sit on and tell it by starlight in the wilderness of New Mexico. William Wilson, if you please, had to be hung twice, they hung him for 9 minutes, put him in a coffin, & a Mexican woman lifted the lid & said he was alive! Lawrence Murphy of the House said he'd been legally hung, they had to let him go, but he couldn't prevent the townsfolk from dragging Wilson from the coffin & hanging him again.

Had I money enough to carry out my land and cattle scheme I could obtain a purchase to break their Irish stranglehold on commerce in this place. You haven't told me yet when your first remittance will come, but I want it *very badly* & in fact, the whole amount. It would ease my mind & facilitate the working of things enormously; I can't *explain* to you, or *express* to you the *strain all this is on me*, I feel like a man on a runaway horse, new dangers appear almost at every stride. I sit & think for an hour or two & get up weary with the tension; & my only consolation is that I am all right at present & the scheme *not spoiled yet*. If you have not sent me the money send it at once on receipt of this, send me the £3200 in drafts of £500 apiece (of course one would have to be for £700) as fast as you conveniently can, then if you think you can let me have £2000 more, write & let me know.

You see I am unable to lay a scheme before you until it is perfected throughout, & in the interim I have nothing to do but bite my nails & fret at the slow flight of time, if you send me the money that I have written for, you will see that I shall invest it in a way that will secure your interest in every shape. Now I think that I have unburdened my mind, which acts as a sort of safety valve to my sanity, I need not repeat the oft told tale of the love I bear you, so I will simply say that I remain as ever, your affectionate son,

John

Lincoln, New Mexico
11th April, 1877

7 Belsize Terrace
Hampstead,
London, England

Much Beloved Parents,

The game is going marvelously well so far, I keep on making my points, but there are some that can't be made without money & *ready money*. Now as regards safety, I am going to execute a small deed & give it into the safe keeping of Dick Brewer, to be opened in case of any accident happening to me & it will be appointing R. A. Widenmann & A. A. McSween as trustees of my property until you could get over here. I shall have the finest property I have seen since I have been in the United States. To hold *unsurveyed land* is a sort of game of "bluff" (Poker) I am willing to undertake, I could run a herd of cattle upon it & call all the best locations "camps" & have men in my employ to represent that they owned them & I should then have force enough to carry out any intentions I might have in regard to them. To run a small herd of cattle will cost as much as it would to run one twice or three times as large, for one needs a cook, if one has but two herders, a stable, a mowing machine, a wagon, a work team, a couple of houses, a cattle corral, camp cooking outfits for the ranch & road, a barn &c &c which cost just as much for the running of 200 as for 1000 head of stock. So you see that the more cattle a man has, the more economically they can be worked. The property I have my closest eye upon you could recover every cent out of in the event of my death that it will cost; & more too; & in my safe I shall always keep full particulars, both of the property acquired & speculations gone into.

Dick Brewer has got over his smallpox & is well & hearty. I am as well as ever. Brewer's father & mother have gone back to Wisconsin so this is a Bachelor's hall, there is nothing very polished about it, but the welcome is as hearty as it can be. You may be interested in knowing that I go by the name of "The Englishman" as a general thing & they say to Dick from time to time, "Confound that Englishman, what is he going to do in this country anyhow?" These are the reported comments of the "House," which Murphy and Dolan are said to make. McSween calls them "Irish scum" but I say tut-tut and tighten his leash.

You are right in supposing that McSween is to be instrumental in working my points & you can take my word for it that my arrangements with him are such as will be the most likely to bring everything out as I wish it. I have all the confidence in him that is necessary, in so important an affair, but nevertheless I never give a chance away or have a corner out of which he could make a cent out of me against my will.

Dear Darling, Much Beloved Sister Lilian, when I read the Dear kind words you wrote to me, I thought I had never wished to go home as much before. I saw a grand, great, bald headed eagle, sailing & sailing & *sailing* round in the sky, above my head; I looked up with my eyes full of tears, & thought, "if only I had that eagle's great, strong wings, how swiftly I would fly across the land & the sea, & how straight I would go, to my Dear Old Sister" then I thought how I should kiss & hug you, till I thought there would be nothing left of you, for I could never make you know how much I love my Dear Little Sisters. I love you *all the time* till my left leg nearly breaks. I never think of being happy unless I think of my Pets; & whenever I *am* happy, I am sorry that you cant share whatever it is that is making me so, whether it is the "drumstick" of some old turkey "gobbler" or a ride on a fine day under a blue sky, & a shining sun. I sometimes dream that I see you all, & I wake up so happy that I nearly cry.

And Dear Darling Mother, don't imagine that I am overcome, from morning till night, with a sense of lonely-ness & depression, or that what seem hardships to you are any inconveniences to me, for that is not the case; my heart always feels as light as a *feather*; ambition will help a man to disregard the *present entirely*, & if you could see me build-ing a fire in a camp under the star spangled (not banner, of Uncle Sam) but vault of heaven, you would probably hear me whistling at the same time (the nearest I could get with my unmusical mouth) "I wish I had a fish with a great long tail" & if the matches would not strike & I had to do with-out the "lambent flame," the expression my "fiz" (physiognomy) would wear, would be far more indicative of wrath at the trouble, than sadness. If I could explain my plans for making money to you, Mother, it would sound like a sort of fairy tale; I have kept up a *"terrible thinking"* (like that speechless parrot) all the time, to puzzle, & twist, & turn & patch, & alter my scheme until I have made it fit my requirements, but I believe that if I had the money I want (I can *make do* with £3200 this year, but could do much more with £5200) you would be astonished at the result.

My health is splendid; nothing seems to hurt me. Smallpox, I guess, hates the sight of me; I sleep every night like a sack & snore & snort like a "grampus" from 9 pm until 5 am. Widenmann does not sleep very well & is I think a musician (although I am not much of a judge of that class of stock) & lies in bed & listens to my solos on the "base vile" until he can't stand it any longer, he then punches me in the ribs or anywhere else that comes handy & tells me he wants to go to sleep, "All right, old fellow, it's a free country, go ahead" I tell him & turn over & pitch it a key lower down, in the morning he blows up about it the way I treat him, but I tell him "I have only got his word for it, as I did not remember waking up after I said goodnight." "Well then, Harry, you're a confounded Galloot" he says & we change the subject. He calls me Harry under the misapprehension that you also know me by my middle name, how he came by this chimerical fancy I haven't the least notion. This is Sunday, Dick Brewer and Widenmann are off on a bear hunt & Widenmann has taken my rifle. God bless you all, my darling darling Pets! Good night!

John

7 Belsize Terrace
Hampstead,
London, England

My Most Beloved Father,

I can't *begin* to express my appreciation of your gener-osity. My present exchequer at last is adequate to the task of *all* my schemes of which you shall have the latest and most surprising news. If things turn out exactly as I expect at the end of the first year, & you could spare more capital, £2500 more capital would nearly double the amount of the profit, but I consider the amount that I have received is as much as one ought to put into stock to *start* with, an addition the next year would be all right though.

I am now going to introduce you to my *latest* scheme for making money, it is a little new to you so open all your ears; & before I start let me tell you that it has been long studied & has my full endorsement. First of all, let me tell you that groceries in this country realise a profit of 50 per-cent on the *return* & they are a cash article; in the second place there are two cash customers for four staple items in this country, viz., the Indian department, & the Army, & the articles they buy are corn, hay, flour, & beef. In the third place, the Mexican is essentially a "borrowing" ani-mal, if anyone will lend he can't help borrowing, any more than the needle can help turning to the pole; but unlike most borrowers, he pays willingly as soon as it is in his power. Fourthly this country is so far away from any other (I mean this *district*) that produce raised here is protected from foreign produce by a tariff of 1½ cents per pound (for it costs 1½ cents per pound for wagon freight from any other produce market). Fifth this district is not large & one can arrive at within a few lbs. of the amount of grain that will be required *by the whole community or any member of it*. Now the question arises, out of the existing circumstances & with these ascertained points, what scheme, if practicable, would catch the ready money of the Indian department, & the Army, & avoid the dangers of too many debtors among a needy & improvident class?

The first part of the question is simple to answer; by having hay, beef, corn, or flour raised within the district, Uncle Sam is compelled to patronise you & pour his almighty dollars into your cap. The answer to the second is simple likewise. Don't credit the poor shiftless wretches with what they can't pay. Now, you see we know what we want to do; we are like the wise men whom Columbus told to balance the egg. The solution I think you will agree is found in the following problem. Tunstall opens a grocery store, Mexican applies for groceries; T. supplies him with groceries in return for promisory notes to deliver x lbs. of grain to his store of fair merchantable quality, upon the 20th day of August, T. having ascertained beyond doubt that the crop planted by M. will (when gathered) equal x. The same problem can be solved in the same way on the flour question. By this means T. can acquire a *controlling* interest in both these articles. The question then arises, is T. sure to get the contracts? perhaps he may not, but whoever does, *must* come to T. to buy, or get "bust," including Murphy and Dolan and their "House."

"But (I hear you say) this is not going into a ranch business at *all*. We don't see what all this means." Just you hold on for a spell till I "shpit on me hands" as Pat said. You see the Mexicans would bring their steers, cows, calves, yearlings, & year-olds, ranches &c &c to trade for groceries just as sure as anyone would sell to them that way. Now you see I would sell for any good property they brought. This is how the "House" does it. If their title was good, I would take their ranch as payment & let it; it would be *splendid* property to hold.

This country is different to any other & if a man is somewhat supple & can accommodate himself to circumstances he can make far more than if he tried to run his affairs just as he would, or could, in an old country. All the fixtures necessary to run my store will be a desk, a scale, & a safe, & I should need all of these if I had nothing but a cattle ranch. My most earnest desire is for success & more on account of my sisters my Pets than for myself; for if I can but win I would be content to cast the fruits of my success at their feet, knowing that I had won the means of smoothing away a vast proportion of the rocks in their path & given them the means of beautifying their lives & I could retire from the scene without a sigh.

You see what I drive at. The ranch scheme and the store scheme are interchangeable. Certain ranches if controlled would control the price of grain & in this country it is more easy to corner the market than in any other part of America. Now to make things stick "to do any good," it is necessary to either get into a ring or to make one out for yourself. *Everything* in New Mexico, that pays *at all* (you may say) is worked by a "ring," there is the "Indian ring," the "army ring," "the political ring," the "legal ring," the "Roman Catholic ring," the "cattle ring," the "horsethieves ring," the "land ring" and half a dozen other rings including Murphy and Dolan's "Irish ring," but theirs is on shaky legs. I have it on good authority that they are close to ruin.

My ring is forming itself as fast & faster than I had ever hoped & in such a way that I now possess nearly 400 cattle and 4,000 acres, the finest plum of the lot as to ranches hereabouts. To which the addition of a store will present a formidable aspect and make every Mexican now beholden to the "House" stiffen & roach his back like a mule & buck through the ring that is using him & into mine instead. Mc-Sween and Widenmann, of course, are my principal allies but in the matter of daily operations, the machinery of the business, which necessitates taking the bit between one's teeth, Dick Brewer has agreed to be my foreman, & his talents are such that he attracts the best "hands." They work for him and thereby work for me. I propose to confine my operations to Lincoln County, but I intend to handle it in such a way as to get the half of every dollar that is made in the county *by anyone*; & with our means we could get things into that shape in three years if we only used two thirds of our capital in the undertaking.

The land scheme will take, as I have told you, £3200 from first to last. The payments have already commenced & will continue to have to be paid until about next Decr. Or Jany. After which there will be only a small payment left to be made about 12 months after that. If these kind of little outlays run me close you must strain every point to keep me supplied as I intend to work things in such a shape (unless my luck leaves me altogether) that I win the game. There is *no* speculation about it, & *nothing* that you can't wash your hands quite clean of in a moment, if you desire it.

Please hug for me my Much Beloved Trinity. Yours as ever,

Most Affectionately,
John

Lincoln, New Mexico
12/77

7 Belsize Terrace
Hampstead,
London, England

Dear Mr. and Mrs. Tunstall,

Your son John is away and is not able to write to you this mail, but is, as he says, "alive and well" after the "rustling" of his horses. He will doubtless send you his letter shortly.

Yours sincerely,
Robert A. Widenmann

P.S. We have been in great trouble but it is now all over.

Lincoln, New Mexico
6th December, 1877

7 Belsize Terrace
Hampstead,
London, England

My Dear Father,

I have had to expose myself a great deal in raking over the country, on expeditions arising out of all that has happened, when I was by no means in a fit state to go; I feel pretty badly used up just now. I don't know whether (like the horses) I shall be able to get on my pins as soon as the new grass comes. When a fellow has to go through what I have done in the last 4 months, & just has sand enough left to play the last card, & wins the odd trick; I can assure you that until the excitement of the next rubber moves him, he feels more like a dead man than a live one; I hardly like to write it, but I feel awfully used up.

I am not by any means "flattened out" I feel more mad than hurt; what flattens the balance of mankind makes me angry & exasperated but it never depresses my spirits. I have been working like a lunatic the last two days from sunup to sundown, branding cattle; it is the hardest work I ever did or looked at; to lasso & throw a heavy wild steer & then hold him down while he is branded takes muscle, skill & nerve & if it is not a little, the finest sport I ever had a hand in, I am very much mistaken.

On the matter of the theft of my horses & stock, I can tell you now that all has been resolved & the beasts recovered. McSween's horses also were stolen by the same men. As I later learned, Mac went to the sheriff & demanded of him that he raise a posse with our Dick Brewer as deputy sheriff, to be furnished with provisions from my store. If I tell you that Sheriff Brady complied with reluctance, you must understand that both Brady & "the Boys" who carried out the theft are in tight with "the House," which has never since I've come to this country ceased to harass me. They have threatened to kill "that Englishman" on sight, they were incited to make these threats by James Dolan and his "House" whose business I have very nearly taken away. When I set out for John Chisum's ranch on the Pecos, to learn news of Dick's posse, a party of riders up ahead came my way, it was the posse with their captives. I must say it did me good to shake Dick Brewer's great paw, I was afraid lest they might have "drilled a hole through him." "Why I thought you boys went out to round up some wild stock," I said to the posse men. Brewer laughed, the captives did too. I was somewhat nonplussed when one of them, mocking me, said "By Jove! He don't know if Dick has got us or we've got him."

The hardest nut in the gang is a character called Tom Hill. "Well," he said, "have you got any whiskey, Englishman?"

"Merely a dram," I answered, my confidence restored. "If you knew me you would know that I don't need any to keep my blood warm, but if you met me at Lincoln, I'd soak you."

"Well, we'll be in the jug (gaol) by then, you get back and you can soak us there if you like." So I knew they'd indeed been captured by Brewer. The posse rode on with their four captives, the rest of "the Boys" remaining at large, & Brewer stayed with me briefly & described the fight that resulted in their capture. "The Boys" being surrounded in a "choaser" (that is a house built over a hole in the ground in such a way that when you are inside, there is as much of the house under, as over the ground), a good many shots were fired, Jesse Evans (one of "the Boys") says he cant tell how he failed to hit Dick as he had three fair, square shots at him, & he was saving his shots for him alone. The bullets struck within 4 or 5 inches of him each time. The end of it was, that some men in Dick's posse who knew these fellows well, told them that they meant taking them dead or alive, & that if they surrendered they would not be lynched, & they surrendered.

They seemed tame enough once in captivity. I can't believe Evans "failed" to hit Dick Brewer as he is a dead shot by all accounts, it could be their ferocity was a mere show to please their sachem James Dolan when he heard the reports. I did give them a bottle of what Americans call whiskey in their cell, they make it from corn, molasses, tobacco juice, chilies, and (good heavens!) strychnine.

When I informed McSween that his horses were recovered he hardly seemed gratified, having other pressing business. A Dolanite named Charles Fritz has filed a petition in probate court demanding that McSween pay insurance money owed him from the death of his brother, a partner in "the House." They threaten to charge him with embezzlement & attach all our property, his & mine, if he doesn't. McSween and I are not formal partners; of the handshake school, rather. The "House" the Irish ring refuse to believe this. Imagine such cheek in *our* blessed plot, father.

In all this, my foreman Dick Brewer has proven his mettle and devotion, as honest and brave as they make them. My men would die for him, & so for me, too. One of these men, a young lad, the finest of the lot, has a quick mind and sunny disposition, he keeps us on the qui vive. I've given him a good horse & saddle & gun, guns being the currency of choice in these parts. He looks scarcely 16. The remarkable thing is that until last month he was on the other side, one of "the Boys." He'd stolen my dapple-gray buggy team & was thrown in gaol but his "compadres" never went his bond. So he sent for me to come to some agreement & said he was willing to rectify the wrong & said that "the Boys" had lulled him into stealing. He touched my heart & I made the proposal that he join my side if I got him out of gaol. He jumped to the occasion & has been with us since. His name is Antrim but (a nod to his appearance) all call him "Kid." A week ago he announced out of the blue that he fancies the name William Bonney now, and enjoined us to so call him. Here in the wilderness names are like hats, a new one is tonic.

The last battle is about over & the waters are calm enough now to settle down & I can see to your investments. Things were so bad I nearly felt home sick (a weakness I never allowed to come over me since I left you) but I had too much fighting on hand, to think about leaving the front. I hope you will have spent a very merry Christmas when you receive this & that a happy new year will follow it. You know you have all my love.

Most affectionately,
John

Lincoln, New Mexico
2/78

7 Belsize Terrace
Hampstead,
London, England

Dear Mr. and Mrs. Tunstall,

Your son is "all right" but we are very busy. The Sheriff has attached his store and threatens to attach his stock. Should anything occur to him you will be sure to hear from me at once.

Yours sincerely,
Robert A. Widenmann

1878

―

Tunstall

Wゃ HAT ARE YOU MEN DOING?"

"Taking inventory."

"Of my property? This is a damned high-handed business. What the devil gives *you* the right —"

"The law, Englishman."

"The law be damned!"

William H. Bonney watched his new boss, who briefly looked ready to fly off the handle then a moment later distractedly appeared like a greenhorn trying to act dangerous. He didn't know what to look like. Bonney and Fred Waite stood at the door of J. H. Tunstall & Co., General Merchandise, Billy with his short-barrel Colt's Thunderer in his right hand, arms menacingly folded across his chest, Fred with his Winchester loosely cradled in his fingers, both watching Mr. Tunstall losing the struggle to adjust his response to the seizure of his store. Billy thought, What next? He could understand Tunstall's jitters, he'd been there himself, he knew what it was like to be bullied by thugs. If a horse won't buck all that's left to it is fussing. Tunstall straightened up, his back seemed to stiffen. Good for him. Across the counter, coolheaded Sheriff Brady clung to a ladder suspended from a rail above the shelves; above *Tunstall's* shelves. Brady'd been dictating to Jim Longwell below him the names and quantities of those items that he plucked from their places and threw back as though he owned them — fourteen boxes of Lamonta hosiery, twenty-three of the Fletcher no. 78 flat white corset laces, ninety spools of black thread, thirty-eight cards of hair ribbons, thirteen bolts of cheap gingham, eight of cotton checks, boxes and boxes of Gauntlet Brand Cream Tartar; the shelves were deep, Billy knew.

At the door, Fred scowled. The scowl was nothing special. Billy had observed that Fred Waite's scowl was more quizzical than threatening, and he often wore it. Beyond Fred, Mr. Tunstall's darkening face and corrugated hair were still as a silhouette while, dancing around him, pear-shaped Rob Widenmann sputtered and fumed in his distinctly un-American fez. When Brady first ordered Tunstall's property attached, Widenmann had turned into a helter-skelter battle-ax and swore he would have those who did this to his friend dead or alive. Now he swung his arms, stormed back and forth, and tried to act salty, to Billy's chagrin. And Mr. Tunstall standing there straight as a wiping stick; he kept himself uneasily inside himself except his protracted silence betrayed him. Dull of tongue, Widenmann jumped in. "Your court order is against Alexander McSween. This is Mr. Tunstall's store."

"They're partners, ain't they?" said Brady.

"How merny times. How many terms — how . . . many terms." At the door, Billy caught Fred's eye. Arms flailing, Widenmann spit it out. "How many *times* did I tell you they are not partners! Tell him, Harry."

John Tunstall looked around at the barrels of nails, spindles of rope, bins of oats and barley, drawers of thread, and Billy followed his gaze. Seventeen iron hoes, twenty-three pails, a dozen axes, more than thirty shovels. Fred had told Billy that these were all commodities their boss had personally bought in St. Louis and arranged to have freighted to Lincoln last year. He lingered near the iron cage with its desk and high stool and account books and ledgers. "You'll hear about this" was all he could say.

"Tell them, Harry, tell them!"

"And those horses and mules out back. They are my personal property, exclusively."

"Then take the damn horses, Englishman. What do I care? I've got work to do."

"Call your men off, then."

"Jim, would you please march around back and tell Peppin and Davis that the Englishman and his friends can take them animals away?"

Jim Longwell strolled toward the Kid and Fred standing on either side of the doorway. Tunstall's store was long and wide, with floors made of wood, three-foot-thick walls, and steel plates inside its shutters. Its entrance was a set of metal doors that opened onto Lincoln's single road. The place was built like a fort; a lot of good that did the Englishman. As Longwell slipped between them, Billy raised the Thunderer so he'd get a good look at it, and opened his mouth and contemptibly hawked, but it sounded too dry. Longwell then paused and they stared at each other while behind him Fred levered his carbine, whose swift collision of sliding metal parts hummed through the wood stock and up any skittish spines within earshot. Longwell spit on the floor and continued. They followed him out.

Other Dolanites stood outside the door or sprawled on the bench, and behind the store five or six of the Boys lingered by the gate to Tunstall's corral. Facing the gate, Bonney's eyes slid incessantly above, behind, and between these former associates, who stared at him smugly. He felt rooted to the spot. Only George Davis nodded. George had taught Billy, when he ran with the Boys, how to breach an adobe corral and take possession of its horses by using ordinary ropes to saw through the wall of hardened mud and straw. Now the Kid worked for Tunstall, their enemy. Their contempt felt religious;

he'd become a heretic. It was a matter of pride for William H. Bonney to mask his discomfort with silent arrogance. He tested a sneer but felt at the same time so conscious of himself peering out from such an unfinished body that he surely would stumble, even drop his gun, if he took another step. Some wiseacre said, "How old are you, Kid? Fourteen? Fifteen?"

"Older than that."

"He don't know how old he is. No one ever told him."

Davis's voice sounded mock-friendly. "You like muscling for the Englishman, Kid? Looks like they fattened you up."

"Mr. Tunstall does not keep a mean table."

"We miss your smart ass."

He'd practiced relentlessly, drawn and shot at whiskey bottles, rehearsed the insults guaranteed to spark rage and make his adversary rashly pluck at his weapon. He'd armored himself with a scowl like Fred's so no one could see the muddle inside. He'd shot a man before, he knew how it felt, and the next time he vowed to be calm as a nun. His intractable cockiness still felt oversized; he wished he'd grow into it now instead of later. He'd run out of patience. He liked to whip himself up. You sons of bitches better watch your backs. Look for a ditch you can die in, Brady. If this don't beat stealing soldiers' horses at three in the morning outside Arizona whorehouses!

Five minutes later, Fred and the Kid led the horses and mules toward McSween's house while the livid John Tunstall strode ahead full steam visibly fuming despite his little victory. He burst into McSween's followed by Rob Widenmann with his open-ass shuffle trying to catch up. Billy and Fred stayed outside to guard the horses. Fred rolled a cigarette and lit it and drew. The Kid's eyes scanned Lincoln's shabby adobes. Even at midday the sun at a slant almost missed the town, the way its only road hid in this valley hanging halfway up the mountains on a February day, with high bare hills and higher peaks behind them upraised on either side. Snubbing posts lined the wide dirt street, stock tied to some, while behind the doby houses were crudely fenced yards with milk cows, goats, pigs, chickens, and sheep, though the fences were porous and most of these creatures had the run of the town. Across the road from McSween's, a patrol of yellow-legs from Fort Stanton had singled out a blanket-wrapped Pueblo Indian and were searching the pannier on his burro's back. Bordered by line-trees, fields climbed the stretched earth up behind the houses to the base of the hills.

The Kid said to his new friend and confederate, "Tell me again what this is all about."

"It's like this," said Fred. He pulled on his cigarette, blew out smoke. His voice was so deep that despite his height, five inches taller than the five-seven Billy, it seemed to well up from the earth at his feet. Fred was half Chickasaw. He'd attended not one college but three, in Illinois, Arkansas, and Missouri. His mustache, not unlike Alexander McSween's, plunged diagonally down from nostrils to chin line, though the Kid and Fred had confidentially agreed that McSween's kinky lip- and chin-hair looked like a Chinaman's — or a blanket Indian's.

Billy ought to talk. His lip was just peach fuzz.

Fred Waite spoke slowly but was so quick of reflex he could easily grab a squirrel off a tree trunk and whip it in circles by its long tail and fling it up dizzy into the topmost branches, the Kid had seen him do it. "Okay. This Emil Fritz was kind of a *jefe* with Murphy and Dolan. He was partners in the House. So he died. And Murphy got laid up. Laid up, all right. They told him go ahead and drink all you want, you got cancer of the stomach. Myself, I've known men who could make themselves stop breathing. Their will was that strong."

"What happened to them?"

"They died. And when Lawrence Murphy dies, Jimmy Dolan will be left the last one of the partnership. He's already in charge of the House by hisself now. So Emil Fritz dies, this was about maybe four years ago — long before Mr. Tunstall shows up, or you neither, Kid — and his family hires Alexander McSween, the only green-bag in town, to clean up the estate. Where the trouble began is Mac is supposed to collect a big policy that Fritz had taken out but the insurance company has gone belly-up by this time. And Dolan says the Fritz estate owes him a pile. They were partners in the House. But Mac claims the opposite, the House owes a lot of money to the estate, and besides there are other heirs, he points out. And this insurance money is eight thousand dollars." Fred looked at the Kid. "Are you following this?"

Billy nodded and shrugged.

"Well, look. Pay attention. This is the part where the soldiers on the ramparts talk about the king's been acting queer lately."

"What king?"

"Never mind. So Mac has to go all the way to New York and find another lawyer there. Together, they get most of the money from the bankrupt insurance company. But he won't pay it out until he determines who gets what and who owes who. Dolan, meantime, goes to court in Mesilla and gets them to believe his side of the story, which is not a surprise given Judge Bristol's being in their pockets. He accuses McSween of embezzlement because he's holding on to money which is owed to him, Dolan. That's why Macky Sween got arrested in December and thrown in the hoosegow. And yesterday, see, Dolan gets Bristol to issue a writ of attachment for eight thousand dollars against McSween. They come racing back to Lincoln and Dolan makes the sheriff go to Mr. Tunstall's store and start seizing his goods because Tunstall's supposed to be partners with McSween. That's what Dolan says. They're in Macky's house too." Fred nodded toward McSween's house. "They're taking inventory there. And next they plan to go to Mr. Tunstall's ranch and attach all his cattle and horses."

"It ain't fair!"

"It's like I always say. When folks lose their heads they get dumb as sheep. You got to rile them up to get any justice."

"I know how to get justice."

"It's just a way to harass Mr. Tunstall through Macky Sween. He's been cutting into Dolan's business something serious. It's the back door they found to sweep Tunstall out of town. McSween they hate, too. But Tunstall has cost them."

"I'm glad I joined up with the Englishman, then."

"You didn't know all this?"

"I knew it like you know about getting someplace without paying much attention."

"And you're Irish, ain't you?"

"That don't mean I'd muscle for a lot of rusty Irish thugs."

"But you used to, didn't you? You ran with the Boys?"

"The Boys weren't working for James Dolan then."

"But you stole Tunstall's horses."

"He forgave me for that."

"So how come you switched sides?"

"How come I switched sides? That's all you ever say. I switched because the Boys never sprung me from jail. Plus, they owed me money. Besides, it wasn't sides before I switched."

"Those are pretty good reasons."

"And Mr. Tunstall paid me a visit in jail and offered to get me out if I returned his buggy horses. He took to me, Fred. He asked me right there if I wanted a job and I said sure, doing what? Working on his ranch. Protecting his interests. Could I shoot a gun, he asked. Is the pope Catholic? He hired me on the spot, in the Lincoln county jail. He's impulsive, that man."

"That's how I hired to him, too. I was staying at Patrón's. You want a job? he says. Why not? I answer. I'm of the same mind, I find him hasty. Or a poor judge of character. Does he strike you as capable? He looked up a tree in there."

"He strikes me as rich. He's always writing home for money. Fred, no one ever gave me anything before. He gave me a gun, a new horse, a saddle. At first I thought who is this milk-knee? He says he won't cook but one time on the Feliz when Saturnino Baca offered to do so Mr. Tunstall confided he would not eat anything that Mexican touched. So he removes his coat and waistcoat and gloves and turns up his sleeves and shakes the frying pan like crazy, dusting its contents with flour, and squats at the fire while coughing the smoke out and rubbing his eyes."

"And that endeared him to you?"

"Well, he's an Englishman. I can understand how he feels about Baca. But he pitches in. He believes in this country. It takes a lot of understanding, he says, because it is new and not even a mining country yet. It has as good a future as California, he says, even if at present it's in a slumber — but things will go ahead with a rush very soon."

"He's right about that. But he got in over his head, I believe. He's a little lost when it comes to cattle. I can see his busy mind adding up the tons of meat. It ain't so much the ranch, it's the store that riled the Dolanites. He's the first real competition they've had."

"He gets you on his side," said Billy, "by way of talking nonstop about all his plans. Pretty soon you feel a stir of something, too. I like it when he shouts, *By the Powers!* and rolls his eyes and makes a little fist and waves it at the ceiling. I can't help from laughing. He came in one night with a cut on his head two inches long when that crazy mule threw him. The confounded treacherous beast of a mule, he screams. Then he gets mad about the harnesses he ordered that never arrived and chews out Dad Gauss as if *he* was the mule. Then he turns around and stands us all a glass of whiskey and says things are going 'swimmingly' and pretty soon we all agree — we're all rolling on the floor. 'To burros,' he says, lifting his glass — 'God's noblest work.'"

"That's pretty good," said Fred. Both men looked around. The flanks of Tunstall's horses wouldn't stop twitching though this was flyless February. Each but one was tied to a snubbing post, and suddenly that one swallowed his neck, rolled on his back, and flexed in the dirt and dust of the street.

"He's square," said Billy.

"But the world is not square."

"I trust him. Don't you?"

"I'd like to know him better."

"A man like that makes you feel like going straight."

"Straight to where?"

"Come on, Fred. Straight to hell." Billy laughed. But he did trust Tunstall. That such a man would just drop from the clouds and think highly of him was surprising enough, but that he'd come to him in jail, to the thief who stole his horses, and offer to spring him, no questions asked — it makes you want to stick around.

"What do you suppose they're doing in there?" Fred nodded at the house.

"Deciding what comes next."

It was natural that you either hated Mr. Tunstall, as James Dolan did, or learned to admire him. Billy took it on principle that people were either friends or enemies; men of their word or low sneaking animals. No one was both, there was no middle ground. Four-square men like the Englishman the Kid took to right away, all the rest could go to hell. Tunstall didn't necessarily look the part — he could have been a banker. And he was swelled up a little over his nationality. Tight, wavy hair, aquiline nose, receding chin-line. It was the way he laughed, the way he spoke his mind. Mr. Tunstall pooh-poohed things like lords and dukes when he talked about England — they had no drive, he claimed — but there was something in his manner of carrying himself, unless he'd slept badly and woke with a crick, something in his lofty soft-heartedness that seemed positively nobby. You could tell from his looks and the way he spoke that he'd wind up rich. He never threw money around but he had it. He didn't soft-soap you. Then why, Billy wondered, can't I look him in the eye?

Because he is a gentleman. He never acts second-rate. He never seems concerned about shielding his cards, he is an open book. He likes horseplay, too, and this they had in common, he and the Kid, who often felt the urge to kick up his heels, to whip around on a crowded dance floor crushed hard against some sweetie pie's hips, he got stiff just thinking it.

"Who's this intoxicant?" Fred was peering up the road.

"My God. It's him." Billy draped his hand around the butt in his holster and Fred raised his carbine, both staring at the man pimp-strutting up the road, Mr. Tunstall's nemesis, James Dolan himself. "C'mon, you son of a bitch," the Kid whispered. "We'll give you a game." And the Irishman did come, he didn't waver, he spotted the two men guarding Tunstall's horses and aimed directly toward them. You could almost hear the drums. In fact, he'd been a drummer boy in the Union army when he met Lawrence Murphy, whose interest in little Jimmy Dolan, the Tunstall side claimed, was more than just fatherly.

On the other hand, the Dolanites insisted that they'd seen the Englishman and Widenmann chasing each other and snapping their towels while bathing buck-naked in a hole on the Bonito.

James Dolan was short, shorter than Billy, and swung his arms like a very tough citizen, balefully smiling as he drew closer. Fred levered his Winchester. Billy watched the man approach. The doughnut-shaped pout around his tight mouth, the John B. hat, the army-tent overcoat, high-heeled boots, and steel-bore expression — and the scornful smile — all buttressed a façade carefully devised to intimi-date pantywaists. His powder-blue eyes looked hard and cold enough to shatter whatever light they admitted. Through his smile could be glimpsed the cratered lava-bed that once had been his teeth. The funny thing was that as he drew closer his stature didn't wax, it con-tracted. He was a death-fist, a bantam, a cocky little midget who'd rip out someone's eyes just for looking at him wrong. "Hello, boys."

Billy watched him.

"Don't I know you? You look familiar."

"I work for John Tunstall," said the Kid.

"And these horses — ?"

"They belong to Mr. Tunstall."

Dolan looked at the animals. "Weren't they attached?"

"Brady said Mr. Tunstall could keep those horses. They're his personal property."

"He said that, did he?" Dolan smiled at the Kid. Then he eyed Fred and reached in his pocket and handed him a card and walked on toward Tunstall's store with a wafture of his hand.

James Dolan

SIZE MATTERS

Box 136, Lincoln, New Mexico

"I've seen this before," said Fred. "He drops it in the laps of cuties he spots — unfulfilled ladies — on ferries and trains and at the gaming tables."

Later, McSween called them inside while Hank Brown and John Middleton took their places on the street guarding the horses. They ate in the winter kitchen with Yginio Salazar, and listened to the sheriff's deputies slowly moving room to room in the other wing, meticulously listing all the lawyer's possessions. The fourteen-year-old Yginio didn't exactly work for John Tunstall; he hung around and ran errands and delivered messages for spare change. Mr. Tunstall and Macky Sween, he told Fred and Billy, were following the deputies to make sure they didn't pilfer. "He wants you to take those horses to the ranch."

"What for?"

"I think he don't know. He's trying to decide. He and Macky, you know — they got aggravations."

Billy said, "Yes."

Macky's house was a large U-shaped adobe with a flat, earthen roof with the usual vigas. Three wings of rooms around a central garden on three long sides. The McSweens had furnished it expensively, tastefully — where *had* they found the money? Billy wondered — with a parlor organ, six stuffed chairs, a sofa, corner racks, lavish mirrors, heavy drapes. In the sitting room, where the deputies now operated, Mac had a hundred law books in sectional glass-fronted shelves to the ceiling. There were five hundred more in his office next door at Mr. Tunstall's store. All this he could lose. Sue McSween's sewing machine, their stoves, lamps and clocks, the library tables and carpeted bedrooms with the tall-boy bureaus and washstands and beds sporting altar-sized headboards — all of it was subject to the writ of attachment.

In the kitchen, Fred and Billy lapsed into silence and overwhelmed the food. Slumgullion stew. It would have to hold them for the rest of the day and the forty-mile ride to Tunstall's ranch on the Feliz.

· 5 ·

1878

Tunstall

Tunstall's ranch house wasn't much: a one-room log structure with a single door and window all of fourteen by fourteen, and a corral. Driven there by Fred and Billy, the seven repossessed horses and two mules now occupied the corral. In a borrow pit outside the corral the Kid shoveled dirt into empty grain sacks to help fortify the place. Somewhere to the east were Tunstall's cattle, he knew, four hundred head on four thousand acres, land that spanned a long stretch of the Feliz River. Fred had told Billy that years before Tunstall arrived in Lincoln this acreage had belonged to the Casey family. But Robert Casey having been killed by William Wilson — who had to be hanged twice — his widow and children were powerless to stop Tunstall and McSween from arrogating their grass and water, since the law is on the side of those who file, not those who squat. Not that Tunstall could file. His friends had to do it, including Fred, because foreigners couldn't legally own land under the Desert Land Act. But Tunstall had put up the twenty-five cents an acre, and made the improvements, and at the end of three years for the further payment of a dollar an acre to the U.S. government, his friends would have title and would transfer it to him.

He'd loaned the widow Casey money to tide her and her children over once they lost the land they thought was theirs forever. Most of Tunstall's cattle had also belonged to Ellen Casey, whose debts to the Englishman became discounted in the form of livestock, which thus became a bargain. All this sounded square to the Kid, since as Mr. Tunstall explained, he'd never expected the sold-up widow to pay back the loans; and this was the way it was done in New Mexico.

Still, he'd come out ahead on that deal. He'd acquired a considerable amount of dirt and meat that belonged to someone else.

The ranch sat in a high desert bowl in the foothills east of the Sacramento Mountains, a place thick with grama grass circled by rolling hills and crushed by blue sky. Sky was most of it, Billy had observed, sky and hills, and hills inside hills, and hills concealing hills, and hills pinching into arroyos and ravines then swelling out into more hills, all bare of trees. The only trees lined the river: clusters of cottonwoods leaning over its bed. A spring at the head of a canyon to the west watered this basin even when the Feliz seemed all but dry, as now in winter. Dick Brewer, Tunstall's foreman, held his boss's ranch to be the most brutal yet singular spot in all of God's forgotten backyard, a place where awe and solitude met, and he'd defend it with his life, he'd declared to Billy, and without consideration of the fact that *his* ranch on the Ruidoso would be claimed next by Tunstall if he were to die.

The Kid filled the grain sacks, Brewer and Fred Waite hauled them to the house and piled them in barricades four feet high, enclosing a space as large again as the house before its front door. "This wants dirt," Brewer said, hefting a sack. "You never will follow the spade for a living."

Billy flushed. "My arms are tired."

Under Rob Widenmann's officious direction, Henry Brown, John Middleton, and Bill McCloskey cut portholes in the ranch house and piled Billy's sacks on the roof to serve as parapets. Tunstall had stayed in Lincoln to strategize with Alexander McSween but they expected him soon. They also expected Sheriff Brady and the Boys.

If the Dolanites could attach their boss's cattle and ranch in addition to his store, what would be left to him? Seven horses, two mules, and a shovel, thought the Kid. When the barricades were complete, he and the others sat inside them on the ground and spooned into their mouths and immediately swallowed, without pausing to taste, the son-of-a-bitch stew cooked by Godfrey Gauss, Mr. Tunstall's gray-bearded, hollow-eyed coosie. Each of them said, "Hey, this is *good*, Dad," but Gauss didn't smile. Leaning back against the wall, Billy sat with his legs straight out and his plate in his lap and his hat on his boots, and Fred asked him why. "It's a quick way to get up if I have to."

"Don't look quick to me. And where'd you get that shirt?"

The blue shirt in question, threadbare and faded but nonetheless distinct through Billy's unbuttoned jacket, sported an anchor whose rope was loosely coiled around its canted shaft. He looked down at it. "Had this since a boy."

"I've had this one a while, too," said Fred. "Sateen." He opened his coat. "Here we are like two five-year-olds comparing our weenies. Don't get me wrong, anyone that wears a sailor shirt is after my own heart. An anchor in the desert makes as much sense as a cuspidor on the ocean. You never thought you'd be socially crucified for it?"

He looked away. "Why should I give a damn?"

The earth thundered to the north. Over a raise came a squall of horses and even from this distance, craning his neck to peer across the wall, the Kid recognized members of the Boys: Jesse Evans, Frank Baker, Billy Morton, Tom Hill, and other former associates. At their head was not Sheriff William Brady but his deputized facto-tum, Billy Matthews, whose glower was unmistakable even through a wall of dust a half-mile away.

Pear-shaped Rob Widenmann suddenly jumped up and climbed over the wall. "Rob!" hissed Dick Brewer.

"I am not afraid. I intend to arrest them."

"You can't arrest those men, you cabbagehead. There's more of them than us. They'll serve you up for supper."

"I have warrants," said Widenmann, walking toward the posse and holding up his hand when they were fifty feet away, and ordering them to stop right there. The man who liked to call John Tunstall "Harry" ordered Matthews to ride forward and state his business. As he'd crowed to Tunstall's men, Widenmann had convinced the U.S. marshal for New Mexico to appoint him as a deputy, and now he would arrest Evans, Baker, and Hill, for those were the very brigands, he'd repeatedly declared, who had stolen some cattle only last year on the Apache reservation. Billy and his compadres watched from the barricades, hands on their weapons. Facing Widenmann, Matthews announced they were an authorized posse and expected his assistance. He produced a document and with downcast eyes pretended to read it, even though it was generally known he couldn't read; instead, Billy guessed, he'd committed it to memory, no doubt under James Dolan's tutelage. While "reading" the court's writ of attachment Matthews sounded like a schoolboy, loud and discomfited, but when he was through he reverted to a beast with red eyes and mossy face, and glared at Widenmann then announced he'd come for the Englishman's stock. "I see the horses," he said, nodding at the corral. "Where's the cattle?"

"Sheriff Brady said we could keep those horses."

"He's changed his mind on that."

"It's been changed for him, you mean," Widenmann snorted. "You know who calls the shots."

"Where's the Englishman? Hiding?"

"Harry's back in Lincoln."

"He wasn't there when we left."

"Maybe you didn't look hard enough."

Matthews folded the writ of attachment and slid it inside his coat. "What's all this?" He waved at the barricades.

Widenmann became huffy. "We are here to protect Harry's interests."

"Then where is he? Where's — *Harry?*" Matthews held the name at arm's length like a rat caught in pie.

All at once, Dick Brewer shouted from the barricade, "Who's hungry out there? We were just about to eat." Matthews and Widenmann looked at each other, eyes suddenly adrift. Matthews shrugged; his posse dismounted. Inside the barricade, Billy muttered to Fred, "What the hell is Brewer doing?"

"Exercising Christian charity."

"Hell, we just fed."

"Pretend to like it again."

"No kidding, Fred, what's he up to anyway?"

"What's he up to? Better to occupy jittery hands with spoons instead of guns."

Standing out there, Widenmann looked lost. The posse hurdled the wall and inside the barricades milled about looking deadly while Gauss handed out the scraped tin plates and pointed at the pot still steaming on the fire and said, "Chuck away." Sheepishly, Widenmann climbed the wall, too. Dick Brewer asked Matthews where Sheriff Brady was. "Wait," said Widenmann.

Matthews turned to him. "Speak up, clot."

"I have warrants for the arrest of Jesse Evans, Frank Baker, and Tom Hill. Some posse you are — with thieves and criminals!"

"We've been deputized," said Matthews.

Jesse Evans tossed his plate aside and approached Widenmann and swung his carbine by the lever all the way around, catching it cocked and pointing inches from his belly. Billy knew Evans; he liked to terrorize people. His gray eyes were dead and his thin lips cracked but his fashion of intimidation was to smile and kindly angle his head with concern. "You've got a warrant for *me?*"

"That is my business. Why are you with this posse?"

"To enforce the law, Gretchen."

"My law takes precedence. I have the authority."

"A gun is pretty good authority."

Leaning back against the barricade, Frank Baker turned to Buckshot Roberts and declared for all to hear, "What's the use of talking? Pitch in and fight and kill these Englishman's catamites." As Evans had, Baker threw his plate aside and playfully swung his pistol on his finger then held it to his cheek and aimed it at Widenmann. Billy drew his gun; his heart was in his neck. The rest of Tunstall's men levered their rifles and also drew, some squatting, some sitting. They were at a disadvantage; only Widenmann stood. Back in Lincoln, Mr. Tunstall had remarked that Baker's face supported the Darwinian theory, and Billy studied it now; his lowering brow and broad nose and thick neck and small pink ears did resemble an ape's. Both he and Buckshot Roberts had been shoveling stew into their mouths as though stoking boilers, although as everyone knew Roberts could barely lift his spoon due to the buckshot he carried in his shoulder.

On Roberts's other side, Billy Morton asked William Bonney, seated next to Fred with his hat on his boots, "You still piss the bed, Kid?"

"I still piss in your mouth."

"You ought to have smelled his blankets in the morning," Morton told the assembly.

"You ought to have smelled his dick," said the Kid, "when he finished with Baker."

Smiling, Jesse Evans still held his rifle inches from Widenmann's jiggling gut. Baker hawked, a cloud crossed the sun. Don't exhale, Billy thought, just quietly leak air. No one moved. Then it was over. As though shaking off a spell, Evans lowered his rifle, the rest looked around and holstered their guns. But Billy had noticed Matthews and Evans exchanging furtive glances and kept his hand on the Thunderer's butt just in case. Matthews announced that he and the posse would ride back to Lincoln and get further instructions from Sheriff Brady. While they climbed the barricade and returned to their horses, Billy stood and dusted off his pants, Fred continued eating, and Widenmann, shaking, turned to Dick Brewer and remonstrated with him about mollycoddling cutthroats. Brewer said, "It was all we could do. It's clear what their intentions are. They don't care about the stock. They're after Mr. Tunstall. It's a simple trick, Rob. Allow him to take those seven horses and mules then arrest him for stealing them. They'll say they were attached."

"Where is Harry now?" Widenmann asked. "He was supposed to be here. Is he in Lincoln?" He searched Brewer's face but the latter turned away. The handsomest man in Lincoln County gazed at the last of the posse riding off, and seemed detached, unperturbed. He's a soothsayer, Billy thought.

The soothsayer made an utterance. "I don't think he's in Lincoln. I'm not sure where he is."

"Why did you help fortify this place if all you wish is to talk?"

"If they come up firing, that's one thing, Rob, even if they do out-number us. Let them take the first shot. I believe they did not intend to waste their bullets unless Mr. Tunstall was among us. They want to arrest him."

Billy looked at Fred. "Is that what this was about?"

"Uh-huh."

Widenmann began to splutter. "If that's the case and they back — get back to Lincoln and find Harry gone they'll just return with more men. You know how those fiends play their cards. They want Harry to fight."

"He's thought of asking John Chisum to borrow some of his wad-dies. Enough of Chisum's men combined with our hands might dis-courage those hotheads."

"So he does intend to fight!"

"He intends to prevent one. It's wise to be strong."

"It's wiser to give no quarter, Richard. Look at me, I feel — I feel like a coward. I feel like a coward! I have the authority to arrest those cattle thieves and I haven't done it."

"Man up, Rob."

"Now they're getting away!"

"Get a hold of yourself. Lower your voice. You've done dandy so far. We'll have our chance."

The Kid watched Dick Brewer. With his strong nose, blue eyes, high brow, mop of curly hair, and iron-clamp jaw, he gave nothing away, you couldn't ruffle the man. That's the way to be. In front of him, Widenmann continued spluttering. Matthews had said he'd get instructions from Brady but Widenmann now declared he knew better, Matthews would go directly to Dolan. In that case, Rob would return to Lincoln, too, he announced to Brewer, and find Harry and get instructions from *him*. Meanwhile, he paced back and forth — Mr. Tunstall's only error in judgment, thought Billy. Rob took out his warrants, read and refolded them, tucked them back in his coat. He'd write a letter to the Boys, he now announced, and to no one in particular he recited its contents. "It would go like this. Dear Messrs. Evans, Baker, and Hill, you *Hunde*, you . . . savages, if you try to collar Harry you will hear the gentle report of my gun, that is the kind of hairpin I am. How does that sound? This thing of horse thieves being on a sheriff's posse may do in some places but it has gotten thin with me. Yours truly, Robert Widenmann."

Fred said, "Try 'Yours on the first dark stormy night, Rob.'"

"'Yours on this side of hell, Rob,'" said Billy.

"That's good," said Widenmann, pointing at the Kid. "'Yours on this side of hell, Rob.'"

◆　◆　◆

MUCH BELOVED FATHER, I am almost used up, I've just about had it, how dare you cut me short with no further emolument? I am still below par, my machinery was compelled to make forced marches from Lincoln to Roswell before going to my ranch when it should have been standing still for repairs, and when shall I ever find the time to rest up and recruit?

Crossing the desert on horseback, Tunstall made a fist and struck his thigh with it. Mormon Pussy's withers indifferently rippled.

I am at death's door, he mentally scribbled, and certified dead if I don't make this effort, sitting on saddle all day and all night without food or water. I really do think I am as tough as anyone, about as tough as any cowboy and as tough as a merchant like you, Beloved Father, who has to beat out competitors just to get his share of market. Have you ever had to commit bloody murder for the sake of a sale? And what did Mother think of that? Or did you merely sit comforted by a glowing fire while your minions carried out your wishes? I've been adamant that nothing should give the other side an occasion for violence, you'd be proud of me, Father. Lots of fellows . . . decent fellows . . . in my shoes would not have done as much. I am of course well established, the Mexicans think that El Inglés does not dress and put on quite as much style as they would do if they *vale tanto* (were worth as much as he) *Pero es muy buen hombre, muy rico* (but he is a first-rate man and very rich). I can think in parentheses and capital letters, even italics, and translate my lingo, I have a clarity of purpose, make my points well, good points, very fine points, against ubiquitous chicanery, against thieves, desperadoes, corrupt officials, and cutthroat Irish, all of whom have had the laws altered to suit their greedy purposes. If you could realize the odds I have had against me you would be astonished that I ever made a point. I will beat them as sure as they live. *As they live.*

The cold sun over Tunstall's right shoulder cast a foreshortened shadow across the yellow track. Before him, the horizon made a perfect semicircle. He was riding into sky.

This winter is a very cold one, Mother, you would not like it. Or else being fagged out and rheumatic I feel it more than I did the last, though I'm able to drive a hard pull against the wind without using gloves so I guess I am as tough as ever. You must think of me as tough, very, very tough, and I cannot regardless be near death's door though I've suffered a good deal with rheumatism on this ride. There is a local peculiarity in the atmosphere that catches a rheumatic subject every time and my knees ached a great deal as I rode across the flatlands on the way to Chisum's ranch. I was on the qui vive, I saw their purported writ of attachment and discovered an irregularity in it and had it set aside, you'd be proud of your son. Those fellows would steal the eyes out of a man's head if he did not have them peeled all the time, they have not, however, so far scored a single point in my game. *Not a single point.* I made this trip to make *a very fine point* and I think I have made it. Chisum thinks so too. I rode down to South Spring to ask his assistance and he generously offered it. A few of John Chisum's jinglebob cowboys would supplement my forces and protect my ranch from the best-armed posse.

This anticipative script reassured Tunstall, though he'd not yet managed to stay the court's writ; nor had he quite arrived at Chisum's ranch. Perhaps forethought would function as a kind of charm and become self-fulfilling when he actually got there.

Mother, please explain to Father that an additional £300 per annum for overhead would secure his investments, for the cost of doing business in a country as peculiarly circumstanced as this one couldn't possibly have been foreseen, Mother. I have so far acquired a great deal of good property that has not yet had time to turn around and pay and I am out of pocket on several turns I have not had time to work because — I mean to say — mind you, this unexpected impediment — I am working out my *original* plan as fast as my circumstances (which look pretty sticky) will — Did you think it would be a jolly bed of roses, Mam? I approached Chisum's ranch in the early part of morning beneath a frozen sun. Fruit trees, orchards, cottonwoods, corrals, all poor and naked in the cruel light. The adobe house seemingly abandoned with its *pretil*, its parapet with the portholes on top, for defense against attack. But no one was about.

Tunstall climbed off his mare. The fifty-mile ride all the way from Lincoln couldn't possibly have been a waste of time, could it? He'd begun last night, ridden all day today, felt dog-tired and bitter, but he would complete the gesture, *by Jove*, what choice did he have? He'd anticipated Chisum's *generous offer* too much to admit he hadn't really expected the man not to be home. When the door swung open and Jim Chisum, not John, stood there smiling — his own comic version of his brother's face dominated by the nose, smiling drearily at Tunstall — his heart shriveled in his chest.

Less than an hour later he was back on the trail having wolfed the eggs and beans the Chisum coosie'd whipped up, having watered and fed poor Mormon Pussy, having . . . come a cropper. With John Chisum not home and the jinglebob cowboys out riding the line, there was no help here and all was wrong with the world. Perhaps the cattle baron had known he was coming and conveniently vanished, now that push had come to shove and Lincoln County seemed on the verge of war. Tunstall plunged his hands into Mormon Pussy's mane heading southwest toward his own ranch, another forty miles away. The wind was from the west, deceptively slack, but he couldn't peel the cold off his ungloved hands, and how foolish of him to leave without gloves!

He pictured himself alone on the prairie as though inching across the face of the moon. In fact, he was alone on the prairie. And indeed, it resembled the face of the moon in its yellow-brown featureless vapidity.

By early afternoon the flat land had opened up, the hills begun to rise. He dropped into the canyon though he knew he was climbing it, the entire folded land rolling up from this point. The wind was now unforgiving and bitter; his hands had grown numb. The sky was the blue of solid ice in the mountains. You can fancy me nearly perished with cold, having a pretty tough time all around, Father. All this stealing of my property has put me back terribly. These are surely matters that a comfortable squire like *you* have always been has *no* conception of, in your warm feather bed. In your paneled office. In your coach and four with blanket and fur hat and the hand- and foot-warmers full of hot coals. The cost of securing investments in a land lawless as to business, though holding up a painted picture of judges and warrants and writs and other documents universally known to be farcical is . . . is . . . I must say . . . It is a byword among these parts, *hem hem*, that men expect to be paid, and well paid at that, for going on the warpath. Just like you, Papa. When I get my dander up, I'm liberal but prejudiced, charming but arrogant, humble but righteous, the spitting image of my pater. I've been known to win favor and popularity while seemingly indifferent, above the fray if you please. Not at all, not at all. I came here because it's where California was twenty years ago, the idea being to strike while the iron's . . . to get in on the ground . . .

He nearly fell off Mormon Pussy but clung to her mane. When his eyes flew open they were facing the sun, cold as a pearl yet sharper than an ice pick. Every joint, every fiber of muscle in his limbs felt hung with sordid weights. Back and forth his mind slogged like an angry piece of music, soothing itself, lashing out, licking wounds, indulging the brutal yet comfortable sorrow of his sole forbidden fruit, self-pity. John Henry Tunstall, upright and square, on the finest California saddle you could imagine, with his blankets rolled and tied and his mahogany travel box nattily secured, in English riding pants and leggings, big-hearted, free — a fine-looking chap, forthright yet modest — but regrettably the victim of Irish savagery and greed . . .

The sun looked to be an hour from setting now. The trail dipsydoodled up over ridges, back down across the river. Cannonball-sized rocks in the riverbed with platforms of ice and tents of snow between them. His resolve began to stiffen. He counted the times his trail crossed the river, after twelve he'd be there. Here, the river had cut a brown corrugated wall at the base of one hill and he found himself ascending through white earth, then red, then dun-colored, brown, then back down through white. The dry brown grass in alluvial valleys was a foot high in places, forage enough for a hundred thousand cattle. We're rich, Beloved Father! He crested a rise and looked down at bare cottonwoods and his bunkered ranch house.

Meager as it was, nonetheless it made a start. And the boys there squatting around a merry fire, his faithful honest gunmen for three dollars a day. And the wide rising valley of brown and yellow earth swaled by the river and filled with dying sunlight.

◆ ◆ ◆

BILLY COULDN'T BELIEVE how ravaged his boss looked, how changed and beaten down. If you rode a hundred miles nonstop for two days you'd look wappered, too, said Fred. "His spirit's beat," said the Kid. "Look at him there with his head in his hands."

Tunstall raised his head and stared into the fire. He'd aged, Billy thought, his mouth appeared crusty, his eyes were dark and sleepy, and the flesh on his face looked as though you could just pull it off piece by piece. He was only, what? — twenty-three or -four years old. His corrugated hair fell in corkscrews to his ears and his fair cheeks and the bottom slope of chin showed erratic burrs of hair. It could be his heart was weak. When your heart's weak your head begins to falter and your strength goes away. The living breathing shadow who used to be Mr. Tunstall had already announced he wouldn't countenance bloodshed. We'll give up the damn horses, he'd said — surrender them to Brady. If we have to fight this out we'll do so in the courts. "Don't worry, boys. We'll best those cowards yet. It may take a while."

Rob Widenmann, too, had recently arrived, having failed to find Tunstall in Lincoln. He listened to his friend and his gospel of surrender with obvious dismay. Like Tunstall, he'd been two long days on the road but this seemed to stir him up instead of weigh him down. Billy thought they compensated for each other; Rob did his damnedest to become Tunstall's courage. He slapped his own shoulders, fisted the air, began uncompleted thoughts of justice and defiance with words like *By George*, then looked sheepishly at "Harry."

Dusk. Overhead, the sky had gone pale with a few strewn stars but their house and barricade of heavy earthen sacks now lay at the bottom of featureless dark. In this dogmatic solitude, the utter silence of the universe was commonplace and enduring. As darkness spread, Brewer divvied up a watch in case the Dolanites tried a night raid.

Billy took the second shift. While the men behind him snored, he sat on the barricade facing a crushing excess of stars. They made the planet seem irrelevant, a mere swirl of shadows. His Winchester lay on his lap. A few of the men slept inside the ranch house, the rest between the barricade and the front door. Footsteps scraped; someone was up. A shape propped its elbows on the wall beside the Kid and took a deep breath. "I can't sleep," said Tunstall. "It's remarkable. I've been on the road for two entire days and am *thoroughly* exhausted yet sleep eludes me."

"Sometimes you're so tired you come out the other side."

"Yes, that's it. I feel utterly depleted yet I'm wide awake. The night air feels so intensely cold and pure it's almost absurd. Do you mind if I stand here? I'll keep my voice low. The cold for some reason hardly seems cold at all. Aren't you tired, I ask myself. Tired? *The devil!*" Tunstall's fist thumped the barricade; it made a distant sound. His mouth moved queerly in its gunny sack of darkness, and his voice sounded corky, very British, and twangless yet fitful in the way it randomly pinched words. "There's a kind of *madness* in scraping back and forth across desert wastes ten thousand miles from home, in quest of what? — I could have married any number of widows back in England if it's money I wanted. Leave those pigs to their wallowing, I said to myself, the pigs who marry wealthy widows. There's more credit for a man when he makes his *own* way, on his *own* hook. Wouldn't you agree?"

"Sure."

"Don't you worry, Kid. We've hit a rough patch but we'll be out of it soon. No need for gunplay. Is it Antrim or Bonney? I get them mixed up."

"Bonney."

"Upon my word, I have faith in our future just as strong as ever.

This is a country where penniless shepherds become millionaires. I met one in California, a former bankrupt named Hollister, who at the outset had just a few acres. With every *penny* he could spare he bought more land and stocked it with sheep. I dare say he's now worth more than three million dollars. He did nothing that is not as well within my reach. I'll be as rich as him and not before long. I look around, I look — on the miseries of others and compare them to my own and regard myself as fortunate. Old chap, I tell myself, these may be rough times but you'll get *your* turn of luck before very long. Really, luck seems to follow me wherever I go."

"The same goes for me. I'm generally lucky. Only, luck mostly happens when you don't need it. When you need it, it jumps to some other lucky fellow standing nearby."

"As at the gaming tables? So luck is paradoxical, eh? You may be right, Kid."

Billy said nothing. He didn't wish to give away not being acquainted with the word *paradoxical*.

"We make a pair, don't we? Smart chap. We'll win this game yet." Tunstall's head shook in the dark as though expelling doubt. The Kid couldn't help it, he felt like a schoolboy whose brand-new teacher was boarding at his house and wished to make the lad's acquaintance. "Look at you, you were born in this country. *Were* you born in this country?"

"Born in New York, come west with my mother."

"New York? Is that so? I landed in New York on the liner *Calabria* when I was nineteen years old. Fearfully ill on that voyage from England — thought I would die. Thank God for champagne! — it settles the stomach, fortifies the heart. I stayed in the St. Nicholas on Broadway."

"I've been on Broadway."

"Splendid pile, upon my word. A fine bath apparatus. Had my first warm bath in ten days there. Have you been inside it?"

"I was just a boy."

"Gad, they had everything. A hairdresser, hosier, glover, hatter, a billiards room with eight tables. A lift going up and down all the day. A marvelous façade, elegant, yes? Upon my word, what a splendid city! The tide of life on Broadway goes at a racing speed. Our Cheapside in London proceeds at such a pace, but your horses are better — I saw that in New York and think it even more true in New Mexico. I suppose you can see that I'm no mindless Chauvin. The first time I walked down Broadway I thought all the men had a restless, hungry look."

"My father liked to lead me and my brother up and down Broadway. Had all we could do to keep up with the man. Smoked a big cigar. Threw the stub on the sidewalk and my brother and me foughten over it but the cattle got snippy. There's so many people traipsing up and down Broadway, every time I see a cattle drive that's what I think of. I like it better here."

"Room to breathe, eh? Did your father come west?"

"Just my mother and me. And my brother Josie."

"And where is she now?"

"In her grave in Silver City."

Tunstall paused. "I am sorry to hear it. I sometimes feel unworthy of a mother's love. We all do, I suppose. Were you close to your mother?"

"She's in my mind a lot."

"What sort of woman was she?"

"She enjoyed life. It was hard to watch her die. Full of vinegar. Pushy. Always trying to keep me up to the mark when I was a boy. I'm afraid I bucked."

"How did she die?"

"Consumption."

"And is your father living?"

"I suppose he died. I never saw him again after leaving New York. My stepfather, Antrim — he's in Silver City."

"Some people have both their father and mother yet grow up devoid of parental affection. My father's gruff and distant but he listens to reason. He lends support to my cause. I've told him repeatedly, *now's* the time to jump in. Land in New Mexico will be *treble* its value at this time next year. New Mexico offers as fine a field to rake in a few dollars as anyone could wish for. This is a *golden* opportunity. Upon my word, when I contemplate the future, it all falls into place. My mind runs ahead, I can *scarcely* catch up. After you boys see me through this crisis, each of you shall have your own little ranch. I promise you that. Some of us, you see, have title to a sufficient number of spots as to allow those whom we favor to settle themselves upon the intervening spaces. It's a patchwork quilt. You boys will fill it in. I dare say we'll make a powerful association. Me, you, Brewer, Waite, Middleton, Brown. You are sensible men of the highest courage and firmness and ambition. I am willing to assist you all as to money. By Jove, we'll be princes! I can buy all the county scrip available at one dollar and sell it at a dollar-fifty. I intend to control it all if I can. County scrip, land and cattle, loans on cattle. Mercantile goods sold at a nice profit. Government contracts for flour and corn. Absolute control of the price of grain — this means cornering the market. Can you imagine it, Kid? The acquisition of titles to a *great* many ranches. We move forward like an army as broad as the land, taking all of the various paths to wealth. I feel like an old bachelor, my mind runs on nothing but dollars and cents and, of course, dodging bullets, *hem hem*. It's a rum business, yes, but we *must* defend ourselves. I am opposed to any violence that isn't absolutely necessary. Fear of my life has never occurred to me. I keep my hand on my — what do you call it? — 'shooting iron' — should trouble arise but that isn't very likely. Did you know I'm nearly blind in my right eye? I dare say, no one knows it. The eye looks *perfectly* normal when you see it. It's quite an advantage, I think, in many ways. Suppose I ever marry — the possibility is not remote — I shall look at my wife with that eye alone in order to believe that she is perfect and unblemished. This is *policy*, not fancy, *hem hem*. All men should do the same. One might call it *zoology*. My mother is a dear, poetical, religious, warmhearted darling. We differ on religion. Hers is the usual C of E claptrap, mine is selfish and hard. My principle is best expressed by Shakespeare: 'To thine own self be true.' As regards to a hereafter, my ideas are cold. I call on no names, past, present, or to come. I *can* say that regarding self-control I have not met my equal, or at least I think not. I'm afraid I talk a lot. Sometimes I can't stop. I know what they say about me, they say that *brown-coated, beef-eating* Englishman and his plans and all his proud talk —"

Tunstall went silent. Billy glanced toward his boss. His half-moon profile, ragged with shadows, flickered into shape inside the night's emulsion. His smile looked hideous. His normally lidded eyes, or eye — only one was visible — had swollen in its socket and the white was even whiter than his pale skin, white inside white. His talk, the Kid sensed, was full of nervous rattle but nonetheless it stirred his young soul — *Can you imagine it?* Yes, I can imagine it. My own ranch and cattle, horses galore. Tunstall had opened a curtain in his mind and the spectacle on stage confused him with excitement. Then again he was tired, both of them were tired. "You need some rest, Mr. Tunstall."

This restarted him. "We're on the homestretch, Antrim. All it takes is holding our heads above water while the land rises and the railroad lays tracks and the people pour in. We'll settle on our ranches, each on his own, and take wives and raise children. It's true, however — *wives!*" Tunstall was nodding his head in the dark. "It's true the female sex is scarce in these parts."

"There's plenty of Mexes."

"You like the Spanish women, eh? Tell me, how do you do it? How do you manage to get them alone? They never leave their daughters five minutes alone, even with a gentleman. A minute after you're ensconced with the lovely one an old hag comes in and sits against the wall and gazes into vacancy." He paused. "By the powers, I'm spent. I'm on my last legs."

"They sneak out at night."

"Who?"

"The daughters. That's how I get them alone."

"Then you know how to obtain the suet from the pudding. I'm afraid I can't ignore their imperfections myself. Their love of display, their slight knowledge of economy. They invariably possess a tribe of poor relations. I know, I know. The young Spanish women are *mighty* nice looking. And a *lusty* young man like yourself —" Tunstall laughed. "I tell all inquiries that I love horses and dogs and that's enough for me."

"It's enough for me, too."

"Then you see lovemaking as quite a waste of time?"

"I wouldn't go that far."

"What you ought to do is marry a girl whose family still holds a Spanish land grant. You'd secure two things at once. But take care she doesn't lower and degrade you, Kid. The proudest man alive can wind up a brute." His voice had grown fainter and now lapsed into silence. Both men allowed their gazes to drag behind the stars pouring over the horizon. They watched without speaking and Billy's fatigue flowered, grew heavy.

Footsteps came behind. "My watch," said Fred Waite.

The Kid swung around and slid off the barricade. "You need sleep, Mr. Tunstall."

"I could use a little sleep. I'm fairly exhausted. Our little chat has done me good, Antrim. I'm grateful to you boys. Upon my word, we'll weather this storm. We'll leave Gauss here in the morning, he's old, they won't hurt him, assuming they return. It's impossible to tell where they'll show up next. In any case, we'll bring the horses back to Lincoln. Let the sheriff have them. Let him bear the costs of feed until the courts restore them to my possession. We ought to clear out at the first crack of dawn."

But at the first crack of dawn when everyone was saddled, John

Tunstall was still fussing with his travel box, a gift from his father, as he'd once told the Kid. As Billy watched, his boss shrank. He no longer was a giant. They couldn't go yet, he had to wind his gold half-hunter pocket watch in its velvet plush drawer in the mahogany box with the silver corner brackets and inlaid silver plates, and he crouched above the watch as though panning for gold. Then he had to primp, cut his fingernails, file them, clean his face, and pomade his hair. The lid of the box contained a mirror inside, and Mr. Tunstall placed the box on the barricade, settling it onto a grain sack of earth like a hen on its nest so it wouldn't fall off, to see himself in the mirror. Inside the box were mysterious fluids and creams, soaps, scissors, nail files, a snuff box — sprays! — most in silver cases or silver brocade encasing glass bottles, and each with the initials prominently embossed, J H T for John Henry Tunstall. Billy felt a pang of dread. Absorbed in himself, the Englishman seemed blithely unaware that others were present and watching him and waiting. He needed a shake. Where's that ranch you promised me? I feel sorry for the man, he's just as green as I am. And Widenmann's a lardy bull in a china shop, and Fred doesn't care. Only Dick Brewer seems to know what's going on.

Tunstall sat on the ground and pulled off his boots and removed his hose and with the silver-and-ivory-handled scissors trimmed his toenails. At last, shod again, he packed away the travel box and signaled the others his readiness to leave.

On the Ham Mills Trail to Lincoln — through bare hills and brown grass, over passes, through canyons — Fred and Billy hung back. Brewer, Tunstall, and Widenmann led, the others kept to the middle with Tunstall's horses and mules, Middleton in their midst in the wagon. "Think the Boys'll come back?" Fred asked his friend.

"Will the sun rise tomorrow?"

"If you ask me, Rob nearly got himself shot. How did you ever get involved with those fellows?"

Billy hesitated. "It was not a choice I made. I was on the dodge then. I just more or less fell in with that crowd and made the best of it."

"On the dodge from what?"

"I had a fuss with a man."

Fred waited. "And?"

"And I killed him."

"Is that so."

"So I left Arizona."

"For where?"

"New Mexico."

"Is that when you met the Boys?"

"No. I roamed around first. I wasn't well-posted on the best ways of getting along in the world just at that time."

"But you are now?"

"I'm getting there. Where I first met Jesse Evans and the Boys was stealing a horse from a church in Mesilla last August or September. They were doing the like. Leading off the best mounts as quiet as mice while their owners inside sang, 'There Is a Happy Land.' I came north with the boys, spent some time at Fort Sumner, partnered up there with a hog farmer named Garrett. Garrett also bardogged at Beaver Smith's saloon. He was tall as a fire pole and me, I'm short, they called us The Long of It and The Short of It. They called us all sorts of things. Both Garrett and me, before he got married, we sugared the women. We had our love scrapes. We had a bushel of fun making the citizens at Sumner think the Boys had come to shoot up the town."

"Had they?"

"No. There are pleasures in that town they wouldn't want to disturb. It was us firing shots at midnight in the air. The Boys did steal some cattle nearby to sell to James Dolan for five dollars a head. He sold them to the army for fifteen."

"Quite a profit."

"The way he does business."

The treeless hills around them broke against a raise with dry yellow grass rising to the horizon, and their horses started steaming. Dick Brewer up ahead tempered their pace. "I've been thinking," said Fred. "First you ran with the Boys and now you're with us. You're like Antony, then."

"Who's he?"

"First he fought for Caesar and the Romans. Then he fought for Cleopatra and the Egyptians. Have you heard of Cleopatra?"

"Everyone's heard of Cleopatra."

"Very pretty."

"What happened to Antony?"

"He was muchwhat a lady's man. Like you. First he's on one side then on the other and then there's a war, just like we got brewing."

"And how did he do?"

"I didn't get that far."

Billy looked at Fred, riding easy to his left. Handsome and tall and fully contained, with his whiskey-barrel voice and permanent scowl and rock-steady eyes. He felt drawn to the man; he had a certain dignity. "Who cares what side you're on?"

"Don't make any difference. Pick one and stick with it."

Was that a reproach? You couldn't tell with Fred. He never changed pitch, never shouted, never whined. "I agree, stick it out."

"And Macky's no saint," Fred continued. "A pettifogging lawyer. Mr. Tunstall, I don't know. I suppose he's square. Here we are fighting for Scotch and English swells against the poor Irish."

"Poor be fucked."

"You're right about that. Both sides are out to get rich off the other."

"I think he has principles. Tunstall, not McSween."

"That's because he's got us to do his dirty work for him."

"Mr. Tunstall pitches in."

Fred wavered. Billy sensed him struggling to agree. "Well, I believe in principles."

"I do, too."

"One time I found two cockroaches in a flapjack. I thought, one's okay but I draw the line at two."

The Kid laughed. "One of my principles is never steal the same horse twice. Even horses know my name."

"Is that why you call yourself William Bonney now? What happened to Antrim?"

"They're looking for a young man in Arizona by the name of Antrim. I thought it would help if that wasn't me."

"Is there a warrant?"

"I didn't wait to find out."

"Why Bonney, then?"

"Why not? It sounds nice."

"But you're not a nice person."

"No, I am not."

"So what's the point?"

"What do you mean?"

"There's gotta be a point."

"Stay alive, that's the point."

Fred appeared to consider this and nodded. He looked unblinkingly ahead. "What I'd like to get out of this is a ranch."

"I've paltered with that idea myself."

"My own, not an Englishman's."

"He told me last night we'll all get ranches, everyone that works for him. I couldn't believe it. You and me, Fred, we could fall in together."

"He said that, did he? Do you have a place in mind?"

"I like that long stretch south of the Peñasco."

"So do I. Below the ridge? Near the big cutbank?"

"That's the one."

They rode in silence for a while. Ahead, their shadows began to grow longer, and the first pines and cedars spotting ridges to the west were backlit by the sun.

"Let's hope we picked the right side, then," said Fred.

"Let's."

The sun in Fred's face had made him cock his hat; he was looking at the Kid. "So what happened with that man you killed?"

"Which one?"

"In Arizona."

"He died."

Fred paused for a long thirty seconds. "I mean, what's the story?"

"It was at Camp Grant. The blacksmith there liked bullyragging me. So I bought a gun and the next time he done it I shot him in the gut. He died the next day and I pulled like hell for New Mexico Territory."

"Where you met the Boys stealing horses from a church."

"There was some roaming in between."

"Is that the only man you killed?"

"More or less."

"When I just asked about it you said, Which one?"

"I must have been thinking about Brady's posse. What would of happened if we started firing. Sometimes when things run through your mind it's almost like you've done them already."

"I know what you mean. So he's the only one you killed?"

"You asked me that already. What are you, some sort of bounty hunter, Fred? Have *you* ever killed a man?"

"No, I haven't. What's it like?"

"It ain't much. I don't know. Sometimes you can't help it."

"How did it feel? Did it make you feel bad?"

"Not bad, not good. I got somewhat excited. Then I settled down."

What he didn't tell Fred was the strange way he'd pictured it just before he fired: percussion of impact, spray of dust and blood, sorrowful groan, man flying backwards. Windy Cahill took an entire day to die, the Kid later learned, but by then he'd fled the territory. Riding next to Fred, he worried his mind back along lines he would have chosen to forget if he'd had a choice — back to Silver City after his mother died. At fourteen, he joined Sombrero Jack's gang and began his life of crime with a certain ignominy: stealing butter from a rancher. Later, George Schaefer stole Charley Sun's revolvers, plus his clothes and blankets, and gave the Kid the clothes to hide in his room, but his landlady saw them and called Sheriff Whitehill to teach him a lesson. All my life, he thought now, riding next to Fred, people tried to teach me lessons; it's time I taught them some.

The wind picked up. The sun was getting colder. Fred seemed content with Billy's answers and said nothing.

He convinced the softy sheriff to let him have the run of the Silver City jail instead of being locked in his cell, then that night escaped through a chimney. Then he fled to Arizona. These events, in his mind, all seemed to accordion, or resemble the broken surface of a lake whose crests hide the troughs, thereby stringing them together across stretches of tedium. He was fifteen, sixteen, and stole some horses around Fort Grant and again was arrested, this time by Miles Wood who, serving as sheriff, dressed himself as a waiter and hid his gun beneath a tray and pulled it on the Kid as he ate breakfast at the Hotel de Luna.

Wood marched him to the guardhouse at Fort Grant. Could it be, he wondered now, that Wood had gotten wind of his first escape? He hired a blacksmith to rivet shackles on the Kid but still he broke out, with the help of John Mackie and a rat-tail file, later returning to the Fort Grant area — like a dog to his vomit, Billy thought now. And who should he run into there but the very blacksmith who'd riveted the shackles? At Atkin's Cantina this man recognized the Kid, knocked him down, slapped his face, mussed his hair, taunted him. He was only a boy! And Windy Cahill was a man, a thirty-two-year-old mick born across the sea in Galway, and Billy didn't have to take it.

What he remembered was the rage: red, blinding, hot. Cahill pinned him down with his knees on his arms but he managed to free one and draw his pistol and thrust it in his belly. You kill just one man and your hand's in the game and the shame and confusion you felt when he whaled you vanish as a bubble pops. And afterwards the deed blooms as if it's happened a thousand times before and could only transpire this way again, following ancient tunnels and channels inside the hidden world, the one we really live in. Deeds did themselves — you were just the messenger. You've been baptized, little boy. And now you're damned for life. The act of killing doesn't stop when the gun's fired because that little bullet on its big errand sucks you out of yourself, right through the barrel, and one damn thing now leads to another and you have to go along and keep on going, if you don't you're — nothing. You don't even leave footprints. And something hard and sharp now skewers your days, those past and those to come, something like an ice pick driven through a deck of cards. "You still there, Fred?"

"That's okay. I'm here."

"You kill someone and alls you want to do is turn a new leaf over."

"Is that what you did? Didn't you say you went back to stealing horses?"

"That's what I mean. You want to but you can't."

"I don't see why not."

"Because you can't. You're someone else now."

"I'm someone else, too, and I never killed a man."

"It's not the same, Fred."

When they came to the wagon road, Fred swapped with John Middleton, taking the wagon alone into Lincoln while John took Fred's mare. The main party rode through Pajarito Flats, passing the springs, watching the shadows cast by the mountains grow longer and spread as the sun began to set. Dick Brewer's cattle wintered on these flats, most of them hidden in timber to the west. Brewer rode ahead between Tunstall and Widenmann in the glow of dying light reflected overhead. Once Fred was gone, Billy rode next to Middleton five or six hundred yards behind the others.

They'd been riding all day. Before them was the rise that fell away to the Ruidoso. When they crested the ridge they saw the Capitans' gray and black profiles ahead in the distance. Overlapping in dusk, receding with the light, the mountains looked scant on a vanishing horizon.

Riding drag, Billy heard the first shots, then the avalanche of horses galloping behind them, spilling over the ridge they'd just crossed. He turned and saw Matthews racing at the head of a posse now increased by about a dozen men. Then he thought, We're strung out. We've let the lead get out of earshot.

He was right. Widenmann and Brewer, ahead of Tunstall now, had spotted turkeys in the brush left of the trail, and in the act of chasing them up a steep slope had debated on their mounts whether hunting wild turkeys wouldn't raise the whole country.

Rob said, "You're unduly alarmed."

"They'll be up about our ears."

"Not likely, Richard."

Then they, too, heard the gunshots.

Below them, on the trail, Tunstall found himself alone. By this time he'd attained his hundred and fortieth mile in three days, and had reached the exalted stage of fatigue in which nothing seemed to matter, his body was abuzz, he could feed on air, he weighed less than dust. Seconds later, he felt like a butchered quarter section hanging from a hook. When the shots grew louder he whirled his horse around. The Kid and John Middleton came galloping toward him and, passing the Englishman, urged him to follow. "For God's sake, move!" Middleton shouted.

"What, John? What, John?"

The vanguard of Matthews's posse split off from the rest and approached the Englishman. He waited, unable to make out their faces in the granular dark. The horses' hooves, slowing, clattered on seams of gray, pocked limestone running through the yellow grass. Tall ponderosas darkened the field beside a chaparral of Gambel oak and junipers. The three men approaching stayed well below the trail, three indistinct shadows. "Buck?" said Tunstall. His hat looked familiar. "Jesse. Tom." Three of the Boys. He'd brought whiskey to their jail cells! He kneed his horse ahead and held up his hand. Thought he heard Hill say, "Let him get closer," though it could have been, "Looks like the lime-juicer." He could see them better now. Billy Morton, Jesse Evans, and Tom Hill — men he knew well. Enemies, sure, but he saw them as straight, at least they weren't two-faced. Well, let them arrest him. They're a posse after all. At least he won't run. He'll rely on the law, yes, that's the only way. The thought wavered briefly through his picky mind that he was too young to be so exhausted. I'm only twenty-four years old.

· 6 ·

April 1881

Escape

ON THIS SIDE of the Capitans, the trail grows more sandy, the
ponderosas thin out. Now it's junipers and piñons comfortably
spaced with scalds of free dirt between isolated trees. Billy Burt's
pony has affably managed to cure his own limp — he must sense feed
ahead. Around a quick bend in the many folds of hills, the scratch-
ankle town of Las Tablas emerges.

Yginio's house is like the handful of others: the usual adobe with
grass on the roof and vigas protruding along the broken roofline. A
doorway, a window. Cottonwoods, walnuts, *carretas* in the yard,
sheep in their pens, goats nuzzling the new bunch grass in the brown
powdered earth. Chickens. A toddler in a shift. "*Viene la gente, Tío!*"
she shouts.

The Kid corrects her. "One people."

Beyond the house, against a bare hill — dark clouds to the north
lit by the vanished sun — he spots Yginio running, the oxen and plow
abandoned behind him. "Bilito! *Nunca, nunca, nunca.* It's a ghost.
You're in jail, Bilicito!"

"Not anymore." Billy finds himself clinging to his mount's neck
and rolling off the horse in undignified fatigue.

"What did you do? I can't believe it. You son of a bitch!"

The two men embrace. Billy keeps muttering, Henio, Henio. "I managed to escape."

Yginio hefts the free shackle on its chain tucked in the Kid's belt. "Mother of God." He's a handsome young man, Yginio Salazar, younger than Billy, which may be why the elder always took to him. Sometimes you get tired of being the lambkin. "Romolo! Romolo! Billy Bonney's here!"

"Romo's around?"

Yginio shrugs. "All the time now." His friend's stepfather, Billy now sees, stands in the doorway. He doesn't approach. Yginio, tall and thin, looks the opposite of Romolo, squat and overweight, although quite strong. Romolo's famous, on holy days and fiestas, for lifting sacks of potatoes with his teeth. Yginio's more wiry; Billy's never seen him sweat. Even caught plowing he's as polished as ever. Soft, distant eyes. A perfect fluke of a mustache that appears freshly combed, brown hair parted neatly, small ears, long cheeks. He can't stop grinning and he's wearing a jacket impervious to dust, or so it seems to Billy. "*Adelante!*" He takes Billy's arm.

Romolo still stands in the doorway. "Hello, Uncle," Billy says.

"I'm not your uncle."

Glancing at Romolo, Yginio says, "He's just being polite."

Romolo disappears before they enter the house and can't be seen inside. No sign either of the child from the yard. "First, eat," says Yginio, before passing through a doorway. Billy can hear a chittering exchange in rapid-fire Spanish through that door, then one of the men stomps off through the back. Minutes later, through the room's only window, he sees Romolo in the dusk behind the two oxen heaving up against the forked plow with ferocious contempt when it meets an obstacle.

Inside, it's growing dark. A bed, some stick chairs, a rough table, its lamp unlit. Walls whitewashed with *jaspe* sporting obscure chromos in bright tin frames. The floor is beaten earth slicked over with mortar, the ceiling oiled canvas pulled to a point where a rope hangs into the mouth of an *olla* in the middle of the floor to catch precious leaks.

Yginio has become a domestic wonder. *Empanaditas*, a *caldillo* with goat meat, *rueditas*, a stack of blue-corn tortillas sprinkled with cheese, onion, and shredded lettuce and covered with red chili. Biscuits, mugs filled with blue *atole* gruel and salted boiled milk. *Morcilla* made from hog's blood fried with pine nuts and raisins. "I've died and gone to heaven," says Billy. His heart swells out to his friend, his eyes water from the chili, and despite being starved he slows down to savor the carnival of tastes, also out of politeness to his better-mannered host. "You'd of made a great woman, Yginio."

"That's what my mother said."

"Mex food beats pig's feet and pickled eggs hands down."

"We know how to enjoy."

"We had these *empanaditas* the last time, no?"

"I knew you like them."

"I do. They're just the same."

"That's because whenever I do something now I always do it the same way exactly."

"How come?"

"Something bad will happen if I don't. I do it very carefully."

"I can understand that. You don't want to rush things."

The dark grows darker and Yginio lights the oil lamp. He serves the foamy chocolate that Billy loves, spiced with cinnamon and ground pecans, and when they finish that he offers, as though he's been saving them for him, two very fine Tepics.

"Same as last time. I say let's smoke 'em."

They smoke the cigars and Billy yawns. Thumps and rattled pots in the kitchen. Romo likes to smoke, too, Billy knows, but he still resolutely fails to appear. Across the table, like a rash, Yginio's grin spreads upon his face again. "How did you escape?"

"Where's José?" asks Billy.

"In Santa Fe."

"What happened to his dream about going to California?"

"I guess it ain't happen. How did you escape? What happened to the deputies?"

"Dead."

"Jesus, Bilito. They won't hang you this time for sure. This time, I believe, they going to crucify you."

"Well, why not? I'm persecuted too. Those Dolanites and Murphs who murdered all those people — they went scot-free. How come it's always me? I'm tired of playing Bad Man from Bitter Creek. I was supposed to get amnesty too, remember? Give a dog a bad name and he'll be blamed for every bite in the whole damn neighborhood. What I want to know is who betrayed me."

"Sheriff Garrett came through here yesterday on his way to White Oaks."

"I know. He left Olinger in charge."

"So you threw down on him?"

"I didn't wait, I just killed him."

"A hard one."

"Hard is not exactly the word. Olinger's a man, if I didn't have to shoot him, I would have preferred to boil in his own piss."

"Lucky Billy," said Yginio.

"How come I'm lucky?"

"Because you get to kill all those people. You get to shoot the mens you want and most of the time you only have to do it once. The rest of us, what we get, is sit around on our asses and say, What was that you just insulted me? Did you say that to *me*? Please apologize. You make me feel bad. Then we get to sit there while they shoot off our toes. You say you shot them both?"

"I did."

"Christ almighty, Kid, I wish I could of seen it."

"I bet he's still lying there. Nobody liked him."

"Olinger?"

"Now, Bell, I didn't want to shoot *him*. But I had no choice. I never shot no one that didn't deserve it. But I feel bad about Bell."

"He's scum like all the rest."

"He was good to me."

"That's just for the looks. He would have shot you like the others."

"Well, that's true. Someone's always holding a gun to your head." Yginio nods, lowering his eyelids like a knowing tomcat — Yginio, who will die three years short of World War II. "Let's not talk about it," says Billy.

"Now what will you do?"

"Go someplace, I don't know."

"You'll have to leave the territory."

"I know."

"Go south. Go to Old Mexico. Garrett can't follow you there."

"I've got things to do in Fort Sumner."

"If you know what's good for you —"

"I know what's good for me. What's good for me is to stick around a pissing while. I plan to kill the man that betrayed me — whoever that is. It must of been a friend. Plus make John Chisum pay me what he owes. I'd love to run into Lew Wallace, too. Break every one of his fucking fingers then he won't write any more books. On top of which I got family in Sumner."

"You mean Paulita?"

"Not just that. You know, friends. They might as well be family."

"Except the one that betrayed you."

"Do you know who that was?"

"No."

"Not Jesús or Juan. Domingo wouldn't do it. Francisco's a true friend."

"Which Francisco?"

"Lobato."

"What about your sweeties? Nasaria, Celsa?"

"Celsa would never do something like that."

"Paulita?"

"She's pregnant! None of them would."

"You just said someone did."

"That's why I want to go there. See for myself."

"But the law will catch up!"

"We're going in circles, Yginio. The law will catch up regardless. They'd follow me to hell."

"Maybe to hell but not across the border."

"I know, I know. I need to think about it. Can I stay here a few days?"

"Of course."

"There's no authority in Lincoln."

"Who's the J.P. now?"

"I think it's still Wilson."

"He would take his time. City clerk?"

"Billy Burt. I got his horse."

"He'll go to Garrett when he get another one. He might come through here."

"I expect he'll go by way of Murphy's ranch. On top of he's a coward."

"Did they know you come here?"

"They know I hit for the hills."

That night he can't sleep. He lies awake on the floor beside his friend's bed hearing rare and strange sounds through the buzz of his consciousness: fine, high-pitched crinkles, pink and green in his ears like old brittle oilcloth. He knows Romo is gone, having left him this silence that ripples like an itch in the back of his mind. Yginio's easy breathing above him begins to drive him loco, too, as though the man hadn't a care in the world. Billy's limbs feel unboned from their long meal, his vessels swollen, the blood coursing through them, and his flesh soft as butter, yet even while he remembers, as though in a fever, the times when he was happy before the Lincoln County War, he senses a hardness, a chisel in his mind. The world was better then. The gay old times at Fort Sumner. How he laughed! The girls came from Santa Rosa, Puerto de Luna, Anton Chico, from ranches fifty miles away, with roses in their hair and pendants on their necks and silk handkerchiefs and ribbons tied around their waists, for the weekly *bailes*. Their bold eyes bluffed then shied behind fans, they made the fans talk, but when he came near them they bunched up like hens. Gallantry flattered them, they didn't get that from waddies. He removed his hat and spoke soothingly low. Feigned ignorance about items on their dresses, embroidered petals and vines, and remarked on colors matching their eyes, or adjusted a ribbon or fingered a locket, even traced a necklace with his gentle fingers across a silky collarbone. Garrett, too, soft-soaped the ladies, and married a beauty — then gave up the dances. He and the Kid would sneak into the back room and loop a chain around one of Beaver Smith's barrels and, setting it on blocks with a dishpan underneath, pull the chain tight and sweat out enough whiskey to last them on the dance floor. Or last them at monte or at the faro tables, where Garrett always lost. I gave him the shirt off my back, Billy thinks. I staked that man plenty more than he staked me, but then again I was handy with the cards, or let's call it skill. Yes, skill. I had the touch.

There's always cheating, said Garrett.

That takes skill, too.

Suddenly, the Kid jumps up in a sweat and rouses Yginio and screams in his face, "You were the one! You betrayed me, you bastard! You told Garrett where I was!" Yet, his friend's eyes stay closed and his breathing unruffled. Billy stands there in his socks. The sheer horror of not knowing — or of forgetting in the morning — whether you're sleeping or awake, if it's midnight or three, if you're in the sorry world and can't get out of it or in a sorrier nightmare.

The next day Billy's stolen horse is gone — back to Billy Burt in Lincoln, no doubt — having pulled loose from the sotol stalk he'd tied him to the day before in hasty fatigue. He can always steal another. He and Yginio work on his shackles with an ax and a rock — Billy's leg resting on a cottonwood stump — and finally get the leg irons off, and he swings the chain around and lets it fly toward the mountains. Then they free his wrists from the heavy manacles and he chafes and slaps his forearms and throws his arms back and forth. He sets up a target range in Yginio's grama grass facing a broken ridge. One lone cholla swelling with buds from sixty feet away. Townspeople come to watch. Yginio stands behind Billy, pockets full of ammunition, to reload for his friend. He knows this will give him standing in the village. The elders here once had been Mexicans, having lived in the region long before its annexation in '45, but now they are Americans, even though they still call the Anglos Americans as though this honorific were the latter's exclusively. And the Anglos still call the Mexicans Mexicans.

"Fuck all," Billy mutters after four shots. "This gun don't shoot for shit. I wish I had my old one." He's been aiming for the buds on the waist-high cholla and hasn't hit a single one. The fifteen or so villagers clap politely anyway. The word has spread, they know he's escaped, they've always been partial to El Chivato. To whom is good to Billy, they say, he is good to them. They stand behind a fence of juniper posts at the edge of the lumberyard — the mill smokes behind them — but now and then children followed by their dogs slip between the posts into the field and lie in the new tender shoots of grama grass to get a better look.

"Whose gun is it?" Yginio asks.

"Bell's."

"Are you sure it's the gun?"

"Of course I'm sure. This gun couldn't hit a barn on the wing." Annoyed, the Kid examines the gun. He runs through the case against it, which he'd snatched from Jim Bell after slabsiding the unfortunate wretch. He'd kicked him down the stairs, fired twice and missed but the ricochet caught him. Blind luck. The gun wasn't cared for, that must be the problem. Neglected guns yaw. No, he hasn't lost his touch. He's heard of hombres who go to ridiculous lengths to correct a failing weapon. Lock it in a vise, heat up the barrel, shove a wrapped poker inside the barrel, and whang it with a hammer. Which queers the bore, of course. "You got a blacksmith here, Yginio?"

"Pedro Silva."

He shakes out his arms. He lets them hang by his side. Elbows slightly bent. As the right arm lifts it will seize the pistol's butt on the way up, with economy of motion, assuming the weapon was properly suspended at a suitable height. A gun raised on a belt cinched to ride through a river and not then restored to the optimum location means the barrel will snag on top of the holster and what sort of flowers do you favor then, *amigo?*

He whips his hand up but it's just average fast, he knows — catches the hammer with his thumb, slides the forefinger through the trigger-guard, fires, and feels the kick as the barrel comes level. A puff of dust blooms in the dirt beside the cholla. "For shit!" He throws the gun down and, hitting the ground, it jumps like a mousetrap, firing in the air, and strikes a squealing puppy over near the fence. A boy grabs the dog and wraps it in his arms and runs toward a house strewing yips and whines.

Yet even this will not impeach his credit with the people of Las Tablas. *Un hombre muy generoso*, Billy the Kid. He give money, horses, drinks. We always glad to see his innocent face. *Su vista penetraba al corazón de toda la gente.*

A thunderous noise comes from the south, from up Las Tablas canyon. Bent over, Billy humps it to the privy behind his friend's house and pulls the door shut as a dust cloud descends and horses approach, whinnying and blowing, and soldiers fill the space between Yginio and the villagers.

Billy left the gun behind. He feels gut-shot, lightheaded. He twists the wooden turnbuckle and contemplates the privy hole. He could hide in the pit if he had to, he knows. Jack Long and the Dummy had done exactly that during the five-day battle behind McSween's house. But upon cool reflection he realizes these soldiers aren't searching for him — they were likely out patrolling even when the Kid escaped and just now heard the shooting and have come to have a look-see. Buffalo soldiers from Fort Stanton. Billy spies them through a knothole. The white lieutenant leans down from his saddle in Yginio's face, who's picked up the gun — dear, loyal Henio! — while his soldiers' black faces impassively survey the brown ones of the townspeople.

And inside the jakes, everything comes out, coils and coils, he just barely got his pants down. He is not the sort of person who goes to the privy because he has to shit. No, he shits because he finds himself in the outhouse, because he couldn't sleep last night, because he can't shoot to save his ass all the sudden. At least he didn't come here to hide like a coward.

"What's going on here? What's all the firing?" To Billy inside the privy, the voices ring clear.

"Target practice," says Yginio.

"Why are they here? What are you people up to?" Billy peers through the knothole and sees the lieutenant gesturing toward the crowd with his glove in his hand. This lieutenant is one he's never seen before; young, buttoned tight, round dumpling cheeks, straight as an Indian on his bay mare. He doesn't speak, he shouts.

"I was practicing my shooting."

"Speak up!"

Yginio repeats himself at exactly the same volume.

"Where's your target?"

"That cholla."

"It looks remarkably unscathed."

"I'm a lousy shot. That's why I need to practice."

"With the whole town watching? These people dropped their chores to watch you shoot at a cholla? See my men? These soldiers? They're doing a job. Long days in the saddle, long nights without sleep. No wonder they resent people like you who sit around dreaming up ways to waste your time. I suppose your fields just plow themselves without you. The sawmill cuts its own boards. I don't buy it for a minute. Why are you here?" He waits. No one speaks. He turns back to Yginio. "What's your name?"

"Yginio."

"Full name."

"Yginio Salazar."

"I've been given a list and I believe your name is on it. It sounds suspiciously familiar. Let me see that gun." Holding the barrel and trigger-guard, Yginio reaches him the gun. The lieutenant is short and Yginio tall but the former being mounted reverses this advantage.

"I've heard all about your vigilance committees, your public executions. Is that why you're here?" He surveys the congregation, mostly women and children and a few ancient men.

"They're here because they want to find out if I've improved my shooting."

"Don't make me laugh. I can see what you're up to. You're trying to make me think you're an object of ridicule. Are you baiting me, mister?"

Yginio says nothing.

"Where do you live?"

"In that house over there."

"Who lives there with you?"

"My stepfather and his niece."

The lieutenant's horse swings around. The gun's on the other side. "It's clear you're a menace to this community."

And Billy watching it all through the knothole, his arms and legs sliced by paper-thin sunbeams shining through the walls like light in a pisspot. The lieutenant doesn't look suspicious or upset or even concerned, he looks pleased with himself and disgusted with the world. "I'm keeping this weapon. It's sequestered. You people go on about your business." He waves the arm with the weapon, finger on the trigger. No one moves. "I often patrol this area," he announces. "I don't intend to hear gunshots again."

◆　◆　◆

HEADING EAST ON a new horse the following morning — again for a second night not having slept — the Kid completes the full circle from jubilant transport for his perilous escape to sheer whipped-dog glumness and meanness and despair. When he couldn't sleep he rose at four A.M. and went out in the dark and two hours later came back with a horse, not from Las Tablas, from a neighboring ranch, out of respect for Yginio. Like a mother, Yginio packed him food. Tins of sardines, *empanaditas, marquezotes*. They embraced, Yginio whispering, "Go to Mexico, Bilito. Go south." From their windows and doorways, people watched him ride out.

Now it all comes crashing down, all the mayhem and loss of the past three years. Tunstall executed, McSween gunned down, Dick Brewer's head blown off, Tom O'Folliard shot in the heart — "Don't shoot, Garrett. I'm already killed" — Charlie Bowdre leg- and gut-shot, mouth filling with blood — "I wish . . . I wish . . ." — and the Regulators broke up, Frank and George Coe pulled out for Colorado, Fred Waite lit off, Hank Brown in Kansas. Chisum still owes me five hundred dollars.

How much?

Five hundred, Ma.

Shoot him.

Sure. The most popular millionaire in Lincoln County.

You're popular, too.

Is that so.

You're famous. You need to take advantage of your good odor.

I already have. The Mexes all like me.

I don't mean that. Write some letters to the papers. Stand up for your rights! Governor Wallace promised you a pardon. You could go to Santa Fe.

I could go south, too. I could go to Mexico. There's advantages in both. Or I could go north to Fort Sumner, Ma.

None of that! I'm wise to you, mister. He wants to see the tart that's carrying his child! For all I give a damn. Go ahead, be my guest. You could shoot her, too. Shoot her in the belly for all I give a damn. Everything I said you always did the opposite. You never did mind well, Henry McCarty. It comes of growing up without a father around. Is that why you shoot people? Headstrong child. Go ahead and eat beans — I'll stick to potatoes. You ever were a bother and how could I help it I loved you so much? I'd say now at least you got plenty of love. That wasn't the problem. Faith, hope, and love. Well, you never had faith. But the greatest is love. The greatest of these.

You loved me so much you got everything I did. I got a toothache, you got a toothache. Remember, Ma? Same tooth, even.

Chilblains, the mumps.

I took to my bed, you took to your bed.

For all you cared. You had your own little world.

I cared. I still do.

Grand way to show it.

Fireweed along the Roswell trail. The sun in his face. Torrey yucca, new evening primrose, cholla everywhere, the resurrection of the grama grass. The earth to his right breaks in successive waves against the north-facing slopes of the Capitans. Green-gray clearings in trees near the summits. He'll be past the mountains soon. Then where to go. Olive-green, mouse-green, yellow-green plains rolling ahead from behind him, around him. Mother dead, too.

· 7 ·

1878

Tunstall

Middleton and billy, leading their horses, scrambled up
the slope to join Widenmann and Brewer, who'd taken cover in an
outcrop of boulders. Below, the shooting had stopped; the posse,
Billy told them, had been firing in the air. Then they heard a single
shot and John Middleton calmly observed, "They've killed Mr. Tunstall." It can't be, thought Billy. Then two more, then the sound of
Tunstall's horses bolting every which way in a panic of darkness. The
Kid, jumping up, could not contain his urine and before he had the
chance to thumb his pecker out he felt a warm thread run down his
leg. By the time he had it aimed, though, nothing emerged. As he
stood there trying to go, from his heart to his toes, everything sank
and a strange calm took over. The ongoing seconds coolly slipped
past the stoppage of time created by the gunshots. It couldn't be
true . . .

Another avalanche of horses: the posse storming off. Maybe they
just arrested Mr. Tunstall, maybe they're taking him with them. The
worm of fear that gnawed Billy's heart refused to abate.

He and the others led their horses down and searched in the darkness, listening for moans. The inky dark swelled in exactly the pock-

ets they thought they'd find a body. At last they rode on, following the steep trail down to the Ruidoso, but Billy and Middleton insisted on stopping at John Newcomb's ranch and sending a search party out the next morning. Pooh, blustered Widenmann; Harry's in jail in Lincoln by now.

But Widenmann was wrong. In the corpse-light of dawn, Ramón Baragón found John Tunstall's body dragged into a thicket beside his dead horse. It was carefully arranged: one blanket underneath him, another on top, his folded overcoat placed under head and neck. His hat had been wedged beneath Mormon Pussy's ear. Tunstall, Billy learned when Baragón returned with the body tied across the back of a mule, had been shot in the breast then shot again in the back of the head and after that his skull bashed, no doubt with a rifle stock. At John Newcomb's ranch they placed him in a cart and freighted him to Lincoln.

The Kid and the others helped Alexander McSween lay out the body on a table in his parlor. Blood pooled in Tunstall's ear had run down his neck, and Billy spit on his bandanna and tried to wipe it off. The skin was cold and hard. Mr. Tunstall's face was misshapen and grayed and the Kid turned his head. Then he turned back and stared at the spectacle. Somehow, on one side, the lower lip had pulled down, the mouth wouldn't close. Billy pinched it together but still it twisted open. He wiped his fingers on his pants.

Soon the word spread, mobs gathered outside. Down the road, someone shot out Dolan's front window. Those who didn't care if they'd be seen by the Dolanites knocked on McSween's door to pay their last respects. One by one they filed past, some averting their eyes from the gray face and crushed head, each greeted by McSween with the same grim words: "Justice will be done." Squire Wilson brought news of the Dolanites' claim that Tunstall'd fired first while running off with horses that had been legally attached. Mac shook his head sadly. "What won't those Irish thugs say?" he asked. "They lie in their teeth, they're cowards and jacklegs, every last one. They can't hold a candle to John! He was a man of his word! Why, John had once —"

Billy Bonney couldn't listen. Next to Fred against the wall inside McSween's parlor, he swore to himself to revenge Tunstall's murder, committed, he knew, by men he'd once run with — most particularly Buck Morton, Jesse Evans, and Tom Hill. That became his litany, chanted in his head as a single word, *Morton-Evans'n-Hill*, for they'd split off from the posse, he'd seen them do that, and rode up to Tunstall and shot him cold. But his purpose embraced their bosses, too, the ones who pulled the strings, men like Dolan, George Hindman, Billy Matthews, Sheriff Brady.

He gave himself the whip over Mr. Tunstall's death. He'd acted like a coward and first-water idiot, thinking the posse was after the horses and maybe at most they might arrest Tunstall, but he should have known better. He should have stayed with the Englishman instead of racing past him, should have fired back. He'd learned his lesson. The world had split in half into those who'd murdered John Henry Tunstall and those with blood in their eyes for revenge, and you couldn't be neither, you had to take sides. Yes, the Englishman had his faults, who didn't, but for the life of him Billy couldn't think of one now. They'd dissolved into the stew of rage and regret boiling in his soul, the coil of wanting and loss, while Mr. Tunstall himself, who'd been good to the Kid, who would always be good, was fixed for the ages, having hardened into marble. And Morton-Evans'n-Hill were buckets of slime each hanging by a string just waiting to be slashed.

He kicked at a chair and it flew across the room and landed on its side. Everyone looked at him. McSween inspected the chair and held up a leg that was knocked clean off. Billy approached and relieved him of the chair and, without a word, carried it through the dining room door to the kitchen and outside. On the hard bare earth at the yard's edge he smashed it into bits and tossed the pieces in the brush leading down to the river.

Back inside, he listened to McSween eulogizing Tunstall. In his lawyer's suit and tie, tall and broad, with hands as large as shovels, and rolling his shoulders as he walked, yet at the same time looking glassy and vague — with his wiry black hair piled on his head and his wishbone mustache lengthening his chin and despite, lamentably, breaking off in mid-sentence as though ambushed by grief, Macky showered accolades on John, praised his generosity, his natural nobility, and his openhearted manner. He was made of bell metal, his heart was pure sterling, he looked down upon us now and approved of our — If anything, he was too soft on the Dolanites. Now they'll see — now they'll see —

"Now they'll see what?" the Kid asked Fred. The growing crowd before them consisted mostly of Mexicans.

"Now they'll see what we do."

"What will we do?"

Fred glanced over at John Tunstall's body. "I imagine we'll have to kill the whole pack of them."

The Reverend Taylor Ealy, sent for by McSween several months ago, offered prayers beside the body. He and his wife, Mary, and their two children had arrived that very morning all the way from Pennsylvania, and planned to board temporarily with the McSweens in their sprawling house before they found their own place. Mary played Sue McSween's parlor organ — Mac's wife was visiting friends in St. Louis — and Squire Wilson translated for the Mexicans such hymns and prayers as they'd never heard before. McSween had told Tunstall's men about Ealy when they carried in the body; he'd been summoned to counter the Catholic influence in Lincoln. And wouldn't you know it? — his five-day journey from the end of the train-line in a wagon and horse had culminated that morning with a welcome from the Dolanites when he and his family rattled into town. Gathered on the porch of James Dolan's store, they'd asked Ealy, driving past, who the hell he was, and when he guilelessly answered they surrounded his wagon and said they'd as soon see a whore come to

Lincoln as a Protestant minister. They had no need of his Bible-thumping, they said, drawing their weapons. Reeking of liquor, Jack Long had leaned into Reverend Ealy's face and informed him that he'd once helped hang a Methodist preacher in Arizona but never tried a Presbyterian, are their necks any tougher?

Now McSween fumed. As the mourners filed past, he declared that the Murphy-Dolan gang was like the Spanish Inquisition, whereas McSween himself and the martyred John Tunstall were like the Covenanters killed in the seventeenth century for defending the Scottish Presbyterian Church.

That night, the Kid, Fred Waite, and Dick Brewer slept on the floor in McSween's dining room, and heard sporadic gunshots outside and hoarse prayers from the parlor, where McSween and Reverend Ealy sat up with the body.

At breakfast, McSween outlined his plans, which became, the more he talked, the more irritatingly legal to the spunked-up Kid. They met in the dining room. Tunstall was still unburied, and at the table Billy just could make out his stocking feet through the open door. Before his sideboard, as he talked, Macky had a habit of making a fist and slamming it into his other palm as though ready to run out and conquer the world, then hesitating and gazing at his hands. He assigned the Kid and Dick to swear affidavits before Squire Wilson, justice of the peace, who would surely issue warrants for the murderers of Tunstall. Wilson, he reminded them, like all the town authorities, was of their own faction, whereas the Dolanites controlled the county government, of which Lincoln was the seat, including Sheriff Brady, District Attorney Rynerson in Las Cruces, and Judge Bristol in Mesilla, who'd issued the unjust writ of attachment that had started this whole mess in the first place. To get justice, said Mac, we'll have to bypass the county, but all the Kid could think was, justice — what is justice? He knew that Mac went unarmed because the gospel said to turn the other cheek, but he was human, wasn't he? By now, wouldn't scenes of bloody revenge have passed through his mind? They'd taken over Billy's: James Dolan clasping Billy's knees begging not to be shot; Sheriff William Brady's lip and large mustache sliced off his ugly face; Billy Matthews dragged through town on a rope behind a manure cart. As he watched the lawyer ramble, though, Billy understood that others did that sort of thing, not McSween.

Others did that sort of thing *for* McSween.

Yet here he was admonishing his men to not allow their grief to fester into brutality. What kind of man was he? Billy brooded over Macky. John's loss meant a loss of income for the lawyer. Was he just a poor actor or, in his own way, oafishly angered? He seemed just as inconsolable over Tunstall's death as over the inevitable stoppage of funds from London, and announced to them now with a sympathetic frown, "I can't pay you boys yet." He looked them each in the eye. "But I will. I will. You'll have to trust me on this one."

No one responded.

One problem, Mac went on, was that Lincoln's town constable, Atanacio Martínez, was just a part-timer, he didn't even wear a badge. "You might have to persuade him to exercise his authority." McSween's eyes grew brighter. "He could deputize you boys."

"I'll persuade him," said the Kid.

Rob Widenmann walked in with a letter in his hand — he'd been writing to Tunstall's family in London in the room he'd shared with "Harry" — and the men filled him in then realized they'd better dissuade him from helping. "You're a hothead, Rob," Dick Brewer said.

"That is not true!" Rob looked down at the ammunition belts draped across his shoulder.

"So what?" Billy said. "We could use a few hotheads."

In the end, it was just Dick Brewer and the Kid who swore the affidavits, and only Fred and Billy who roused Martínez from his bed to deputize them so they could help serve the warrants. Martínez demurred. They'll kill me, he said. Billy in turn told Martínez that he'd better take that chance because if he didn't he would kill him himself. So the next day they set out for Dolan's store: Billy, Fred Waite, and the reluctant Martínez.

It was morning in Lincoln. Wood and charcoal smoke hung in the air. The throat-scratching dust of Lincoln's single street was so perniciously fine it rose like a vapor when disturbed by marching heels. People watched from their porches and weedy yards when the three men of justice swaggered up the road past Tunstall's store, rifles cradled in their arms. The Dolans and Murphs were still inside that store attaching Tunstall's property even though he was dead. At the door, Jim Longwell spit brown chew on the street and caught Billy's eye as he passed; the Kid sneered. Ahead, the Dolan store sat at the end of town, the only two-story building for many miles around — it would later become the county courthouse — and Billy observed that its front porch and door had been placed under guard by buffalo soldiers. The Negro men in blue stared without expression as Fred and Billy approached, Martínez trailing behind. Their white Lieutenant DeLany ordered them to halt. Martínez caught up and stepped forward. "We have warrants to arrest some men inside this store."

"What men?"

He read the list: Jesse Evans, Tom Hill, George Hindman, James Dolan, Billy Morton, and others not identified by the witnesses.

"How can you arrest unidentified men?"

"We'll know them when we see them," Billy said.

"None of the men you name are here."

"This is Dolan's store. Dolan must be here."

"Mr. Dolan's life would not be worth a farthing if turned over to you."

Deadpan, the buffalo soldiers watched. Martínez, trying to look fierce, nearly shrieked, "How is it Dolan rates protection from the army when he's wanted for murder? Please explain that to me."

"He ain't wanted for murder. You got a drunken *alcalde* to issue those warrants and they don't mean dick. I'm just doing a job here. I'm here to prevent the destruction of property and the loss of more lives. Last night a mob fired on my men and killed a horse. You want to go in there? Go ahead and go in there. These men are intemperate —" The lieutenant now shifted his attention to a crowd who'd followed the three, raising his voice. "You are my witnesses. I tried to protect them but they won't listen. Well, it's their funeral." He grandly stepped aside and ordered his men to make way for this "posse," contemptuously placing the word inside quotes, and Martínez marched forward, followed by Fred and Billy.

Eight or nine rifles simultaneously levered when they kicked the door open. Martínez made his announcement anyway. "We have reason to believe there is murderers in here. I intend to serve these papers."

"Go ahead and serve them."

Billy looked around. Stumpy James Dolan stood behind the counter, his doughnut lips smiling. Gauded up in a California hat and a black sateen shirt whose placket was laced with flat leather strings underneath his wool coat, he sighted down his six-gun directly at the Kid. To one side was Buck Morton on the end of a Winchester, to the other Sheriff Brady, while fanning out around them, some behind the counter, some five feet away on the sanded floor, some behind pickle barrels, one before a coffee mill with large iron wheels, each with a carbine, a rifle, or a pistol, were the other Dolanites all drawing beads. A dozen fingers on a dozen polished triggers, a dozen squinty eyes, a dozen hard pricks, a dozen tight scrotums, a dozen oscillating knees. Martínez took a giant step and put his papers on the counter. "Well. I'll save my spit."

"Don't you want to read them?" Brady asked.

"It says to arrest you. Every man jack."

"You can't arrest a duly authorized posse. You ought to know that, Constable. But I can arrest you. I've done it all the time. You come here to terrorize peaceful citizens and I won't have it."

Billy looked at William Brady, senior statesman of the Dolanites. "Peaceful be fucked."

"Who's this lick-twat?" asked Dolan. "Is that you, Antrim? I remember you now. You're Judas to my Jesus, I've been told."

"Kiss my ass."

"Surrender your guns," Sheriff Brady said.

"Go ahead and take them, you son of a bitch."

The three were disarmed of their pistols and rifles, including Billy's favorite Winchester. He stood in the middle of James Dolan's store, eyes feeling sneaky, not entirely sure what to do with his hands or how to reestablish his swaggering airs or at least maintain his dignity of bearing when his heart was in his boots. This was not how they'd planned it. Billy Matthews lowered his carbine and slapped Fred's shoulder and tried to raise the tone. "You boys given us a good meal down there at the Englishman's ranch and we would like to reciprocate before we have you ironed. We're low on chuck but would whiskey do the trick?"

Fred looked at a wall. "I'm not normally a drinker."

"Just because we don't hold with John Bull ways and you're a bunch of limey heathens and one of you's a turncoat don't mean we can't be friends. Fetch that bucket, Billy."

"Fetch it yourself."

"Fetch the goddamn bucket!"

Matthews wasn't looking at anyone named Billy but he did sound impatient. All the others had lowered their weapons. Men began to move. The pail in question sat beside a saddle rack beyond the counter's edge. The Kid shrugged, dragged his feet, tried to swagger toward the whiskey but his quick hand caught the handle of the bucket simultaneously with Morton's, who'd strolled behind the counter at an equal clip. The two glared at each other — Tunstall's friend and Tunstall's killer. "He said Billy," said the Kid.

"Well, my name is Billy," Buck Morton said. "You ain't no Billy. You're Kid Antrim."

"I go by Kid but my name is William Bonney."

"You're pulling my leg. I know your name."

"Just bring me the cocksucking bucket, would you please?" Both men lifted the bucket and started for Matthews but one Billy geed while the other hawed and some whiskey sloshed out. "And take care with it, would you?"

Morton said, "Folks around here call me Buck but all of you know that my given name is Billy."

"I didn't know that."

"Which one's Billy, then?" asked Dolan.

"I am."

"Me."

"My given name is Jacob," said Matthews. "My daddy just started calling me Billy. Some folks, though, it don't make any difference what their given name is. They'll change it and think everyone is fooled."

"That's true," said Brady. "I myself favor William. Billy's always sounded gutter rat to me. Why anyone would choose it?"

Both men looked at the Kid.

"Here, moisten your tongue," Matthews said to Martínez, handing him a cup. "Drink it down."

"What do you call this whiskey?" asked Martínez.

"I call it, 'Mother I'm Dying Can I Have a Piece of Pie.'" Matthews tried to smile but his pinched face just sneered. His overgrown mustache hung halfway to his chin and the V of his brow gripped his glower hard and caused the end of his fat nose to buckle.

Billy Morton, on the other hand, looked handsome and young, being only twenty-two. A choirboy smile — just like the Kid. But he'd been the one to fire first at Mr. Tunstall, the Kid felt sure of it. Cherubically, Morton cocked his head and frowned and took the cup from Matthews — the one intended for Martínez — and sucked it down, then looked at the constable. "Will you drink some now? It's not poisoned, I guess. It will moisten your tongue."

"It's moist enough already."

"Give the crawthumper some." The Kid nodded at Dolan. "Then we'll know for sure if it's poisoned or not."

"You got a sassy mouth."

"And you got a big one. Size matters."

A head above Dolan, standing behind him, Sheriff Brady laughed in his boots.

The drinks were passed around. For every half cup thrown down by Dolan's men, the trio drank two — that was the rule of hospitality announced by Billy Matthews. "What proof is this?" Fred slurred at one point.

"Muchwhat a hundred," Billy Matthews said.

By the time they were marched through Lincoln to the jail, Billy, Fred, and the constable were slittering like gut-shots. They couldn't keep a straight line. The whole town fell out to watch the parade and the Dolanite triumph. Even in his cups, Billy knew there was a reason Dolan's store and Sheriff Brady's office were at one end of town and the jail at the other: it was these public processionals, these caravans of shame, displayed before the citizens. One Dolanite, John Hurley, stomped down the road dancing and twirling and shouting, "Ya-haa! Three turkeys in a hole." Inside the jail, when Brady opened the trapdoor and shoved his captives down the ladder then pulled the ladder up and looked down at the three, he calmly observed, "You got a lot to learn, boys."

◆ ◆ ◆

"I THOUGHT WE could just arrest those bastards. I thought alls we need's a warrant."

"Just like Macky," Fred said.

"Don't equate me with him. His game is not mine."

"What do you mean?" In the darkness, Fred's voice sounded even deeper: a rumble-drone filling the gorge in his throat.

"My game," said the Kid, "is to march right up to that miserable wart and shoot him in the teeth."

"You mean Morton?"

"Morton-Evans'n-Hill. James Dolan. Sheriff Brady. All of them, especially Morton. He fired the first shot at Mr. Tunstall, Fred."

"How do you know?"

"I can see it in his eyes. He's a son of a bitch. He thought I was muscling in on his girl last year at one of Dolan's cow camps."

"Morton did?"

"Yes."

"And that's why you think he fired the first shot?"

The Lincoln jail was a *chosa*, ten feet deep. No light. Heavy square timbers lined the underground wall to which their shackles were bolted. The dirt floor on which they sat was cold and smelly — the brimming thunder-mug stank — and the air felt both damp and dry in winter: damp inside bones, dry on a throat. One thing, it sobered you up pretty quick. Leaning back against the wall, their heads in a vise, their dry tongues tasting of carrion and muck, all Billy and Fred could manage was talk. Martínez was gone. Brady had returned after just a few hours and released him without a word to the others. "What about us?" Billy shouted. "I know what they're planning," he told Fred now. "They're footing up in their minds how much it costs to feed us. It would be cheaper for them to cut Juan Patrón's *acequia* and flood this damn dungeon and drown us good."

"That's one way not to have to feed prisoners," said Fred. "The other way is set them free and tell them to run and shoot them in the back. Ham Mills did that with a nigger he arrested because he didn't want to guard him all night. He had a dance to go to. What was that all about at Dolan's store?"

"What was what all about?"

"You and Billy Morton."

"He's like a little brother. He thinks the way to get your goat is to copy what you say. 'I'm Billy.' 'I'm Billy.'"

"He said it first."

"Both of us is Billies. There's plenty of Billies."

"I've been thinking about that. There's so many Billies if someone's on the dodge alls he has to do is name himself Billy. Best way to lose yourself to the law."

"That's what I did."

"Or name yourself Kid."

"I did that too."

"Billy Bevens. Heard of him?"

"Can't say that I have."

"Him and Billy Webster in Wyoming. They run with Sam Bass for a while. Bill Heffridge in Nebraska, also a Basser. Bill Bailey, shot on the street in Newton, Kansas. Curly Bill Brocius in Tombstone. Captain Billy Coe in Colorado."

"Is he kin to George and Frank?"

"Not that I know of. Billy Mullin. Billy Grounds. John Wesley Hardin's sidekick, Billy Cohron. Billy Dixon, also part of Hardin's crew. Lucky Bill Thorrington in Nevada and his chum Billy Edwards, both hung by vigilantes. Fly-specked Billy in South Dakota. There's a shitload of Billies. Wild Bill Hickok, you've heard of him."

"Of course."

"Billy Mayfield in Carson City, who carved a big hole in Sheriff Blackburn's belly. Texas Billy Thompson in Abilene. Bill Anderson in Wichita. Bill Bowen in Texas. Wild Bill Longley in Texas. Billy Sutton, also in Texas. 'I will wash my hands in Billy Sutton's blood,' said Jim Taylor, and he did, too. Billy Wren of Lampasas. Hurricane Bill Martin from Abilene. Bully Bill Brooks of Dodge City who wore a star when he wasn't stealing horses. There's a Billy the Kid in Tombstone, Billy; last name, Clairborne."

"Never heard of him."

"Billy Leroy in Colorado, also referred to as Billy the Kid. You could fool a lot of people if you called yourself that."

"I'm pretty happy with William H. Bonney."

"Where'd you get that name, anyway?"

"Picked it out of a hat. I don't know, I can't recall. There's a lot of Franks, too, ain't it?"

"I haven't made a study of that. There's a lot of Kids. Kid this, Kid that. Kid Dobbs, the Catfish Kid, Harry the Kid, the Mormon Kid, Kid Wade, Kid Vance, the Pockmarked Kid. Plenty of Kids."

"Fine with me."

"Around here there's Billy Matthews, Sheriff William Brady, Buck Morton says his name is Billy, Bill McCloskey, Billy Wier — I'm leaving some out. Billy Burt. There's Billy Campbell, the one that shot Tom King. There was Billy Wilson. He shotten Robert Casey, remember? Had to be hung twice? Now there's another Billy Wilson entirely, up to Fort Sumner. And he calls himself the Kid."

"I've met him. There was a Billy Wilson in Silver City too."

"Then you're just another Billy. Is that what you're after?"

"I don't know what I'm after."

"Men are like shadows."

"Shadows of what?"

Fred didn't answer. Billy raised his arms and waved them around to keep up the circulation.

"So which are you?" Fred asked.

"Which what?"

"Which Billy?"

"I'm the made-up one."

Both men sat in silence. After a while, Fred asked, "You don't feel like a fraud?"

"No sir."

"I do all the time."

"That doesn't mean I do."

"What's that breeze?"

"I'm moving my arms."

"Can't you keep still? You're as restless as a bedbug."

"I didn't know Billy Wilson had to be hung twice."

"This Mexican woman opens the coffin and screams he's alive. So they hang him again."

"What a way to die."

"There's worse. Being burned at the stake, I wouldn't like that."

"I saw a gambler once got his head chopped off. It took three or four good whacks. The head was still trying to scream when it was off."

"A doctor during the French Revolution measured the time a head stayed alive after it was guillotined. Some, the eyes move around, the mouth whispers something. Some of them stayed alive for fifteen seconds. But every time the doctor puts his ear to a mouth he can't quite hear the whisper. Can't make out what he's saying."

"Fred, how come you know about so many Billies? You sure as hell have quite an equipment of names."

"So do you, Kid. I've kicked around a lot. I've been all over. You pick it up gradually, all the names people say. I began in Indian Territory first, wandered to Texas."

"Did you cowboy there?"

"I never took to that life."

"Nor I."

"I hunted buffalo instead."

"What was that like?"

"A pretty good living until one morning you wake up and look around and there's no more buffalo. And just last week you saw a regular ocean of red and white carcasses rotting on the plains. I've seen their bodies so thick after being skinned it looked like a bunch of logs from a hurricane. And before that, see, when they were alive, you never saw so many buffalo. They covered the plains from here to the horizon. You'd look out there and see the ground itself moving. I suppose it never occurred to us then that we could use them all up."

"What did you have for a weapon?"

"Well, the Springfields was too much like the army. I tried that Sharps that fired the three eighty grain bullet but it wasn't accurate. They fixed it to a forty-four caliber with less lead but the trouble with that was the cartridge case leaked. It blinded some men. So they drop it down to a forty caliber and put the lead back up to three hundred and eighty with a hundred and twenty grains of powder and this one has a cartridge case that's straight instead of bottlenecked. That's the one I used. It was good. Too good. I shot and shot and never thought about a thing and eventually shot myself out of a job."

Darkness. Silence. Time either passed or found itself becalmed. When Fred spoke again a bright red mouth opened deep inside Billy's sleeping brain. "So you're from Arizona."

"Silver City, Fred. Arizona was a breather."

"I forgot Silver City."

"And Kansas before that."

"Kansas?"

"Wichita. And before that, Indiana. And New York City before Indiana. But I prefer here."

"New York? I've always heard about that place. What's it like there?"

"It's like castrating elephants."

· 8 ·

1878

War

Outside in the dark, Juan Patrón's *acequia* thinned to a silence. The water still flowed but its unyielding sameness had drained it of sound. Like whittling a stick till there's nothing left to whittle — that's how Billy understood it. To be conscious of not consciously hearing a sound that nonetheless is somehow clearly there could drive you crazy, just the same. Best not to think about it. "Did the Greeks get paid?" he asked.

"I haven't researched that."

"First time I ever got paid for sitting in a jail."

"How much did Macky promise us?"

"Three dollars a day."

Fred had been telling him about the Trojans and the Greeks but in the middle of the night it sounded like a dream. The Kid judged it must be the middle of the night from the waves of unconsciousness lapping his mind, not from the lack of light — the jail was pitch-dark both day and night. And Fred's deep voice always sounded dreamy. The jail felt warmer now. Night air didn't penetrate its underground pit, whose uniform temperature resembled a root cellar's. The Trojans and Greeks foughten a big war and no one was paid, instead they whacked up the spoils. The Trojans were under siege in their palace and the Greeks were attacking them. "So which are we?"

"I guess we'll find out," said Fred. "We're the English, they're the Irish."

"McSween's a Scotchman."

"Same thing."

"And you're a redskin."

"My grandmother."

"A war like that your children have to finish. Tell me one thing. Who won? The Trojans or the Greeks?"

"I didn't get that far."

"You never get that far, Fred."

"Alls you ever want to know is how it turned out. That's not what's important."

◆　◆　◆

"You have family in Indian Territory, Fred?"

"Yes."

"Brothers or sisters?"

"Two sisters. What about you?"

"I got an older brother in Texas."

"What's his name?"

"Josie. Are your parents still alive?"

"Yes."

"Both? Your ma?"

"That's what I said."

"What about your pa?"

"Last I heard."

◆　◆　◆

"THAT MAN YOU killed, Kid."

"What about him?"

"Did you watch him die?"

"I told you, I lit out. It took him a while."

"I'd much rather get it over with myself."

"So would I."

"How come you shot him in the gut?"

"It was the only place available. His knees were on my arms. The bastard was bending over me, Fred. I'll tell you one thing."

"What?"

"I ever get shot there, do me in the head."

"That would be my choice, too."

◆ ◆ ◆

"WE ARE CUTTHROATS in this town. We'll do anything for money."

"Well, they're cutthroats, too. They're bloodthirsty animals."

"It won't come to any good."

"No, it won't. If the sun blew up, that would solve all our problems."

Did Fred really say that? Billy grew confused. The mind fog washed back and he thought he was sleeping when a scald of light burst behind his eyes. Not the sun blowing up, just the trapdoor flying open. Sam Perry, one of Brady's deputies, lowered a ladder. "You boys can go."

"Who sprung us?" asked Fred.

"No one. We were drying you out on account of public drunkenness."

Billy climbed up first. "Where's my Winchester?"

"Confiscated by Brady."

"He can't do that."

"Of course he can, he's the sheriff."

Lincoln was overcast but still blinded the Kid when he stepped into the street. It was afternoon already, they'd missed Tunstall's funeral. He learned this when José Chávez y Chávez, riding out of town, told them they'd gotten out of digging a hole. Billy didn't find this funny. You throw in with the law, try to serve a legal warrant, and wind up unable to pay your respects to the man who gave you your horse and handsome saddle and the rifle now in Sheriff Brady's possession — the man who promised you a ranch! They headed for Mc-Sween's, passing José Montano's, Saturnino Baca's. Outside the Torreón, originally built to watch for raiding Indians, four Apaches from the reservation sat behind a pile of deer and antelope hides and bickered with a Mex, who sorted through the skins. A fifth Apache had been pulled aside by soldiers who were asking for his pass. He pretended not to understand. "Pass. *Pass!* To leave the reservation!" The impatient lieutenant shouting at the Apache was Millard Goodwin, who nodded at Fred and Billy. "We'll be there shortly."

Once they were out of earshot, Billy asked Fred: "Be where?"

"Something must be up."

At McSween's, in the kitchen, everyone was present — Dick Brewer, John Middleton, Henry Brown, plus some newcomers, townspeople and local ranchers sympathetic to their cause. While Fred and Billy were in jail last night, these men had attended a meeting at Macky's house then stayed on to join up. "Join what?" asked the Kid. Rolling his big shoulders, swinging his long arms, McSween approached the two liberated prisoners and embraced each one. Martínez, he told them, returned his papers unserved; but honest Dick Brewer, true as steel — tall, handsome, and square — marched back to Justice Wilson, who wrote out a new set of warrants and appointed Dick himself as a special constable empowered to arrest Tunstall's murderers. And these men here were now his deputies. "What about us?" Billy couldn't bleach the impatience from his voice.

"Raise your right hands."

So the law had recrudesced and Billy and Fred were its deputies, too, and even U.S. Deputy Marshal Rob Widenmann appeared at the door between the sitting room and kitchen, cartridge belts slung over his shoulders, pen and paper in hand — he'd been writing more letters to London — and announced that he also had warrants to serve and that Lieutenant Goodwin, having no choice, had agreed to assist him in searching Dolan's store, also Tunstall's — still under occupation — for John Tunstall's killers. Behind Rob, when he entered, pausing at the door, was Tunstall's bulldog, Punch. With rheumy eyes, wheezing, he surveyed the room for food, sniffed Billy's foot, and settled with a grunt, rear legs first, on a filthy rag rug. Rob had often told the story, with fondness and a chuckle, of the time he once overcoddled Harry when the latter felt poorly, and Harry grew impatient and set Punch on Rob for not ceasing his treatment, and the poor dog, confused, barked and slobbered at Rob with Harry holding him back and Rob shouting hysterically, "Call him off, for pity's sake!" and Harry laughing all the while.

◆ ◆ ◆

MARCH 6. FRED AND BILLY saddled up. Acting on a tip that one, maybe two, of the murderers they sought were down on the Pecos near the Peñasco, they rode out of town with Dick Brewer and the others, their number now swelled to eleven. Only Rob Widenmann stayed back in Lincoln, to hold down the fort. Fred was last in line — he ate dust. Past the stubble of cornfields, under spreading box elders and walnuts and cottonwoods that in summer created an overhead canopy blocking the sun — in March, though, they spidered the gray cloudy sky with ominous black scrawls — they rode east on the Lincoln-Roswell road and, from the rear, Fred noticed up ahead what appeared to be a snow squall. Then he saw that in passing the old Valencia ranch one of their number had taken out his skinner and ripped open some featherbeds set out to air across the fence. It was Charlie Bowdre. He spun around on his pony and raised the knife and the whole gang whooped, for this seemed quite the show. Charlie had his tail up, all of them did, he'd caught a whiff of blood, and even if it was only featherbeds, his zeal had impelled him to air out some innards. When they'd all but passed except for

stolid Fred, a woman ran out of the house behind the fence, screaming in Spanish and waving her arms, to retrieve her maimed bedding.

They rode down to the Hondo, following the canyon descending
through the foothills, rode until their horses were in a perfect foam
and they had to stop and breathe them. The yellow-brown hills gave
out at this point to a treeless plain beneath high cirrus clouds running clear to the Pecos, forty miles away. Fred imagined their prey in
the unsubmissive distance seeking out their holes in apprehension
of a scrape. Here come the Regulators, he thought — for that's what
they called themselves, Regulators of the Law — watch out, here we
come! Oh, we are ferocious. Our boss is Dick Brewer, we chose him
ourselves, because he is of irreproachable character; because his
good looks are the fame of the county; because his name to us is a
tube of paint out of which squeeze only the truest colors; and best of
all, because he'll clean your fucking plows. We are not just a duly
authorized posse with a special constable, although we are that, we're
a vigilance committee, we have elected officers and each of us has
taken an iron-clad oath not to tattle on the others or give away our
operations. We call ourselves Regulators, also Iron-Clads, but you
can nominate us your ticket to hell — eleven men united by a pen-
chant to hang lofty trees with assorted body parts.

Regulators, he thought. It sounded important. When you stopped
to think about it, what exciting work this was. To know you might die
in its performance only improved your flagging concentration. It's
exciting to get discountenanced, abused, thrown in jail, shot at, ambushed, hung, dismembered, isn't it? — to ride around all day with a
target on your back, to check all the locks, sleep with your guns.
Probably the world cried out for regulating, Fred wasn't sure. For
one thing, the law ought to take care of that. But the law itself could
use the same medicine. The law was too patient.

Back in Lincoln, Fred knew, Macky Sween had fled. He was living in the mountains. Because the other side, too, had resorted to law and obtained an alias warrant against the lawyer for his failure to post bond on charges of embezzlement. If Mac had not departed, Sheriff Brady would have nabbed him and forced him to stew in Lincoln's underground jail for six or seven weeks until the court's spring term. And once in that jail, Fred was certain, Brady would have called in cutthroat Jesse Evans to do his part. Yet, Brady too had been arrested, by Constable Martínez, for stealing hay from Tunstall's corral to feed the Englishman's horses that Brady had attached, or so McSween claimed. He'd been forced to post bond, much to the Regulators' joy. And with the help of a military escort, Rob Widenmann had ransacked Dolan's store searching for Harry's murderers and when he couldn't find them he marched up the street, Lieutenant Goodwin and his platoon in tow, and entered Tunstall's store and routed the Dolanites with their ladders and clipboards, still attaching the merchandise. He reoccupied the store for the Tunstall-McSweens and launched his own inventory to see how much they'd stolen and made preparations to fortify the place.

So the law was on our side, thought Fred, eating some jerky as they remounted. The law was on both of our sides, he thought again, a notion that impelled him to both scowl and smile while nodding his head. They'd decided at this point to cut southeast across the plains instead of going straight to Roswell then turning south. Their way looked flat from here but all of them knew there were swells and declivities that would fatigue their horses. Nonetheless, they'd save time. It comforted Fred to think they were being rational despite the blood in their eyes, and that the law was on their side. But if the law was on Dolan's side, too, where did that leave the law? The law, Fred supposed, had always been a crafty stallion you had to break before you rode it. The law, it appeared, did not reflect what was right. If it did, one side would be the good citizens, the other the scofflaws, and you'd have moral clarity. Instead, what was right was what the law said, and both sides were right, and the way to break the law was to do whatever you damn well pleased; and the way to obey it was to be guilty.

Late that afternoon they spotted some men at the mouth of the Peñasco and fired their first rounds. The Kid identified Billy Morton and Frank Baker and three more he only spottily knew racing for their horses and splashing through the Peñasco and flying south on the road alongside the Pecos. Two men split off — of no interest to the posse — and the Regulators chased Morton, Baker, and a third, Dick Lloyd, and a hundred shots were fired — Billy knew, he counted, counting calmed him down — before Lloyd's horse collapsed. They sped right past Lloyd, Lloyd was small potatoes, and pursued Billy Morton, the one who'd killed Tunstall, the one who'd leg-pulled the Kid about his new name, the one who'd mouth-lashed him last year at a cow camp for trying to steal his girl. In a thick stand of bulrushes and rivercane, Morton and Baker tried to lose themselves, but the river was behind them, they had nowhere to go. "Save your powder, boys," Dick Brewer said, dismounting and pulling out his sulphur matches. He set the dry tule on fire.

Smoke billowed. Brewer posted watches at either end of this alluvial thicket where the Pecos goosenecked. As they waited, the Kid dismounted and paced, kicked at the dirt, doffed his hat. I'm on the prod, he thought. My high brow and black Irish eyes are disordered by ire, I don't look pretty anymore. I'm a city boy who's become a stump jumper, I wear an ugly sneer! When Morton and Baker finally broke through the brush, rubbing their eyes and coughing and staggering while trying to raise their arms, Billy threw down on them and cocked his Colt's Thunderer, though it was a self-cocker. But Dick Brewer ordered him to ease the hammer back. "Hell," said the Kid, "let's finish them now." No one spoke. Brewer relieved the two men of their weapons. Morton looked cowed; with his undercooked face, he looked like a baby-cheeked blue-eyed little boy who didn't want to piss his pants. Frank Baker, on the other hand, loured at everyone with his beetling brows and enormous nose and mouth and small ears and slanted brow and hairy hands and neck. His very appearance invited them to kill him. Billy felt he could easily grant the request but Brewer spoke up. "I would have preferred that we shot it out, you cowards," Dick told the two. "But we've taken you alive and that's that."

◆ ◆ ◆

ALL THE FOLLOWING DAY, and the day after that, as they trotted up the Pecos with the prisoners in front, Billy boiled with indignation. Justice isn't justice, he thought, if you have only a taste; you've got to eat the whole pie. Bill McCloskey joined them at one of the cow camps they passed. Just two weeks ago, before Tunstall's murder, McCloskey was part of the crew at Tunstall's ranch, but he'd also been friends with Billy Morton, everyone knew that. You had to wonder what he was doing here, the Kid observed to Fred, as they rode north. Which side was McCloskey on?

Fred shrugged. Familiar ring to this question. "He's keeping an eye on us. Throwing in with his friend."

"We could disarm him."

Frank McNab, a Regulator riding on the other side of Fred, turned away and spat a long snake of tobacco juice; it balled in the dust. He was lanky and long-chinned, with a pinched, corky mouth, a high reedy voice, and a sweet or sour face, depending on the provocation. His friends had learned to beware of the sweetness. "Disarm him, hell," he said, looking back. "Just shoot the damned traitor."

When they pulled into Roswell, Billy said to Dick Brewer, "We ought to kill them today. They're just eating our food."

"I'm a constable now. I've got a job to do."

"What jail will you put them in?"

"The only one in Lincoln."

"Then you can be sure the sheriff will release them."

"In that case I'll rearrest them. Maybe next time they'd prefer to shoot it out."

"We could shoot it out now."

Tall in his saddle, straight as a snubbing post, Dick shrugged and looked away.

Morton and Baker must have heard this exchange, as Billy Morton asked permission to write a letter to his cousin. Where's your cousin? asked Brewer. In Virginia. He was educated, Morton, as the Kid knew, his family was actually Richmond blue blood. Brewer said he could write it if they read it over first, so at the P.O. in Roswell Morton asked for pen and paper, and Brewer, the Kid, and Fred read his letter, and Brewer gave him permission to mail it — for all the good it would do him, Billy thought.

Roswell, New Mexico
March 8, 1878

H. H. Marshall
Richmond, Virginia

Dear cousin Henry,

The 6th of March I was arrested by a Constable party accused of the murder of Tunstall. Nearly all the sheriff's party fired at him and it is impossible for any one to say who killed him. When the party which came to arrest me and one man who was with me first saw us about one hundred yards distant we started in another direction when they (eleven in number) fired nearly one hundred shots at us. We ran about five miles when both of our horses fell and we made a stand when they came up they told us if we would give up they would not harm us; after talking awhile we gave up our arms and were made prisoners. There was one man in the party who wanted to kill me after I had surrendered, and was restrained with the greatest difficulty by others of the party. The constable himself said he was sorry we gave up as he had not wished to take us alive. We arrived here last night en route to Lincoln. I have heard that we were not to be taken alive to that place. I am not at all afraid of their killing me, but if they should do so I wish that the matter should be investigated and the parties dealt with according to law. If you do not hear from me in four days after receipt of this I would like you to make inquiries about the affair.

Your cousin Billy

They rode out of Roswell on a cold blue day a little past noon. Morton kept saying it wasn't just him, it was the whole damn crew that had killed Mr. Tunstall. But Billy Bonney knew better: the other Dolanites had scattered Tunstall's friends while Morton-Evans'n-Hill accosted the Englishman.

Frost on the ground. The earth crepitated beneath their mounts' hooves. The fine ash and powder of frozen winter growth along the edge of the road bleached its shoulders white. The road itself was muck-skinned with ice beneath the hard mud. Yet the sun burned their necks.

Ten miles west of Roswell they turned up a trail to Blackwater Draw, the army's shortcut to Fort Stanton. It bypassed Lincoln but you could double-back to town along the Bonito. The Kid wondered why they were taking this route and caught up with Brewer. "If the Dolanites send a rescue party out from Lincoln, they'll miss us," Dick explained.

And if we kill Morton and Baker, no one will hear the gunshots.

Billy kept his trap shut. He felt jumpy, alert. The solution to jitters was anger, he knew, anger always whipped fear. He, as Fred had, thought of the law — and of justice, what is justice? The question had festered since McSween raised it. Justice was when you did unto others what they did unto you. You paid them back in kind. Can the law do that? The law is too big even for its own britches. The law is a coat that fits all sizes so fits no one at all. It has too many buttons. The law had deputized them, issued their warrants, and restrained Dick Brewer, yet it had failed to restrain the other side. Alexander McSween believed in the law but he'd run off from an alias writ. Sometimes the only go was to tear off the law, pop all its buttons. The law had no feelings — it was cold as to justice. When you got your mad up the last thing you wished to have in your hand was a goddamn law book. And Billy was mad, he was so full of mad he felt scared of himself. He was trembling, he noticed, and tried to calm down. At the same time, he thought, surprising himself, he was making distinctions. Distinctions are important. I'm making a distinction between the law and justice. He laughed out loud.

Beside him, Fred glanced at his friend and smiled.

Those men, including Morton, didn't just kill Mr. Tunstall, they shot him off his horse, grabbed his own gun, put two bullets in the dying man's head, and for good measure bashed in his skull. They covered Mr. Tunstall, a respectable man, a man with polish, with his sweaty horse blanket. They stole his saddle. They shot his horse, too, and stuffed the Englishman's California hat beneath its head for a pillow. It wasn't only a murder, it was a taunting execution, it made death into mockery. And, watching Billy Morton, who looked pale this afternoon, who squitched at the sun beneath his John B., the Kid worked himself up into hating the bastard, hating him worse than he ever had before, hating him to a hair because he would kill him.

Cinchweed, sage, yucca, grass, cholla. As they climbed, the brown grass rattled when they passed, the clear air grew warmer. Dick Brewer rode ahead, then came Frank McNab beside Bill McCloskey. Fred and Billy followed with the captives close behind, and the other Regulators brought up the rear. They passed rising hills, the Kid looked around, he'd been here before. Blackwater Draw never did seem to start before it deepened around you; a furrow in the earth, the stray lost cliff, some cottonwoods and junipers springing from folds. The snakes in his head made his thoughts scatter. When he saw the cottonwoods clustered in arroyos he thought of pubic hair that grows in damp creases; of human bodies and their soft folds, of their foggy, vague, futile resistance to force. Skin was a barrier for the eye, nothing else. The softest touch kills. If it wasn't for the atmospheric pressure, Fred once had told him, you would likely explode just from swatting a mosquito.

A *cuesta* lengthened on their right, a high yellow cliff slapped up against a raise, as they ascended a parabolic valley toward Blackwater Holes. Here, a damp gouge defined the draw's shifting axis, now east and now south, and cottonwoods nubbed its ill-defined banks, and growing shadows crossed them. Averting his eyes, Billy registered the sun edging steadily toward the gray-blue Capitans. He saw, looking back at Morton and Baker, sunlight casting their shadows in the dust their horses raised and thought all men are shadows — one of Fred's saws. Here we are in shadowland, even shadows have shadows.

He swiveled back and faced west just as a jackrabbit crossed Fred's path, one ear standing up stiff as a wiping stick, the other flapdoodling nearly to the ground. You could just see the light shining through his raised ear as the rabbit disappeared into the brush. It would shine through your hand. All at once the light collapsed. The sun slipped behind Capitan Mountain and its yellow-orange glow darkened the peak, steeling its outline. It was late afternoon. Rising moisture in the air. Spokes of sunlight behind Capitan's helmet wheeled into the sky, and the mountain turned into air and white fire. The larger peak behind outlined Sunset Peak in front, its volatile shadow containing it perfectly, exactly like a helmet on a darkened head, and the posse stopped, awestruck. With a smile, Frank McNab shot McCloskey in the ear, the red gout of blood spat by his other ear sparkling in the sun, suspended in air, the intact portion of his hair catching fire, McNab saying as he shot, "You are the turn-coat that has got to die before harm can come to these fellows, are you?"

He was talking to a corpse. As McCloskey fell his horse bolted. Morton and Baker spurred their blown mounts, clinging to their necks, and Billy fired wildly, his heart going crazy. At the head of the valley, where a pair of inlets formed Blackwater Draw, the seep from a spring had muddied the ground, and this slowed the fleeing horses. Too late, boys. You should have seen the willows. Billy raced up and, calming himself, fired through Baker's thigh, through his saddle, through his horse, whose eye-whites ballooned as he folded going down. The horse landed on Baker, pinning his legs. Then the Kid fired at Morton who, on his mount, had just spun around, dropping his jaw. The ball shattered his teeth, severed his tongue, and drove into his brain before he could scream. He landed in mud.

Billy dismounted, approached Frank Baker, took off his hat, knocked the dust from his pants. He did feel calmer now but just to be certain he stuffed the hat into the armpit of his gun hand and held out the free hand with its palm down, staring it into level immobility. Without lowering the hand, he walked slowly toward Baker, tongue jutting from his mouth, and pointed his pistol. The hat dropped. Legs pinned by his horse, Baker was propped on one shaky elbow, pale as milk, but he sneered at the Kid. The man whose face supported the Darwinian theory waved his free arm, both defiant and cowed, his meaty paw rubbing a notional canvas as though to erase his puny assassin. The first shot ripped the flesh between his thumb and finger, baring the bones. The thumb hung limp. An artery was shred. Still waving back and forth, his hand became a hose. The second pulped his eye, and blood from the eye filled the hairs of his beard, gluing them together, and ran down his neck. Only when he seemed to grasp that he was dead did he collapse.

The others rode up and fired into the bodies. Their communion of lead. Not much that Dick Brewer could do about it now. His shots were the last two, one for each corpse. The Kid remounted, they rode back to McCloskey, Billy raving all the while about why McCloskey did it, went and got himself shot, he should have known better, he wasn't altogether vile. A sharp hand at monte. Too bad he turned tail. "Fucking Judas," Billy said in a spasm of bitterness. His shoulders and arms were trembling again, enough to beat the band, he couldn't stop them if he wanted.

Then he slowly withdrew — retracted his soul — a process that entailed his eyes hooding over and narrowing to slits, his mind contracting to a hard little stone, his body feeling annoyed at every little fidget from his scared horse. It would not be that awful to be the only person left alive in the universe.

Henry Brown rode off to catch McCloskey's horse, the rest on their nervous mounts looked down at his body. From where McCloskey lay they could peer up the valley to the other two corpses draining into earth, and to Baker's horse kicking, the shadows crawling toward them, Capitan on fire, the rest of the world having gone into hiding inside hills and rocks and crepuscular grass and sparse trees and willows. If you sent your eye out it wouldn't see things, it would see light and water moving through folds of matter. One of McCloskey's eyes was wide open, the other closed, telling fibs.

All at once Billy felt an afflatus. He swelled like a bladder, rose in the air, his edges expanded and touched the horizon, and now he looked down at the others from above. He spotted Fred Waite looking angry and confused, swiveling his head — staring off into the distance. And Dick Brewer impassive, John Middleton grinning. And the others on horses who sensed their impatience and swung around repeatedly, anxious to return to Lincoln like their riders, who would tell their fellow citizens what had transpired here once they got their stories straight.

· 9 ·

1878

War

BILLY AND THE REGULATORS rode on to Francisco Gutiérrez's sheep camp, and Dick Brewer promised him money from Alexander McSween if he'd bury the bodies — bury them fast. But it wasn't fast enough. When the word spread, Sheriff Brady and his deputies rushed to Blackwater Draw and counted eleven bullets in Morton's body, one for each Regulator — the same number in Baker's — and found McCloskey's brains still dripping from the single hole in his head. Gutiérrez and his sons had just begun the graves. In Lincoln, the Kid and the other Regulators spread manure for the populace. The captives were shot while escaping, they said, and Morton himself shot Bill McCloskey before making a run. Later they heard about Brady's response. Morton shot his best friend? the sheriff sneered. Shot him with what? — he was being held a prisoner. With a gun he had hidden about his person, was the story. That would have to be a derringer, Brady concluded, and derringer exit holes at close range are large and ugly. McCloskey's, he said, was small and clean.

It would be laughable, said Brady, this story they've invented, if it did not involve such bloodthirsty deeds.

The Regulators made their way to San Patricio and holed up there in Dow's store. They couldn't stay in Lincoln. The governor himself,

Samuel B. Axtell, had revoked Squire Wilson's appointment as justice of the peace, and Widenmann's as deputy U.S. marshal, thus invalidating their arrest warrants. The Regulators were no longer a duly authorized posse, overnight their stripes had changed, they were a gang of assassins. Now Dolan rode herd on his sheriff, William Brady, to stir his stumps pronto and round up these so-called Regulators and arrest their employer, Alexander McSween. And if they try to escape, you know what to do.

Word reached Dow's store that someone — John Chisum? Alexander McSween? — might not object if Sheriff Brady were killed and might even remember the five hundred dollars he'd squirreled away in an old shoebox, which he just might award to the executionists. The Kid and his chums, bunking at the store in a backroom, sat on empty barrels and lip-chewed this rumor. The killing got easier each time, Billy knew, it was a self-fulfilling prophecy, but this Brady reward, he asked the others; now, whose idea was it? Chisum, the respected rancher and businessman? Alexander McSween, the esteemed attorney? McSween was their overboss. What was really driving him? With a criminal charge of embezzlement against Macky, a civil process of attachment still in effect, and the sheriff and a patrol of soldiers scouring the area, trying to flush him out, Mac had informed them he was pushing the limit. And his wife was back, Brewer pointed out, back from St. Louis. Both of them holed up at Chisum's ranch. She's the whip hand, said Billy. She eggs Macky on, she must be the one. And five hundred dollars! The McSweens don't even have five hundred dollars.

"How do you know?" asked Dick.

"What if Chisum's backing him?"

"Chisum plays his cards close."

Fred Waite asked, "When did that woman come back?"

"Sue McSween arrives when and where she pleases."

"And she's egging him on? She's a Lady Macbeth?"

"Who's that?"

"This haggish woman that washed her hands of murder and it wouldn't come off."

"Is that history, Fred?"

"Maybe Sue's putting up the five hundred dollars."

"Sue McSween?" said Jim French. "Sue puts out, she don't have to put up."

Inertia. No one knew what to do. Then wheels began to turn as though of their own accord. At John Chisum's ranch, McSween climbed into a buckboard with his wife — Chisum and some traveling merchants followed in a second wagon — and drove west to Lincoln for the commencement of the April term of court, to give himself up. If you fought in the courts as opposed to the wilderness, at least like the gods the law could be wheedled. But ten miles from Lincoln the weather grew sleety and Sue insisted that they put up in La Junta. And up the road in San Pat, Billy Bonney roused the others and, minus Dick Brewer, who didn't like the smell of this, they loaded up and snuck out and soft-pedaled it to Lincoln, tying gunny sacks around their horses' feet when they reached the edge of town. The new twelve-foot-high defensive wall Macky had started around his house was still unfinished in back, and the Kid stepped across the footers and knocked. On the last night of March, in solid dark raked by horizontal sleet, he was met by Rob Widenmann at the kitchen door. "Where's Mac?" asked Rob.

"Still at Chisum's," said Billy. He and the others brushed past Rob, swaggered through the kitchen, and landed in the parlor, muddy boots and all, where John Middleton said, "I suppose all you got is skink?" Rob replied, "Hardly," and found the Pike's Magnolia that Sue McSween kept hidden in her desk, for her husband was a teetotaler. Only Billy and Fred didn't drink. The rest of the boys freely blew it in, although in perfect silence; it wouldn't do to betray their presence in Lincoln.

"Brewer did not come?" Widenmann asked.

Fred said, "No."

Billy bucked monte with Fred at a table. Fred was El Montero. Middleton sat before Sue McSween's organ and drummed the cover on the keys pretending to play; he couldn't play regardless. Rob Widenmann drew an imaginary bow across the fiddle wedged beneath his chin, flexing the bow arm like a swan's neck, and Frank McNab and Henry Brown danced — cantered back and forth, swung each other around — but slowly, miming stateliness and pomp. Candle- and lamplight cast their shadows on the wall. Fred showed the gate and the Kid shoved a button across the table toward his expressionless friend. They weren't playing for money; Billy had found Sue McSween's cigar box of buttons on her desk. He spotted a young girl at the far door watching the silent musicians and dancers; it was Pearl, he knew, Reverend Ealy's daughter. The missionary from Pennsylvania and his brood still lived in a wing of McSween's house. Her eyes were wide open. He wondered what she saw. Crusaders for justice or bloodthirsty savages? Bloodthirsty savages make a lot of noise, so Pearl must be watching justice take a breather. Jim French leaned his head against the wall, closed his eyes, and softly hummed — the only sound in the room. When he opened his eyes, Billy saw he was smiling and beckoning to Pearl but she shook her head and vanished. Around two A.M., the Kid asked Widenmann, "Have you got any spoons?"

"How many?"

"Seven."

Widenmann held out a fan of spoons as the gang filed out the back door with their rifles. Each chose a spoon — his ticket to hell. "Harry's grinding wheel is still in the store," said Rob. "Beside the axes." They crept through looming cottonwoods to Tunstall's shuttered store and saw overhead that the clouds had blown out. The cold dry stars sliding above them just skimmed the bare branches. Rob unlocked the store, relocked it behind them, lit an oil lamp. Billy went first; he sharpened his spoon, Fred cranking the wheel. When Widenmann cracked the back door open, Tunstall's dog,

Punch, in the corral barked and howled to beat all, and Rob ran out there and pretty soon the dog stopped. Outside, Billy saw he'd tethered the animal in the far corner before his food dish, then muzzled him; so much for the food. Surrounded by a six-foot-high adobe wall, the corral was attached to the back of the store, extending beyond it to the east. This was where Tunstall had kept his prize mounts, where Brady and the Dolanites had first set up camp to attach the Englishman's merchandise and horses. East of the store, the high thick wall for about twenty feet faced Lincoln's single road, and here by starlight the Kid stretched himself out on the ground and set to work. Adobe, he knew, was thick and heavy stuff but somewhat yielding to patience. Using his spoon, he gouged a porthole in the wall, and the others as they exited the store with their sharpened spoons spread out along the wall and followed suit, a hole for each man. The only sound in the night was the scritch of digging spoons in the dried mud, straw, and clay, plus their whispered curses. Your hole, Billy said, must be large enough to sight an accurate bead but not so large as to be seen from the road.

As they finished, one by one, the men dropped their spoons and leaned back against the wall, rifles in their arms, to sleep off the Pike's Magnolia.

Dawn. Faint light in the sky but a shadow on earth, as though the sky itself had cast it; then a fading gray felt; then whiskey-colored air; then the cold-pressing sky weakening to blue. "Rattle your hocks," William Bonney said, and six rough-looking customers clawed sand from their eyes, unglued their tongues, rubbed their leaden brows. Some were still drunk, which helped them endure the taste of rotten spit. The Kid, however, was sober as a judge and tense and disgusted by his rank comrades. Someone had to do it. Someone had to keep an edge and narrow his bead and maintain cold ideas as to leveling the score.

Lincoln woke up. Lying at his porthole, Billy watched the town stir, smelled the charcoal, heard roosters. A wagon chirped and rattled up the road, hissing through puddles left from last evening's sleet. Odors hung in the air. Sweet piñon smoke, smell of coffee. Sheep and goats bleated. From the west end of town, a commotion of legs and barking dogs and good mornings moved in their direction but the store blocked his view. Widenmann, at the far wall of the corral, kept watch standing on a barrel. "They're coming," he announced.

Billy levered his rifle. Five echoes followed. To those behind the wall it was a bone-crushing sound but on the street no one turned, not Billy Matthews nor George Peppin, carbines cradled in their arms. "Hold your water," said the Kid. Then came George Hindman and Sheriff Brady twenty feet behind, Brady's red face beaming like a lantern as he marched through his town. Reaching to his chin, entirely embracing the bottom half of his face, his mustache resembled a well-fed rodent. A familiar Winchester lay across his arms, and Billy flushed — it was his, the one the sheriff had sequestered when he threw him in jail. He dug his boot-toes in the dirt. Brady's little procession, he knew, was headed for the courthouse to post a notice for the April term of court, and the first-water fools weaved around puddles trying not to muddy their freshly shined boots. A waste of polish if you're dead. The sun found a notch in the hills to the south and raised the soggy road just as Brady's coat jumped like a sack of frogs, his arm flipping funny, and the Kid realized they'd already fired. And who gave the order? Apparently no intentionality was involved. All of them had fired and from their portholes it was easy: Brady and his men were half-pint figurines, gewgaws on a shelf, and they shattered into bits. They fired again, and this time the noise and smoke slammed against the wall, obscuring Billy's porthole. People were shouting. Brady, he saw through drifting dust, sat in the road. Someone had rushed out and lifted George Hindman and held a cup to his mouth. "Oh, Lord," Brady groaned, trying to rise, then all fired a third time and Hindman was ripped from his ministrant's arms while closer to their wall Brady fell back. Close or far, it didn't matter.

Hindman lay still. Later, Billy learned that a stray bullet had crossed the road, sped over a field, found Squire Wilson hoeing his onion patch, and passed through his buttocks.

Brady half sat, half lay there kicking. Dark bloody flowers aghast in earth around him. On an impulse, the Kid hurdled the wall and ran into the road to recover his rifle, the Winchester Mr. Tunstall had made him a gift of. And as he ran out and as Jim French followed, as they beelined for the street, William Brady, who'd ridden in from his ranch that morning; who was born in County Cavan the eldest of eight and took communion habitually from the age of seven and crossed the ocean from Ireland, joined the Union army, served in Texas as a sergeant for a five-year hitch, then reenlisted for another five years, only to be discharged when the Civil War started; who joined the Second New Mexico Volunteer Infantry as first lieutenant, rising to command of Fort Stanton by war's end; who was mustered out as a captain with a brevet of major; who married Maria Bonifacio Chaves Montoya and fathered nine children, the ninth still in her belly on this April morning; who served as sheriff, U.S. commissioner, and Lincoln's first elected representative in the territorial legislature; who was forty-eight years old; died.

A shot grazed Billy's leg and passed through French's thigh and the two raced back to Tunstall's corral, Billy with his Winchester, French lunge-trotting behind. The Regulators mounted and rode out of town but French fell off his horse; he couldn't grip it with his knees. The Kid helped him hide inside an opening in the floor of a room in the back of J. H. Tunstall & Co., General Merchandise, where he lay face-up in the two-foot-high space, a gun in each hand, beneath the reinserted boards and the repositioned bed, then snuck out that night under cover of darkness.

Later, Billy learned that Macky Sween arrived when the corpses still lay there draining in the street, blood unspooling into mud. The new sheriff, George Peppin, wished to arrest *both* Mr. and Mrs. Mc-

Sween but could not. Mac refused to recognize Peppin's authority — the governor hadn't confirmed his appointment — and refused
to be taken to Lincoln's deathtrap jail, surrendering instead to the
buffalo soldiers, who brought him and Sue back to Fort Stanton
where they'd be safe in its jail until the spring court convened. Rob
Widenmann joined them there; he'd been arrested, too.

◆ ◆ ◆

AFTER THAT, it was a cavalcade of killings. With Macky in custody
and the town torn apart — the meek and the crafty getting out while
they could — Billy and the others headed south to the Apache reservation hunting for those remaining Dolanites who'd taken to the
hills. They'd swelled to fifteen and Dick Brewer once again was head
of the crew but Brewer hadn't been at the Brady kill-feast, he'd fallen
a notch in the others' esteem; and Billy Bonney had risen.

They put up at Blazer's Mill in a pocket of the foothills to the Sacramento Mountains. The two-story adobe was no longer a mill, more
like a village in a box: store, post office, Indian agency, boarding
house, eatery, and meeting place. Here, they ordered a meal. With
their horses corralled behind high plank walls and the men inside
eating, anyone entering the valley just then might have sworn the
place was empty.

And here comes Buckshot Roberts riding a mule, his legs nearly
scraping the ground on either side. He's bullish and short and carries in his right shoulder a painful load of buckshot that impedes his
range of motion; he can't raise that arm. Still, he's learned to fire
from the hip, or prone behind a rifle, and he's a crack shot, having
once been a hunter for Buffalo Bill. He was Frank Baker's friend before Billy shot Baker, and a member of the posse that had pursued
and killed Tunstall. But he'd just sold his farm outside of Lincoln
and planned to fog out of the county for good now that it had become a battlefield, after first checking at the Blazer's Mill P.O. to see

if his money from the sale had arrived. As he snubbed his mule and drew his Winchester out of its scabbard, the mill's door opened and Roberts found himself before Frank Coe, a Regulator and friend of the Kid. "We have a warrant for your arrest," said Coe.

"The hell you have."

"I'm glad you showed up. We don't have to hunt you down. You best come inside and see Brewer and surrender."

"Me? Surrender?" Roberts laughed, winced.

"What choice do you have? We're fifteen to one."

"We'll see about that."

"Ain't there been enough bloodshed? Do you want to get yourself killed? Come inside and surrender."

"I'll be killed if I surrender."

"What makes you think that?"

"I know damn well who's inside there. I know what they done."

"If you give me your gun, I'll stand by you. I'll make sure you're not hurt."

"Don't make me laugh. Laughing hurts my shoulder."

"This is no joke. Surrender while you can."

"Not by a long jump. You must think I'm pathetic or a gullible fool. Well, Frank Coe, it's been a grand talk. Now I'll be on my way."

Billy spilled out the door sparring with his friends like a boy at a *baile*. Then they saw Roberts. "You son of a bitch, throw up your hands!" Charlie Bowdre yelled.

"Not much, Maryann." Roberts swung his Winchester up from his hip and fired at Bowdre, who shot simultaneously ten feet away. Roberts's ball traveled eight hundred miles an hour straight for Charlie's belt buckle and merely knocked him on his ass. Bowdre's shot, however, skewered Roberts's viscera, the Kid spotted it flying out his backside.

The shot to Bowdre's buckle ricocheted and shattered George Coe's right hand, removed his trigger finger.

Roberts shot again and hit John Middleton square in the chest, shredding his lung, just missing his heart.

He shot a third time and struck Doc Scurlock's pistol, still in its holster, for all of this happened in supercooled time. The ball burrowed down Scurlock's leg.

He shot once more and skinned Billy's arm and now the smoke was everywhere, it had absorbed the space between them. Gut-shot, Roberts backed across the road and stumbled into Dr. Blazer's private house. His rifle was empty. He found, on the far wall of Blazer's office, a single-shot Springfield, officer's model, .45-70 caliber, and a box of ammunition on the desk beneath it. In a corner of the room stood a three-quarter bed. He dragged the mattress off the bed, belly-humped it to the door, all the time leaking blood and fecal matter, and settled in for the long haul. But the effort cost him; his eyeballs swung back, a hurlwind in his head seemed to spiral down his spine. The mattress lay against the bottom half of the door. Sprawling behind it, Roberts rallied himself. His large and windy belly had spare capacity, that's what he figured, it would keep him alive, dispensing fat into his system long enough to have a game, and what else could matter now?

Across the road, outside the mill, Dick Brewer ordered Dr. Blazer's foreman to go pull that wounded bastard out of the house but he refused. Shots came from the doorway; everyone took cover. Brewer ordered Blazer to do it himself and Blazer said, You. "I'll burn the fucking place down," the sterling Brewer declared, but he didn't; he forted up instead in a pile of firewood beside the two-story mill building and he, too, hackles raised, trying nonetheless to keep sane and steady, and clinging all the while to the logic of amends that had brought them to this impasse, settled in for a siege.

Middleton was down. He coughed up blood. George Coe had wrapped his shattered hand in a shirt, Charlie Bowdre had had the wind knocked out of him and was crawling toward the mill gasping all the way. At a window in the mill, Billy passed his rifle to Fred to reload and while waiting fired with his pistol six shots so rapid, whomping Roberts's mattress, that his gun burned his hand and he had to throw it down. "He's licking us," he said.

"Yes, he is," said Fred.

"He's just a sneaks-by, no?"

"Hardly. I suppose he's hopping mad."

In his pile of logs, Brewer fired his carbine and saw the doorjamb splinter next to Roberts's face. Roberts meanwhile spotted Brewer's puff of smoke and drew a careful bead and squeezed just as Dick raised his handsome head. As it entered his blue eye, the ball snagged a patch of Dick's fine brown eyebrow and, lifting him bodily, drove him back across the firewood. The part of his brain still thinking "lucky shot" went flying behind him, the rest stayed in his skull. And, tall as a maypole, true as steel, the soul of honor, plucky and reliable, of irreproachable character, the man whose good looks were the fame of the county no longer had a head, its top was blown off, including the bulk of his black curly hair that plenty of painted fingernails had plowed.

That did it. Roberts resumed dying — it took another day — and Billy and the Regulators, pragmatists all, left him in his hidey-hole, left Dick Brewer's body where it was, too, sprawled across a pile of wood — unburied — and John Middleton in agony writhing on the ground. The bullet in his lung took eight more years to kill him. They just up and rode off while they still could, having had it up to here. No one said a word. A single, collective, head-foremost sensation somewhat akin to disgrace kept butting them along, and their bluster was depleted but only for the interregnum, which didn't last long. They already had a new leader — William Bonney — who understood that disgrace was like everything else, something you waited out. Brewer'd cashed in and Billy had survived and the killing was inescapable now.

· 10 ·

May 1881

Escape

WHICH WAY, WHICH WAY? It all looks the same. Fireweed along the Roswell trail, the sun in his face. Torrey yucca, new evening primrose, cholla everywhere, the resurrection of the grama grass. The earth to his right breaks in successive waves against the north-facing slopes of the Capitans. Green-gray clearings in trees near the summits. He'll be past the mountains soon. Then where to go. North to Fort Sumner. South to Mexico.

Go to Mexico, Henry, you'll have your fill of chicas there.

Or they'll have their fill of me, he wants to answer, but it never will do to potty-mouth his mother. I'm Billy now, Ma.

To me, you'll always be Henry.

Fans of erosion up there in the mountains. Pale yellow dust. It's as dry as sin here. He wishes Yginio had come with him a ways just for the companionship. Alone, his mind flounders. To keep going east is to avoid studying the matter, is to dilly-dally shamelessly. He can't listen to his mother. Her disgust unmans him. She scraps them right back, Ma always did, she's a proudy, that one. I say one thing, she says the other, then I drop down a hole. I lick the dust, cowed. It happens every time. *Sleep in your own piss and shit, Henry Antrim, for all I give a damn.* His table manners at home were never as good as they were out in company, once she took to bed. She lay on her deathbed for three long months in the house in Silver City, turning more and more gray, spitting up gouts of blood, while thirteen-year-old Henry found a hundred occasions, a constant press of business, distractions galore, which happened to prevent him from going home and opening the gate and knocking on that awful door and softly entering that terrible room, as was his duty, and sitting there with her. *Look at you, you're a mess. How often do you change your underwear, Henry?*

Underwear?

Blankets of bluebottle flies ripple from the stinking hides when Henry passes the butcher's. A man sorting through the stacks is pulling some out to freight to his tanning pits and needs the boy's help. Two bits. The tanning pits are south of town in what they call Chihuahua, Silver City's Mex hill — how can Henry go home? The school ceiling collapses in the heavy rains and the older children have to help with repairs. Henry must rehearse for the minstrel show, in which he'll dress as a girl and dance in the chorus of Buffalo Gals, to raise money for the school, which regrettably chops his time at home short. Henry and Tony Conner smell joss sticks on Hudson Street passing a building that Henry calls a boarding house. Tony demurs. That ain't no boarding house. It's what my mother called it, says Henry, indignant, she had a friend there she much liked to visit. Some friend, says Tony. Your mother's friend was the opium pipe.

They must stone a Chinaman and of course that eats up time. He wishes he could steal the costume jewelry from Derbyshire's window and bring it home to his mother, and he lingers there staring. He lingers and lingers, Silver City invites it. He must race the street Arabs. He must visit his stepfather at the mine where he works a few miles above Silver. Antrim stands in a smashscape outside the shaft house holding his wheelbarrow filled with gray gangue as his stepson approaches. How is she? he asks. Tired most always, Henry informs him, when will you come home? She's as thin as a straw, she coughs all the time.

I wouldn't like to see that, Bill Antrim says. He doesn't set down the wheelbarrow.

Henry stares at the man who, a year or so ago, married his mother and loaned him his surname. He knows what Antrim thinks: some things have to be just because they have to be; there's nothing *I* can do about it. He remembers firing a shotgun in the hills near this mine under Antrim's supervision, he and his brother, Josie, when they moved to Silver City. They were shooting at pumpkins placed on a stump in a pinscape of stumps, for all the spruces and firs around Silver City had been cut down for timbering the mines. A slight boy, only twelve, when Henry's turn came he thought for a moment that the burro he and Josie had ridden to this place had kicked him in the chest. He'd fallen — been walloped — on his skinny ass upon pulling the trigger, and lay there as though just having woken up from a Rip Van Winkle sleep. It wasn't only the shock of being knocked over; it was the deafening sound inches from his ear that left a ringing blank and cracked the world in two. Did I die? he asked, and Antrim and Josie laughed, looking down.

Consider that a rehearsal, said Bill Antrim. Everyone dies. Everyone's bullet has been assigned. You might as well get up. This ain't your time yet.

When is my time?

Nobody knows. It was writ down somewheres a long time ago. It's your destiny, said Antrim. You can't do much about it.

Poor shaken Henry climbed to his feet and brushed off his pants. The shotgun lay there on the ground.

Both of you boys ought to know right now the way the world runs. Some things happen because they have to happen. You can't change them or stop them. No use of crying about what never was or could of been. Never say *if only* or *would of* or *could of*. There's no going back. Your votes were cast a long time ago and they weren't cast by you.

Henry asked, Who were they cast by?

By the armies that foughten the war when you were born. Oh yes, there was a war. A war in the heavens.

Who won?

Henry's stepfather laughed. I suppose you'll find out when you die, you little shit.

You'd think that Antrim was a hard man for saying such things, the Kid thought years later — for telling young Henry his bullet was fired the moment he was born and would follow him all his life, taking every turn he took. But he wasn't, he was soft, as soft as cream pie. He was helpless — that was Antrim's dirty secret. His nose and chin appeared to pinch together, buffered by his mustache, and his voice went so low his stepson could barely hear it. The same thing happens when Henry finds him at the mine and tells him about Catherine and asks when he's coming home. After a pause and gentle frown accompanied by a downward cast of eyes, in a voice less voice than a rustle of leaves and a scraping of twigs, William Antrim, wheelbarrow still hanging from his arms, says of his wife lying on her deathbed, I wouldn't like to see that. That's not the Catherine I remember.

Mother has friends who look in, Henry knows, and Josie still lives there, she doesn't need Bill Antrim. Or himself, for that matter. He takes to sleeping in the warm ashes outside the ovens at the brickyards — to stealing pig's feet at the Blue Goose and boiled eggs at the Orleans Club, and to doing chores for Mary Richards, the teacher, who can write equally well with either hand and whose cheeks are not cadaverous. It is Mary who insists that he sit with his mother. Mary who threatens to take him by the hand all the way to the cabin at the end of the bridge across the big ditch, which would kill him with shame. I'll go myself, he says. Bring me a lock of her hair, says Miss Richards. Mary says she remembers just a year ago Catherine singing and dancing the Highland fling. She baked bread, she cooked for the children at school, she took in laundry, she laughed like a schoolgirl. Goodness, her voice would charm hardened criminals! Well, he'd figured on moving back anyway, is why he pulls the latchstring on the cabin, pads into the room, stumbles on a boot, eye-strings on the strain. Windows all shawled, unlit candle by the bed. *Henry*, she whispers. *Is that you, Henry?*

Where's Josie? he asks.

He moved in at the butcher's.

How come?

He couldn't stomach the smell.

He feeds her the chicken broth she instructs him on making. He helps her to the jakes. He holds one of her hands in both of his and squeezes it repeatedly and, in pain from the consumption, she squeezes back. Then one day she yanks out her hand, points at the ceiling, and sputtering the sharp tool that once had been her voice, exclaims, *He's smiling!* She looks frightened, excited, amazed, a little puzzled, and sinks back on her pillow. Then shoots up and desperately blares, *She's* smiling! *She's* smiling!

Henry peers up at the cracked beams and water-stained boards. Who, Ma?

Her lungs fill with fluid. A young priest arrives, summoned by their neighbor Mrs. Conner, and mumbles some prayers, and Catherine's breathing grows more rattled and hoarse. She hyperventilates, her keyhole-shaped mouth voraciously open, can't get enough air. Then she falls into a sleep and will not be woken up. Henry holds her limp hand. She breathes slow and even, fizzing her lips upon the exhale like an infant making bubbles. This lasts all day until late afternoon when, as though stung, she suddenly winces. Henry thinks the pain has returned and squeezes her hand; no response. He's seen that wince a thousand times before, when she pricked her finger sewing or touched her wrist to a stove. Usually she'd say, *Cripes* or *Oh shoot.* Her hand begins to cool.

Outside, he spots two dogs going at it and ferociously, blindly, pelts them with stones.

And this is the way he sees her even now in a sanctum of his mind:

behind a splintered door in darkness, pinched dirt flindering down from the ceiling. Clothes piled on the bed. Her ashen face. Always a membrane of moisture on her skin, even now, in death. Hair matted and wet. Head slumped forward, eyes softly closed, though the white of one eye bulges like an egg forcing open the parted lids just a sliver. She summons him there, to her side, once again. Sometimes he locks her up in that room in his mind or finds himself playing jackstraws with Josie when she calls them out the window, not in Silver City now, now it's the tenement in New York, and he and his brother squatting in the dirt outside the school sinks. *Don't look me in*, she says. *Remember I said don't let anyone cheat you and if you do, settle it yourself?*

I don't hold with any other way.

The dead had left her alone, she always said. It wasn't the living who'd abandoned poor Catherine, it was the dead, and she vowed not to do the same. In her opinion, the dead ought to stick around. Stay with you. Be dead. But *be* there, alongside. *When I stepped off the ship I had no idea who I was or where I'd come from. I wasn't even sure what the buttons of my shoes were supposed to do. When I first saw that place, the ant hill in the sky, I promised myself never to die there. It was no kind of place for any man or woman and one thing I noticed they didn't say potato, no, they said podado. I remember holding you in the palm of my hand, no larger than a squash, little Henry McCarty.*

Henry Antrim.

Antrim came later. If you suffered from something, from a toothache or the flux, why, I would come down with the same blessed thing just by feeling bad about it, by imagining how you felt in my mind, so best keep away. It works both ways. What a small nut we lived in on Cherry Street, Henry. What a hot place in summer and the North Pole in winter.

He still holds her hand. Still feels it growing colder. Ma, can I have a lock of your hair?

To remember me by? It's just a mess of dry grass.

He has his own penknife. He reaches out and saws, pulling on a tress, appalled as the skin lifts from her smooth scalp and stretches to a point, and frightened by the eye-white bulging through its lids, a big dry eye as round as a cow's, though just a paring of it shows. How did he get here, what should he do, who crammed so much grief and confoundment in his heart? *He's after going out west,* he remembers she told him and Josie one day coming home from the market.

Who, Ma?

Mr. Antrim.

That had to be before they moved to Wichita. By the time she married Antrim in the church in Santa Fe, Henry could sign his name with either hand, the first thing his teacher Mary Richards noticed when they arrived in Silver City. He and his brother signed the marriage book as witnesses: Henry McCarty, Josie McCarty. But who the dickens was McCarty?

Never you mind. Old carrion, so.

Billy looks around. He's done it again. He's decided what to do without deciding what to do. He's rounded the Capitans toward Agua Azul, heading south, not north. *Good for you, boy.* And he continues. Why not? Neither way makes more sense than the other. Besides, goers-backward never come out ahead. And anyway he's tired. The insupportable vexation of always being on the move only gets balmed by not thinking about it. There's a hard glassy edge to everything he sees, a brittle sense of melancholic dislocation, though he knows this land well. The blur to the east could be sandstorms or haze, hard to tell which. Between here and there: sharp outline of hill, south-facing slopes beginning to green, two or three wind-battered trees in a hollow alone with their buds. A pungency in the air. Crushed cinchweed on this little-used trail. So he's going to Mexico. He concludes it must be that. Even though it feels like a version of himself tied to an ankle and stuffed with sawdust that has made this decision. There's no forward spill. It impedes his sense of urgency. How mortifyingly slow everything happens, how sluggishly his carcass gets dragged by events. Just one damn thing after another, and who gives a shit?

A bright cube of rolling thread tumbles in air, catches the light, elongates, contracts, like some caught thing underwater. Then another. Another. The air's crazy with them, slowly trembling and spinning. Now and then Billy glimpses inside the gauzy cages a squirt of black spider. Spiders swim past piloting their aircraft and there's not a breath of wind. Their tumbling outlines and boxes of light shift in the air in diminishing stairways from here to the horizon.

He spots on the ground, in the lengthening shadow of his horse, four red blossoms arranged in a wheel just opening as the shadow falls across them, or maybe one blossom, four petals. Each is almond-shaped. Then, bending from the horse, he sees it is not a flower at all. It's four bird-chicks opening their mouths, thinking the shadow is their ma's, come to feed them. Here, the land gently troughs and cottonwoods appear and half a dozen cattle erratically maunder through a basin below. One walks into a tree trunk, veers, makes a circle, walks into another. Another lows as the Kid approaches, and swings his head around, and Billy's gullet clenches. The steer's eyes are sewn shut; pus leaks through the stitches. He's heard about this but hasn't seen it till now. It makes wandering cattle stay closer to home.

A faint wagon road runs through this valley, and more trees appear, Gambel oaks and willows, grass and hard mud cracked into octagons. A fence. A stone hut, long ago abandoned. The valley widens, loses definition, a *bosque* rises out of the dancing heat lines. An adobe, corrals, broken gates, a fallow garden. *Carretas*, forked plows abandoned on their sides. The house a burnt shell. Adobe walls broken, timbers caved in, mud roof cracked apart and sitting on the floor, cold smell of scorched wood. Another casualty of the Lincoln County War. Sprawled in the yard beside the *horno* in back is the corpse of a man, his features burned off. His splayed arms and legs are charred stumps: a black star. The headless skeleton of a boy reclines against a tree, strips of clothing and flesh still hanging from his bones. His head has rolled off and is arranged in the dirt with a cigar in its mouth.

An hour or so later, Billy's horse bogs down, his hooves suck mud. Then he notices the willows and recognizes where he is and it comes with a shock: Blackwater Holes. This is where he shot Morton and Baker, where McCloskey got killed, where it all became unstoppable. Coming on it now from the opposite direction, his mind must adjust its panels and mirrors. Yellow cliffs of that *cuesta* ahead where the draw swings south. Bare cottonwoods below. New grass, willows blowing over into yellow, tule shooting up.

Eyes moving everywhere, nowhere, stuck. His horse stops. There's something wrong with my mind. Who was it called me malignant and cruel, a minion of the devil? He leaves the trail, skirts La Junta, decides to miss the canyon where Mr. Tunstall was murdered and pulls for a shortcut to the Ham Mills Trail. This unexpected tour of old abominations is taking its toll. Where Tunstall was murdered in cold blood. *Is there any other way except cold, young man?*

Down and bloody, Ma. Hot. Drunk on killing.

Suddenly he remembers he doesn't have a weapon. The whole day must be revised. Caution flows back like an acid to burn the complacency off his journey from Las Tablas. He feels a goneness on his hip. He stops, looks behind, listens for a while. Same old vigilance. Yet now he feels naked.

Sun to the southwest long in the sky so hot on his face it burns like ice. The cattle in the new grass in Pajarito Flats are undoubtedly the same as three years ago but no longer belong to Dick Brewer, of course. Nothing belongs to Dick Brewer anymore; and he belongs to nothing, he's just a troubled thought. The long day gives the Kid a second helping of time and this horse, at least, humps it. By sundown he's crossing the trickling Feliz below Mr. Tunstall's ranch; it now belongs to James Dolan. It's still faintly light when he ties to the snubbing pole at John Meadows's log cabin on the Peñasco. He can't hallo the house. Must be careful. Tries peeking in a window but it's so filthy all he sees is scrabbled murk and yellow light inside obscured by many gouges. He approaches the door, knocks meekly, backs off, then steps behind a cottonwood. Behind the door, Meadows closes his twelve-gauge with a *shlang*, which Billy hears clearly. Exactly the point. "*Who?*" he growls.

"The Kid," says the Kid.

Meadows lifts the bar and squints outside.

◆ ◆ ◆

"FUCK. Missed again."

"Try the Le Mat."

"Christ, John, that cocksucker weighs three or four pounds."

"I'll take out the shot."

"It still weighs a shitload. It's not a practical weapon."

"At least you could try it."

Billy hands Meadows the odd-looking Trantor. Its butt is too narrow, it doesn't feel right. Why invent a chamber to hold five shots when it could just as easily hold six? Suppose you failed with the first five, what then? In fact, he has. At fifty feet, he's missed the empty whiskey bottle five times, the errant shots displaying no pattern.

Meadows puts the Trantor in his gunny sack and gives Billy the Le Mat. Always the clown, even vexed as he is, the Kid staggers forward, rescuing his right hand with the left, acting like the weapon's as heavy as an anvil. "Draw, you sucker." His arm lifts out of an imaginary holster with painful slowness, as though underwater. They're in a gravel hollow behind Meadows's cabin; the river once looped around a ridge here but sometime in the previous millennium it cut itself a shorter neck and isolated this gully. Presumably, the sound of the gunshots will rise instead of spreading horizontally and alerting the countryside. He fires and the shot is so wide of the mark he can't even detect the eruption of dust. It could have flown straight up, too.

Five more miscarry. It's not him, it's the gun. "You could reload the buckshot," says Meadows.

"It never seemed right to me. Pistols firing shot."

"Lawmen like it. You share out the shot with the underneath barrel if you're facing a crowd, then pick off the ones that are left with the upper."

"Well, you'd have to keep a hold of it every blessed minute. You'd be dead before you raised. Let me try that Smith and Wesson."

He tries the Smith and Wesson, Meadows standing beside him. John Meadows is slight, with big ears, a large mustache, and high, hairy eyebrows. How he's managed to keep himself out of the Lincoln County War is by mindful circumspection and hardly leaving his ranch. He's a rancher, sure, but a small one with no employees; he does everything himself. I've always wanted to ranch, Billy told him last night, it just never worked out. It's a good life, said John. Pick of horses to ride. Deer in the mountains, antelope on the prairie, ducks in the river, cattle on the range. Choice of weapons to fire — I've got weapons to spare. That was Billy's opening. I could use a pistol, John, but I can't pay you for it. That's all right, Kid. You can take it on tick.

Billy fires six rapid shots in succession; the bottle doesn't even tremble. And when he breaks it to reload the weapon seems to come apart, pieces flying in the air, and he drops the thing. It was just the shell-extractor, he belatedly recalls. Some smartass named King decided it would save you precious seconds to not have to dump expended loads via gravity.

Meadows picks up the gun. It isn't so much the gift of a weapon as the waste of cartridges that's beginning to grate him. "Your best bet's the Colt's Navy."

"Let me try it again."

He reaches in the gunny sack and hands out the pistol by its long barrel. The length of the barrel on a Colt's Navy has always bothered

Billy. Being used to a Thunderer, he knows that in drawing this cannon of a weapon he'll catch it on the holster. But drawing's overrated, he also knows that. Accuracy beats a quick draw hands down.

He fires and misses.

This model's a conversion, firing .38-caliber metal cartridges, of which Meadows has a stock in his gunny sack that Billy seems bent on depleting. He fires again and misses. Rounds *is* expensive. Fires and misses. "Shit!" This weapon is beautifully balanced, the Kid knows. The butt feels lovely; obliging to the hand, graceful as a swan, smooth but not slippy. Then why can't I hit the bottle. He brings the weapon to his face, holds it with both hands, extends his arms slowly, sighting down the barrel, then lowers it. "Christ. I feel like a little boy." He raises it again, stiff-armed, and aims, and the bottle explodes when he fires.

"There you go."

"Light trigger."

"Reliable weapon."

"I guess I'll take this."

"You'll want to carry it in your waistband."

"I know."

"Keep one chamber empty."

"You mean the quick trigger? I'm not worried on that."

"You could lose your manhood."

"I think I lost it already."

"You're just tired."

"More tired than you know, John."

Later, they climb a grassy knoll and talk, the river spluttering below them. Some of Meadows's stock on the other bank low now and then. Sing to me, cowboys. "I bought the right dirt. I learned *that* when a boy. Buy sweet and buy low, my father taught me."

"I used to have my eye on some land upriver. Me and Fred Waite."

"I never saw land go back one cent in value all my life. I worked for years till I got a little money and slapped it into land quicker than lightning. Where is the war that can carry off land? Where's the thief who can steal it? No sir, land is land, and when you have that your money is safe."

"They stole Tunstall's land."

"I bought land and kept on buying. Now I have all I need."

"How much is all you need?"

"It just lacks a thousand acres."

"That's not an awful lot. Don't you have trouble with your neighbor's cattle?"

"It's plenty for me."

Sitting there beside Meadows, the Kid begins to feel like he's been left behind. You could spend all your life on a thousand acres and never know want. Never change your clothes. Eat brisket, drink buttermilk, sleep on a featherbed. Meadows does smell a little riper than most but where's the harm in that? He smells of wood smoke and layers of sweat, new on top of old, old soaked into wool shirts and leather vests and britches, new — Billy pictures it — a kind of softly crawling crust on his skin and in his hair. Well, better a close smell on your own land than no smell at all. Better to die in the same place you live instead of roaming the world becoming more and more a fanciful creature. Given time — given rootlessness — men pick up pieces of themselves from what's around them, from whatever's at hand. They become made up.

"Where's your next stop?" asks Meadows.

"Maybe John Chisum's."

"I thought you were going to Mexico, Kid."

"I don't know about that. I'm changing my mind."

"You'll have sheriffs and deputies up about your ears."

"What would I do in Mexico without any money? I'll have to get a little somewhere. Go back and see my friends."

"Where?"

"Fort Sumner."

"Sure as you go there, Garrett will get you."

"I don't believe he will. I can stay there awhile and get money enough and then go to Mexico."

"You'll get caught or be killed. He'll just kill you this time. You ought to go south while the going is good."

"You sound like Yginio. Go to Mexico, go to Mexico. I've given up that notion."

"You've departed from your faculties."

"Don't worry about it."

"I'm not the worrying type."

In the silence that follows, Billy pictures the bed behind the door in his mind. He removes his boots, pads backwards slowly, makes it to the porch, then lights out without a word. She must have died again, mothers always die. Then they stay with you. The next morning, once more not having slept at all — not having eaten much either, his stomach a permanent hollow mass thick as to lining, thin as to contents — he tucks his Colt's Navy into his shrinking waistband and shakes Meadows's hand and rides east toward the Pecos.

11

1878

War

JULY 18. In Alexander McSween's besieged adobe house, Billy pulled on his blue anchor shirt, clawed his thicket of hair, and rose from the parlor floor. Yginio Salazar and Tom O'Folliard lay on their backs beside the tasseled couch but the couch itself was empty of Fred. He must have slipped past the many bodies on the floor without waking a soul. "Where's Fred?" the Kid asked McSween in the kitchen.

"The jakes."

"He'll get shot."

"It's too early. Coffee's on the stove."

As Billy poured a mug Fred walked in the door and barred it behind him. Others shuffled into the kitchen: Jim French and Tom. McSween wouldn't sit, he paced back and forth, and provided the men with news of the siege: Lallycooler Crawford, who'd been shot through both hips while trying to sneak down from the hills around Lincoln and get a bead on the privy that Fred had just visited, now lay dying at Fort Stanton.

"How many is that, then?" asked Billy.

"Two if you count Dan Huff."

"He was poisoned. He's not in this war."

"You heard all the shooting last night I assume?" Standing before them, McSween, in tie and collar, waistcoat, and worsteds, though this was high summer, crossed his legs awkwardly as though trying to relax then stumbled and uncrossed them. "Wilson and Reverend Ealy were carrying Huff past the Torreón and the brutes inside detected their footsteps and opened fire. There's no one in this town who is not in this war. There are no innocent bystanders."

Unless you counted Macky Sween, thought the Kid. At the table he pulled out a chair then stood there trying to decide what to do. Piss outside or here, in a jar? Fred was staring at his shirt, which he'd worn every day of the siege for good luck, and Billy mentally dared him to smile. A sailor shirt scarcely comported with his stature, he knew, yet nothing comported, nothing answered the purpose or tallied or matched in this wreckage of circumstance. At least the shirt smelled of man-sweat. This made him feel less boyish. Everyone smelled pretty rank by now, since water for baths was scarce, as was privacy. The coffee had wrapped a steel band around his head, and he had to pee badly, and McSween in his duds with his fatuous airs annoyed him, as usual. On the kitchen wall a photo of John Tunstall, taken in San Francisco, appeared to mock them all. How many times had Billy tried to picture John Henry Tunstall since he'd been murdered? Whenever he did, the man's face broke up into granulated bulbs that drifted apart. Then he'd gaze at this photograph on McSween's wall of the perfect stranger who'd opened the flood gates, and now here they were caught in a current that no one could buck. They couldn't stop now, if you stopped you'd be dead. I've stepped outside myself, Billy thought, I'm in the wash. I'm up to my neck and cut off and exposed and I never could swim and it's all I can do to keep my head above water. I could climb out to shore but they'd shred me like lettuce.

Outside, he ducked and ran to the privy through the dry light of morning but no shots came. Isolated near the fence in back of the house, it made an especially risky destination. The day was hot already and dust from his tracks tunneled the sunlight. Beyond the privy's warped boards, gullied and gray, cedars and piñons descended to the river.

Back in the kitchen, Billy barred the door and sat at the oilclothed table next to Tom. He listened to McSween ramble on about everything and, equally, nothing — the decline of the world, the intentions of the Dolanites, the comfort of friends. "When do we get paid?" asked Fred. Tom blew on his coffee. Elizabeth Shield's ten-year-old, Minnie, came racing through the kitchen, chased by her older brother Davy, a pimpled adolescent, and she whomped right into Macky, who did not appear to notice. Davy swung a dead rat tied to a string into his sister's face until his uncle, as though through a fog, began to discover the disturbance below him and the sneaky boy hastily stuffed it in his britches. Elizabeth Shield was Sue Mc-Sween's sister. She'd come from Missouri with her family of six including Minnie and Davy to live with Mac and Sue. Two months ago Billy had helped the preacher Taylor Ealy and his brood move into Tunstall's store next door, making room in Macky's house for the Shields. Like McSween, Elizabeth's husband was a lawyer, and a Scotsman to boot, thus another irritant to the Church of Rome in Lincoln, and Mac's firm now had become McSween and Shield. David Shield was presently visiting Santa Fe — fortunate man, thought Billy. McSween heard a muffled scream at his feet and spotted a child-blur, and Billy witnessed on his boss's face the fraction of his brain allotted to the present moment putting two and two together. But what Mac said was addressed to his men. "Don't you worry about it. We've got more pressing matters. I'll pay you boys everything you're owed as soon as we're out of this."

Fred asked, "How much is that, then?"

"Foot it up yourselves. I trust all you boys. Put it in writing and show me your figures. Not today — do it when we're out of this."

The children ran off. The Kid thought of Macky's *this* — the thing they weren't out of — the final, decisive, stick-to-one's-guns, never-say-die, holdout for ascendancy, once and for all between Dolan's boys and Tunstall's avengers. You'd think clearing Macky's name would have made a difference. Two weeks after Dick Brewer's death the grand jury in Lincoln had found Mac and Rob Widenmann innocent of all charges, including embezzlement. And public opinion had swung to Macky's side! Widenmann, just the same, had fogged out to Mesilla, in fear of his life, for the war still continued as though nothing had changed, and now Billy thought maybe Rob had been wise. On Dolan's side, ruddy George Peppin, confirmed as sheriff by the governor, had augmented the Boys with men from Seven Rivers, a town south of Lincoln near the Texas border. These desperadoes and hoodlums had been cowing the populace even before Sheriff Peppin had them deputized, and those of them who were vets of the Modoc War in California had scornfully applied a new name to the Regulators: the Modocs. Billy swore it wouldn't stick. The Modocs were a tribe of bloodthirsty Indians and the Regulators were righters of wrongs. The red devils in this business weren't the Tunstall loyalists but these new Irish savages from Texas, who had robbed old ladies, ripped the roofs off of stores, thrown the goods into the streets, and shot the horses outside. They'd ambushed Frank McNab at the Fritz ranch and chased him up a gully and shot him in the back. No wonder people were fleeing the territory. Squire Wilson, after offering the courthouse and its land for sale to Taylor Ealy for two thousand dollars, and after Ealy demurred, had lowered the price to seven hundred dollars and a span of mules but still hadn't made a sale. Meanwhile, McSween had mortgaged his wife's brand-new nine-hundred-dollar piano, and where *had* he found the money to buy it in the first place? He'd mortgaged it to pay his loyal men, and still they hadn't seen a cent. "Kid, when this is over, I'll set you up pretty. You, Jim, and Fred. You'll get that ranch Mr. Tunstall promised."

"What about Tom?"

"Tom, too. The whole lot." Across the table from Billy, Tom

O'Folliard raised one furry eyebrow — the outer limit of his silent eloquence. He was Billy's new mate, the factotum who followed him everywhere he went, much to Fred Waite's amusement. Billy still ran with Fred; but the six-foot-one Tom with a torch of red hair and moribund eyes who brought the Kid his coffee, who loaded his weapons and wiped down his horses, what wouldn't he do? — now was Billy's shadow, and Fred had become more like an older brother. Tom patiently watched, even held, Billy's bay outside gambling dens, whorewallows, and saloons.

"Did you have a place in mind?"

"In what respect?" asked Macky.

"That ranch," said the Kid.

"They'll be ripe to pluck when Dolan's ring is broken. His men dead or in jail. There'll be plenty of opportunities then, boys. Land and stock galore."

From the dining room came the screams of bored, trapped children and the sound of a crash.

Nearly two dozen Regulators had forted up in Mac's house. They slept on his floors and ate his food and filled his bedpans. Others occupied the grain warehouse in the back of Tunstall's store while Taylor Ealy and his family inhabited the living quarters in front. Many of Billy's Mexican friends had camped inside José Montaño's store and Juan Patrón's house further down the street, and a dozen more Regulators, including Frank Coe, Charlie Bowdre, and John Middleton, were at the Ellis store. Total Modocs: sixty-three.

The Dolanites, on the other hand, numbered only forty, but their cutthroat ways made them doubly effective. Only blood for blood would stop them, Billy knew. Between the Boys and Peppin's crew from Seven Rivers, Dolan had assembled as nasty a collection of human spittoons as the Kid had ever seen. Even their names were grotesque: Lallycooler Crawford, Roxy Rose, Rustling Bob Bryant, Ameredith Olinger. Or what about "the Dummy," who passed for deaf and dumb but looked for all the world like a stitched-together hybrid of Irish gorilla and hump-shouldered, bloody-eyed ox? The Kid pictured these murderers diked out in chicken claws, dead crows, and the teeth of Texas Rangers. He'd never seen monsters like them in Arizona. They were the muscle, Dolan and his inner circle the cunning. They fought with guns and knives, Dolan with affidavits and warrants. Words could serve as effectively as bullets, as James Dolan had shown, words, lies, and tricks — he walked the lie straight. They'd do anything, the Dolanites; they'd avail themselves of law, of the governor, the D.A., the army, Judge Bristol, to exceed restraint of law. Why, thought the Kid, did sliminess have such passionate advocates and surrender no quarter whereas fair play and justice, under Macky's supervision, was always willing to negotiate and compromise? They had holed up at the Wortley Hotel across from Dolan's store.

Sporadic firing had occurred on both sides for the last several days. Apron-men and bystanders had been wounded in the street. Dolan had had the nerve to send Jack Long calling on McSween the first day of the siege with arrest warrants for the Kid and nine or ten others but the Regulators met him with a fusillade of bullets and he turned tail. Messengers had gone back and forth between Dolan's crew and Fort Stanton ten miles away, McSween had informed them; but thus far only one trooper had showed up in town, and claimed to have been fired upon from Mac's house. Meanwhile, snipers surrounded McSween's, some behind other houses, some in the hills. Once everyone was up and the morning was over, no one dared go outside to the privy anymore — except Sue McSween. Her theory was that even savages and barbarians would not shoot a woman. The others used bedpans that Macky's Negro servant, George Washington, crept out at night to empty.

George Washington now entered the kitchen to start the first shift of breakfast. Behind him strutted fifteen-year-old Yginio Salazar.

"Ah," said McSween. "Comes the leaden messenger."

Yginio announced that Mrs. McSween would like to see her husband right now in the parlor. Looking plucky and gay, Mac strolled to the door. "Henio," said Billy. "Sit. Have some coffee."

Someone had managed to smuggle an old *Las Vegas Optic* into the house, and Yginio held it up. "Hey, Kid. Says in here an outlaw named Billy the Kid robbed a buckboard down at Captain Pope's Crossing. Was that you?"

"How could it be me? I'm here, ain't I?"

"This was last week. Says he's from Silver City."

"Lots of people are from Silver City."

Yginio shrugged. He looked at the door. "Is the yoo-hoo still safe?"

"That's not what we call it, Yginio."

"Mrs. Macky Swain calls it a yoo-hoo."

"We just call it the jakes. She was being cute."

"Is it safe?"

"I wouldn't go out there," said Billy.

"She may be cute but she's a tough one," said Fred. "Tough as leather. She stands up to the Dolanites."

"She's got balls," said the Kid. Yginio laughed. "How come do you suppose she never had children?"

"Maybe she ate them."

"Two weeks ago, did you hear what happened, Fred? She found out the Boys stolen Macky's horses and thought one of them was her mare, Pet. Then she thought Macky's dead — that must be it. He was holed up in San Pat at the time and that's where they got the horses. So she grabs her Greener and loads both barrels and runs down to Dolan's store and screams she wants her Pet back or someone will die."

"So she was more upset about Pet than her husband, is that your point? I know she dotes on that horse."

"That could be true but they assumed she meant Mac. John Kinney told her, I haven't killed him yet. But I've killed fourteen men and I'll get to him presently."

"He didn't know she don't care about Mac. It was the mare that drove her there."

"I disagree. If nothing else, she's loyal to her husband."

"What do you think, Tom?" Fred looked across the table.

"I don't think."

"The Dolanites have a man called the Dummy," said Fred. "That's what we ought to call you."

"Talk's overrated," said the Kid.

"Is it true what they said about Tunstall?" asked Fred. He lowered his voice and looked toward the parlor door. "You know. Him and Sue?"

"It's true about Francisco Gómez."

"I thought she didn't like greasers."

"She's just after her greens," said Billy. "If it has a cock, she'll take it. In the mouth or up the ass — that's all she likes."

"Not so loud," said Fred. He sounded peeved. "How do you know?"

"A little bird told me."

"That just goes to show she's never been properly fucked."

"They say he found her in a whorehouse. He was bent on redeeming her."

"That's not how she tells it. How she accounts for it, she was living in a convent. Where was this whorehouse?"

"Near St. Louis."

"That's where the convent. And what the hell was Macky Sween doing in a whorehouse?"

"Preaching the gospel. Ramming the fear of the Lord into the girls."

"McSween couldn't ram a goat with his boots on and its rear legs inside them."

"Can't you just see it? Feeding her pussy and reading the good book."

"Plus, where do you think she picked up those airs? Not in a whorehouse."

"She got them from Macky."

"Oh sure. Mr. Fumblemump."

"Minnie!" said Yginio, minatorily loud. The girl had appeared beside them at their table as though suddenly embodied. Fred and Billy glanced at each other and Fred changed horses.

"Now *we're* the Trojans, Kid."

"What do you mean?"

"We're holed up in here. We're the ones under siege from the Greeks out there." Fred sipped his coffee. The smell of ham had filled the room, mixed with the piñon smoke from the stove. George Washington waved at the smoke with his spatula.

"I thought you said before that we were the Greeks."

"Not anymore. And Sue McSween — she's Hecuba."

"Who's that?"

"The Trojan queen."

Minnie stared at Tom O'Folliard, who couldn't help smiling. Mule-faced Tom had found a sweetheart. "Can I see your gun?" she asked. She climbed into his lap and he lurched to one side to reach for his holster but Fred lurched across the table and clamped Tom's arm.

"Christ almighty, Tom, don't be such a fool. She's just a child."

"Oh."

"I may be crazy but you take the cake."

Tom sat there, tongue-tied. He was a large pile of shoulders, arms, and head, with a monolithic face — slit-eyed, thin-lipped, jug-eared, iron-chinned — but he, too, was just a child, the Kid thought. His head might have been twice the size of little Minnie's but it was honeycombed. All of us are children. "Tom, where were you when they passed out the horse sense?"

Tom said nothing.

Yginio circled the table to Tom and lifted Minnie from his lap. He took her by the hand and led her out of the kitchen just as Doc Scurlock and Charlie Bowdre walked in and poured themselves coffee. Next door, at Tunstall's store, Punch was barking like a bell that would never stop ringing. With Rob Widenmann gone, no one fed him anymore on a dutiful basis, and no one living at the store dared to approach and muzzle the beast, so he barked all day, especially mornings. It had become a leitmotif; it made them think of the Englishman. "Mr. Tunstall would have liked Minnie," said the Kid. "His sister was the same age."

"Tom, you really don't have to rob the cradle," said Fred. "There's always Mrs. McSween."

"She's not as cute as Minnie. Right, Tom?" Billy grinned.

Tom stood then sat, blushing red as a carrot. Yginio came back and he and Doc and Jim stood around the table. "There's a soldier on the street."

"So now they're rousting up the soldiers."

"You know what this is like?" asked Fred. He looked around. "It's like two groups of porcupines. It gets cold, we close in and huddle together but right away both sides feel the other's quills so we have to move away. But then we're cold again and decide to come together and we get stabbed again and have to move apart and it's the same damn thing over and over. We can't be together and can't be apart."

"You means us and the Dolanites?" said Doc.

"Well. It's universal. It could equally apply to Macky Sween and Sue."

"To Minnie and Tom."

"Learn to laugh. That's the answer."

"Who could have made such a balled-up world?"

"Some pin-butt," said Fred. "It wasn't exactly *made*, in my opinion. Or if it was, they left out a few pieces or employed defective goods. The world's a mistake, that's what I think. It should have been one thing or the other; God or Satan; clean living or devilment. Instead, what you got is this muckheap, this mess. You got honey from corpses and rot from pretty mouths. Each day, it gets made over again and each night the darkness comes back and takes charge. Somewhere along the line I guess something happened. Some sort of malice aforethought, someone did something wrong. A fly in the ointment, I suppose — I don't know. It's like the rocks and the dirt and the wind by themselves stopped pulling their freight and just went to smash. Myself, I'm broke of trying to mend it. You just have to go along. Learn to laugh. That's the answer."

◆ ◆ ◆

IN THE PARLOR, McSween avoided watching his wife as though she were the sun, but she looked bullets at him. He was tall and foggy, Sue short, pert, and puffy. "And something else. Your nephew is terrorizing his sister with a dead rat. Kitty wants to know would you get rid of the thing."

"His father's prerogative."

"His father is in Santa Fe." Everything Sue said had the sting of common sense laced with curt civility. "He has broken an oil lamp."

"Which one?"

"The Swiss. Vicente swept up the pieces. It warms my heart to see the old and the young, the brown and the white, getting along so well."

Her faint white mustache lifted when she smirked. Mac knew she didn't like so many Mexicans about. After five years of marriage, he and Sue no longer bothered to correct, or even object to, each other's behavior, they just referenced it icily. The machinery of courtesy they'd gradually constructed took over when they talked, with the odd squeak and thump. They even smiled — sometimes. But Sue, his *bona roba*, always made up and corseted like a big doll, and carefully composed, hair rigidly curled, bubble-eyed, lace-collared, upright, beflowered, her round cheeks saucy, her smile inviting, her warm neck lovely, had not been intimate with her chalky husband for over two years. Instead, they talked business, and the makeshift engine clanked. They'd once loved each other; then hated; then both. Then, with accusatory lapses, spasms of blame for lost affection, and periods of silence, they slowly passed into indifference. At first, their cold politeness seemed to function only in the vicinity of others; now *they* were the others. Poor Mac; his wife's bosom heaved in his presence but he knew it wasn't desire. It was laced-mutton willfulness, pride, her preeminence, plus her high dudgeon at being married to a sponge. He was taller than her by a good foot yet he withered in her presence. His long ropy mustache felt incidental. His handsome good looks — the big chin, the sharp nose, the wide eyes, the empurpled Scottish complexion — didn't seem to help. He'd seen chromos of Victorio, the renegade Apache, whose mustache looked like a parody of Mac's, bitter and thin. And if the red devils really *were* a lost tribe of Welsh — even of Israelites — perhaps there was a Celtic-Semitic-Apache blood connection in the matter of facial hair . . . ?

The other thing about Sue was her uncanny ability to read his every thought. "Hairless little monkeys," she observed now. Her niece and nephew?

"And what are we? The hairy sort?"

In drifting apart, he and Sue had created a third thing in their wake, a straw man between them. Their toxic knowledge of each other occupied this being, hence their wary small talk and refusal to touch. Lately, Mac had realized that the straw man was himself. It didn't exist when they weren't together but when they were he was the scarecrow caught in the middle. It was not unlike this war, he thought — a collective lunacy jointly upheld by all involved, a hopeless mess of maniacs of the deepest dye, and Macky caught in the middle, always in the middle. He'd seen cattle pile up crossing a river and the weak ones get climbed on and die in a line, not being able to go any further, consequently forming a bridge for the living to cross upon. That was him, Macky Sween — crushed by the mindless need of others. Nail me to the cross, boys. And they put me as boss. The water climbs, the earth moves, the cattle panic, and I'm boss.

How long had Kitty been standing in the doorway? Sue's sister Elizabeth was nothing like his wife. Flatiron face, sunken eyes, high brow. Short and squat, she hardly suited his conception of a woman, never having flirted with Mac, or with anyone for that matter. Perhaps he should have married *her*. She had Davy by the collar and led him to McSween, who'd have to search the boy's pockets and find the dead rat. "Mac, this boy needs a talking-to. I'm blue in the face."

Mac felt an utter lack of control. At the same time, he had to affect authority. And he was broke, he thought now, descending headlong into his mind's last pit. Their money was gone, every last penny; he'd hit bottom at last. Even Sue didn't know. The piano was the last straw. Mac had been euchred, that's what it came down to. His creditors would get him if the Dolanites didn't, and his creditors were mostly Dolanites anyway. He slapped the boy's pockets, feeling for the rat. Reached into one, felt a string, gave a tug. It was down his leg. Davy had cut a hole in his pocket. Handy for many things, as Mac discovered, to his chagrin — the boy had an erection.

After Kitty and her son left, Mac stood there in the parlor holding on to the string. The rat hung by its tail. Sue sat at her desk. She was writing, he could tell by the press of her shoulders. Sue had recourse to expedients. Her life did not lack, even in the midst of war, for consolations. And Mac had learned to avail himself of her comforts, if only by proxy. For example, she kept parallel diaries, one official, one private. One in a cubby of her rolltop desk, the other in a velvet box hidden inside a false-bottomed drawer with her Pike's Magnolia. One for daylight, one for night. One innocuous, one shameful. One to be discovered and read by her husband, the other a secret, but he'd discovered them both. He could even tell which she was writing now. Her shoulder bore down but didn't crab up, this must have been the public one.

◆ ◆ ◆

JULY 18, 1878. *It is the Murphy-Dolan crowd who is to blame for our boys adopting this way of getting a living. Fred Waite, the Kid, good-natured Tom O'Folliard — what would they be without this wretched war? They are all good-natured, rollicking boys, always singing and full of fun. Mr. McSween, of course, did not approve at all of the killing of Sheriff Brady. Quite naturally, the killing of the representative of justice has turned many friends against us and did our side much harm in the public mind. Those of the party who did this shooting, and have bragged of the fact, now must defend us, and this situation we must accept. Nor was Andrew L. Roberts's death anything but senseless; he was on his way out of the territory at the time. In our eye-for-an-eye world, it resulted in the murder of Richard Brewer, as fine a young man as ever lived. On the other side is the fact that Brady and Roberts, William Morton, Frank Baker, Manuel Segovia, Charles Crawford, Mr. Hindman, all were hand and glove with the Dolan faction, which openly flaunts justice and law. In their effort to check the inroads that Mr. McSween and Mr. Tunstall were making into their schemes to get money by hook or crook, they deliberately planned the murder of both of them.*

And now, we wait. We wait for Armageddon, for that is what it amounts to. There are rumors that the soldiers will enter the town to restore law and order. If it were that, I would welcome them. But everyone knows that Colonel Dudley, too, is James Dolan's puppet. I shudder to think of what will happen to us, and of what our own natural desire for revenge will lead to if unleashed.

◆ ◆ ◆

MY CONQUEROR, WHO, *as he afterwards told me, had been struck with my appearance, kissed me in such a manner that his intent was*

· 174 ·

unmistakable. But even new-born love opposed so sudden a surrender;
and the fear of being surprised by my husband was a bar to my compli-
ance. Not for long, however. After being rebuffed, he lay motionless
beside me, and the perfection of his manly limbs, even fully
clothed — his vermilion lips, pouting and swelling to the touch — his
long feminine eyelashes and black curly hair — all conspired to weaken
my resolve, despite my natural modesty. I could not help but observe
that his condition was such as to require that his trousers be "taken
out." And, though not a tailor, or a doting mother, it did fall to me to
relieve him of the pressure such a swelling entailed by opening his but-
tons. And, oh! It emerged with a stiffness! a hardness! an upward bent
of erection! and was to all appearances as pretty a piece of woman's
meat as ever I should see, and of a size as to feed a convent and a half.
In the sequent, he, stretched upon his length, chin on my buttocks (me
kneeling bent forward), fumbled with his fingers to unlace my stays,
his ungraceful skill such that the stays wouldn't loosen, until with a
sudden spring of release my bosom tumbled forward, he in his impa-
tience having sliced all the laces with one sweeping motion of his
Green River skinner. With my bosom fully bare, the firm hard swell of
a pair of white breasts rose to his cupped hands when they circled my
torso, whilst in my nether vessels the flow of sluices commenced . . .

♦   ♦   ♦

THAT NIGHT AT two A.M. Billy heard sounds. He'd been sleeping
in the parlor on the floor beside Tom. It came from the west wing,
from Mac and Sue's quarters, and could have been a Dolanite crawling in a window. They'd already tried once to set fire to the house.
In granitic dark he threw off the blankets, padded toward the door.
No corridors in Macky Sween's house; the rooms simply opened into
each other. He crept through the parlor and the sitting room, step-
ping over and around sleeping Regulators, into Mrs. Shield's bedroom — she snored behind a screen barely visible in darkness. Walking through this house was like walking through a train whose cars

had been stopped on a horseshoe bend. Gradually, his eyes adjusted; and his ears devoured noises now loud, now soft, now rhythmic, now knocking. Moaning squealing gag-croaking sounds, splinters of noise, bed ticks softly smashed. He passed through more rooms into the west wing and discerned a bent figure lurking at a doorway and stopped and backpedaled. It was Macky's silhouette. Curled around a doorframe, Billy watched Mac crane toward the lit crack of a barely open door. The sounds came from in there, unmistakable lamentations of pleasure and pain, and the squealing of bedsprings. Mac didn't move a muscle.

The Kid heard a squeak behind him. At this room's other door he saw Tom O'Folliard, watching him watching Mac. And Macky watching Sue, no doubt, but with whom? And behind Tom, if Billy could have seen her, Minnie Shield watching Tom watching Billy watching Mac watching Sue and her lover.

◆ ◆ ◆

JULY 19. In the morning Billy saw the couch was empty and learned that Fred Waite had racked out sometime during the night. At breakfast, he watched Macky and Sue to see if anything was amiss. Mac seemed content, Sue well-nourished. The doings of night greased the common business of day, it appeared. Once again, they ate in shifts. A boarding-house breakfast: steak, fried eggs, biscuits, gravy, coffee, things had always been nice and foody at Mac's. Then Macky announced to all at the table that he'd written a note to the postmaster in Roswell requesting stamps. All was right with the world! After all, the Kid knew, they outnumbered the Dolanites. And José Chávez y Chávez, Lincoln's new constable, was a member of their party and carried around wherever he went — to breakfast, to bed, to the privy at night — a tall stack of warrants for George Peppin and every member of his posse, for all of the Boys, for James Dolan, too, for the whole lot. Who knows, this could be the day they were arrested.

When little Minnie took Mac's note outside to post, Billy moved into the parlor to observe her from the window. Others followed. "What's that dust?" someone said. Then she came back and told Uncle Mac that soldiers were marching through town from the west. Sure enough, there they were, on foot and mounted, raising dust, scaring cats, causing dogs to bark: Colonel Dudley himself with his thick mustache running into burnsides, Captain George Purrington, four other officers, a company of Negro cavalry, and another of white infantry, thirty-five men in all. Behind them, on a wagon, a Gatling gun and a twelve-pound howitzer.

"What the devil's going on?" Mac asked.

Sue remarked, "The Congress has prohibited military intervention in civilian affairs. He knows that."

"Go remind him, why don't you?" Doc Scurlock said.

"Maybe I will."

"Who's that?" said the Kid. "That ain't no soldier. See that, Jim? — that's Jesse Evans. With a goddamn cavalry cap."

"Don't look like Jesse Evans."

"It sure as shit is."

All five of Kitty Shield's bedlam children were jumping up and down behind the Regulators grouped around the window, trying to spot the army troops. "Listen," said Jim French to no one in particular. "They can't take sides. I may be crazy but Dudley's not stupid. They'll all of them be court-martialed if they do."

"Colonel Dudley," said Sue, "is a whiskey barrel in the morning and a barrel of whiskey at night."

"But he ain't stupid is all I'm saying."

"He ain't stupid, no," said the Kid. "He can't take sides, sure. But lookit. See what they're doing? He's got the howitzer pointed at José's."

It was true. The troops had camped across the road from Montaño's little store and had trained the twelve-pounder at its front door.

The door opened and someone emerged. He'd thrown a blanket over his head and raced east down the road, out of sight. Within seconds, a dozen others ran out, also hidden under blankets. Next door, the Patrón house emptied out just as quickly, and those men, too, fled down the Lincoln-Roswell road. And shots were being fired, not by the soldiers, no, they were nonpartisan, but by Dolanites in the hills, Dolanites to the west. Nothing now prevented them from closing in. "That son of a bitch," Sue McSween hissed. "Do something, Mac."

McSween in the parlor sat to his desk and, obscurely enraged, wrote a note to Dudley:

> Genl Dudley USA. Would you have the kindness to tell me why soldiers surround my house?
> Before blowing up my property, I would like to know the reason. The constable is here and has warrants for the arrest of Sheriff Peppin and posse for murder and larceny.
> Respectfully, A. A. McSween

Over Kitty's objections, he gave the note to little Minnie to take outside to Dudley, and Billy watched from the window the brave young girl bouncing up the road to the crusty commander. "If anything happens to her," said her mother, "I'll shoot you myself." Macky's vague and glassy posture and blankness of face created the impression that he simply didn't hear her.

Ten minutes later, Minnie returned clutching a reply. Her brother Davy attempted to snatch it from her hand. Squeals of the children, shouts of the Regulators, Punch barking next door. And, outside, a contingent of soldiers surrounding Sheriff Peppin as he marched down the road. Shots in the distance. Suddenly, a madness had swept the world, it seemed. Macky read the answer and handed it to Billy:

> A. A. McSween, Sir. I am directed by the Commanding Officer to inform you that no troops have surrounded your

house, and that he desires to hold no correspondence with you. He directed me to say that if you desire to blow up your house he has no objection providing you do not injure any of his command by doing so.

Lt. Millard Goodwin

Mac looked around the room, at the men, the children, Sue, the parlor organ, a chromo of a country church on the wall. He looked around seemingly searching for something but lacking the foggiest notion of what. He dropped into a Morris chair. From several rooms away came the sound of breaking glass. Macky jumped up, Billy and the others ran toward the sound, in the doorway the Kid warned them to keep clear, stay back. At the front of the house, the window in Mrs. Shield's room had been shattered top to bottom and its barricade of adobes knocked to the floor. "McSween!" someone outside the window shouted.

"What do you want?"

"It's Marion Turner. I have warrants for you and the others in the house. Will you surrender?"

"We have warrants for *you*." But Macky sounded addled.

"Who issued your warrants? Let me see them! Come to the window!"

Jim French suddenly pushed past McSween and fired at the window with his Colt's Army, inching forward as he repeatedly shot. "Here's our warrants!" he bellowed. "You cocksucking sons of bitches." Outside, the fleeing men chopped gravel with their boots.

Out the window Billy saw that more soldiers in the street mounted on their ponies were escorting more Dolanites riding toward the east. They were after those blanketed men, he thought. McSween nudged him aside. One by one, with care and precision, Mac piled the adobe bricks back in the window. He pushed one in place, tried to pull it back, removed the bricks below it, then fit them in again. Sue said, "Macky, what the hell are you doing?"

"Fixing this barricade."

"I'm going out there." She stared at her husband. He opened his mouth but nothing came out, and she bolted from the room.

Outside, Sue McSween crawled on hands and knees along the half-finished adobe wall beside her house. In the street, she raised up and strutted east with arms swinging. She marched straight down the road and no one tried to stop her. Colonel Dudley had dismounted and stood in the roadside next to his wagon with the howitzer and Gatling gun. They'd set up camp in a weedy empty lot across the road from José Montaño's store. Soldiers milled about, Lieutenant Goodwin approached. "Halt," he barked, and she stomped through the dirt and dust right past him.

"I have business with the colonel."

Colonel Dudley erected. "Mrs. McSween."

She stared darkly at him — his cratered eyes, hairy ears, anticlinal cheeks. His nose seemed to have gotten a toehold on this face, which was pale as a chalk bluff. Quite a paunch on Dudley, and he made a failure lifting it to the level of his chest when he saw Sue approaching; no shelf to hold it. "My husband and I wish to know what you are doing in town on such a day."

"I am not aware, madam" — fluttering medals, night-cat glare, the sun overhead so directly above them that no one cast a shadow — "that I have to report my movements to you. However, I'll answer you. People from Lincoln have been coming to the fort for protection for months. I am here to protect women and children and anyone else who requires protection."

"Protect them from whom?"

"From belligerents on both sides."

"Then why do your soldiers escort the belligerents from only one side?"

"If your husband wishes it, we'll escort him, too."

"Escort him to jail!"

"Do you expect my protection? When you allow such men as Kid

Antrim, Jim French, and others of like character to be in your house? I will send my soldiers where I please."

"Why is your cannon pointed at my house?"

"If you will look more closely you will perceive — do you see? — that it is pointed precisely in the opposite direction."

"I have been told you will blow up my house."

"You have been misinformed. I have a letter right here sent to me by your husband stating that he intends to blow his house up himself."

"My husband would never write such a letter!"

Above them, the leaves of cottonwoods and walnuts stirred sluggishly in a breeze that did not relieve the heat. They lightly showered dust back on the road that the soldiers had raised an hour or so before. Gunshots came from Sue's house. She turned and tried to peer around the buzzing soldiers who had managed to surround her. "Mrs. McSween," harrumphed the colonel. He pulled Macky's note from the pocket of his coat and read it aloud.

Sue turned back to him. "I don't believe my husband wrote that."

The colonel held it up, that she might scrutinize the scratches. It surely was Mac's notepaper: *Law Office of McSween and Shield* across the top. But when Sue reached out he snatched it away. "Ah, Mrs. McSween. You must think me a nincompoop." Bloating his eyes, he turned to Sergeant Baker standing beside them. "If this woman attempts to take this letter from my hand, you are to shoot her." And he continued to flaunt it like a boy playing keep-away.

More gunshots. Sue swung around again to look at her house. With her back to the colonel she barked, "Then you won't help us?"

"If your husband will surrender to me, I give you my word of honor, as an officer of the army, that he will not be molested or in any way hurt."

She turned to face Dudley, wild-eyed and haggish — her freshness rubbed off — raising her voice, on the verge of tears. "Everything you say sounds pretty thin to me."

"Excuse me. I don't comprehend what you said."

"I said it looks a little too thin."

"I don't understand such slang, Mrs. McSween. The ladies I associate with do not use such language. I don't know what you mean by the phrase 'too thin.'"

"I mean despite your blubber I can see right through you."

◆ ◆ ◆

THAT EVENING, Mac and Sue sat in the parlor. From the bowels of the house came sounds of a commotion. "What's that smell?" asked Sue but Mac didn't answer. He didn't wish to answer, it was his privilege. A few hours ago, Jack Long and the Dummy had snuck up on the house and set the kitchen door on fire but Kitty and her daughter had doused it with water. Macky's men in Tunstall's store had spotted the arsonists, who'd fled to the privy under their gunfire, and they continued to shoot, shredding the boards. For all anyone knew Dolan's two thugs were still in there now, either dead as four o'clock or huddled down inside the pit. "I smell smoke again, Mac!" Sue had jumped up and now crossed the floor sniffing. When she fled toward the back of the house Macky followed.

Through the east wing, through the Shields' quarters, through their own wing, all the way to the storehouse were Billy and the others bunched up like cattle at the rear door. "They tried another fire," said the Kid. "Run off our horses, pulled boards from the stable, and set this room ablaze from the shed but we're putting it out." A fusillade of gunshots came from outside. Jim French, Yginio Salazar, Florencio Chávez, and Ignacio Gonzales burst through the door, smoke and bullets trailing them. All coughed and backed away. "They're in the stable," said Jim, blinking as he spoke. "The flames is straight in their line of fire."

"But you extinguished them?"

"We couldn't."

Soon, the fire grew. Mac had always assumed that adobe didn't burn, and, of course, it did not. Could dirt itself burn? But the beams and framework could, the vigas, the floor, the furniture inside. And once it got started, as he now learned, you couldn't get at it, it burned in the marrows and was impossible to stop. Like a slow fever, it grew and spread methodically; it transformed the very house into an oven. Plus, the smoldering fumes and smoke and oily residue seeped torturously through every crack and seam, down from the ceiling, up from the floor. Backing off, they shut the door to the burning storeroom and Billy and Yginio pushed a dresser against it.

They'd been, by now, in this house for five days. More than one hundred hours. Their usual malodorous bodies and clothes had ripened like fruit to a state beyond rot. To Mac, who had always sought explanations for his trials, nothing made sense, except he was embedded, nailed into the moment, then the next one, then the next. He was in a familiar place, in the middle. Do not speak of existence when it comes to Macky's bearings, speak of the mess. The clutter, the noise, the bullets all the time snapping into the house — this was all to be expected. The firing now relentless. Punch barking. Please feed him. Macky realized that their entire entourage had wound up in Sue's sitting room, and below him, on a table, her sketchbook was open to a pen-and-ink drawing of Lincoln's Torreón spread across two pages. The Torreón was not a symbol for anything, save artful intention. Nor were the flowers on the piano, the framed photos of houses Mac had never seen, of boys and girls he'd never met. Was one of them Sue? And gimcracks and knickknacks and little carved figures and waxed apples and pears, a herbarium, old brocade on the stuffed chairs. Sue had even bought a prie-dieu for this room, dear pious Sue. The flowers had never wilted here, had they? The wickedness of the world even rewrote nature. Macky noticed a place low on the wall just above the floor where the adobes appeared to have decomposed, and he thought, I must speak to Romolo. More *jaspe* perhaps. And the bowl going round. No, it couldn't be. Not now, not here. McSween took a seat and propped his head in his hands. Faults in his mind shifted, blocks of thought fractured; it was almost a relief. The fragments were such that he could occupy one, whatever its contents, as long as he pleased. *Parties knowing themselves indebted to the Lantier estate are requested to call at my office and settle. Produce of every kind taken as payment. Delinquents will be forced. Request aid of the sheriff while the bowl goes round.*

They were singing. *While the bowl goes round, while the bowl goes round.* Sue played the mortgaged keys, all sang the borrowed songs, and Yginio fiddled. Tunstall's favorite song was "The Tear," by Gumbert, Mac suddenly remembered. "Sing 'Factory Girl,'" someone said.

> *Pity me my darling*
> *Pity me, I say:*
> *Pity me my darling,*
> *And carry me away.*

How brave of Sue! She was playing the piano to keep their spirits up. The assembled sang the chorus, she warbled the verses, and fifteen-year-old Yginio sawed his violin. The children sang, too, save when distracted. And was that a real ax in little Davy's hand, who once more was chasing his sister? Sue's dresser rose, gems and money showered down, smoke filled the room; the sound of an explosion. Fire in the burst doorway. "Heave," someone said. A dozen men surrounded the Beatty grand piano and tipped it on its side and it floated through the door. Macky found himself collecting dollar bills, jewelry. Someone screamed in his face, "Is there any more powder kegs?"

"Powder kegs?"

Coughing and retching, they moved clothes, the prie-dieu, a chair, carved figurines into Sue's bedroom. Somebody took Macky's arm to guide him through the door and they found a black satchel for the treasure in his hands. Sue's lovely voice was at it again. *Some folks do*, they sang. The notes of the piano tumbled down an incline as though it hadn't been properly uprighted, or the house was on its side, or gravity had been suspended — tumbled down, burst away, became smoke and air. The grace of God, David Shield once had said, won't carry a man through such troubles as these, it takes powder and ball. Then he went to Santa Fe. The only palliation those Irish admit of is bullets, I'm afraid, he'd told Mac on another occasion. Their pernicious stimulants give them a wild purpose which prayer cannot defeat, my friend. Do not wonder at the fact that once having tasted the evil sweets of sin and unrestrained behavior, on returning to the haunts of law-abiding folk they languish and pine for the irresponsible solitudes where neither laws nor restrictions imposed by morality have the least effect on their —

At one juncture, Mac found himself lifted up bodily as they moved from room to room, down the west wing, across the front portion, up the east wing to the kitchen, taking Sue's piano with them as they went, also her bedding, clothes, items of furniture, and, in Macky's satchel, her jewelry and cash. The house methodically devoured itself behind them. Sue played a new song in each new room — "Old Memories," "The Mill," "Ellen Bayne," "Wilt Thou Be True?" — but soon the chorus lost interest. Children screamed, smoke billowed, more windows burst, and Mac vaguely recalled, just after it happened, watching through the parlor window his wife and her sister and Lizzy's five children racing for a wagon outside on the street. In the wagon were Taylor Ealy and his family, fleeing Tunstall's store. Soldiers surrounded it. Twilight in Lincoln. Dark hills, white sky. The fire sent its heat ahead of itself, through the walls, beneath the floors, as though scouting fuel. The air grew heavier, smoke clung to their clothing, coughing and retching they slatterpouched themselves.

All at once William Bonney yanked Macky's head from his hands by the hair and slapped his greasy face. They were in the kitchen now — the last room left. "Pull yourself together, man!" But all Mac could do was stare at a blue shirt with an anchor and a rope and, hand across his mouth, suppress a giggle. He raised his eyes to Billy's. The boy's expression had struck a fleeting mean between panic and rage, and his hat was on his head, his black hair licked and curled around his ears, he'd tied a bandanna around his skinny neck. "Jesus Christ, Macky!" He grabbed Mac's arms and shook them. Then, clapping his hands, he raced through the kitchen kicking soppy butts, shouting, "Get a leg on! Stir your sticks, turkeys!"

"I've lost my mind, boys," Mac heard himself say. Bonney, Tom, José, Harvey Morris, and Jim French raced out the door to a riptide of bullets parting the air. Dark figures in the yard, light cast by the fire, an outer darkness beyond. Francisco Zamora and Vicente Romero went next. Then Yginio Salazar and Florencio Chávez, one on either side, took McSween's arms and passed through the door and were in the hellish light. Mac recognized Harvey Morris on the ground draining into earth. Why weren't they moving? Across the yard, the Kid shoved the barrel of his Colt's into Robert Beckwith's mouth while Bob Ollinger behind them, the mountain gorilla, reloaded his Whitney. Yginio went down. "Surrender, McSween!" someone shouted from the fence.

"I surrender!" he boomed, but ahead of him Vicente and Florencio were dashing for the chicken house, firing at whatever moved. No one held his arms. Obscure figures all around, running shadows, smoke, repeated flash of muzzles, zipsting of bullets. The chicken house jumped, its planks splintering and shredding. "I shall never surrender!" Mac heard himself recant while entering the hailstorm, and he found that he was spared. The bullets must have missed. Warm spit filled his mouth. He ran like hell until nothing was before him, he tumbled through darkness, and happened to fall on top of Robert Beckwith, rolling over on his legs, stars and smoke above his face. Now it was Macky's turn to stop existing. The stars and the smoke were inside a vacancy. He owed David Shield a saddle, he recalled, and posted the note in his mental files. The following morning, chickens could be seen pecking out Alexander McSween's eyes.

When the surviving Dolanites examined the bodies they laughed at the bullet holes. The dead were not outraged. Their bones would become New Mexico dust breathed by future tourists. They flipped Yginio over. "I'd like to plant one more bullet right between this greaser's eyes," John Kinney said.

"No," said Milo Pierce. "He's dead but his face looks pretty good. Let's leave him alone. His mother might want to remember what he looked like."

"Fuck-all," said Kinney, walking away. He picked up a loose adobe brick, turned around, and heaved it at Yginio, striking his hip. "Dead as a herring."

Later, Yginio crawled through the gate, scrabbled through brush and yucca to the river, dragged himself along the riverbank. He reached the house of his sister-in-law a half-mile away with a bullet in his back and another in his shoulder and managed to live another fifty-eight years.

12

1878

War

THE KID RAN bent over crashing through brush down toward the Bonito below the burning house. Once beyond the circle of light he was forced to go blind and trip and grope. Branches of Gambel oaks whipped his ear. Trunks of cottonwoods loomed sufficiently dark inside the greater darkness to caution him to slow. His boots caught on sage, yucca stalks grazed his neck and snapped through his legs. Turpentine smell of the needling junipers he was forced to blunder through to gain the river, and the wafting acrid odor of Macky's burning timbers underlying that. Then the soft sand. Mud-suck. Trickle of water. And Billy mucking through to reach the other bank and traverse the open fields and begin the slow climb toward a faint illumination on the northern slopes cast by the fire. The shooting hadn't stopped. Who was there left to shoot? Crossing open ground, he knew that the danger now was stray bullets whizzing past and thumping into earth, or worse, striking rocks. Zig and zag; they follow you, regardless. Rocks and boulders in the way, more sage, bladed yucca. Once in the hills, with hoarse burning throat he jog-stumbled up. His Colt's Thunderer, he noticed, was still in his hand. Best to keep it there. Then he tripped on a rock and, sputtering forward, changed his mind and holstered the pistol so as not to shoot his foot off. He vaguely made out a bank of low clouds the higher he climbed; they obscured the stars. And he perceived, looking up, the wounded reflection of McSween's burning house swirling in the sky.

What to do now? Blow up the world? He felt helpless, confused. The perception of impotence compelled him to check his weapon again, to break it open, rotate the cylinder, feel each round with the pads of his fingers. Shouts and laughter came from below. Glancing down, in the light of the red oily smoke pouring from the house, he saw shadows of men burdened with goods passing between Tunstall's store and the road. They were looting the store. It looked like someone'd found Yginio's fiddle and begun a reel because peanut-size phantoms danced in the lurid light, yellow devils from hell. Another fire in a barrel further down the road where Dudley's soldiers huddled lit up their button-faces. And Billy climbing higher. Where had the others gone? Did Macky make it out alive, where were Tom, Yginio, Charlie Bowdre, Jim French? The higher he climbed the darker it became and he soon began to feel the warm moisture of the clouds. Now he angled east. He wasn't lost but he felt it. He stumbled, tripped, lurched up against a cliff but it seemed to give way. He tried to step back but couldn't stop from spilling forward and tumbling down with groping hands through a needling softness and the oily smell again and, sinking gently, grabbing for branches, foundering, gliding, he lowered himself, floating, it seemed, then found he was blundering down a declivity, found his legs dancing rock to rock, the rocks moving, too, rolling beneath him, with him, around him, then grinding to a stop.

He sat. Ankles sore. Covered with dirt, some sliding down his neck. Stayed there a blessed while. The while stretched to hours; he'd curled on the ground. What happened down there, he wondered, sitting up, what had they done? Had Tunstall's avengers lost everything now? He couldn't see the fire. Bosky here, he sensed. Smell of piñon. He might be in a draw. He jumped up, continued, then felt his heart snap when, stopping at a sound, he heard footsteps in the dark, stumble-prone thumps. They were searching for him. He drew the Thunderer and padded softly forward expecting dogs to bark, torches to appear. "Who's there?" No answer. The heavy foot-steps continued. There was nowhere to go. He didn't move. He ab-sorbed more than saw a large hulking shadow approaching through the darkness, and cocked the Colt's. "Is that you, Tom?"

"It's me."

"Christ's sake, O'Folliard, how come you didn't answer?"

"I wasn't sure who it was."

"You almost got yourself shot."

"That would have been unfortunate. Jim found the horses."

"Our horses? Where?"

"Downstream. Almost to the Hondo."

"Where is he now?"

"Waiting over to Tinnie. It ain't all the horses. Only six."

"Only six? Who else is with him?"

"José and Charlie."

"So everyone made it?"

"Saw Harvey Morris fall."

"What about McSween?"

"I think he surrendered."

◆　◆　◆

FOUR WERE KILLED escaping the house, he later learned, most notably Macky. Two more dead inside from the fighting. Lallycooler Crawford took another week to die. Total, six Regulators, two Dolan-ites, and now Dolan and his men with a headlock on the town. Now the brush-poppers from Seven Rivers, emboldened by their triumph, began to terrorize the countryside. They'd been deputized by Sheriff Peppin and assisted by Colonel Dudley and the army but with the Regulators routed they were no longer needed and, the Kid sus-pected, they felt the lack of all the fun. They'd become a band of brothers. To them, normal life was dull by comparison to pillage and mayhem, so they stuck together and went on the warpath, and Billy couldn't get the Regulators to stop them. The Regulators could not even bury McSween, Lincoln was closed to them, townsfolk had to do it. Billy later learned he was laid beside Tunstall behind the latter's store — *grassed down*, folk said on their native island. But here no grass grew to cover the dirt.

The store itself had been plundered by the Dolanites. Fearing for her life, Sue McSween had fled to Las Vegas.

The crew from Seven Rivers decided to call themselves Wrestlers, or Rustlers, identical words if your mouth was full of chew, and they no longer merely robbed old ladies, tore the roofs off of stores, or shot Regulators' horses. Instead, under the leadership of a man named John Collins, they wrecked Will Hudgen's saloon in White Oaks, abused Hudgen's wife and sister, then ransacked Lincoln looking for Sue McSween. Billy insisted to the Coes and Fred Waite that they regroup and fight this scourge. This was no time to quit. Those hatchet men and murderers, those weasels, those —

"What about them?" said Fred. "They won, didn't they?"

"It ain't over yet."

The Wrestlers broke into houses, stole horses, burned ranches, trashed stores, shot to cripple. They looted and burned the Coe ranch on the Hondo, and rode up to three adolescent boys cutting hay in the fields on José Chávez's ranch and murdered all three and ran off with their horses. At Martin Sanchez's farm, they wounded a farmhand and shot Martin's fourteen-year-old son, Gregorio, through the heart. Two days later, under a black moon on the Bonito, they dragged the wives of two employees at Bartlett's gristmill into the bushes, held knives to their throats, and took turns raping them.

Then like scorpions in a jar they turned on each other. As Billy heard it, John Collins was poisoned by God knows who, and John Selman and Ed Hart aspired for his position. While Hart's wife cooked dinner, the victorious Selman shot her husband through the brow, splattering his brains into the skillet that held their sizzling steaks.

As at Macky's house, Billy found himself rousting up sponges when he rallied the Regulators. It was like trying to throw snakes into a gunny sack. Then, exactly like the Wrestlers, or Rustlers, all they could really do was pillage, for when rage overflows and thins as it spreads it finds expression in happenstance. The Regulators accosted a traveler on the Roswell road and took his horse and money. They raided the Casey ranch and stole more stock and at Charles Fritz's ranch they stampeded a hundred and fifty head of cattle and rounded up fifteen horses. They placed pistols to the heads of Fritz's two sons, and Fred Waite asked Billy, "Are you sure you want to do this?"

"Any excuse for a party," he said.

"You mean these are the fellows who killed Mr. Tunstall?"

They weren't, of course. The Kid ordered them released. He wasn't sure what to do and sometimes he didn't care. The war wasn't over, he blared to the others, but even he saw it had become a war by proxy, for when you can't kill the principals then you terrorize their sympathizers. Or just lash out at anyone. They stole every horse at the Mescalero Apache Reservation Agency and killed the agency clerk, Morris Bernstein. Or Bernstein rode into the crossfire between the Regulators and a band of Indians, and wound up dead. But who turned out his pockets? Who took his rifle, pistol, and cartridge belts? Events were in the saddle, you hung on for the ride, and often Billy thought that the wood tick in his ear that always told him what to do had died and tumbled out like a piece of cold wax. Then he thought, no he hadn't. If he died I wouldn't know it. The fact that I'm thinking about him in this manner means he's still there.

I never listened to him anyway.

The more gadfly he grew the more he hated himself. Reasoning creatures began to vacate the county. The Beckwiths fled. Buck Powell and Lewis Paxton pulled up stakes and decamped. In Roswell and Seven Rivers, the post offices were closed. A contingent of Mormons who'd immigrated to Lincoln County sold their ranches and left; this was no place for a Stake of Zion, they said. Much to Billy's dismay, John Middleton racked out for Kansas and Henry Brown for Texas. In Washington, President Rutherford Hayes removed Governor Axtell from office and appointed the Civil War general and novelist Lew Wallace as the new governor of New Mexico Territory.

Even Frank and George Coe, two of the Kid's oldest friends, announced they'd sold their ranch and would pull for Colorado. They'd had enough of the outlaw life and urged Billy to join them. All still had warrants against them and now a new governor would make sure they were enforced.

"You can't go," Billy said. "I'm the decider. I'm still after the mob that murdered Mr. Tunstall."

"It's a done deal," said George, holding up his hand. He wiggled the stump of the finger shot off by Buckshot Roberts at Blazer's Mill. "We sold out. We're gone. Come with us, Kid."

The taste in Billy's mouth was wormwood and gall. "I'm no quitter."

In late September, the Kid, Fred Waite, and Tom O'Folliard rode east from San Pat with a stolen remuda. Outside La Junta, they passed señoritas with *ollas* balanced on their heads. The walnuts, box elders, and cottonwoods overhead on the Lincoln-Roswell road were heavy with leaves, which cooled the hot day. Mexicans at one farm had begun their threshing: on a circle of ground outside their adobe, they'd leveled the earth and spread it with straw and splashed on water and allowed the mud to harden. Now goats and mules, driven in circles, trampled the sheaves in the afternoon sun. Behind them, Billy saw, boys with pitchforks made from forked branches threw up the crushed wheat to catch in the wind, and gradually the chaff idled toward the edges in circular windrows like ripples in water. He knew the grain left behind would be tossed in the air with long-handled shovels to free it from goat dung then washed and spread on a canvas to dry before being carted in sacks to the gristmill.

Further down the road, outside a barn, women beat corn in wooden *cernidors* to separate the kernels, which fell on lengths of canvas. Men cut needle grass with short-handled sickles on the banks of the river and sang as they cut. The Kid had cut grass in exactly this manner, helping out his friends Yginio and José. As the men below him sprang up and bent down, sprang up and bent down, he felt his body absorbing their rhythms, his own back and arms going through the same motions. The grass lay in long rows. The wind whipped through this valley. A mule pulled a *carreta* driven by a young boy — he looked all of seven — toward the rows of cut grass. And on a fence, magpies laughed; why hadn't this behavior, their mocking seemed to say, been blown to smithereens like every other thing of duty and custom inside Lincoln County? Why hadn't it, too, become ashes and debris?

Billy and his friends could have been riding through the Bible.

Now and then beyond the farmers he glimpsed a river, the Hondo, that had grown too shy on water to flow; instead, it pooled between rocks.

They would take their stolen horses to west Texas by way of Los Portales and sell them there; then steal more horses on the Llano and bring them east to White Oaks and sell them to the miners. East and west, back and forth: a Sisyphean life. The Kid thought, I'm just a horse thief again. As they emerged from the foothills it was cockshut time on the flatlands below: beginning twilight. The prairie flared up like an all-body rash which the shadow of the Capitans, creeping east, slowly balmed. Billy led them north skirting Blackwater Draw and continuing northeast across darkening plains. When it was dark enough they camped underneath the stars, burning sage and old booshwa in this seldom-crossed land. Tom brewed some coffee and brought Billy a cup. After a while, the fire declined to ashes and short-lived coals, the day's surviving heat cooled. "Has anyone ever counted those stars?" the Kid asked Fred.

"I did once."

"How many did you get?"

"One thousand eight hundred and thirty-two. But by the time you get a count there's new ones come up. The sky continues turning. You must keep on adding stars. I've never had the patience to keep it up for very long. I've tried different ways. Divide the sky in quadrants, count the stars in a quadrant, multiply by four. The trouble with that is they aren't spread out even. Look at your Milky Way — one long string of clusters. Anyways, a Frenchman thought he figured it out. He did a scientific count, got forty-seven thousand, three hundred ninety."

"That many?"

"That many. But then an Englishman got over ninety thousand. And a German after that come up with three hundred twenty-four thousand. It just keeps on growing. Like frog eggs in a pond. And there's plenty we don't see. They're too far away. Counting's important but what you see now — we're just scratching the surface."

They watched the sky in silence.

The next morning, removing the hobbles from the horses, Billy said, "Where's that Appaloosa?"

Fred and Tom looked around at the emptiness. Flattened out by hidden powers, by a cosmic rolling pin, the desert's false limits suggested immensities. Only to the west, where the mountains got pushed, did distance seem real.

"And the croppy? I only count twelve. We began with fourteen. You hobbled every one, Tom?"

Tom nodded and shrugged.

"I see tracks going west."

"You want to follow them?" asked Fred.

Billy couldn't decide. "That won't bring us to our milk."

The following morning they struck the wagon road leading to Fort

Sumner and held it for a while. But it made the Kid nervous; there could be other traffic. They strayed north toward evening, the sun at their backs growing weaker as it set. Already, its strength was in the other direction. It was circling the world to come all the way around and summon their shadows strung out before them. A cloudbank to the east looked so low in the sky it could have been a dust storm, though the air hardly stirred. The sun against this cloudbank gave it knobby contours, it shifted erratically, drifting in all directions. They heard a crepitating rumble. As wide as the desert, behind a sudden wall of wind, the cloud overtook them and they were plunged into a furnace whose whining roar and screech of dry wings sounded uncannily like actual fire. Fred waved his hat, Tom pulled his jacket over his head, his mount spinning around, but Billy just sat there unmoving on his horse laved by the grasshoppers brushing his eyebrows, catching in his shirt, trying to squeeze into his mouth. The air had gone black with them. They crawled through his mare's mane, devoured mites in her ears, and would not be shaken out. In a gesture as ancient as petitioning redress or expressing ecstasy, Billy flung his arms out to the sky and one landed on his hand and he brought it to his face: bucket-headed, pop-eyed, caparisoned, strapped, with muscular, buttressed, piston-femur legs, fully charged in its stillness, slime-green and black. Hello. He'd seen them like this in huge swarms before but mostly through windows. He'd watched them cover the roofs, doors, and shutters of stables and barns, and strip a field within minutes of everything but stalks. He'd even seen them peel fences and boards. They stripped objects so bare they no longer had names. The grasshopper snapped from his hand into shrapnel and the air ripped around him. These were angry beasts; there was nothing here for them. In the absence of crops, they'd become a din of beggars sounding clack dishes. He detected a tremble. The earth or his horse? A worm of fear began to spiral. It could be they'd lost their compass, they'd be stuck here for hours. You want to keep going west to the Rio Grande valley where green things still grow, he urged them. And as he thought it, they rivered. The shattered pieces scrolled and light leapt from earth and the blind cloud flooded the sky and was gone, its roar shrunk to nothing.

The three men were left speechless. Oddly enough, the world at their feet still swarmed with nameless spirits and imps, though the plague had now passed. The world's secret architecture had burst — its lost prayer etched on a speck of dust. Billy pictured apes, rats, and frogs boiling from the desert, teeming around him. It had something to do with his destiny, he felt, that destiny written before he was born. Composed in code, its detail was exhausting, and the president of heaven had cached it away in an underground cave and conveniently forgotten it. Each clattering hopper, born in the earth, had whispered a piece of that incomplete story but in their rush to proclaim it they'd drowned each other out. They'd produced only babble. Their dream of chaos, then, was not the world's dawn come to haunt its settled ways. It was just more noise.

The face of the world has changed since that time. It was older then; wrinkles and cracks spidered every landform; the earth carried hidden scrolls. Since then we've learned the use of machines to seal it up safely as smooth as an egg.

The boys looked around and spotted something strange: a herd of pronghorns grazing on the prairie as though not even interrupted. They were faster than the hoppers, they could have outrun them, instead they'd just ignored them — they didn't exist. The Kid began to wonder whether anything had happened.

Meanwhile, their remuda had scattered, mostly west. They could see the plumes of dust. But when they'd succeeded in rounding them up, three more were missing: a zebra dun and two sorrels. And the sun had set; it was growing dark already. Either these were especially far-ranging horses or someone'd been picking them off, Billy thought. How dare some rustler steal horses that had been already stolen fair and square by himself? This time they picketed instead of hobbling the horses, in a wide grassy swale breaking to the west, guarded on the north by a bottlecap bluff. Three or four cottonwoods, their leaves turning yellow, grew in this valley. The ground was broken here; they could camp at a distance and make a big fire so he'd think it was safe — but split a night watch from the top of the bluff.

Billy took the last watch. At dawn — pale sky, dark earth, purple ribbon where sky and earth met — he spotted a shadow approaching the horses, whose tails had started jumping. The thief was tugging at a picket when Billy scurried down, drawing his pistol. "You son of a bitch, raise up your arms. Where's the rest of my herd?"

The man backed up against the trunk of a cottonwood, leering at the Kid. In the uncertain light, this cocky little cowboy struck a sassy pose broadcasting dissipation. Hips slung forward, arms bowed apart, one hand resting on his Winchester's barrel. He tilted his head, his mouth hung loose. The slouchy wool sweater bagged at the wrists was two sizes too large, and the buckskin vest filthy. The worst thing about him was his slack-jawed arrogance. The way his wet mouth, stained with tobacco, loosely cracked open. The fuck-you smirk. "Who the hell are you?" asked the Kid.

"A man. Who are you?"

"You can be damn well sure I am not a woman."

"I am not a woman, either. I am a man and I like bad men."

"Is that so? Then you ought to like me. I'll kill any cocksucker that dares steal my horses."

"I take what I want. I aim to steal myself a living."

"Not from me, you don't."

"I'll show you!" the man yelled. "Look at me! Look!" He began to raise his rifle.

"Lower that weapon," Billy calmly said. But he didn't feel calm. His Thunderer locked on the man's chest. The sweet feathered flags of the grama grass around them took on a red tinge as the sun broke the sky, as did the tansy asters on their dead stalks. Only ten feet away from this smirking horse thief, Billy's gun began to shake. The world had slightly turned, that's all it takes, and now someone else tastes with my tongue. The impudent shit. His arms were still spread but the Winchester's barrel now inched upward, seeking a level. "Goddamnit, what's your name?"

The man at the tree said, "I am Billy the Kid."

The Colt's Thunderer fired in rapid succession, six clustered shots in 2.8 seconds, and dust flew from the holes as though from a rug thrown over a fence. Wisps of smoke rose from the splintery hull of the man's chest. Look. He's still smirking. He's still propped against the tree. Somebody woke up the wrong man this morning. His rifle fell clatterwhack while he himself leaned against the cottonwood tree, more insolent than ever, head lolled back. Billy reloaded and gingerly approached and kicked out his ankles. He dropped straight down. The Kid leaned over and stared long and hard into his eyes, which hadn't snapped shut.

Then he fingered his sweater, thick as bear fur. I could use a good sweater what with these cool nights. He surveyed the corpse, admired the new boots. They were V cuts, sharp . . .

◆ ◆ ◆

FRED WAITE ANNOUNCED he'd decided to leave. He said he'd go back to Indian Territory, he was fed up with running from the law. He wanted to see his family, wanted to own his own farm. "You want, you want," said the Kid. "Why don't you just take what you want like everyone else? We've got everything here."

"Well, I'm shut of that now."

"Don't you want to get the Englishman's killers?"

"That makes me no nevermind. It's over. How come it's so important to you? He's not the only one that died."

"Mr. Tunstall was good to me. He gave me a horse, a saddle —"

"I know, a gun."

"I liked him. The man had a heart."

"You hardly even knew him."

"I knew him good enough. He had polish. He was different."

"He wasn't that different to you and me, Kid. He was after the same things. So was James Dolan. Stick it to the Mexes. Make yourself all the *dinero* you can. Get rich and get out."

"That's not true. He was good to the Mexes. He let them buy things on tick."

"So did Dolan. The difference was Mr. Tunstall never lived long enough to take it out on their hides like Dolan did."

"How can you say that? Goddamnit, Fred, to hear you talk, you'd think there's nothing good in the world."

"There's good in the world and there's bad in the world and they're wound up together. You know the buffalo bird? The one that lays an egg in some other bird's nest? The other eggs in the nest are half the size of this monster but their mother's got to feed it once the scummy thing hatches. All it does is squawk and eat all the food and starve out her own chicks. The good feeds the bad and the bad grows fat. But it's part of the family. Inseparable."

"You say the damnedest things."

"Do I, now? You're the one that switched sides."

"Suck my dick, Fred! I thought you were my friend."

"I'm sorry, Kid. I was just saying."

"What the hell does switching sides have to do with anything?"

"Well, you wouldn't have done it without you divided the world in equal parts. Good and bad, white and black. That's not a regular world."

Fred and Billy's horses rubber-nosed each other, facing at an angle. Their riders fell silent. They were just a few miles from the Fort Sumner road where the shortcut to Los Portales forked east. Tom O'Folliard climbed off his horse and walked him a ways, making a circle. Clouds had blown in, threatening rain. A chill was in the air, they'd pulled on their gloves. Under a wide and endless gray sky, the yellow earth rippled and spread to the horizon, barren and flat. More rocks here than dirt, more dirt than vegetation. Fred swiveled his head, took in the wasted plains. "Well, Kid. I'm sorry. You know how it goes. I'm out to find some good, too. I just haven't found it here."

"Forget good. I'm after justice."

"Good luck on that."

"Alls I ever did was shoot a few people."

"I know, I know. You never wanted to hurt them."

"I've learned a lot, Fred."

"I have, too. The main thing I've learned is how to live with myself."

"Yes." Billy coughed; sighed. He turned away. "Well." He sighed again — blew out a tub of air. "It was a time, wasn't it?" He turned back and watched Fred, whose eyebrows had furrowed. With his mustache, they made a big X across his face. His startled scowl hadn't changed since they'd met — he always looked mad yet never got mad. "You have to say that, Fred. Good or bad, it was a time. Don't you think it was a time?"

"I suppose."

"It was. You gotta say it."

"Was what?"

"Quite the time."

"You make it sound like it's over."

"Go on. It was a time."

Fred paused. "'It was a time.'"

"Sometimes don't it all seem like a dream?"

"You want me to say that, too?"

The Kid couldn't help it, he felt his eyes widen like a little boy's, looking at Fred.

"Okay, okay. It feels like a dream. Where'd you get that sweater?"

"I've always had it."

Fred swung his horse around and made toward Los Portales leaving Billy feeling irked, uncompleted. When he was fifty feet away he turned and waved his hat without stopping. "Adios, boys!"

"Hey, Fred, hold up! I was wondering something."

"What?"

The Kid had to holler. "Was that you with Sue McSween the night before Macky died?"

Fred was still trotting off. A wind had come up. "What did you say?" he shouted as he diminished.

You and Sue McSween!

He scowled and repeated, "Me and Sue?" and stopped and said something but the wind intercepted and blew it away. Then he turned and Billy watched him grow smaller out there below the world's turning rim. He thought about how Fred often went missing when the shooting began. He'd taken the wagon road, splitting from the group, when Tunstall was shot. He did put a bullet into Morton and Baker at Blackwater Draw after they were dead — or did he? He could have shot into the ground. He could have missed Brady. And he'd slipped out of Macky's house after boarding Sue — if that was him in Sue's room. He grew smaller and smaller, small as a chigger out there on the desert, and finally vanished. The Kid turned his horse and made for Fort Sumner and never thought of him again.

· 13 ·

1879

Peace

Whereas it has been made to appear to me, that by reason of unlawful combinations and assemblages of persons to arms, it has become impracticable to enforce by the ordinary course of judicial proceedings the laws of the United States within the Territory of New Mexico, and especially within Lincoln County thereof, and that the laws of the United States have been therein forcibly opposed, and the execution thereof forcibly resisted; and

Whereas, the laws of the United States require that whenever it may be necessary, in the judgment of the President, to use the military force for the purpose of enforcing the faithful execution of the laws of the United States, he shall forthwith, by proclamation, command such insurgents to disperse and retire peaceably to their respective abodes within a limited time;

Now, therefore, I, RUTHERFORD B. HAYES, President of the United States, do hereby admonish all good citizens against aiding, countenancing, abetting, or taking part in any such unlawful proceedings; and I do hereby warn all persons engaged in or connected with said obstruction of the laws to disperse and retire peaceably to their respective homes on or before noon of the 13th day of October instant.

A PROCLAMATION

For the information of the people of the United States, and of the citizens of the Territory of New Mexico in especial, the undersigned announces that the disorders lately prevalent in Lincoln County in said Territory, have been happily brought to an end. Persons having business and property interests therein and who are themselves peaceably disposed, may go to and from the County without hindrance or molestation. Individuals resident there but who have been driven away, or who from choice sought safety elsewhere, are invited to return, under assurance that ample measures have been taken and are now and will be continued in force, to make them secure in person and property. And that the people of Lincoln County may be helped more speedily to the management of their civil affairs, as contemplated by law, and to induce them to lay aside forever the divisions and feuds which, by national notoriety, have been so prejudicial to their locality and the whole Territory, the undersigned, by virtue of authority in him vested, further proclaims a general pardon for misdemeanors and offenses committed in the said County of Lincoln against the laws of said Territory in connection with the aforesaid disorders, between the first day of February, 1878, and the date of this proclamation.

And it is expressly understood that the foregoing pardon is upon the conditions and limitations following:

It shall not apply except to officers of the United States

Army stationed in the said County during the said disorders, and to persons who, at the time of the commission of the offense or misdemeanor of which they may be accused were with good intent, resident citizens of the said Territory, and who shall have hereafter kept the peace, and conducted themselves in all respect as becomes good citizens.

Neither shall it be pleaded by any person in bar of conviction under indictment now found and returned for any such crimes or misdemeanors, nor operate the release of any party undergoing pains and penalties consequent upon sentence heretofore had for any crime or misdemeanor.

Lew Wallace, Governor of New Mexico,
13 November, 1878

Mesilla Independent, January 11, 1879
Lincoln, New Mexico

Gentlemen: I see by an article in your paper in which you predict that the peace in this country is by no means assured, Sirs, if you will be so kind as to publish this answer to your article I will state that to the best of my knowledge that there are no serious troubles existing in the county at the moment.

I speak from personal knowledge when I say that many persons of the two parties heretofore at war with each other are getting together and settling all old difficulties, several such reconciliations having taken place in my office within the last few days, and through my advice have become friends again and as far as I can judge it is the intention of all parties to use their best efforts to settle and forget old quarrels and disputes, and again become friends and aid the enforcement of the law. Our board of County Commissioners has been in session four days regulating the County. The corn contractors are filling their contracts with fine American corn such as this country can boast of raising in great abundance. I can safely say that we are now enjoying peace and plenty and those who doubt it can come and see for themselves.

J. B. Wilson, Justice of the Peace

Law Office of Chapman & Quinton
Las Vegas, New Mexico

February 10, 1879

J. P. Tunstall
7 Belsize Terrace
Hampstead,
London, England

My Dear Sir,

You will please pardon me for presuming so much upon an entire stranger but as the subject of this letter is in regard to your interest as well as that of Mrs. Alexander McSween, I have taken the liberty of writing to you. As attorney to Mrs. McSween I have had occasion to make myself familiar with the business relations that existed between your son and Mr. McSween during their lifetime, and also as to the estate left by your son. I have been busily engaged during the last three months collecting evidence in regard to the murder of your son and Mr. McSween and to the robbing of your son's store with a view to bringing the guilty parties to trial, and I feel quite certain that I will be able to convict the men who committed the murders at the next term of court, which will convene in April. Mrs. McSween has expended considerable money in collecting evidence and is very determined to have the murder punished. I think that for a foul murder that of your son is without parallel and the general public demand that his murderers should be punished.

I desire to call your attention to the estate of your son that you may make such steps as will protect it. In company with Mrs. McSween I went to Lincoln County in November last for the purpose of probating her husband's will, and upon our arrival there we found that Mr. Widenmann's bondsmen had commenced proceedings to have the letters of administration granted originally to Widenmann as administrator of your son's estate revoked, and that Mr. Widenmann had given the bondsmen a mortgage on the whole estate in order to secure him, and under this mortgage they were going to take charge of the whole estate. The mortgage that Mr. Widenmann gave had no effect in law only as against yourself but not against the creditors. After examining into matters I advised Mrs. McSween to take charge of your son's estate and had her appointed administratrix believing this to be the only way to protect your interests and those of Mrs. McSween, as much of the property was owned jointly by your son and McSween.

I find that your son was owner of 2,300 acres of land entered under the Desert Land Law, all of which is in the names of other men, and unless immediate steps are taken all or most of this land will be lost. I think Mr. Widenmann is derelict in his duty in not appointing someone to look after your son's estate in his absence. The charge and management of the real estate remain with the heirs, and if you desire to have the title to the land claimed by your son perfected, you should send power of attorney to Mrs. McSween authorising her to take charge of the land for you. I am certain that you could not trust the management to a more competent and careful person, and one who was a true and devoted friend to your son.

We have taken steps to have Colonel Nathan Dudley tried for the part he took in the murder of McSween and the robbing of your son's store, and I am confident of convicting him, which will make the government responsible for the value of the goods taken from your son's store. It is necessary to convict Dudley and Peppin to make the government responsible.

I also desire to call your attention to the circumstances in which are left the men who fought for your son and who have done all in their power to avenge his murder. They have been indicted for killing some of the murderers of your son and are without any means of defending themselves when the trial comes on. They were promised both by McSween and Widenmann that they should receive pay for hunting down the murderers of your son, but they do not ask any pay, but I think that something ought to be done to assist them out of their present trouble, as it would be a vindication of your son. If you can do anything for them, I think they deserve it. They have requested me to write and explain their situation to you, and you can take such action as you think proper.

I shall leave here tomorrow for Lincoln and shall do all in my power to protect the estate of your son. I hope that you will not delay in answering this letter and advising Mrs. McSween what to do.

Very truly your much obliged friend and servant,
Huston I. Chapman

◆ ◆ ◆

SUE MCSWEEN'S RETURN to Lincoln occurred after nightfall. No one greeted her, no parades were held, but neither was she stoned. Her house was gone. The fire had spared nothing. Her grand piano, prie-dieu, knickknacks, beds, and chairs were utterly destroyed, and the only things left were a discandied kitchen stove inside the broken outline of charred adobe walls. She and Attorney Chapman moved into Saturnino Baca's old place beside the Torreón, and furnished it meagerly with what could be salvaged from John Tunstall's store. Its cramped quarters, low ceilings, and dark rooms were a cross she had to bear, but she had Huston's help. When reports spread of her arrival, old friends helped, too. Former Regulators called and welcomed her home, and Billy Bonney sat before her now. Without leaning back, he perched on the edge of the day bed in their parlor while Huston raved on in his Morris chair. They'd been discussing the peace. Peace without justice, the lawyer declared, is hollow and tawdry, and the murderers of Tunstall and Alexander McSween must be made to stand trial for their crimes. "What bothers me," said Billy, "is all I ever got for pursuing those snakes was a stack of indictments."

"But who is there to arrest you?" Chapman said. "Peppin's resigned. Kimbrell has no heart to pursue old feuds."

"You never know who's going to serve you with paper. It's hanging over my head."

"The situation as it stands hangs over all our heads. It cries out for resolution, not the bromide 'peace.'"

On her rocker, Sue turned and looked at Huston Chapman. She turned her whole body instead of the head, slowly, as though afraid she might spill. Stiff-necked, iron-jointed, straight as a poker, she nonetheless cringed at the lawyer's woody face, broken and red and growing redder as he spoke. One entire cheek and brow was blistered with shingles, made worse by his three-day exposure to the cold on the ride from Las Vegas in Sue's open buggy, and he picked at the crust surrounding his eye — picked with his right arm, the left no longer was. Its sleeve was pinned up. He'd told her the story: cleaning a shotgun at age thirteen, he'd accidentally blasted that arm, and the doctor amputated three inches from the shoulder. A missing arm, a leper's face — you'd think he was all used up, thought Sue. But he hardly cared or noticed. In their amorous moments as well as in their attorney-client conferences, he'd pooh-poohed the idea that he couldn't accomplish with one arm and scaly face anything that others could with two and smooth cheeks. And his credentials proved his point. Chief surveyor for the new city of Portland, Oregon Territory; assistant engineer for the Southern Pacific; bridge engineer for the Atchison, Topeka, and Santa Fe; private attorney in Las Vegas, New Mexico; indefatigable lover. If anything he needed taking down a peg, Sue had sensed that right away. She would punish him tonight and that would show him, she thought, punish him for the blight on his face, for his mustard, his pride. For daring to approach her with his one arm, for touching her with fingers that minutes before had been lovingly probing his scabby incrustations. Yes, she'd discipline him. She frowned at him now. Frowning excited him. A painted, goat-in-heat grin wouldn't do. She'd settle his hash. And he'd rise to the occasion. How would you feel if you were *me*, Sue thought.

For Sue McSween, to unbend was unthinkable. Pieces of her would litter this room if she did not each morning wire them into place. Maneuvering herself around to face Billy, she was careful not to rock, her chair was a trigger. Gravity itself was a kind of disease that required inoculation, and Huston Chapman was her doctor. Already, wattles had begun to appear on the line of her chin, and chicken tracks ran between her hairline and eyes. Lumbago, bursitis, fallen arches would follow. It was Macky's death that had hastened this process, plus the loss of her house, of all her precious things. And how to express her sadness and grief without succumbing to premature decline? "The world is such a cold and selfish place," she'd said to Billy when he knocked at their door and asked how she was doing.

"Yes, ma'am."

She'd bristled. Gone icy. Gestured at the day bed, waved him into place. He'd always called her "Sue," never "ma'am," before. He jerked up his pant legs and sat on the day bed while she sank into the rocker without so much as dislodging it a hair. Was this what she had to look forward to now? Respect and veneration for her age and sex? Better to join her life companion in the home they'd been promised long ago beyond this sorry life, in that beautiful land of which Mr. McSween had many times spoken. And she would, she'd join him now, were it not for the lessons she taught each night to the naughty Huston Chapman.

Now Billy wavered. "Fred's gone. Hank, John Middleton, both of the Coes. Charlie's talking about he just wants to be a farmer."

Sue melted a little. "And what would you do if all this were over?"

"I don't know. Settle down. Trade horses. Start myself a ranch."

Chapman rested his chin in his hand. "I thought you wanted Tunstall's murderers to hang."

"I do. It's just —"

"As far as being paid, it's virtually a certainty. I've written to Tunstall's father on the matter."

"It's not just that, it's all the slaughter. It gets so you forget why you're even doing it. I thought you could get those warrants thrown out. The ones against me."

"I'll see what I can do."

"It would be nice to be able to steal a few horses now and then without someone all the time blowing your head off."

"Ha ha. Very good."

"I thought this was America. Land of the free."

"If they're free to blow your head off, you're free to blow off theirs."

"They don't like me to be so free, Mr. Chapman."

"An eye for an eye. That's how it works."

"Isn't that just the problem?" Sue's eyes clouded over looking at Billy. She rocked forward once, gripped the arms, stopped herself. "I would be very sorry to see you wind up in Richard Brewer's shoes. You're too nice a boy."

"I'd be very sorry to rot in prison myself."

"John Henry Tunstall admired you to distraction. He often told me so. My husband, too. He adored you. All of you boys worked so hard for our cause."

"And look where it got us."

"Oh, please don't say that. I've had a hard enough time coming back here as it is. Just sleeping at night in this poisoned atmosphere. Knowing what might have been. Those men stopped at nothing. You fought the noble fight."

For free, Billy thought.

"My dear, you make it sound like it's over. It isn't over yet," Huston Chapman pointed out.

"It is for me," said the Kid. "There's no percentage in it."

"There's rumor of a reward in your case," Chapman said.

"Reward for what?"

"For your hide."

"Has a figure been proposed?"

"I am privy to Governor Wallace's plans. He has mentioned one thousand dollars."

"A thousand dollars for me? Christ, I'm not worth it."

"He seems to think you are."

"All the more reason to settle this now."

"Wallace is coming to Lincoln," said Chapman. "I've convinced him that his presence is crucial to ensure a just outcome in this place. You can settle it with him."

"I've got others to settle with, too. When's he coming?"

"He'll be here in two weeks."

Lost in thought, Billy stared at Huston Chapman's pinned-up sleeve. Stared so much the lawyer squirmed. "How do you" — the Kid almost said *fuck her* — "put on a shirt?"

"Teeth come in handy. Or a helpmeet."

"I don't suppose you have trouble riding a horse."

"I prefer buggies."

The next morning, the Kid wrote to Jesse Evans. That evening, they met on either side of the wall of the corral behind John Tunstall's store: Billy, Tom O'Folliard, Doc Scurlock, José Salazar, and George Bowers on one side; Jesse Evans, James Dolan, Edgar Walz, Billy Matthews, and the newcomer Billy Campbell on the other. Dark shadows, bare trees, cold moon in the sky. The high adobe wall acted as a mask: they told each other the truth. "I wouldn't run with you cocksuckers ever again for a thousand dollars," said the Kid. The sum had wormed into his mind overnight.

"Nor I with you," said Jesse Evans. "You're a goddamn turncoat."

"Boys, boys," said Edgar Walz. Being brother-in-law to Thomas Catron, the putative leader of the Santa Fe ring, Walz saw to Catron's interests in Lincoln, Billy knew. "It does not make sense to perpetuate this row. Times are changing. No one's suggesting you throw in together. Just live and let live. That's what this is all about."

The Kid said, "That's right. That's all I want. Leave each other alone."

"Not a lot of chin music."

"You can mouth-fight all you want, I'm sick of it myself."

After a while, like boys in a schoolyard, they were scraping their feet in the cold dirt and looking down at their boots. On either side of the wall, they sagged toward the gate, threw it open, lined up. One by one, beginning with Billy, the Regulators stepped forward and shook hands with the Dolanites, each man coldly smiling. Those inclined to look away did not see James Dolan take out a pink hanky and wipe his little palm and short fingers but Billy did. Dolan flashed him a grin.

They repaired to the Wortley and at a long table drew up their treaty, Walz acting as scribe. The wording of the agreement was dictated by Dolan. One, no one can kill a member of the other party without first giving notice of withdrawal from the treaty. Two, all persons who are friends to either side are included in the treaty and not to be molested. Three, no soldiers will be killed for anything they've done before this pact was made. Four, no person will give evidence against a member of the other party in court at any time. Five, each side will assist the other in resisting arrest upon civil warrants. And six. If any person fails to carry out this compact which he has sworn to and signed, he shall be killed on sight.

Then they gave their word as men of honor to comply with these terms. Men of honor, thought Billy. He would give but never take that sort of security, and surely not from these men. He squirmed in his seat, refused their refreshment when Walz ordered a round, and wondered if he'd done the right thing.

"Let's celebrate," said Evans.

"How shall we celebrate?"

"We could shoot someone." This remark from Campbell set them all to laughing and stamping their feet and jumping up to hug each other, and the Kid went along with it. Soon, most were drunk and had spilled out the door and their revels could be heard, punctuated by song, gay shots fired in the air, and eternal oaths of friendship, up and down the town. Even Billy fired his gun. It's done with. Hoopee. They were heading arm-in-arm for Frank McCullum's oyster house, taking up the whole road — make way, nancies! — when in his great-coat and wide fedora hat, James Dolan said to the Kid with a grin, "You were always a pissant."

"And you a cocksucker. I mean that sincerely."

"Then we make a pair. We're some for our inches."

"Go fall on your face, Dolan, you're shorter than me."

"Not with our hats off."

"You won't admit it, will you? Every man has his own hell. In this life, I mean, not in the next."

"In the next it don't matter if you're a pipsqueak?"

"Let's find out about this one."

They broke off from the group. The collars on Dolan's double-breasted greatcoat seemed larger than staysails on a stumpy craft, and his black hat rested squarely on his ears sharp enough to slice the fingers that dared pluck it off. He had a dragonfly eminence — the eyes topped a spine — and this disconcerted Billy. Dolan's frowning smile with its smoldering pout seemed to know that the eyes had mesmeric qualities and thought this a hilarity. The man had a certain power, no doubt about that. He had bigness in his small-ness — the oversized coat emphasized this, as did, in a strange way, the pale-as-milk face. He removed his hat with two careful hands and ten deliberate stubs and the Kid whipped off his and they stood back to back in the middle of the road, but the parade had left without them and there was no one to judge. Billy felt a little foolish. The whole shebang was a charade. Finally, both hoofed it up the road to overtake the others, the raw son of Erin and the grubby horse thief with an instinct for survival and as much genius for depopulation as for seeding new replacements. He of all the company had not touched a drink and was itching to get this over with and leave.

Dogs barked. Homeowners barred their doors and closed their shutters. Sheriff Kimbrell had heard the promiscuous firing and lit out for Fort Stanton to request assistance of the military.

As the two gangs clamored toward futility, the Kid spotted in the shadows a noodle-limbed man with a lantern in his one arm dashing past beneath the trees. Billy Campbell stopped him. "Who the hell are you and where are you going?"

"My name is Chapman and I am attending to my business."

The Kid held back behind those who surrounded Sue McSween's lawyer, cringing on the man's behalf. The other Regulators lingered at the edges. Tom O'Folliard slipped away into the dark. Underlit by his lantern, Chapman looked ridiculous. He'd poulticed one side of his face with bread, the downroping bandages holding it in place lurid and loose; they resembled flayed skin. He set the lantern down with his one arm and scowled at the men, impatiently blinking.

"Well, Mr. Chapman, will you celebrate with us?" Campbell drew his pistol and pointed it at Chapman, waving the barrel in interrogatory circles inches from his chest.

"I don't propose to celebrate with a drunken mob."

"Watch how you talk. We'll make you, goddamnit." Chapman tugged his cataplasm; it evidently obscured his view. It looked hastily wrapped and the Kid guessed he'd been racing from the apothecary home to Sue's ministering arms. Campbell poked him with the gun. Chapman didn't flinch, though his eyes widened. They appeared to turn yellow in the waxy light. "You're just cake on both sides, ain't it?" said Campbell.

"You can't scare me, boys. You've tried it before. I presume your name is Dolan? You with the gun?"

"You're not talking to Dolan," Jesse Evans said. "But this man is a damned good friend of James Dolan."

Before the Kid could stop him, short-stuff James Dolan, showing his teeth, stepped forward in his oversized tent-coat and fired point-blank at Chapman, flaming the dark. Billy Campbell fired, too, the shots rang as one. Campbell's pistol downpoured smoke and Chapman cried out, "My God. I am killed!" In the moment it took him to topple over backwards his clothes caught fire from the flash of the powder. The burning wool stank. The men standing there gave him some space, all looking down at the spectacle. He burned on his back on a dark street in Lincoln, the fire already charring his flesh, and the nauseating smell nearly made Billy retch.

They repaired to McCullum's, ate oysters, drank beer. By now, all the Regulators had vanished save the Kid. "I promised my God and General Dudley that I would kill Chapman before he made more trouble, and now it's done," said Billy Campbell. He was shaking, fired up. Seated at the round table, James Dolan reached down, pulled up his pant leg, and produced a pistol. He offered it to Walz. "Go out there and put this in his hand." Walz looked disgusted and sniffed and turned his head.

"I'll do it," said the Kid.

Dolan grinned. He handed Billy the derringer and the latter jumped up, scrambled to the door, and ran out to the road. Chapman's whole body was in flames by now, lighting up the faces of children and dogs at the side of the street who had gathered to watch. Billy raced up the road in the opposite direction to where Tom O'Folliard held the reins of his horse. They rode out of town east, heading for San Pat. Five miles from Lincoln, he heaved the derringer in the river.

◆ ◆ ◆

> San Patricio
> Lincoln County
> Thursday 7th 1879

To his Excellency, General Lew Wallace,
Governor of New Mexico.

Dear Sir:

I have heard that you will give one thousand $ dollars for my body which as I can understand it means alive as a Witness. I know it is as a witness against those that Murdered Mr. Chapman. if it was so as that I could appear at Court I could give the desired information, but I have indictments against me for things that happened in the late Lincoln County War and am afraid to give up because my Enemies would Kill me. the day Mr. Chapman was murdered I was in Lincoln, at the request of good Citizens to meet Mr. J. J. Dolan, to meet as Friends, so as to be able to lay aside our arms and go to Work. I was present when Mr. Chapman was Murdered and know who did it and if it were not for those indictments I would have made it clear before now. if it is in your power to Annully those indictments I hope you will do so as to give me a chance to explain. please send me an annser telling me what you can do You can send annser by bearer I have no Wish to fight any more indeed I have not raised an arm since Your proclamation. as to my Character I refer to any of the Citizens, for the majority of them are my Friends and have been helping me all they could. I am called Kid Antrim but Antrim is my stepfathers name. Waiting for an annser I remain Your Obedeint Servant,

W. H. Bonney

Lincoln, March 15, 1879

W. H. Bonney.

Come to the house of old Squire Wilson (not the lawyer) at nine (9) o'clock next Monday night alone. I don't mean his office, but his residence. Follow along the foot of the mountains south of the town, come in on that side, and knock on the east door. I have authority to exempt you from prosecution, if you will testify to what you say you know.

The object of the meeting at Squire Wilson's is to arrange the matter in a way to make your life safe. To do that the utmost secrecy is to be used. So *come alone*. Don't tell anybody — not a living soul — where you are coming or the object. If you could trust Jesse Evans, you can trust me.

Lew Wallace

· 14 ·

1879

Wallace

MARCH 17. NINE P.M. J. B. Wilson's squalid one-room *jacal* in
the trees behind the courthouse. Old man Wilson sprawled on his
bed, Governor Lew Wallace majestically seated in a chair beside it.
The shutters down and latched, to cut the cold. On the table by Wallace a coal oil lamp that cast a feeble yellow light. Trash on the plank
floor: newspapers, oily sardine cans, a hoe, discarded shirts, one boot.
Even for the governor, Wilson hadn't picked up. Why clean if it only
gets dirty the next day? Wilson wore filthy pants but a fresh collar,
tie, and black jacket, his marrying clothes, for he was justice of the
peace.

Wallace sat there in a dark broadcloth suit with papers in his hand
and glasses on his nose, a portrait of himself. The Civil War general
wore a thick dark goatee shaped like an iron wedge. Heavy broad
mustache, bare spidered cheeks, high forehead, a thin rage of gray-
ing hair thrown across the brow. Tall and wide of beam, he heavily
stood and marched to the door and peered out into the night. When
he sat down again, his piercing right eye, the black one, the sentry,
stayed fixed on that door. His attention was divided; he was like two
people. Wallace had a theory about our *double nature* — the real and
the acquired. The latter was garniture, the former foundational. The

latter was invariably the result of education, but the former, like the divinity of Christ, as his novel-in-progress dutifully explained, was what we are at the core. And at *his* core, Wallace was an artist. This could be seen in the sensuous lips barely visible through the mass of facial hair, or noted in the large Roman nose and finely drawn nostrils, gaunt cheeks, sculpted ears. The sensitive might also have detected its hint in the dreamy left eye, the bland one, like a woman's, which displayed a pregnant absence, for it did not see this world, the yellow-gray room filled with trash, the old man on his filthy blankets audibly gumming a barely cooked chicken held by greasy fingers. Instead, it inwardly surveyed a scene as exotic as a harem: the market at Joppa. It conjured up balconies, gardens, silken tents. It sketched for a rude audience the donkeys dozing under panniers full of lentils, onions, beans, and cucumbers; the sandals and un-dyed blankets of the merchants; the earthen jars of the veiled women, the produce from Galilee, the half-naked children, their brown bodies, raisin eyes, and thick black hair attesting to the blood of Israel. Plus the brawny fellows with their dirty tunics, the bottles of wine lashed on their backs, and the doves and ducks, the singing bulbul, or nightingale, perched on a fig tree — Wait. This was daylight. Scratch the nightingale. Or perhaps . . . yes, a bird *market*, why not? That's the ticket, bright birds in bamboo cages. Buyers, whose purchases fluttered in their nets, scattering colored feathers, seldom failed to think of the perilous lives of the brave birdcatchers, who boldly climbed cliffs, hung by a single hand and foot from a precipice, or swung in a basket down the mountain's craggy face.

Wallace had also demonstrated in his novel, in the part he'd just begun — Book Eighth — that most of us lack hearts roomy enough for more than one absorbing passion. In one passion's blaze others may live but only as lesser lights. This came from experience. His passion lay halfway across the world, in the ancient civilizations of Rome and Judea; in Roman coliseums, chariot races, the gladiatorial combat, slave ships, pirates, the gastronomy of figs, and ultimately in the coming of the Christ. But not in this alkali wasteland of New Mexico, in these mountains grim and fixed as walls of adamant, in these horrible dust storms and hideous people, bedraggled and unfriendly, dirty, always babbling. They bent over their hoes, they ate the bitter dust, they cowered in their wagons. They found themselves at the mercy of outlaws who held life cheap and did nothing about it; instead they wanted *him* to bring them peace and order.

They judged General Wallace harshly in the war. At Shiloh, it was said, his division arrived at the battle so late the Union army nearly lost. He was relieved of his command, unfairly, unjustly, and had bristled ever since at the thought that he'd been scapegoated. He bristled now in his chair at the prospect, once again, of being blamed if the lawlessness in New Mexico continued, and consulted the scribbled pages in his hand, then pulled out his pocket watch; nearly nine-thirty. Squire Wilson, beside him, tossed his chicken bones on the floor, wiped his fingers on his blankets. Wallace fiercely reassumed his eagle look and watched the door and listened for footsteps. The mail-order kitchen chair in which he sat, with the flimsy arms, was carved with eastern squirrels. Ah, by Bacchus! he thought. Is he not handsome? And how splendid his chariot!

"He'll be late," said Wilson.

"He is late," said Wallace. From his leather portfolio, he pulled out more paper and with his Faber began a furious assault. Yes, a bird market . . .

When the knock finally came it was several hours later. Squire Wilson unbarred the door, swung it open. The Kid slunk in, wary, eyes searching the room. "I was to meet the governor here."

"I am here."

In Billy's left hand was his Colt's Thunderer, in his right the Winchester. "Your note promised absolute protection."

"I have been true to my promise. This man and myself are the only persons present."

Billy nodded at Wilson, who grinned, showing gaps in his nubby yellow teeth. "Squire." This was the same J. B. Wilson who'd issued the warrants the Kid and Fred served on the Dolanite faction before landing in jail; the same justice of the peace fired by Governor Axtell only to be reinstated later; the same old man wounded in the buttocks in his onion patch when the Regulators shot Brady.

Wallace stood to shake his guest's hand, who first leaned his rifle against the foot of Wilson's bed and holstered his pistol. He wrapped both of his hands around Billy's one, he wasn't certain why. A sudden rush of fatherly feeling for someone he thought would look brutish and imposing and instead was just a boy? He'd expected Ben-Hur, the eponymous hero of his novel-in-progress, or maybe Mallach or Messala, and got this comely-looking creature instead; got Jesus, not a hulking exotic. "You call yourself William Bonney? The Kid?"

"Yes."

"The newspapers have christened you 'Billy the Kid.'"

"They're always trying to pick a fuss. They prank up their stories."

"But you are the notorious brigand they write of? The young daredevil whose escape from a burning house surrounded by gunmen is still on everyone's lips?"

Billy shrugged.

"How did you do it?"

"Luck as much as anything."

"It took considerable bravado."

"I didn't have much choice."

"And you're the one who shot Morris Bernstein?"

"That wasn't me. That was some other Billy. The papers said I robbed a buckboard down in Texas, too, but that was someone else that took my name."

"How do I know you didn't take *his* name?"

"You don't."

"Did you shoot William Brady?"

"That's what the warrant says."

"And Andrew A. Roberts?"

Billy glanced away.

"Please sit." The Kid took off his hat and, hat on knees, sat on a kitchen chair facing the governor, who — thoughtfully, gently — tapped his massy brow. "I cannot help thinking — I mean to say, in my work, the most loathsome, wretched, appalling specimens of humanity parade before my desk. This nationality is like a hive of human bees. The vermin almost devour me. You've seen them yourself, I don't doubt. I cannot help thinking that you are above the norm. I know to what extremity you've been reduced. You have it in your power to — to clear your name."

"That's all I want."

"When I came to this territory, I found that the law was practically a nullity and had no way of asserting itself. Even a governor's powers are limited. I could not possibly have stopped the troubles in this place by civil means. I needed the military. I am a military man. I have never heard music as fascinating and grand as that of a battle. But your military here is one more faction, I am afraid it's taken sides."

"You can say that again."

"The president has agreed to declare martial law if all else fails. In my view, it should have been done long ago. There have been more than a hundred murders in this county alone in the last year. I have found that every calculation based on experience elsewhere fails in New Mexico. Still, permit me to think — I judge from your appearance — that your motives have not been without honor. This country was not made for civilized men. It is a wilderness without the manna, shall we say?"

"Sure."

"Yet, it contains some of the best grazing lands in the whole United States. The outlaws and rustlers will lose in the long run. The people of America need beef. It is inevitable that land holdings will become larger and beef production rationalized and made more efficient. With peace and the restoration of law, this territory will prosper, and I am determined that it do so. We were making progress; your wars in this county seemed to be over. Then Attorney Chapman was shot. It was cold-blooded murder. I knew the man, we'd met several times and corresponded extensively. In truth, he'd fired a salvo of letters at me and at others demanding Colonel Dudley's arrest. Perhaps he made himself a target. But the very public nature of this crime is all the more reason to arrest its perpetrators. We are at the pivot point. I wish to put an absolute stop to the resurgence of your deplorable 'wars,' and I intend to use every means at my disposal. Here is my offer: testify before the grand jury and a court of law — convict the murderers of Huston Chapman — and I will let you go scot-free with a pardon in your pocket for all your misdeeds."

Wallace watched Billy glance around the room. Squire Wilson had fallen asleep on the covers of his bed. It was cold in this shack. The governor stood, slipped his overcoat off the chair back, and wrapped it around himself. "If I do that, they'll kill me," said the Kid.

"We can prevent it. I have a plan. We seize you while you're sleeping. To all appearances, this capture will be genuine." Wallace sat.

"Who does the seizing?"

"You may choose the men."

"You ought to go ahead and get Jimmy Dolan before you seize me. He and Campbell done it."

"Campbell and Evans are locked up now."

"Not for long. They're bound to escape. And when they do, you won't easily find them. Watch the Fritz place, Baca's ranch, the brewery. They'll either go to Seven Rivers or the Jicarilla Mountains. Also, what I want you to do when you arrest me is put me in irons."

"I understand. You're afraid of the loss of your reputation as a desperate man. Are you still bent on vengeance?"

"I'm tired of all the killing."

"Why is it you know so much about these people?"

"I ran with them once."

"And now you've changed your mind? You were on their side once and you had a change of heart and now you think them bad characters?"

"I thought they were bad a long time ago."

"Are they angry at your — your turnaround?"

"Not unless they find out about this. What's that you're writing down?"

"The information you've given me about Dolan and Campbell." Wallace stared at the Kid with his black eye, the sentry, but the other was drifting. This precious specimen before him had killed how many men? The papers said one for every year of his life but of course they overstated. "Your duty is plain," he mumbled while writing, but even as he spoke he felt a touch of disdain. The Kid looked leery. He'd placed his hat on the floor, his knee jacked up and down, he kept swiveling his head. "We will put you in irons if that is your wish. Don't you worry about it. We'll hold you at Fort Stanton, how's that? Surely, that will not injure you in the public estimation."

"The only thing I'm afraid of on the fort is they could poison me there. Or shoot me through a window at night. I am not afraid to die like a man fighting but I would not like to be killed like a dog unarmed."

"I'll arrange that no harm come to you."

"Arrest Tom, too."

"Tom?"

"Tom O'Folliard. There's indictments for him. He'd be lost without me."

"Are you still bent on vengeance?" Wallace asked him again. "I've been told all this began when you swore to kill the murderers of a man named Tunstall."

"That's right. They murdered him, see, and I could have prevented it. I should of stopped them. Mr. Tunstall was a respectable man. He treated me square."

"And you're still angry about it?"

"I've calmed down a little. I'm sick of all the fighting. It still gets to me, though. You wouldn't know it sometimes because I make a lot of jokes. I'm not really a killer. I may be a general spiteful fellow, I've never been satisfied anywhere I was, but I have got some pride. These newspapers don't know the first thing about me. 'He will go down in history.' Well, if that's true, they better get it right. I'm not a cold-blooded tough. I want things to square up, that's all I want. Those people that killed Mr. Tunstall ought to pay."

"Attorney Chapman, too."

"The same damn men."

"Yes, your former friends."

"That rankles me, too. I made it up with them and look at what they did."

"I understand. You'd like your name to be cleared. You don't wish to be a scapegoat." Wallace smiled, the dreamy eye glowed. All at once his heart melted. "I'll level with you, Mr. Bonney. 'Kid.'" He held up some scribbled pages. "This is not the information you've given me. *That* is stored away in here." He tapped his forehead. "No, this is part of a book I am writing. *This* is where my heart lies. I have been writing it in my spare time in Santa Fe since becoming governor. Writing it in the Palace of Governors. Ha! Palace! Have you ever seen the place? Hardly a palace. But it has been my" — he sniffed — "my portal to a different world. The second door from the west end plaza-front opens into a spacious passage. Take the first left-hand door in that passage, pass through my office, and there is a room with one small window, grimy walls, undressed boards, and rain-stained cedar rafters. The ceiling bends beneath the weight of many tons of wet mud. Palace! I submit to you, this so-called palace is more like a cave. A place built when William Shakespeare was alive! It leaks on rainy days, I must have a fire to counteract the damp. But once there, at my rough pine table — not unlike this one — I am the Count of Monte Cristo in his dungeon of stone, lost to the world. I lock the door, bolt the windows, and bury myself in these very pages." He rattled the foolscap. "I know no happier way of passing the time in these dangerous wilds. It takes me so completely out of the present world."

Wallace smiled at Billy.

"My book is what they call a toga novel. The hero is a rebel and a fighter. He's much like you — impetuous. And he also seeks revenge. It is nearly his undoing. He is a Jew, you see, and the Jews are rebelling against their Roman oppressors. His father's long dead; he has inherited the estate; they were quite rich. Judah Ben-Hur — for that is his name — searches for another father in the course of the narrative. Various elders essentially adopt him: Quintus Arrius, a Roman; Balthasar, an Egyptian. I realize these names mean nothing to you. He comes into his own under their love and guidance but never manages to expel the hatred from his heart. Like you, Ben-Hur finds himself in a predicament. He hates a man who had been his closest friend when they were young, a Roman named Messala. This man turns on Ben-Hur, has him arrested. He sells him into slavery, confiscates his wealth, imprisons his mother and sister. And when the chance presents itself — I shall not go into details, but my hero, through the agency of a father figure, regains his freedom from slavery — when the chance presents itself, Ben-Hur crushes his former friend, his great strength and cunning leaving his antagonist a cripple for life. And note the exquisite irony, 'Kid.'" Wallace couldn't help placing Billy's sobriquet in quotes. "Messala had made his former friend a slave, and the latter acquired his strength as an oarsman on a Roman galley. Are you following the sinuous turns of my plot? Now he uses that strength to defeat his antagonist in a chariot race. While overtaking Messala, he snags the Roman's wheel with the iron-shod point of his axle. In the ensuing violent crash, Messala almost dies. Of course, he lives on to plot against his enemy but his power is diminished. There you have my story, or the extent of it thus far. I've researched it impeccably. It has a charming picturesqueness in its descriptions of scenery, persons, and customs. Its philosophy is sound and its moral and religious tone is pure. And it teems with adventure as well, 'Kid.' Adventure and love. In her jocular manner, my spouse refers to my novel as 'Christ and a horse race.' The Christ, you see, appears in my book. A daring feat for a novelist."

"A horse race?" said Billy.

"Yes, exactly." Wallace grew excited. Smiled, widened his eyes. Dry spittle webbed the corners of his mouth and he wiped them with his forefinger and thumb. "You would enjoy it thoroughly. You're a horseman, are you not? 'On, Altair! On, Rigel! What, Antares! Dost thou linger now? Good horse — oho, Aldebaran. Well done! Ha, ha!'"

"What sort of names are those?"

"Arabian. They are Arabian horses. 'Ben-Hur! Ben-Hur!' shout the common people, cheering on the race. Among the Romans under the consul's awning, it is a different story. 'By Hercules!' says one. 'The dog throws all his weight on the bits.'"

"The dog?"

"Let me put to you a question, Mr. Bonney. Ben-Hur has had his revenge; his enemy lies broken. But the Romans still govern his beloved homeland. He secretly raises three legions of Jews and trains them to fight and drive the Romans from Judea. But one evening he receives a letter from a friend. The letter tells him about a new king, a savior, who will lead the Jews from bondage. Imagine his disappointment, then, when he finds this man dressed not as a real king but as a common carpenter, with sun-scorched hair and ordinary sandals. What should he do? The question to me is hardly academic. This is the fork in my story right now. Should he fight against the Romans or follow this so-called king in the desert?"

"I know what you're driving at. It's Jesus, right?"

"Exactly! The Christ!"

"Well, he had his revenge, he might as well go ahead and repent."

"It's not a matter of repenting. The Romans occupy his land."

"Why not kick them out first then follow Jesus?"

"Is that how you would do it? Remember, this king is his spiritual father. He's been searching for a father all his life."

"I don't know why he'd do that. I never missed having a father myself. Fathers be fucked. All they ever do is put in a gay time and crawl out the back window. If they run into money, that's it right there, you never see them again. I'll tell you what you ought to do. This Ben ought to make a secret meeting with the emperor. The emperor gets himself up as an ordinary man and sneaks out of his palace and meets him in a shack like this one here. It's late at night. Midnight. Just a lantern on the table. And your Ben shows up and the emperor waiting there offers him a bargain. I'll leave you alone if you turn in the rebels, that's what he could say. It depends on if Ben is still in it for revenge or if he's for himself now. Sometimes there comes a time when your best friend is yourself and to hell with all the rest. Jesus Christ doesn't have a damn thing to do with it. Some people won't let you live your own life. You have to haul freight or make yourself an arrangement. Once you discover there is no hell, your job is to make it soft on yourself, hot for everyone else. Give that a try, Governor. That's how you could write it."

"What's that noise?" Wallace jumped up. The Kid grabbed his Winchester, Wallace warily padded to the door. "Singing," he announced. "Someone's singing outside." He unbarred the door, swung it open, peered into the night. In the dark outside, illuminated by torches, a handful of Mexicans, women and men, serenaded the shack. Wrapped in serapes, one man played a guitar, another sawed on a fiddle. The young women wore long silver earrings and silk-embroidered shawls; ringlet curls hanging from their piled hair had been pasted to their foreheads with wet sugar.

> *Por la luna doy un peso,*
> *por el lucero un tostón*
> *Por Bilicito famoso —*
> *mi vida y mi corazón.*

Wallace and the Kid stood at the door. "So you're a hero, is that it? A man of the people?" The governor's eyebrows wedged across his nose.

"They're my friends."

"An object of tender regard, I suppose. A good brave boy?"

Billy shrugged.

"Our meeting tonight was supposed to be a secret. You were not to breathe a word."

"Well, I told them. Just in case."

"You're the one not to be trusted, then. How can I know you'll keep our bargain?"

They stared at each other. Wallace filled with disgust. The three-day journey from Santa Fe, this filthy shack offensive to the nostrils, the snoring justice of the peace. When you consort with blackguards this is what you get. He'd already, in his mind, begun washing his hands of the cherubic "Kid," then he thought of Pontius Pilate. Don't be too hasty, General. When vacillation raised her six drooling heads he called himself general to precipitate resolve.

As for Billy, watching this fatuous man, he thought of all the chances he'd let slip. The chance to stay with Tunstall instead of racing past him the day he was murdered. The chance to kill Dolan when they stood back to back in the street the other night. James Dolan's grin was sheer you-be-damned; his life's purpose was making other people feel worthless. Dolan wouldn't keep their so-called pact any more than a sieve keeps water. "Go ahead and arrest me. You'll see what I do. I'll be at Gutiérrez's place near San Pat. Send Kimbrell with men you can depend on. I'll testify when the court meets in April."

15

May 1881

―――

Escape

Lᴇᴡ ᴡᴀʟʟᴀᴄᴇ, ᴡʜᴀᴛ ᴀ ʙʟᴏᴡʜᴀʀᴅ. Riding north along the Pecos, Billy admits he should have seen it coming. When he broods on Wallace, as he can't help doing now, halfway between John Meadows's little ranch and John Chisum's enormous one, the urge claws his heart and he has to choke it off, the urge to go to Santa Fe and take the second entrance from the plaza-front and knock on the door to the left in that passage and walk through the general's office into his cave with the single window and the weight of many tons of mud overhead and the rough pine table where the flannelmouth governor writes his darling books and tap him on the shoulder and when he turns around blow off his head.

He'd be guarded.

I know. It's too late for that now.

He sweet-talked you, Henry.

He never intended to hold up his end.

And you held up yours.

Shows you what a sucker, Ma.

Cotton drifts on the air from the trees along the river. Pronghorn tracks through a muddy draw lead to the water, high and fast from spring rain. Beyond the road ahead, black anvil clouds rise above the horizon. The cotton's everywhere, on his clothes, in his mouth. It scoots in lacy throws across the wagon road, thickens to folds. Iron-trunked cottonwoods growing high beside the river produce the thready stuff.

He testified as agreed against James Dolan, even Colonel Dudley. And Dolan was indicted, though his venue got changed to Doña Ana County. And once Billy'd spilled the beans and his own case came up, District Attorney Rynerson, a Dolanite, challenged the governor's right to grant him immunity, and Wallace never fought it. By then he was back at his palace in Santa Fe. The Kid got indicted for Sheriff Brady's murder, also Buckshot Roberts's, and was held under house arrest at Juan Patrón's in Lincoln. Holed up in his backroom, writing *Ben-Hur: A Tale of the Christ*, how could Wallace be bothered with a cocky *pistolero* in a starving desert where romance never flowered and Christ never walked? I wrote to him, Ma. I bugged him on his promises and never got so much as a thank you, no thanks. So I skinned out.

And look what it got you.

It bought me some time before Garrett caught me. It got me where I am. As long as I'm alive.

It brought you right back to a stealing whoring life.

Don't forget passing counterfeit money.

You never listened to me. You were always stubborn.

Don't start, Ma.

I want this, I want that. I want a piece of bread. You didn't ask for it, you screamed. Don't say I want, Henry, I said, be polite, say please. Please, Mother, may I have a piece of bread? I want it, I want it, I want it, you'd scream. I remember your brother got tired of your screaming and knocked you down and straddled your chest and there he was braining you on the kitchen floor. Say please, he's screaming, say please, say please! I had to pull him off. Remember that?

No.

Would you listen for a minute? No, Mother. No, sir. No, ma'am. You never listen.

No, Mother.

I always felt hard done by. You never would listen. Wash your hands, say your prayers. Don't touch that, it's filthy. Eat your fish, mind your manners, dress warm, clean your nails. I'd take you to the fish market and people would say, What a pretty young man. I've never seen such a pretty young man.

That's enough, Ma.

Lot of good it does him, says I, he's the devil incarnate. A boy that pretty? It isn't possible, they'd say.

Mother, please.

Then once you stayed in bed all day. Remember that?

Yes, ma'am.

You were eight years old, maybe seven, I don't know. You would not get out of bed, not that day nor the next. I had to pretend I didn't care at first but after a while I couldn't help myself. Get out of bed, I said. Say please, you said. Please, I said, Henry, please get out of bed. I'll think about it, you said.

Mother.

I was peeling you spuds. Boiled them up the way you liked. Never any coal. Cold stove, cold rooms. Is that why you did it? You were cold, so?

Mother, that's enough.

I was at my wits' end. Don't get up just to make me happy, I said. Do it because you want to get up. I cried, I paced the floor. You were such a cruel child. At last you said, All right, then, I'll get up. Happy, Ma? I shook my head. Are you doing it for me? — well, don't. It's all right, Ma, I'll do it for myself, I want to get up. Don't eat dirt, I said. Our people don't eat dirt. I was bringing you food, if you remember. Serving your majesty. Eat some more peelers. One day, you jumped off the table in the kitchen just to see if I'd catch you. Watch this, Ma!

Made a lump this big. Yours truly had to heat up a razor and cut out the lump. Remember that?

Yes'm.

You were brave, so, I'll say that. Lay there while I cut, never shed a tear. That's the stubbornness, too. Was it Josie or you got the coals down your sleeve? You were swinging the censer at mass, remember? And the lid was loose and two or three coals fell down your sleeve? High mass, if I recall. Of course this would happen right at the conse-cration and you couldn't cry out or stop swinging the incense, even as the coals burned through your flesh.

Ma. That's enough.

You must have thought then that God was sending you a message. I remember the shock on your cute little face. And that was just a taste. A few coals, that's all, not the fiery pit itself. I'm burning up, Ma. Make it stop. Make it stop. Mother, may I cry out? May I shoot that man, Mother? Shoot them all, Henry dear, every last one, what differ-ence does it make? Clean your gun, child . . .

A drumbling of earth comes from the road behind him. He finds a break in the sandy bluff above the river and descends through the *carrizo*. Dismounts, holds the reins. The hammering of hooves grows louder, breaks the air. Through the cane, he spots ten or fifteen Apaches under care of their agent, whom he doesn't recognize. Ever since Victorio lit out to old Mexico, those Apaches left behind have simmered down. They sit on their mounts upright as posts unswerv-ingly watching the road before them. Presumably on a buffalo hunt. A hunt for the sacred buffalo whose once-flood of meat has dried up entirely. Still, it has to feel good to get out for a change.

Further north, approaching Roswell, he spots a lone figure ahead on the road. This lump approaches strangely, without growing larger. The Kid begins to realize he's walking — unhorsed — not even driv-ing a buggy; hence his slow rate of inflation as he nears. He brokenly flap-steps. No threat, Billy senses. A peddler, he sees, pushing his cart. He's dressed odd, too. Chinese sun hat, linen duster, bandanna, sturdy black shoes. The bandanna's been raised across his nose and mouth but he pulls it down, exposing his face, as Billy draws closer. He looks as though both of his eyes have been blackened. Then the Kid sees it's just a pair of tinted spectacles. "Good day," he says, smiling. Short man, long coat. Wide nose, crooked teeth, a rash of black bristles. The two-handled cart on wheels is a cross between a trunk and wheelbarrow.

They've both stopped. "Good day," the Kid answers.

"I suppose you're another one of Chisum's cowboys?" His croak-infested voice sounds querulous, amused.

"No."

"You're a friend of Mr. Chisum?"

"Not no more," says Billy. "You're coming from there?"

"It's another ten miles."

"I know how far it is."

"Now I see you up close, I can tell you're not a cowboy."

"How so?"

"No leggings, no gloves, no rope. Nor, these." He removes his spectacles.

"What's those?"

"Dark nippers. Tinted specs. The latest thing, essential for cowboys. I sold bushels of these at Mr. Chisum's ranch."

"Why would anyone buy such a thing?"

"So as not to squint."

"What's wrong with squinting?"

The man widely smiles. "You're a sly devil, ain't it? Tell me — no. Let me guess. You've cowed before, haven't you? You're not a cowboy *now*."

"That's the state of the case."

"You've done your share of squinting, in other words. A hat doesn't help. It shows on your face."

"Shows how?"

"Gullies across the forehead, young man. Lines at the eyes. How old are you, son?"

"Old enough."

"Damage from the sun has caused men not much older than you to go blind."

"I enjoy to squint. What would I be without my facial squint? I wouldn't know myself."

"Squinting's not half of it. Sunbeams, dust. They molder the eye-strings, canker the ball. Spectacles like these are a salve for the eye. One day, you'll waken up and find your very sight decayed, like a cloth. You'll no longer see through it, you'll merely see the ragged ends." He opens the lid of his box on wheels revealing tinted glasses on a velvet display board.

"That all you sell?"

"There are ribbons, pins, needles, buttonhooks, and other such sundry underneath. It was a glad day in this starving country when I found products I could sell to the male sex, too. Men outnumber women here ten to one."

"How much are the glasses?"

"Two for five dollars."

"I will take five."

The peddler grins, wraps the glasses in tissue, bundles them with paper, ties it with string. When he hands up the package, Billy's Colt's Navy is pointed at his nose. His eyes widen, nostrils flare. His face holds the smile by force but goes dark. Billy slips the glasses inside his saddle bag.

"Hand that pistol up, too. The one in your left armpit, inside the shoulder harness. Reach inside your coat and draw it out very slow. When it's out of the holster, keep it flat against your chest. Then take it by the barrel with your left hand. Do you understand these instructions?"

He nods.

"Then reach it up to me butt-end first. And if you've ever practiced the road-agent's spin I hope to God you'll tell me first what to carve on your stone." The man hands up the gun. Good Lord, it's a Thunderer. I must have done something right. Thank you, Mother. "Close up that box." The peddler closes his box. "Go on. You can go."

"You've done worse than burgle me. You've wounded my pride, robbed me of manhood. What will I tell Cynthia?"

"Who's Cynthia?"

"My fiancée."

"Tell her you got robbed by Billy the Kid."

The man begins to hustle, pushing his cart. Billy lifts and cocks the Colt's Navy, *glick*, and sights down the barrel just to see him squirm, for he keeps on looking back. He skips, he runs, he turns to the side, he jerks left and right, heaving the cart ahead. The Kid's face stays dead. He feels it like a leaden mask. He watches the peddler shrink down the road growing smaller than a cockroach.

◆ ◆ ◆

IT WOULD BE nice to do Chisum some grievous bodily harm. Those chickadees over there in the tule. Suppose John Chisum was a pretty little bird and suppose that bird in the bulrushes was him — if I shot the bird, why then it would be murder.

He fires. Blasts the little birdy's head off. It's the Thunderer, he thinks. It's not me, it's the gun. He looks around at the sage, the grass, the low bluff, and spots a junco. Let's give old John another chance. He shoots again and this bird explodes. How gratifying to have a Thunderer again! Then he continues on the road into the cattle baron's ranch, soon hearing the rumble of hooves up ahead. His gunfire has brought the jinglebob cowboys galloping toward him in a large cloud of dust, about a dozen in all. They warily watch him, all having pulled their carbines and rifles out of their scabbards. "Jeffrey," says the Kid. "Andrew. Jim." He neither restrains nor hastens the easy canter of his horse.

They keep close behind as he approaches Chisum's house. The plank boards that cover its thick walls, Billy knows, are there to prevent assailants in the night from cutting gaps in the adobes. The clay roof is flat with a three-foot parapet sporting portholes, for defense. Alone in these wilds with dozens of cowboys and more or less a hundred thousand cattle to mother, Chisum is a guarded man; always has been. He's the man behind the scenes, as everyone says; he's made a habit of playing both sides against the middle. Advisor to Tunstall, partner to McSween, he nonetheless failed to come to the rescue when Mac's house was burning down. Claimed he didn't know. He'd once paid Dolan's Boys to steal horses from the Apache reservation, with Macky as his agent! The Dolanites in turn stole Chisum's cattle and altered their brands from long rails to arrows, though you couldn't alter jinglebobbed ears — you had to cut them off entirely, Billy knows — he'd done so himself. Chisum had even given the Regulators permission to steal a heifer now and then, if they were hungry or restless, since he knew they'd do it anyway. Not the steers, though; steers he could sell. How much John Chisum had to do with Billy's capture at Stinking Springs is unclear to the Kid but he has his hunches. Pat Garrett lives in Roswell, a few miles from Chisum's ranch. It was generally known that, once elected sheriff, Garrett was hired by the PSA, the Panhandle Stock Association, to capture or kill Billy the Kid, and Chisum may have thrown in with that crowd. He must have, Billy thought. Was it Chisum's idea, or Macky's — or Sue's — to offer five hundred dollars for Sheriff Brady's murder? It would be just like Chisum to bruit the notion abroad then back off as an innocent once the deed was done, for he'd never seen the money. The Kid had once threatened to shoot Chisum's cowboys at five dollars each until he reached the promised five hundred dollars, but he'd thought better of that. They shell around him now, the jinglebob waddies, hanging weights on his heels, as he climbs off his horse, as he snubs it, unlatches the gate on the fence, walks to the front gallery, knocks on Chisum's door. Cocky, yes. Hard as nails. The Kid does have something, does he not, of the air of Napoleon?

Sallie Chisum answers and turns beet-red. Billy once gave her "two candi hearts," as she carefully noted in the little red book she showed him in the parlor. She and the Kid had taken savage rides down the shallow Pecos holding hands on the gallop, but he's worked up now, he won't acknowledge their history. He narrows his eyes, peers across her shoulder. "Your uncle John here?" Chisum never married, though he's handsome, Billy grudges. And he's one of many men said to have used his friendship with Macky to help himself to Sue McSween.

Bootsteps in the parlor. Sallie's driven-forward chin and down-curved mouth and straw-blond hair swing around and there's her uncle, who is not exactly smiling as he approaches, more like indulging amused suspicion. Mainly what you notice on John Chisum's face is his strong sharp nose and his mustache tapering to twisted ends and his squinty warm eyes. The gray-haired, flap-eared, over-cooked head is what happens to cowboys who live long enough; but inside all that wreckage of skin, Billy knows, lies an angular man still softly magnetic. "I see you met our friend." Chisum points at Billy's eyes with a rolled-up newspaper.

The Kid removes his tinted spectacles. "He says he sold a bunch to your cowboys."

"He didn't sell us any. We laughed him off the place."

"May I come in?" Shit. How come he feels buffaloed?

Chisum ushers him into the parlor: tasseled sofa, horsehair chairs, filthy rag rugs, plank floor. A cast-iron stove with nickel foot-plates smells of soot and charred wood. The broken arms of a rocker beside it have been wired back on. The white walls show water stains behind framed lithographs of European monuments; the Kid spots a Greek temple. Sallie watches from the door then disappears outside.

"We've just been reading about you," says her uncle. He hands Billy the paper, a *Las Vegas Daily Optic*, and sits on the sofa. Why is rage so fleeting? Billy's been in this parlor a thousand times before, drunk Chisum's coffee, eaten his beef. Part of the cattle baron's charm, he knows, is a distracting hospitality, a refusal to stint. Do something quick before he trundles out the food. He sits in a stuffed chair and glances at the paper. "Billy Bonney," says the heading. It's dated last week.

Socorro, N.M. May 2. — 4:15 P.M. —
　　Advices from Lincoln bring the intelligence of the escape of "Billy, the Kid," the daring young desperado, the murderer of Bob Olinger and J. W. Bell, officers in charge. As near as can be ascertained Billy "the Kid," was in an upstairs room in the hotel at Lincoln, and watching his opportunity, slipped his handcuffs. He then knocked Deputy Sheriff Bell down, and snatching his revolver, killed the gallant young officer dead. Bob Olinger, one of the guards, hearing the shot, and with the remark, "the Kid has tried to escape and Bell has shot him," rushed upstairs. The moment he reached the top of the stairs the Kid fired, killing him instantly. He then went downstairs and at the muzzle of the deadly six shooter forced the landlord to saddle the fastest horse in the stable, on which he mounted and made his escape. Several men were at the house at the time but dared not offer any resistance. This is the report on the street, and I think it is in the main correct.
　　(The report of Billy's bold dash for liberty is confirmed by a private letter from Roswell-on-the-Pecos. The break was made on Thursday night, and the information has had time to reach Las Vegas by this time. Rumors are current that after his escape, Billy killed two men who took it upon themselves to recapture him. The men, Bell and Olinger, are well known in Las Vegas and have friends all over the Territory who should see that their horrible deaths are avenged. The governor will offer a reward for the re-capture of Kid, who was to have been executed on the 13th inst. — EDITOR OPTIC.)

"Hotel?"

"They have the courthouse confused with the Wortley," says Chisum.

"Newspaper men will print anything," says Billy. "Who wrote this letter from Roswell they talk about? You?"

"That paper came yesterday. It is four days old. This is the first I've heard of it, Kid. Did you kill two more men after you escaped?"

"Not yet. Plus, Olinger got it outside, not on the stairs. With his own shotgun." The Kid scours the paper but senses Chisum watching him. "Says here Governor Wallace will offer a reward."

"He already did."

"I expected a pardon from the damn governor. I ought to kill him, too. I expected Macky Sween to pay me. Tunstall was going to hook me up with a ranch. And you —" He raises his head, elevates his voice. "You owe me money, John. I don't care how you figure it. Mac promised us three dollars a day and we never saw a cent. Well, you're his partner, ain't it? Then word came down that anyone who killed Brady would get five hundred dollars."

Chisum rolls a cigarette. His stare never threatens. The thin-lipped smile makes sense, Billy thinks; he may keep a full table but he's mean on obligations.

A knock and the door swings open from the porch. It's a Chisum waddie, cradling his rifle. "Everything all right?"

"Yes, Frank."

"We're outside, Mr. Chisum."

"That's fine. There's no problem."

Like the late Macky Sween, Chisum never goes armed, he leaves that to others. In Billy's estimation, this also indicates pride; he thinks he can soft-mouth his way out of anything. He's one of those men who even while he talks you'd swear he was winking. He pretends to be on your side no matter what. "Now, Kid, listen up. If you talked about it till your hair was white as mine, you still couldn't convince me that I owed you money." He lights up his cigarette, draws on it easy, allows the smoke to scarf evenly from his wide mouth.

"We risked our damn lives. We murdered men for you."

"And I let you hole up here. I gave you whatever you needed on credit and never asked to be paid."

"Never asked to be paid! Never asked to be paid!" The Kid pulls his Thunderer and glares at the trim face, the slack-skinned chin and neck. Chisum's disconcerting secret is that he's thin and wiry and a hard worker, yet a voluptuary. The way he lights a cigarette, his care with the smoke, his flat-ass way of walking. He performs every action with forethought and precision and always a know-it-all smile on his face. Even now, with the Kid throwing down on him, he crosses his legs, leans back on the sofa.

This is John Chisum. The famous cattle baron. An idol of clay.

An entire slice of time has gone missing, it appears, for Billy's arm is around Chisum's neck and the barrel of his Thunderer inside the man's ear. They're sprawled on the tasseled blue sofa, legs tangled, boots kicking to get a purchase on the floor. "It was you who betrayed me!"

Chisum's face is red; he is still trying to smile, eyes darting around. "Betrayed you? I never betrayed you, son. You wouldn't shoot an honest man, would you? A man who always looked you square in the eye?" His breath comes in gulps, he's talking in gasps. "I know you've killed a few men but they needed killing."

"You son of a bitch. You're the cause of plenty of dead men yourself. All better than you."

"I always looked out for your welfare, Kid. Don't equate me with Wallace." His broken voice chokes and he looks pathetic — this large man in the smaller one's grip. His thin hair's going bald. Billy manages to stand, Chisum's pointy head locked against his hip, his gun still inside that rowboat ear. "When they run McSween and you boys out of Lincoln, where did you stay? Here. I fed you, I gave you the run of the place. Ease up a bit, would you?" Billy eases up. "I'll write to the papers. I'll write to the governor, remind him about the promises he made." The Kid lets go and Chisum drops, his large ear glowing red. Billy storms to the door, holstering his weapon. "You're not even worth killing, you bastard. I'll take it out on your cattle."

Riding north to Fort Sumner, he feels slimy, soiled, for menacing Chisum. He was right, he'd helped them out. Not enough, though. And he hadn't betrayed him to Garrett, he couldn't have, for he'd never got on with the PSA. The Kid remembers now, when Tunstall was alive, John Chisum railing against those Texas stockmen, who'd plagued him with lawsuits. He'd looked the other way when Billy sparked Sallie, though they'd stopped short of doing the natural thing, much to Sallie's regret. It was owing to her uncle. Billy used to admire him. His heart continues its plunge yet the rage mounts. He almost wishes Chisum *had* been the Judas, then he could have killed him. On an impulse, he gropes for John Meadows's biscuits inside his saddle bag and runs across a packed meal: salted beef, bread, a tin of sardines. Inside a fold of paper is twenty-five dollars. Sallie, of course.

He rides in the shallows of the river instead of on the road. Keeps listening for Chisum's cowboys behind. The world slides past without him. A turtle bellies down the bank into the Pecos. The bluff above the river, the lowering clouds, the sand dunes, the mud.

At Bosque Grande, he sleeps on his saddle at the edge of the trees. Here, the river widens, the grama grass thickens. Blue moonlight seeps through the outpouring branches. He double-wraps his blanket but the cold drills his bones, cold earth pouring into him, deep as an ice pick. In the gray-blue morning, the trees drip with fog rising from the river. Bosky used to be a beautiful spot but now it looks dead in this corpse-light. Everything shagged with icy gray drip.

Late that evening he rides into Fort Sumner and crosses the parade grounds past the old barracks, past the quartermaster's storehouse, toward Pete Maxwell's house. Pete lives in the former officers' quarters converted by his late father into a home, and approaching the picket fence around the house the Kid hears music from the dance hall. Must be the weekend; they're having a *baile*. The fence extends past both house and dance hall all the way to the orchard. Red storms of dried chilis hang from Pete's covered porch next to a side of beef. Billy snubs his horse on the road, opens the gate, climbs the steps. His friend answers the knock in bare feet and drawers; he's just lit his lamp; the twilight now creeps inside his corner bedroom and fills its nooks and pockets with shadows.

They embrace but Billy feels Pete's heart isn't in it. He's tall but dumpy, with lynx-whiskers thinly fringing his lip-top. Pete is not exactly a desperate character with hard ways and steely eyes. His gaze won't meet Billy's, keeps sliding to the side. "Jesus, Kid, how come you came back here?"

"Because of the food. I'm tired of canned salmon."

"Garrett's bound to find you here."

"Assuming I stay."

"Where would you go?"

"There's sheep camps all around."

Pete pulls on his britches and thumbs the suspenders up across his shoulders. Just throws on a jacket across the wool flannel undershirt. Sits on his bed and pulls on his boots. Both men know why Billy came.

"Is Paulita at the *baile*?"

"She's dressing up for it. Deluvina's helping her."

"Is she showing yet?"

"I'm afraid so, Kid."

"She shouldn't go."

"She always does."

Billy looks around. "Sounds like quite a kick-up they're having."

"The usual."

The Kid blurts out all at once, "Goddamnit, Pete, this is my family. You, me, Paulita, Juan, Jesús Silva. That's why I came back."

Pete says nothing.

"You'd think I'd be welcomed."

"I remember when you were nothing. Just a boy."

Billy hesitates. "What are you saying? Are you saying I got too big for my britches?"

"I'm not saying jack."

"You wouldn't betray me, would you, Pete?"

"I'd sooner shoot my own mother."

"Do you think I'm still a boy? Is that it?"

"Hell's bells, Kid, take it easy, would you? I think you're my friend. You know what one of the papers reported? Said you dyed your skin and let your beard grow so's you'd look like a greaser."

"You mean since I escaped? I grew a beard in a week?"

"You can't believe a word they say."

"Do you have that paper here?"

"Not that one. I got others. Go ahead, cut your own throat." Pete waves at the round oak table by his bed, and Billy thumbs through a stack of *Optics*, all filled with the Kid, or Billy the Kid, or Billy Bonney and his daring escape.

Las Vegas Daily Optic, Wednesday, May 4, 1881:

THE DARE DEVIL DESPERADO

The tragedy at Lincoln on the night of the 28th ult., in which two men were killed and a notorious outlaw escaped from justice, is greatly to be regretted, for many reasons. Two efficient officers, in the discharge of their duties, were cut down in the prime of rife manhood, and while death is ever sad, this picture of ruthless murder in a stronghold dedicated to justice, is sad beyond portrayal by our weak words. To this young demon, death is but a name for a condition beyond our knowledge, and not a direful means whereby the hopes and aspirations of the soul are ended. To him the drooping forms of widows and the tearstained eyes of orphans, give no token of the anguish within. Older in crime than Mathusala was in days, he is at once the terror and the disgrace of New Mexico. For years a flagrant violator of every law, and a murderer from infancy, he has, until within the last six months, undisturbed by efforts at his arrest, enjoyed the privileges of a tyrant. His name has long been the synonym of all that is malignant and cruel, and yet such is the inconsistency of human action, that his friends and admirers have been neither lacking in applause nor weak in numbers. Urged by a spirit as hideous as hell, he has well nigh exhausted the boldness of courage and the ingenuity of cunning to inflict suffering upon all around him. With a heart untouched to pity by misfortune, and with a character possessing the attributes of the damned, he has reveled in brutal murder and gloried in his shame. He has broken more loving hearts and filled more untimely graves than he has lived years, and that he is again turned loose like some devouring beast upon the public is cause at once for consternation and regret. For a few brief months he was confined, but regaining his freedom by a daring unequaled before, his unnatural desire to murder again is manifested in the killing of William Matthews and an unknown man, prompted by no motive save the black malice burning in his heart. With an impudence stimulated by past immunity he has singled out the distinguished executive of this Territory as the next victim of his wrath, and has boldly declared his intention of murdering him. Can such things be in a country where law and order presumably prevail? In the name of all the citizens of New Mexico; in the name of its interest and good name; in the name of children made orphans and wives made widows by this fiend; and in the name of that army of specters who accuse him from the other shore, we call upon all the officers of the Territory to unite in his re-capture.

"Would you listen to this. A murderer from infancy."

"Slight exaggeration," says Pete.

"'His unnatural desire to murder again is manifested in the killing of William Matthews and an unknown man.' I never killed Matthews."

"Maybe someone else did."

"I seriously doubt it. And an unknown man. Unknown to me, too. I'd like to shove all these papers down this scribbler's throat." But Billy keeps reading. He reads the accompanying article, then the one for the next day: IS THE KID KILLED? That gives him a good laugh. It seems that someone named Marshal Studemier has gunned Billy the Kid down on the streets of El Paso. And he's a Torquemado now! Whatever Torquemados are.

16

1867

New York City

THE HORSE THAT REARS up has just seen a rat, though how he spotted the vermin down there amid the boots, wheels, wagon tongues, skirts, handbills, canes, dogs, newspapers, legs, pushcarts, sandwich signs, single-trees, double-trees, the occasional pig, unlit lanterns hung beneath rear axles — not to mention nosebags, bustles, parcels, market baskets, baseball bats, grain sacks freighted on hand-carts, wheelbarrows spilling feathers — and street Arabs ducking be-tween and among crinolined dresses, chasing guttersnipes — and gouts of tobacco juice aimed at the interstices — is anyone's guess. Perhaps he imagined it. In rearing, he panics the mob in his path which, squeezing together, squirts a little girl into a cop's arms, while behind the rising horse his cart raises up, barely a foot, but that's enough to eject several sacks of coal. They smash open in the dirt. Like birds to seed, boys flock to the scattered coal on the street, fill-ing their pockets. Several have pails. The city cop with the girl in his arms pats her on the bum back to her mother but the crowd is so dense his meaty hand is forced to linger. This side-whiskered police-man then looks to the coal, and Henry and Josie duck behind a fruit cart. Their pockets are full. The rules regarding spillage are not their concern. Spillage goes to the poor; the poor are everyone. No, it's not the coal that worries Henry McCarty, it's the way that frog had been eyeing him and Josie, the something in his look. Josie says the police are paid fifty cents for each delinquent boy they hand over to the Protestants. That's why Henry's brother always keeps a lump of lead tied inside a hanky in his pocket.

The Protestants wait on side streets off of Hester, away from the mobs. Josie often points them out. They look upright and wealthy, wear claw-hammer coats, sport burnsides, wear spectacles. Their sisters in the Lord wear high-necked dresses with long sleeves and gloves but eschew corsets. They are ogres. They eat little boys. The Children's Aid Society, for which they work, first catches loose urchins with the help of policemen then questions them severely on their parents and religion and if they have either. Catholics get locked in a special room at the so-called House of Refuge, according to Josie. There, they convert you. They throw you in a cage and burn you with pokers until you give up the pope and if you don't they cook you good. If you do, they put you on an orphan train filled with others like yourself and ship you out west. Past the Mississippi, at each station they stop at, farmers and mine-owners stroll through the cars looking over the child-flesh. They pinch your arms and legs, pry open your mouths, examine your teeth. Those they want, they buy to work in a mine or slave on a farm and if they catch you being Catholic there's hell to pay.

"How can they catch you being Catholic?"

Henry asked this question that morning outside their Cherry Street tenement. In answer, Josie reached down his brother's shirt and pulled out his scapular. "See, as long as you wear this you're a Catholic. So suppose when they catch you, you manage to hide it? If they find it, you're dead. Those farmers in Nebraska — they'll tie you to a tree and burn you alive." Holding on to the scapular, he pulled Henry's neck, and swung him by the cord at the mouth of their alley.

"Quit it!"

He yanked Henry toward him, slapped his left ear with an open hand, released him. The ringing in Henry's ears wouldn't stop. He crouched there for a minute, jaw hanging open, clutching both ears, scapular swinging.

Now, the cop starts toward them and they run. Pockets bulging with coal, they run east on Hester but it's a desperate dream of running attempted underwater against a tide of bipeds. Their arms pump and grope, weakly prying breaches, their feet skip and slitter. Elbows whack Henry's head, he's used to it though, Josie McCarty has ever loved to smack his brother. Time about-faces; they're going so slow, against the current of flesh, it seems they've washed backwards. But so has the policeman. In fact, he's receded. Could be he's not chasing them at all. He's snatched a prerogative apple from a cart and his head swings back and mouth opens wide as though not to bite but engulf it entirely. But the brothers run regardless, from sheer doggedness and pluck, just to keep the ball rolling — from the fierce and all but animal pleasure of ducking under carts and dodging swift kicks and racing past shouts and ordinary clatter, snatching fruit themselves. At one point, strong hands lift Henry high and toss the little monkey over heads and shoulders, and he sinks through the hats, he gently subsides, lowering dreamily, he's ahead of Josie now. At a break in the crowd, he dashes ahead and waits on Allen Street near the corner of Hester, warily eyeing a pinch-necked man in collar and tails conferring with an oldish woman. They stand beside a lamppost, she grips a parasol, and he thumbs through a notebook that both of them consult.

Josie catches up. Here, the noise of the market — the rumble of wheels and scrape of clothing and murmur of voices and cries of the hawkers — is its own separate whale with a loose skin around it sliding down Hester Street. One noise trumps the rest: a large woman on the corner behind a barrel of oysters, screaming, "Alive in the shell! Alive in the shell!"

"I'd love one of those snots," Josie says. Henry hangs back but Josie draws closer to the woman on the corner, who faces away. With swift flicks of her hands, one holding the knife, she opens oysters left and right. The long wavy queue before her — kelp along the shore — laps against the mob moving through Hester Street. One by one, she takes their coins and slips them in her apron while offering half-shells like communion wafers to their open mouths. The arm with the knife swings a wild arc at Josie's backside when he darts past. Henry can't help but admire his crafty brother. He's managed to nick three oysters from the barrel in one quick strike and now he's flying back. Then Henry's breath catches. Josie's flying all right, he flies straight into the Children's Aid Society man — for that's all he could be — whose thin lips sneer. He's dropped the notebook to seize Josie by the collar, holding him out at arm's length like a fish. Josie flails and kicks; one oyster falls. When the arm weakens, Josie aims a kick on his shins below the knee with boot-toes, Henry knows, that are sharded with glass. The man howls and grabs his leg and hops on one foot, Josie lands on his feet, and Josie and Henry race full-chisel down Allen Street to Pike.

On Pike Street, they crack their two oysters with paving stones and pick out the bits of shell. They bite the salty cartilaginous plugs off at the base.

Cherry Street's an omnium-gatherum of tenements, dying shacks, cheap hotels in old colonial residences now in shabby disrepair, saloons, dance halls, and empty lots where mansions once stood with just the carriage house left converted to a brothel. Fire escapes geometrically festoon the row of seven-story tenements past Clinton Street. Ash barrels on the street. Wash hangs from windows and on the iron balconies morning glories grow in cheese- and lard-boxes. Lace curtains on some windows, burlap on others. They pass down an alley to their tenement behind its twin on Cherry Street, picking their way through garbage, trash, paving stones, a dead cat, foul rags, unmentionable deposits. Laundered sheets on lines over their heads cross every which way. In an alcove of their building, behind a fence of dismantled packing crates, a pig litter snuffles its overfat mother. Sharp stink of pigshit; then coal soot and dust and something else smelling like eggs poached in ammonia. Their home's in the basement, down narrow stairs to which the darkness clings like a blanketing fuzz, even at midday. Each step going down has a pressed-iron tread but you have to be mindful, loosened treads can snag toes. The stench of soot and urine overpowers down here. From wet, oozing walls, roaches slip out of cracks to sniff passing children. Sound of coughing, puddles on the floor, colonies of slugs and worms in wet corners. They locate their door by feel. Josie kicks it open and the two brothers unload the coal from their pockets into the scuttle on the floor. "Who's that, then?" The hoarse squeaky voice is one they haven't heard before.

"Is our mother here?"

"She's marketing," says the man. They vaguely make him out at the kitchen table with his white ghostly arms and hairy bare chest. Neither burlap nor lace hangs on the windows in their dark kitchen, for the windows up near the ceiling are small, the size of narrow shelves. Burlap has other uses; the walls themselves are burlap, varnished with linseed oil. Above a cup of steaming tea, the man at the table twists himself toward the boys. "Which one's Josie?"

"That's me."

"She said to take your bath."

"I'll do it later. We're off, so. Give Catherine our love."

"Done that already."

"Smartass," mumbles Josie.

Where was he this morning? wonders Henry. Back on Cherry Street, they aim west for Broadway. Today's Saturday, market day, bathe-in-the-tenement's-slop-sink day for Henry. His mother had washed him this morning when they rose, and no man was there then, unless still in her bed. She used reclaiming powder, the only soap in the house; his raw skin still stings. Saturday was when, until a year or so ago, he'd held his mother's hand to the market and back, but now it's the day he roams the city with Josie. And even that will change soon. Next week, Josie begins his first job: cutting heels at the shoe factory down on Water Street. No more scrounging rusted pins to clean in coal oil and wrap inside papers and sell for pennies at the market. No more, for that matter, annually massacreeing sparrows and robins with their fellow guttersnipes on the first day of May. It was always grand, a spring ritual for urchins, to march up Broadway past Wood's Museum where the shabby farms and squatters' shacks began and the trees grew more plentiful and the lilacs were blowing and cows mooed in fields. The bright sunlight and smell of unsupervised earth and perfume of apple blossoms will, in their memories, be forever fused with the slaughter of birds by means of slingshots and pea-shooters expertly wielded until their sacks were stuffed full. Then they carried them back to sell in Five Points. Henry's never asked whether Josie would miss it.

◆ ◆ ◆

"THERE HE IS."

"Who?"

"The one in the cape. I knew he'd be here."

"Who is he?"

Josie whacks the side of Henry's head. "He's your father, dumbbell. You didn't know you had a father?"

Confused, vaguely fearful, Henry peers through the window. It's a cigar store. The man is busy sniffing a balsa-wood container, whose dome he's just removed. Other gentlemen like him in black coats and plug hats float through the store but he's the most striking. His cutaway cloak is bordered with silk and his white wing collar looks stiff as a board. The black tie sports a diamond tiepin matched by diamond cuff buttons. His hair falls to his shoulders; a thin precise mustache and elegant goatee highlight his long face. He's amazingly handsome; shadows chisel the features. He removes a cigar from the container and lovingly runs it underneath his nose.

"Don't he look respectable?" says Josie. "Got polish, I'd say."

Henry just stares. This man — their father? The very concept of a father had been a morass of confusion for Henry when younger. Naturally, he knew what a mother was. A mother was someone you could never love enough. The ache of love he felt for his mother often seemed like a strong wind blowing through a world with nothing vertical to meet it, a wind across an empty desert. Fortunately, they lived not in a vacant but a teeming world, and mothers were everywhere — *his* mother was everywhere — and when her mercurial humors allowed her, she swept him up and waltzed him along and raised his little face and neck to her lips. She sang, she danced, she let him help her dress. He rubbed rouge into her cheeks and brushed her red hair and painted her nails and scratched her back on the sofa. Sometimes Henry ran the pads of his fingers across the mysterious map of her face (she would close her eyes), always landing at her smiling lips and teeth. He still slept in her bed — as long as no one else was there — when Josie kicked him out of theirs after a walloping. The full presence of Catherine threw the very idea of a father into murky shadows. What, for example, would a father's face feel like? That was inconceivable. Given the little he'd heard about fathers, it was easy to imagine that what people called a father was just another phase of his prodigious mother, her morning person after a bad night, or her sudden dark moods; I am not a good mother. Or her status when she stood at the kitchen table as the headwater of a course of admonitions: eat your biscuits, comb your hair, wash your face, smile. No one ever rose in this sorry world without a smile, Henry. Later, when he learned more about motherhood, though still not enough — about babies growing inside a mother's body, mainly

— he thought that mothers also made fathers inside themselves and the process had something to do with rubbing, which was the natural outgrowth of a mother's work, such as doing laundry.

At the same time, he thought that Josie was his father. He lacked a clear notion of scrapping that idea, it just seemed to vanish. When had he stopped thinking he'd grow up and marry Josie and live with him in a cabin north of Wood's Museum? Maybe the time Josie pummeled him so much his eye swelled up and closed. He came home and told Catherine a bully had done it and she grabbed him by the hand and pulled him out the door and up the stairs and together they ran through streets and alleys looking for the bully. Henry had to direct her this way and that. They searched the piers and wharves. This is where it happened; he ran in this direction; I don't know where he is.

What's his name?

I don't know. Would she thrash the bully for him? Was that his mother's intention? She enjoyed this, her bosom heaved as they ran, her red hair flew, eyes flashed. He couldn't tell her it was Josie; his mother would fly off the handle, he knew, and his brother would kill him.

But he could tell Hop-along Sweeney, the notorious hackum who worked for Kit Burns at the Rat Pit on Water Street. He could tell him it was Josie who'd snuck into their cellar and tapped a keg of whiskey, draining its contents into bottles he'd collected, which he then corked and sold on the street for a quarter. He did it; he told him. Sweeney was amused, looking down at little Henry at the door to the Rat Pit. And when Sweeney administered his careful beating of Josie, with a rolled-up newspaper soaked in plaster and allowed to half dry, expertly bruising every inch of his body while not breaking any bones, as two assistants held his arms, thus changing the color of the boy's skin from white to dark turnip, so that Josie had to wear high-buttoned shirts and jackets for weeks and hide the painful nature of his attempts to seat himself at supper and wield spoons and forks normally and clear his dishes from the table — when Sweeney did this, Henry watched from a crack of the door in his cubby in the row of school sinks back of Gouverneur Slip, where bodily wastes splashed into the river directly below. He watched seated on the hole. Watched and felt satisfied with the fairness of life.

"There he goes!"

The tall polished man with the grand sweep of step emerges from the door and strides up Broadway. Though not as packed as Hester Street, Broadway has its own soggy spissitude of persons. The difference here is they make way for urchins. Whether bucking the crowd or carried on the stream, Henry and Josie in their coster caps have the power of lepers — people magically part — and can keep him in their sights. When he stops to converse with a lady on the sidewalk, tipping his plug hat, they stop, too, and dangle at a window. Broadway's a clamorous, sluggardized swarm. It's a buzz of velvet tongues and gay sparks and high muck-a-mucks. The sidewalks are paved, as is the wide street, with uneven blocks of granite set in sand, and the line between sidewalk and street is dubious. Two-wheeled hansom cabs encroach upon the walk, scuttlers outflank the sluggish crowds into the street. One must be careful in the roadway, however — the pavement is yellow with flattened horseshit. It smells like a farm; the air's blue and dusty. Large green and yellow mail trucks, ice wagons, omnibuses, long vans, and flat-bedded drays piled high with casks swell the road, rattle teeth. A van with a painted scene from the late war — the surrender at Appomattox — has halted on the street, unable to move behind a dray trying to circle an unloading stage. Signs fill the air at every level of sight: Hats, Hatter, Photography Studio, Marvin Safe Company, Crouch and Fitzgerald, L. Sauter & Co., Band Rings, Hamilton & Hamilton, Fine Rolled Plate Chains, Dunlap & Co., J. B. Richardson & Co., Makers of the Royal Button, Lace Pins Etc., A. N. Lockwood, District Agent, Imported Saddlery, Arnold Webster, Gold Rings and Lockets.

Josie has found other fathers before. "This one's real, ain't he, Josie?"

"Of course he is, nit."

"How do you know?"

"I just do."

Cigar smoke enamels the air as they follow; he's lit up his purchase. His plug hat is nearly a full head taller than the other stovepipes, bowlers, and porkpies bobbing up the sidewalk. He swings a silver-tipped walking stick. Past cast-iron arcades, glass gazingstocks of dresses, hats, muffs, and gloves, past City Hall Park, the Marble Palace, the Broadway Tabernacle. Crossing Houston Street, they're flanked by Harry Hill's Dance Hall on the right, across the street, and the Gaiety beside them on the left, outside of which the person they're following stops and tosses his half-smoked cigar. Josie races ahead to salvage it. He offers it to Henry, who jerks back his head at the wet, chewed end just inches from his lips. Josie cocks his cap, thrusts the still-smoking cigar into his mouth, darts across Houston and struts up Broadway, Henry dragging behind. Their prey turns on Third Street, takes the Bowery north, pauses outside Paresis Hall, glancing back. Oblivious, Josie plows through the crowds half inside a trailing envelope of smoke. The man has marched ahead again when Josie and Henry stop outside the same dance hall and, waving at the door, Josie tells his brother there are exhibitions in there of a character that would shame even Adam and Eve. "Like what?" his brother asks.

"Like men dancing with men."

"Why would that shame even Adam and Eve?"

"There he goes. Look, he's crossing again."

They follow him up Eighth back to Broadway, which he crosses on the fly. When he ducks into Taylor's Saloon at the St. Denis on the corner of Eleventh, they watch from the arcade, through the high Venetian windows, watch him at the long bar tilt the saddle rocks and blue points down his jacking throat. He glances toward the window. They flush, turn their backs, kick their heels, stroll away.

They wait behind a column. He saunters out the door, strides through the colonnade on legs twice as long as theirs. They must scramble to keep up. Crossing Twelfth, it's little Henry who spots the bright fragment dropping from the man's hand, and who darts past legs and parasols and skirts to retrieve it: a silver ring. Josie says, "Give it here."

"No." Henry runs. He sees his presumptive father up ahead crossing Broadway at Thirteenth with long, loping strides. In the middle of the block, Henry breaks from the sidewalk and crosses Broadway, too, dodging hansoms, drays, omnibuses, pushcarts. Josie follows, screams his brother's name. Henry turns on Thirteenth and crosses again and runs up an alley, Josie at his heels. The man disappears into a door that slams shut in Henry's face. Josie lunges for his brother's hand, tries to pry the fist open. Henry pushes him away. Josie slams Henry's ear and shouts, "Give it here, rat-ass." Henry bangs on the door. Above it, a sign says, "Stage Door — Wallack's." They're still struggling in the alley when the door opens and strong hands and arms force them apart. "*Basta!*" says the man. It's not *him*, it's a doorkeeper, a squat and burly scaldhead in white shirt, baggy pants, a vest, and bandanna.

"What's this?" The pearly voice, deep, chiseled, and strong, comes from the open door, and the others freeze.

"You dropped this on Broadway." Henry holds out his fist.

With dignity, he steps into the alley, extends his palm to Henry. "Ah." He holds up the ring. Smiles with indulgence. Slips it on the vacant pinky of his right hand, his long dramatic face melting its own bladed features. "Two honest young men. Or is it just one?" He looks from Henry to Josie, whose eyes have dropped. Henry flushes.

This alley is nothing like their alley at home. It's paved and freshly swept, not a dead cat in sight. On the brick wall on one side, under glass, a poster says,

He slips the ring on his finger. "Tell him," whispers Henry to Josie. "Tell him who we are."

"Who are you?" says the man, who has evidently heard. Then he tugs up his pant legs and crouches in the alley, hands on knees, before the brothers. "Who could you be? Just another pair of urchins?"

The boys keep mum. The doorkeeper watches.

"Well, your hearts are true blue. From the bottom of my heart, I thank you for your honesty." He removes Henry's hat and rubs his curly head and with both of his hands snugs the hat back on, bill backward this time. "There. How does that look?" He smiles, winks. "You may think me a softy, but there's a story to that ring. When I first came to New York, I had in my employ a young valet, a lad not much older than the pair of you. I had grown very fond of him and had begun to feel like a father to the boy. I was sorry to hear him one day announce he would be forced to leave me. He was wanted on the farm. The laddie wished in some way to show his appreciation of all I had done for him but he was poor. So he took a dime, and with a punch he managed to make a hole in its center. With this as a start, he pounded it and battered it and worked at it for days until he had transformed that dime into a ring. This, he brought to me when he came to say goodbye, with tears in his eyes." The soothing voice rises, widens in volume. "And he presented me with that ring, saying, 'Mr. Bonné, this is all I have to give you to show my appreciation of your kindness to me.' You see, boys, you've recovered a most important keepsake, one I cherish with my life. This ring is not worth much, I know, but I value it because of the way it came to me. He wanted me to wear the ring as long as I lived, and I always shall, even though, sad to say, that boy has since died. He fell from a wagon and landed on his noggin. Such are the vicissitudes of fortune. Nonetheless, I can't thank you enough. Manuel," he says to the doorman. "Bring me two passes."

The doorkeeper disappears inside. "You're William Bonné?" Henry asks.

"Don't pretend you didn't know." He places both hands on Henry's little shoulders. Wide-eyed Henry looks pleadingly at Josie, who shakes his head furtively. The doorkeeper returns and hands Bonné two tickets and the latter sticks them into the belt of Henry's cap. "That will be all, Manuel."

He waits. The door closes.

Bonné looks at Henry, glances calmly at Josie, then cuts back to Henry and skewers his eyes. "You little sons of bitches. You scum." Still crouched before the boy, his powerful grip squeezes Henry's dinky shoulders, each the size of an egg. "I know what you're after, you little whores. You think I can be blackmailed? Is that what you're planning? I've had my eye on you since Fulton Street, you pups. Where was it?" he asks, his face grotesquely twisted. His eyes wobble in their sockets, his mouth has downcurved, spittle flies from his lips. He snatches the tickets from Henry's hat and tears them in half. From underneath his cloak, he produces a hunting knife. "Where was it? The Slide? Battery Park? I know — the Golden Rule. Where's your lipstick, little minx?" Bonné holds the knife before Henry's mouth, pressing the tip of the blade to his lip. And Henry can't help it; the very horizon sinks inside his body; his britches grow wet. Meanwhile, Josie's backing toward the entrance of the alley. "I wouldn't, if I were you, young man. Your little friend is in my power. Stay right where you are. Listen while you can. If I see you two again, if I ever run across you, I'll castrate the two of you. You're familiar with the word?"

The wide-eyed boys shake their little heads.

"It means cut off your balls. I've castrated beasties larger than you, I've castrated elephants. You'll be easy — your little pellets. I won't even need a knife, my teeth will do the trick." Retracting his lips, he flashes those implements, which indeed look very sharp. "Is that understood?"

17

May–July 1881

Fort Sumner

Hᴇ ꜰᴏᴜɴᴅ ᴅᴇʟᴜᴠɪɴᴀ ᴍᴀxᴡᴇʟʟ and she fixed him a feast — roast chicken stuffed with pine nuts, minced meat and spices, a *morcilla* almost as good as Yginio's, stacks of tortillas, dried melons, dried plums — then he went to the *baile*. Around the oblong room groups of men lounged, all in serapes, some on chairs, some in groups. On benches, the *muchachas* peeked out from their fans, watching the dancers, and beside them the wrinkled *abuelitas* cuddled their grandchildren under black shawls. The light was faint — candles on the crossed arms of the *arañas* hanging from the ceiling — but not so faint they couldn't see him. Children racing around or dancing by themselves stopped cold when he walked in, then the guitars, fiddle, and drum stopped, too. He watched the news of his arrival spread like a rash, saw the beauties with their fans and gaudy *enaguas* forget for a moment their various acts of painstaking coquetry, and the men leave their sweethearts and approach and crowd around him, and his heart swelled. "Juan. Domingo. José, where've you been!"

"We know where *you* been." Laughter, shaking heads.

"Where's Francisco?"

"His sheep camp."

As they talked and embraced and shared *cigarillos*, he spotted Paulita on a bench against the wall, biting her tongue — that's what it looked like. Pete sat beside her. He kept her in view while greeting old friends and answering their questions. He held forth on his escape. No, he never killed Matthews, just Olinger and Bell but he felt bad about Bell, he didn't *want* to kill Bell, the man wouldn't surrender. "You boys know I'm fair."

A chorus of *Sí*'s.

"He wouldn't stop when I told him. He'd of raised the whole town."

Domingo Swabacker asked, "How did Olinger die?"

"Like a rat."

A red-haired boy pushed through the crowd and ran up to Billy, shouting, "El Chivato! El Chivato!" The Kid thought of Tom O'Folliard, also a redhead, and reached down to muss the boy's hair then thought better of it. He looked odd, almost chinless, and he stared up at Billy with dark, sunken eyes. "Bang!" he shouted. Then a woman reached out and grabbed him by the arm, hissing, "¡Chist! Stay away from that man."

The men around him laughed. "You're a bad egg, Bilito."

"I'm here to steal your children. I'll rape all your daughters." They laughed again but not for long — a few simply watched him. Everyone in the dance hall was watching him, he saw, and at the door two men he didn't recognize whispered as they watched. "Who are those men?" he asked.

"Cattle inspectors," said Domingo.

The music started up again and who should walk in with a clutch of *amigas* but Celsa Gutiérrez. The Kid asked Domingo, "Where's Saval?"

"He got a sheep camp, too."

On an impulse Billy strutted up to these beauties, who squealed when they saw him and hid behind their fans. He took Celsa's hand, even though she was married — married to his friend Saval. Celsa had taken Paulita's place, everyone knew it, but she and the Kid had always met in the shadows, never on the dance floor, and she flushed, her eyes flamed, she tugged back against him while her little feet in their little *zapatitos* had a mind of their own and followed him like puppies. The dancers cleared a space. "It's El Espinado," said Celsa. Billy couldn't help it, his heart was in his mouth when, hopping to the music, she bent down and mimed picking thorns from her heels while in her flirty way, with lovely sheep's eyes, she glanced up at him and smiled. But he couldn't, like her, submit to this dance, he was too worked up, look at me, El Chivato! He leapt in the air — here I am, look at me! As he romped like a very demon from hell, as he jumped high and spun and stomped booted feet and raised storms of dust, the music followed his lead, it picked up the pace, and Celsa did, too. He swung her high and, flushed, she twirled in crazy circles, flashing her teeth, dreamy-eyed, laughing, this bird-boned woman with the high bosom, thin arms, dark eyes, and darker eyebrows — with the tightly curled hair and the silver *coquetas* and prominent cheekbones painted with red *carmin* — with the long lovely neck coated with white *abayalde*. Her silk *rebozo* luffed and billowed when she twirled. Whirlwinds of color, floating handkerchiefs and scarves. He knew that she knew that all the *muchachas* peeking out from their fans were talking about them. He could have had his pick! Celsa's laugh defied their tongues. It wasn't that long ago, back before his capture, when in quieter moments he'd shared with her his dreams about a happy, settled life and a large contented family and a hundred thousand cattle. Too bad she was married.

But he hadn't talked to her about her sister, not yet. That Celsa's older sister, Apolinaria, was Pat Garrett's wife had nothing to do with this. It was a dead heat for Billy: an angry Paulita could betray his whereabouts to Garrett just as easily as a love-struck Celsa could warn the Kid of his approach. They canceled out, he figured.

The music slowed and in sweaty elegance they danced a *vals re-*

dondo. His ability to leap, she teased, probably reminded the elders and *abuelitas* of the late Kit Carson, also a *chopito.*

"Don't call me a *chopito.* I'm taller than he was."

At a break in the music he left Celsa on the dance floor and walked toward Paulita. Heads turned; eyes followed. Against the walls, the crones all dressed in black were the very army of specters from the other shore described by the *Optic* that he'd read in Pete's room, and they gave him the willies; they were calling him to come. He reached in his pocket and pulled out his tinted specs while fixing on Paulita. He could make out her glare, the bullets in her eyes, and observed that the closer he approached the more livid she grew. Her face looked red. But the Kid worked his magic. She glanced around, began to melt, he could tell from the way she raised her fan to hide her mouth, he could see it in her eyes. "Can I bring you anything?"

"No."

"It's hard to see you sitting here like this."

"I imagine it must be."

"Remember we came to these dances every week?"

"They still have them every week."

"Hey, look at that, Pauley. They just filled the bowl."

"Then you better go get some."

He stood beside her chair. She kept turning away. When the music came back they stared at the dancers, and Billy said, "Every once in a while I took a look-see at you and got a chill down my spine."

"She's standing near the door."

"Who?"

"I don't want her coming over here, Billy."

They watched Celsa pretending not to look in their direction. Beside his sister, Pete asked the Kid, "What about Saval?"

Paulita said to no one, "He don't care."

"Guess who I saw? John Meadows," said Billy.

"He still alive?"

"He's got a new clock. What's he need a clock for? I suspect he never learned how to wind it."

Paulita fanned herself. "Wasn't it running?"

"Said eleven o'clock all the time I was there." He couldn't look at her belly. The last thing he wished to do was ask about the child and stir up more sass. He'd sometimes thought about the tadpole inside her, but as he stood there the tail ends of his vision told him it was hardly a tadpole, nor a bullfrog — more like a large bear cub, he thought. His mother used to say she'd wanted a girl. Then he was born and the doctor wrapped him up and said to Catherine, it's not what you think, and she forced back her tears. That's what she'd told him. What difference did it make anyway? he thought. Girl or boy, this is no place for either. It's a brutal, ruthless world, he somberly mused. "How have you been feeling?"

Pete said, "She can't keep anything down."

His heart began to melt. "We had some times, you and me."

"You can't just talk about days gone by and turn back the hands of time." Her nostrils flared, she pursed her lips.

"I was just saying."

"Things are different now."

"How are they different?"

"People can't always be shooting each other."

"Tell it to the gazetteers."

"I mean it, Billy. Someone's got to do it."

"Do what?"

"Stand up for civilization against savagery. Don't it make you feel rotten?"

Beside her chair he kept shifting his posture. Heat crept up his neck. "What is it that's supposed to make me feel rotten?"

"Shooting Bob Olinger."

"Olinger? Hell! I regret shooting Jim Bell but Olinger was a bucket of pus! Nobody liked him."

"Lily did. She's my friend."

"Lily who?"

"Lily Casey was engaged to Robert Olinger."

Olinger? Engaged? Will wonders never cease. The Kid experienced one of those revelations of another world embedded in this one that he'd been completely blind to. It was not unlike, while engaged in gunplay, hearing hoot owls call to each other. "Well, some women like dangerous men."

"And some women see through them."

"What's that supposed to mean? You mean to where they're cowards?"

"You don't have to stay with me, *Billy the Kid*, you must be tired of standing there. Maybe you've got some personal business to conduct?"

"That's all right."

"Suit yourself. You look tired."

"I am."

He found Celsa near the door. "Here's your *chopito*." Outside, he took her hand and they crossed the parade grounds. Her profile in moonlight contracted to a cameo. Torches and *luminarias* bordered the parade grounds and Billy guided her toward a torch stuck in the earth, released her hand, rolled a cigarette without spilling a flake, and lit it. Some boys from families living at the fort, four- and five-year-olds who should have been in bed, came running toward them. "El Chivato," they shouted. "Bilicito! *Hola*, Billy!"

"Hey."

"Bang bang!" one yelled, and Billy spat out his cigarette.

"Whoa. That fellow there shot out my snipe."

The boy asked, "What will you do?"

"Roll another."

The stumpy little toddler gazed up at the Kid as though at the Virgin Mary. Billy recognized the yellow-black rings around his eyes, the crepe-paper nostrils, and semiformed chin, yellow and crimped like the edge of a lettuce leaf — the boy on the dance floor. He saw that his red hair matched the bandanna tied around his neck. "Who was that?" he asked when they'd left him behind.

"Beatriz Meléndez's boy."

"He's got red hair, no?"

"So does Thomas Connelley."

"And what does Miguel say to that?"

"Miguel say he kill him. He shot at him once outside Hargrove's and missed. He's mostly gone now. Living with his sister in Belen."

"He's out late, that boy."

"She told me one time he never sleep, he's a devil. If Beatriz lock him inside when she go out he break everything around, then when she come back he cry for her to fix it."

"Must be the hair." The Kid pictured a door, a hand on the latch, a deathbed in the dark. *Who's this one, Henry?* He released Celsa's hand.

She looked at him, smirking. "And why is red hair so bad?"

"It's not bad, it's just red." *Who's that slut you're with now?* "See, my mother was a redhead. They scrap you right back."

They found the peach orchard and Celsa ran off in the warm night air and returned with a blanket. The papers said black malice burns in his heart but no, he thought, it's love. He cupped her chin, she put her hand to his mouth. He sucked her middle finger. Both were sweaty from the dance, and Celsa's *carmin* had smeared. She unbuttoned his pants, pulled off his boots, and he crawled on top of her. "What's this?" His fingers skimmed a scab on her thigh.

"Nothing."

Her shoulders were almost as loamy as his; they tasted like plows. Slow and easy, he thought — like climbing a wall. Sliding up her warm thigh and rooting inside her, he suffered himself to sob at the knowledge, deep in his mind, that he was back where he began, in a woman's flesh and blood, instead of hanging from a gallows. The space between her damp breasts smelled of copper. She wasn't like the others. She threw her head back, mouth wide open, and pulled him in as thirsty ground pulls in rain. After a while he whispered, "You first."

◆ ◆ ◆

"BOO! I'm Billy the Kid."

"I know who you are."

"Your sheep look fat, Francisco."

"Good bunchgrass."

Billy dismounted at the edge of the herd. Hot as blazes out here, and Francisco Lobato had found the best shade, but that meant he had to share it with the sheep who'd pressed around him. The Kid wedged through the crowd. "They're all wet."

"From the river. This is why they look fat. Fat with wet wool."

Billy looked around. The color of the empty prairie and hills kept changing when the sun ducked behind clouds — green, yellow, gray. Overhead and to the west, the clouds resembled sheep. He laughed. But far to the east one long black cloud was swelling like a corpse. It could have been fifty miles long, he thought, and it lay stretched behind a low mesa on the horizon. The mesa was in sunlight and all behind it black.

The sun was hotter than shame. Surrounded by sheep, sitting underneath a half-dead cottonwood, Francisco didn't rise when Billy approached, let alone embrace him or shake his hand. Beyond the tree was the Pecos; the water was high yet hardly seemed to move in the absence of banks. Francisco's wagon and mule both stood beside the river, and across it, raked toward them, lay a long plain lonely with sage and meadowlarks — he knew, he'd ridden through it to get here.

"These sheep are full of ticks, Francisco."

"They're not the only ones." His friend reached behind and tugged the back of his collar down and, in front of Billy, leaned forward. "See?" Just below the hairline, running down his neck, were five or six ticks, swollen gray buttons. Their color belied the red blood inside them. The Kid had never seen them that large; would they suck until they burst?

"I can get those off for you."

"Why bother? As soon as you leave I'll just get more." He leaned back against the base of the tree, his round copper face looking up at the Kid without expression. "How come you came back?"

"How come I came back? How come everyone asks that? You'd think they were let down I didn't hang."

Francisco shrugged. The full face and lips, the ram's horn nose with the high curled wings, the wide stringy mustache and brown raisin eyes betrayed nothing. He could have been pissing in a river, Billy thought. Then again, herding sheep depleted your social skills. Yet it wasn't long ago that Francisco and the Kid had bucked endless monte, hunted for squirrels, altered brands, dressed hides, docked sheep, and shared whores. Francisco had taught Billy the fine art of gelding rams with his teeth.

"You heard I escaped?"

"Of course I heard you escaped. I heard you were at Sumner."

"I was there for a while. Then the rumors started. Like Garrett had sent some cattle inspectors to hang around the place and look out for me. And Manuel Brazil come to town to sell his wool and asked too many questions. Plus the *Optic* reported my presence at Sumner. They won't leave me alone. Someone told me Juan Roibal was in touch with Garrett. He's a friend of mine, Francisco."

"He ain't your friend."

Billy looked in Francisco's eyes and waited. Then he decided he didn't want to wait, bad news just put him out of humor, and he glanced away. "I found my old cave outside Los Portales. Spent some time at Saval's camp. Can I stay here a while?"

"I have to get these sheep shorn. I'm gonna bring them in soon."

"Maybe I'll go with you."

"Back to Sumner?"

"Why not?"

Francisco said nothing. Suddenly he stood and all the sheep stared. Those lying down climbed to their feet and faced in his direction. "C'mere, Kid." He walked around the tree, threading motionless sheep, and descended to the river. Beside it, Billy spotted a ewe on her back, hooves straight up in the air. She wasn't moving. "Dumb as shit, sheep. They run like hell into the river and don't know enough to come out. They race to new pasture and suddenly stop and do not move at all. A big storm make 'em panic. They mash together up against a fence and crush their insides. Just die pressed together."

"What happened to this one?"

"Found her like that this morning," he said. "She just get waterlogged, you know? Roll on her back and can't find her feet. Then she bloat up and die. Watch this." Next to them, the river hardly made a sound. They were on a sandy alluvial flat strewn with rocks and pebbles. Back by the tree, all the sheep were watching them, several hundred at least. Francisco, Billy saw, had an ice pick in his hand. An ice pick in the summer. Bending over the dead ewe, he fumbled in his pocket for a match, lit it on his pants, raised the pick high, and brought it straight down on the sheep's taut belly. It hardly moved; you could see it was swollen. As his friend removed the ice pick a faint hissing sound began, and he held the match to the bloodless hole. A blue flame popped and burned as they watched, rising in the air while the belly deflated. "You could probably cook an egg over that."

When the flame went out, Francisco pulled a knife from his belt and cut a line from the ewe's neck to her anus. Ribbons of blood oozed into her coat. Then he skinned the dead sheep, reaching inside up to his elbows and cutting holes around the legs.

When he'd first arrived at Sumner, before the Lincoln County War, the Kid had helped Francisco with his lambing one spring and seen him jacket lambs. A ewe's lamb dies and another one has twins and how to get the ewe to accept a new lamb? Francisco's solution, passed down from his father, was to skin the dead lamb, cut holes for the head and the four legs, and pull this bloody jacket over one of the twins and bring him to the baffled mother. For good measure, he cut out the dead lamb's liver and rubbed it on the pelt then stuffed it inside the jacket. The Kid observed the whole process. The suspicious ewe after sniffing this changeling and walking off — after being repeatedly presented with this sorry spectacle of lamb — at last grudgingly accepted it and gave it suck, and several days later, once the ruse gained a footing, Francisco cut the jacket off.

I could do that, thought the Kid. There's my solution. Shoot a drunk in the face, skin him, dress myself in his body-jacket. I could get Francisco to bury the corpse and say it was me, then light out for Texas and start a new life and find a new mother. "People are sheep," he observed.

"Not me. Don't call me a sheep."

"I mean people in general."

That night, Francisco shared his mutton *caldillo* with the Kid. Billy was explaining his philosophy of life. "You have to be hard."

Francisco yawned. "Me, I'm soft."

"In Silver City," said the Kid, "I was just a boy, and one time I picked up a scorpion. My mother had married a man named Bill Antrim, and at the time he was still living with us. Don't move, he says. Hold out your hand, keep it out from your body, don't drop it, now. Give it to me, he says, be careful, go slow, don't get scared, don't drop it. Drop it in my hand, he says. No, he says, don't. I just stood there like a statue. Finally I saw a pair of scissors on the table and snipped off its tail. My stepfather says to my mother, 'He's hard. Some folks are just meant to be hard.'"

"Don't sound like he was one of them."

"She didn't want to hear it. She takes me by the ear and pulls my face against her breasts."

"Mothers," said Francisco.

They stared at the fire. Its smoke rose into the sky, underlit by the flames, and would never stop rising, like a heaven-bound soul, Billy thought. "What kind of fire is this, Francisco?"

"What do you mean?"

"A redskin fire?"

"It's better than that, it's a Mexican fire. White man makes a bonfire and burns up everything at once. You can't even get close enough to warm yourself good. Indian puts the ends of the logs together in the flames and pushes them in so they gradually burn. Mexican fire's in between — it's the best."

Billy stirred the fire with a stick. "What did you mean about Juan Roibal?"

"What about Juan?"

"You said he's no friend of mine."

"You said yourself he's in touch with Garrett."

"Have you heard that too?"

"Out here in the desert?"

"So what did you mean?"

"I didn't mean nothing."

"Was it him that betrayed me?"

Francisco looked away. Burst of sparks from a log. "Juan would never do that."

Billy looked at Francisco. "At least it wasn't you."

◆ ◆ ◆

SEVERAL WEEKS LATER back at Fort Sumner, the Kid was on a bench outside Beaver Smith's saloon when he spotted Francisco across the parade grounds walking into Hargrove's. So he'd brought in his sheep. But had he seen Billy? He wasn't alone, either, someone was with him: short and squat Juan Roibal, who also disappeared inside.

It was five o'clock, the hottest part of the day, and well into July, and Billy felt strange. A gluey taste filled his mouth. I've changed, he thought. I'm not seeing red. Everything is different now, nothing's the same. He'd been talking with his friend Jesús Silva, recounting the story of his escape for the hundredth time, and he felt like a pest. Was it true, as someone had complained, that he'd tell it at the drop of a hat to anyone who'd listen? Had he become one of those? You're just a swell-head, Kid. He cut the story short. He wasn't sure that was Juan entering Hargrove's, Juan lived in Puerto de Luna, he knew. A huge wing of fear all at once brushed his heart, it came out of nowhere. To resist dark suspicions had never been that difficult, though sometimes it was like nailing rats in a box. It took willful indifference, the stiff-necked conviction that what other folks intended was no concern of his and all he had to do was hold up his end. But this time around he couldn't stop it, he *felt* it — the wing of a bird as large as a dragon. The creature sank inside his body, picked the marrow from his bones. His heart flew around and he felt for the butt of his pistol like a boy feeling for his pud, to make sure it was there. Then the fear took off like a raven from a corpse and once again he was fine. But he still felt suspicious. Jesús beside him, anyone on the parade grounds, the men at Hargrove's, he mistrusted them all. He didn't care; let them plot. He'd always been able to look himself in the mirror without turning away. I can sleep at night, can't I? It's no concern of mine if Juan and Francisco go places together, they've always been friends. The world can go to hell. I'm not what I am. Sometimes you might as well just ditch your own past. What people like about me is my lack of hesitation — he's quick, that boy. If he feels like shooting something that's what he does, no questions asked. Laws don't apply to him, trying to catch Billy would be like trying to hold water in your fingers. How easy it would be to kill everyone he meets!

Then he sees, outside Hargrove's, across the parade ground, the man he thought was Juan walking toward the post office, and wonders how he ever made that mistake. He's not even a Mex; it's Barney Mason's cousin.

Jesús had to go now, he stood up and paused. "What you doing tonight, Kid?"

"Why do you ask?"

"You could throw in with me."

He searched his eyes. "That's all right. I'm meeting a friend. I do have a few left."

"Friends, you mean? Everyone here's your friend, Bilito."

But as Jesús walked off, Billy raised his voice. "This place ain't what it used to be, Jesús."

Later that night he whispered to Celsa, "Let's do it again."

"Don't you have to wait?"

"Does it look like I have to wait?"

"You going to have me crying out for help, Bilicito."

"It's me that cries out. That's the way I am."

In the orchard their proceedings disturbed an errant stinkbug caught beneath the blanket. The bug scuttled out with his ass in the air and headed for the brush at the base of a peach tree. Behind him, the blanket smelled of kerosene, but neither Billy nor Celsa, yoked together, noticed. Near the edge of the orchard, sphinx moths gathered nectar from the lemony flowers, larger than bugles, of the sacred datura. A datura beetle poisoned himself by gorging on the plant's delicious stems and leaves. A three-quarter moon bathed the branches of the peach trees, splashed the earth, flecked their blanket. They heard horses on the road. "Who's that?" whispered Celsa.

"Someone headed for the *baile*."

"There's no *baile* tonight."

"Someone going home, then." Talking, he knew, was a living demonstration of their separate existence, but that only sharpened the sensation of being joined, one flesh.

"El Chivato!"

Celsa reached down and tried to tug up their blanket.

"Who is it?"

"That redhead."

"Bang! Bang!"

"Bang yourself, pardie. Vamoose. ¡*Fuera!*" Billy shifted his weight to his left arm, found a rock in the dark, and threw it at the shadow over near the fence. It didn't move. He grabbed a fistful of rocks and threw them hard, but it was Celsa who yelped when the thrust drove him in. At last the shadow vanished.

They picked up the pace. Celsa hummed with each stroke. She whispered in his ear, "Everyone wants to be El Chivato."

"Not me."

Later, on his back, with Celsa's damp length buttered against him, Billy asked Celsa, "Has Apolinaria said anything about Garrett?"

"I don't know."

"Maybe you could find out."

"She's in Roswell, not here. I never see her."

"You could write. Don't you sisters write all the time?"

She shrugged. "You shouldn't ask me such things."

"Why not?" He grabbed her arm, tried looking in her eyes — she kept turning away.

"You're hurting me," she said.

He felt badly used but what could he do? His heart wasn't in it, he regretted even asking. He said, "I'm starved," and jumped to his feet but his knees buckled. He stamped the sleeping leg to shake out the needles.

"I got some boiled eggs back at my place. Nobody's there."

"I'll go get them."

"Take my knife in the drawer. There's a quarter section on Pete's porch."

"I'll get some of that, too."

· 18 ·

July 1881

Garrett

THE PAPERS MAY CALL me an atheist, John, but my thoughts on the matter are more of a whipsaw. You can be sure that if we kill or capture the Kid I won't be an atheist, I'll be a hero. And so will you." We were north of Roswell on the Sumner Road at dusk, myself and my deputies, John Poe and Kip McKinney. Those in the know claimed the Kid was back at Sumner. He'd haunted Fort Sumner for the better part of June, or so said my informant, staying with Celsa Gutiérrez when her husband, Saval, was out herding sheep, and racking out when Saval returned. Now he was there even with Saval around, for they were old friends and had learned to share; or so claimed the informant. It seemed incredible to me that Billy Bonney should linger in the territory. There was a great deal of talk about the Kid that didn't go, and folks gave statements without vouching for them, and I scarcely wished for the public to have a laugh on me if I showed up at Sumner and he wasn't there. People saw him everywhere. He was the theme of every tongue. The fact of men answering to his description, with *carabinas* strapped on their backs, and on horses like his, riding into town and acting suspicious and talking to persons known as partisans of the Kid, only multiplied his feats, for the bed is longer than the man that stretches on it. I've fellowshipped several Billy the Kids and observed that Kid Antrim was the one that prevailed. He's the one we were after.

Dust from the horses. New Mexico dust, I believe, keeps me healthy, they ought to bag it for lungers. In several directions, saddle-shaped thunderheads in the twilight's white sky shook off black curtains, but all was dry around us.

On my right, John Poe was a monster. A barrel of beef. He could spear you with those minatory eyes under beetling brows set atop a nose as wide and thick as my hand. To my left, McKinney was more rabbity, lean. He was either sneaky or callow, I couldn't tell. Of all things, he wore a New York bowler hat and his bushy eyes beneath it caught every grain of dust. "What do you mean, whipsaw?" asked Poe.

"I mean it goes back and forth. I'm not a decider. I believe in God sometimes but I also believe he's a horse's ass. Consider this man, Billy the Kid. He's been known to kill persons just to keep his hand in. What kind of god would make something like that?"

"I thought you used to be friends."

"We knew each other briefly."

"I heard you once rode to the door of a church and made your horse kneel just to rile up the flock."

"To amuse the children, John. I wanted to see if a horse could pray, too."

McKinney asked, "How long do you intend to ride tonight?"

"Long enough not to be seen. We can bed down across the river at dawn. Away from the road."

"Tell me again how much we get for this."

"The reward is five hundred dollars," I said.

"He's lost value," said Kip. "It was a thousand the first time."

"It was never a thousand."

"I'm a washed-in-the-blood-of-the-lamber myself," John Poe announced. "I shouldn't be partnering with the likes of you."

"Well, I'm an anythingarian, you can partner with me."

"Do you ever go to church?"

"I have my own church. Church of the Disappointed."

"Is that hard-shell or soft-shell?"

"Hard as to creed, soft as to ways of the world. I live among people of unclean lips, so mine are unclean, too."

"Are you referring to me?"

"I'll tell you how I started up this church, John. My uncle came from Ohio. He told me a story about his church, which was the Millerites."

"Ah," said Poe. "'Behold, the bridegroom cometh.'"

"You know about the Millerites? Then you know that the bridegroom never cameth. My uncle was a child, ten years old. It was 1843, the last year of time. His mother was a follower of William Miller, who had studied the Bible and footed up the numbers based on all the prophecies, especial those in Daniel and Revelations. Father Miller concluded that on the twenty-third of April, 1843, Christ would come in the glory of the Lord, with clouds at his feet and surrounded by angels, and raise the body of his dead saints, and change the bodies of the living, and both would be caught up to meet him in the air. Meanwhile, down below, the works of man would be destroyed. Fire would consume the earth, the bodies of the wicked be burned to ashes, and Satan and his fallen angels be cast into a bottomless pit and shut up with a seal set upon it, that he should not deceive the nations until a thousand years had passed. And after that he'd be loosed a little season."

"Quite a die-up," said Poe.

"And as we plunged into eternity, we'd all laugh the holy laugh and dance the holy dance, said my uncle. He told me all this in Louisiana when he come to stay with us. At the time he was a child, his family lived in Indiana with a clutch of Millerites. He remembered the fervor of their preparation. To a boy of ten, who never knew better, all this was a certainty, he said, it was as normal as pie. Besides, preparation was more or less a vacation. Since the world was going to end, people sold their farms or just stopped working them. Laborers quit their jobs. Preachers told their flocks to sell all their property and scatter the proceeds. He heard tell of a grocer that burned all his goods, refusing to even save any for his family. No need for food. One task that made sense to my uncle, and to me when he told it, was to find a high hill so the Lord wouldn't miss you down there on the earth raising up your hands, crying, 'Me! Me next!' There was one a half-mile from their iron-dirt farm with a grassy slope on top. The thing of it was, when the day come, my uncle hadn't changed; he was still a child. He and the other children run around and played prisoner's base and pulled each other's hair and the boys spit at one another — the usual. Anyway, as you know, the world did not end — unless this life we live now is a dream. Night fell, it got cold, and they all drifted home a few folks at a time, all disappointed. But the preachers were not to be buffaloed that easy. They reformed their calculations. Uh-oh, they said, we forgot a few months, and when they toted it up a new date was announced: October twenty-first, 1844. By then, my uncle's family had moved to Ohio. One woman in Ohio murdered all five of her children to give them a head start and that did give my uncle's people pause, but most folks dismissed it and shook their smiling heads. My uncle said the believers were all drunk on hope. They couldn't see straight. He himself was a year older now and fed a little more off the grown people's range. This was to be the great year of jubilees, when all the bondsmen of the world shall be set free. October came. Same preparations, same search for a hill, same orgy of giveaways and quitting of jobs and mad frenzies of conviction. Wild-eyed men running around, acting like children themselves, said my uncle. Comes October twenty-first. Same climb up a hill, this time in the rain, but when the clouds part a great cry goes up. The sun emerges from the clouds! People laugh and cry, start to hugging each other! Children on their daddies' shoulders. But the shoulders get tired. Same long wait, same fatigue, same sinking of the heart when twilight is over and night has fallen. Same sagging walk home after midnight. Same scoffers taunting my uncle and his people, same gangs of toughs throwing eggs at their house.

"Had the Bible proved a failure? Was there no God, no heaven, no golden home-city? No paradise? Was all they had believed but a cunning fable? The grownups tried to figure it out and come up with some answers. After the little book is eaten, and sweet in the mouth, there will be bitterness, they said, quoting Revelations, and they decided that that's what they had now. It was pride and over-zealousness that did them in, they said. And, lo, a little light began to break through. They saw that there was to be a waiting time, a long midnight before the Lord would appear. Thus, they came into the tarrying time. We're in it now, he said. As for me, this story made me look at the world in a different light. Eventually, I made my way west, hunted buffalo in Texas, fought redskins, cowed. The way I see it now, the world did indeed come to an end, it's just that nothing changed. It still looks the same. The difference is the disappoint-ment. This has certain rewards. In my church, we do without climb-ing hills and reaching for the Lord."

"That's an awful story."

"You're welcome to join."

"Do you believe in justice?"

It was dark by now. My tailbone monitored the gait of my mount. I suspect he'd caught a stone in the frog of his foot. In the darkness, the desert swallowed up sound, making heavy clops sound like snap-ping toothpicks. "Justice, I believe, is for them of stiff backs not afraid to be disappointed. What is disappointment but a hungry calf suck-ing up his mother's grief? Even Christ was disappointed. 'My God, my God, why hast thou forsaken me?' Me, I wake up disappointed, do my business disappointed, go to bed disappointed. If I start feeling good, all I need do is tell myself it won't last and right away I'm back where I started — disappointed. I'm disappointed when I'm happy, disappointed when I'm glum, disappointed when I'm disappointed. I don't know how I'd live without it."

John Poe said, "I shouldn't have come. You're no kind of lawman. Do you expect to be disappointed on this business?"

"Of course I do. Either way."

"What do you mean, either way?"

"We kill him or he kills us."

♦ ♦ ♦

I'D WRITTEN TO Manuel Brazil to meet us at the Tayban Arroyo on the night of the thirteenth but he was not there. When morning came, I asked John Poe if he'd ever been to Sumner; was he known around the place?

"Hardly," he answered. "Liked even less."

"People have to know a man before they can dislike him."

"Not sheriff's deputies."

I sent him ahead to the fort to scout the lay. He come back that night with uncertain information. He hadn't seen the Kid and did not want to appear overcurious about him, though from all indications he thought he might be about. Billy Bonney was not an unadulterated fool. It wasn't but last week the reports were given out that he was living with Celsa, but his ability to slip in and out of a place was known throughout the county. "Did anyone recognize you?" I asked.

"They wouldn't know me from Adam's off ox."

We pulled for the fort after dark and unhorsed at its edge. On foot, we lingered near Hargrove's saloon close by the orchard. From there we kept a sharp lookout on the door in the old quartermaster storehouse where Celsa lived. It was necessary to keep in mind he might have known we were there and was trying to work us. A man rose up from the orchard to our right, too obscure to identify, and jumped the fence and walked off. As our sequel will show, although I didn't know it then, this was the Kid himself. I realize now he was with Celsa in their love-bower, which they used when Saval was back from the sheep camps. I changed my notion and told Kip and

John we ought to go down to Pete Maxwell's house, but by circling the fort, not proceeding through it. It had occurred to me to question Pete on the Kid's whereabouts. John Poe by now was disgusted with my ways and thought our caution foolish and I was acting in a manner half froze, half scared to death. At Pete's, I left Poe and McKinney outside, the former by the gate, McKinney on the steps leading to the porch still in his bowler hat. A rattle of chilis shaped like a plumb bob hung on the porch and beside them a quarter section of beef. Pete's room was on the corner. His name is Pete but all call him Pedro. I softly knocked. "¿*Quién es?*" he said, and I identified myself and walked inside more by memory than sight, for all was perfect darkness in there, then found Pete's bed against the far wall and sat at the head of the bed beside him. "Is he here?" I asked. "Talk English."

"Is that you, Garrett? Hold on a minute, let me wake up."

There were footsteps on the porch. It could have been Kip or John. My hands shook, and I thought of the overlong barrel on my Peacemaker, its blued steel. It wasn't something a person could rush into play. The door flew open and a man barged inside, I could tell his back was toward us by the oddly distant voice. "¿*Quién es?*" he said to someone on the porch. He padded backwards in our general direction, a weapon in his right hand, a skinner in his left, his form barely visible in the lesser darkness outlined by the door. I didn't dare speak. I could see he was turning. "¿*Pedro, quiénes son estos hombres afuera?*"

"That's him," whispered Pete into my ear, and when he said this I fumbled for my gun. I couldn't pull it from the holster. I suspected all at once, as he swung around, that he felt or saw the presence of another man at the head of Pete's bed. Within a foot of my breast he raised his pistol while concurrently edging back toward the door, and he appeared to hesitate. Somehow I fired, not having consciously retrieved my weapon. I threw myself aside and felt but didn't hear the concussion of the air as a ball passed my head. A .45 makes such a noise in a room that your ears keep on ringing, you can't hear a damn thing. I shot a second time even as his body fell. These events took a mere fraction of time. Later, Poe and McKinney told me three shots were heard, which confirmed that he'd fired between my two volleys, but we never could find a mark on the wall. And in the chamber of his Thunderer, when we examined it afterwards, though the hammer was resting on a shell, it was clearly an old one fired some time ago; and I knew for a certainty that the Kid, like many others, carried his weapon in this very manner, for reasons of safety. So where the third bullet came from, and whence it went, still remains for me a mystery.

As we later learned, he'd ventured onto Pete's porch to cut a slice of meat from a quarter section hanging there; and spotting Poe and McKinney on the steps, he burst into Pete's room to ask who they were. The timing was propitious; a minute earlier or later and I'd not have been there.

At my feet, he kicked. He lay on his face wheezing and coughing like a dog being strangled. His breath foamed then ceased. I didn't feel much at all. Yet, I shook like a pup. Christ, what a wide-eyed lamb, I thought, looking down at his body. He's just a lost child. But a cocky little shit. At last, I told myself, he's Billy the Kid. And I am Pat Garrett.

Kicking off his blankets, Pete shot across his bed and ran for the door and I quickly followed. I hardly knew where I was. Pete kept on running at a lively gait all the way down the porch, and after that day the Mexes all called him (behind his back) "Don Chootme." At the door, Poe cried, What the hell's going on. Behind him, Kip was trying to peer into the room. "That was the Kid, and I think I have got him."

"That's not possible," said John. "You've shot the wrong man."

"It's him," I said. "I know his voice well."

"Are you sure he's dead?"

"I think so." I stepped onto the porch and as my shaking slowed gently shut the door behind me. Pete, who had made for his mother's room, soon returned with a candle, since the gunfire had stopped. He held it to the window. In the light it cast inside, we saw that the Kid lay on his face motionless. An edge of blood as thick as a pelt slid out from beneath him even as we watched. Behind us others came, having heard the shots. Deluvina Maxwell was first, the family's Navajo slave. She'd been captured as a child in the Canyon de Chelly by the Jicarilla Apaches and traded long ago for ten horses to Lucien, Pete's late father, and now bore the family surname. "You son of a bitch!" she screamed when I turned. She pounded my chest and I stood there and let her, my face hard as stone. I felt far away. "You pisspot!" she wailed. "Goddamn your soul! Why did you do it? He never hurt you, he was a better man than you!" Her high strong brow could split skulls, I knew, she'd eaten considerably larger men than me. Celsa Gutiérrez was wailing behind her and Deluvina turned to console both her and Paulita Maxwell, who'd thrown a blanket over her nightclothes before venturing out. The curses and wails these three women made were a chorus of misery; everyone around me was breaking down, it seemed. I thought of how oxen bellow over dead mates. But as the crowd grew there were some there who thanked me. "All mankind rejoices," said a white man. Most cursed and hurled insults at us, and it occurred to me that people wanting vermin wiped out often find they miss its company. I spotted someone crossing the parade grounds out there in the dark with a burning arm raised. Of course it was a torch.

Dogs barked. The three-quarter moon hung just above the trees, and shouts came from various parts of the fort.

"Pedro," I said. "Who's the coroner here?"

"We got Alejandro Seguro and Milnor Rudulph."

"Where are they?"

"Sunnyside."

"John, you go to Sunnyside and get those two men. Kip, we need a carpenter. Someone to make a coffin. I used to know Jesús Silva, Pedro."

"He's still here. Over to the old hospital."

"Go wake him up, Kip."

◆ ◆ ◆

WHEN THE CROWD broke up, though some snarling *bandas* of boys and young men followed our course with rocks in their hands, Saval Gutiérrez among them, Jesús Silva and I dragged the body to Pete's carpenter shop in the old quartermaster's buildings. Despite their shouts of vituperation, they never threw the rocks; they did not wish to damage the body, I imagine. I wondered about Saval. It could be he was swelled up a bit over the Kid's liaison with his wife. Could be a mark of foolish pride, despite all the Mexes' talk about honor. McKinney had vanished. I believe he thought we'd all be lynched. I felt anxious for the time when all of this would pass into well-merited oblivion.

"It's hard to believe," said Jesús. He had one arm, me the other. "I was talking to him just a couple hours ago. He wasn't worry about nothing."

"What was he doing?"

"Sitting outside Beaver Smith's saloon." Jesús was crying; I heard his voice catch.

"His time was up, that's all. What would he have done if I hadn't shot him? Change his name again? Move somewhere else, become a family man, live quiet and steady? That wasn't him."

"It's a good life, Garrett."

"Depends what you mean by good," I said.

"I mean you do good. You don't do bad things."

"He did bad things."

"But he was wet behind the ears. He thought they were good. His heart was in the right place, that's what counts."

"Sometimes it does," I said. "Sometimes it doesn't."

We lay the body on a table in the carpenter's shop, and Jesús said he'd get his tools. I told him he might as well wait until morning. He left, and by the light of an oil lamp I proceeded to strip the clothes off his flesh. We'd reholstered his pistol before dragging him here and now I removed it and set it on a packing crate close by the door. He wore no shirt; the ball had entered his breast just above the heart, and his hairless chest was smeared with blood and dust. The hole was clean. His gabardine pants seemed a tad long, and the socks slipped off easy. He'd been in his stocking feet. Once fully naked, he appeared chopped short. I saw that his cock was not any special size. His pale skin stopped at the hands and neck, which were tawny as a greaser's. On top of each shoulder was a calcified knob about the size of a thimble. His body was as lean and tight as a mule deer's. I thought of those times we'd served up the drinks at Beaver Smith's saloon, of the two of us on our knees on the ground outside around a horse blanket bucking monte. I realized I'd averted my eyes from his face and looked at it now. It did not appear menacing. Still a smooth-faced boy. Jesús had closed the eyes before we took him. The high freckled forehead looked intelligent, I thought, as did the dark eyes, and the skin possessed a peculiar cast as of a caul or web stretched across the skull; it looked burned and self-repaired. I placed my fingers on the eyelids. Then on an impulse I touched his limp cock, which to my alarm began to stir. The whole body gave a sigh. His lips were partly open, I saw, and in my shaken state I imagined his soul had been caught between his teeth but now was released and its runnel ran down and got pulled through the floorboards, dragged down to hell. Then I remembered there is no hell.

Who told you I was here?

A little dicky-bird.

No, really.

Do you think I would really tell you who it was? I don't hold anyone's life that cheap.

You held mine cheap.

I was doing a job.

Through the wall I heard voices outside. Someone knocked and

I slid the bar out and opened the door and thought, Oh shit. Two women stood there with towels and a pail, Deluvina Maxwell and Beatriz Meléndez. A boy with red hair held Beatriz's hand. "We've come to wash the body," Deluvina said. She looked at me hard but didn't snap.

"Give me a little more time," I said. And then with anxious grandeur: "I haven't prayed yet." Beatriz's boy stared at the table with the Kid upon it. A red bandanna around his neck matched the color of his hair. Something looked wrong with his face, I thought, though he was hardly more than five. "What's your name, son?" He seemed mesmerized; he wouldn't look at me. Deluvina also stared at the table and set down the pail and walked to the body and gazed long and hard at its face, then began once more to sob uncontrollably. I followed behind and stood beside her, looking down. Her whole body was shaking. She spread a towel across the face. Deluvina, too, had been one of Billy's sweethearts. It was not that long ago when the Kid favored women with powerful hams who would buck him all night. He'd told me all about it. I was a good listener. Once again Deluvina started beating my chest and I had to hold her wrists. "He never did nothing to you, you bastard!" she cried before, unaccountably, laying her trembling head on my breast. "You used to be friends," she sobbed. Taking her by the arm, I kindly escorted her back to the door but she shook me off. Beatriz had left; she was outside in the dark. Deluvina kicked the pail of water she'd brought and it sailed out the door and Beatriz shouted, "¡Mierda!" Deluvina stormed out.

I shut the door, barred it, exhaled, shook my head, and returned to the corpse. I thought about praying and how I might go about it. Ways to circumcise the foreskin of my heart. Where is the Lord that led us through the wilderness, through a land of drought and the shadow of death? When I took this job, I thought, I had no religious sentiment. Now, however —

A shot concussed the air, ripped its fabric apart, and I instinctively ducked, felt for my weapon, smelled the hot stink of powder — all the while wondering if I'd been killed. I hadn't. At the edge of the light cast by the oil lamp, Beatriz's boy held the Kid's pistol with his two hands. He lifted it heavily. "My God," I whispered. The boy with red hair and dark rings around his eyes from behind a dense cloud raised the smoking barrel. "Boy," I said. "Son. You don't want to do this. Lower the pistol."

He pointed it at me.

"Point that thing away! Put it down, son!"

His face creased in half. He began to cry but all there was for him to cling to was the Thunderer. Its foreign weight at the end of his arms, large and alive, looked fused to his hands.

I found a calmer voice. "Put it down, son." As anyone could imagine, I felt nervous as a hen, but I managed to produce a tone of composure, even balmed it for the child. "Lay it there on the floor."

The boy cried harder, sat on the floor, and the heavy pistol wavered. I took a step closer. "Did I shot him?" he asked.

"That's fine. Yes, you did. Don't worry about it. I won't tell your mother."

"Is he in heaven?"

"Put the gun down, son. Yes, he's in heaven. Just put the gun down and I'll say that I did it. No one will ever know."

"*Mamá* don't know?" Sobbing, the boy laid the weapon on the floor. I stepped forward and retrieved it and weighed it in my hand. A few threads of smoke still lingered at the barrel. Outside came the sound of footsteps and shouts; someone banged on the door.

"Sure thing, she won't know. I'll say that I did it."

"El Chivato?"

"That's right. El Chivato's in heaven."

"I shot him," said the boy.

"No, you did not. I'm the sheriff here. I'm the one that shot him."

"The sheriff?"

"That's right. See?" I thumbed out my star and, pulling up my pant legs, squatted before him, while the door rattled on its hinges;

behind it came a torrent of Spanish. "Everything's fine now. The sheriff's here. You want to stand up now? Come with me?" The boy reached up and took my hand and climbed to his feet and we walked to the door. I put the gun on the packing crate. "What's your name, son?"

"Billy."

SANTA FE WEEKLY DEMOCRAT

JULY 21, 1881

Billy Bonney, alias Antrim, alias Billy the Kid, a 21 year old desperado, who is known to have killed sixteen men, and who boasted that he had killed a man for every year of his life, will no more take deliberate aim at his fellow man and kill him, just to keep himself in practice. He is dead: and he died so suddenly that he did not have time to be interviewed by a preacher, or to sing hymns, or pray, before that vital spark had flown, so we cannot say positively that he has clum the shining ladder and entered the pearly gates.

The bullet that struck him left a pistol in the hands of Pat Garrett, at Fort Sumner, last Saturday morning, about half-past 12 A.M. in the room of Pete Maxwell. Governor Lew Wallace will now breathe easier, as well as many others whom he has threatened to shoot on sight.

No sooner had the floor caught the descending form, which had a pistol in one hand and a knife in the other, than there was a strong odor of brimstone in the air, and a dark figure, with the wings of a dragon, claws like a tiger, eyes like balls of fire, and horns like a bison, hovered over the corpse for a moment, and with a fiendish laugh, said, "Ha, Ha! This is my meat!" and then sailed off through the window. He did not leave his card, but he is a gentleman well known to us by reputation, and thereby hangs a "tail."

AFTERWORD

The two exclusively fictional characters in this novel are William Bonné and the red-haired boy. All the others are based on historical figures, "based" meaning I learned what I could about them from the historical record and extrapolated — but also invented — starting with that foundation. The details of the Lincoln County War, and of William Bonney's participation in it, are as accurate as I could make them. Readers should understand that many aspects of that war and of Bonney's career are in dispute. For those interested, the best historical overview I've consulted is Frederick Nolan's *The West of Billy the Kid*. A recent biography by Michael Wallis, *Billy the Kid: The Endless Ride*, was published too late for my research.

The source of my information about the famous tintype of Billy is Bob Boze Bell's excellent *The Illustrated Life and Times of Billy the Kid*. Several sentences and phrases from my two Garrett chapters are borrowed from the historical Pat Garrett's *The Authentic Life of Billy the Kid*, a book at least partially ghostwritten by the Roswell, New Mexico, postmaster Ash Upson. In chapter 3, the letters of John Tunstall to his family in London are based upon the actual letters of the historical John Tunstall to his family in London, as published in Frederick Nolan's *The Life & Death of John Henry Tunstall* and *The*

Lincoln County War: A Documentary History. I have combined some letters, altered dates, and provided fictional bridges (including Tunstall's explicit reference to William Bonney on page 50), all for the purpose of using these remarkable documents to help tell my story. Portions of Tunstall's interior monologue and dialogue with Billy in chapter 5 are also based on these letters. Finally, some of the language in Sue McSween's private journal (chapter 11) is taken from a passage in John Cleland's *Fanny Hill.*

The proclamations of President Hayes and Governor Wallace, the letters of Billy Morton, Alexander McSween, Millard Goodwin, J. B. Wilson, Huston Chapman, William Bonney, and Lew Wallace, and all the newspaper articles quoted in the novel, are taken from the historical record.

Whether the historical Billy the Kid was born in New York City and lived there as a child has recently been questioned by historians. But the historical and the legendary Billy the Kid are joined at the hip; and my fictional Billy, being rooted in both, is unequivocally a native of Manhattan.

I would like to thank the English department at Binghamton University for awarding me a Newman Travel Grant for my research. Thanks are also due to the people of Lincoln, New Mexico, for their help with this project, particularly Dee Kessler and Tim Hagaman, former proprietor of the still-thriving Wortley Hotel. Special thanks to Anthony G. Lozano for helping me with the novel's Spanish. And my deepest thanks to Frank Bergon, Bob Mooney, and Anton Mueller for their comments on successive drafts of this novel.